PRINCE OF DEMONS

DEMON'S MARK II

NORA ASH

ABOUT NORA ASH

I write romance that Hurts So Good.

Visit my website to learn more about my upcoming books.

WWW.NORA-ASH.COM

Content Advisory

This is a dark fantasy romance. It contains graphic violence, including scenes of skull-crushing, brain consumption, and general demonic brutality.

There is also (non-penetrative) assault **not** perpetrated by the hero. While Kesh is violently protective and never harms the heroine, the world she's trapped in before he finds her is not kind—and parts of her journey are disturbing and traumatic.

1

GEORGIA

"Your brother is dying."

Those were the words that ended Georgia's world.

She stared at her mom's drawn face, the pale skin taut on her too-prominent features. She'd hardly slept, hardly eaten in the month since Larry's hospitalization. Georgia had done her best to care for her mom while she coped with the news of Larry's aggressive cancer, but there was only so much she could do to ease her mother's life while her youngest child went through chemo with a less than five percent chance of survival.

And now, even that small ray of light had been extinguished.

Georgia clutched her hands in her lap as her mother sank down on the waiting-room chair next to her and buried her face in her palms. She didn't cry—she hadn't since the diagnosis—but Georgia knew she was quietly breaking apart from the inside.

She knew, because she was, too.

He was only nineteen years old. Nineteen, and so full of life and light. How could something so horrible as *cancer* take away the kindest, brightest person in a hundred mile radius?

How was that fair? How was that *right?*

"How long?" she asked, voice soft despite the urge to scream until she blacked out.

"They think maybe two weeks, if we're lucky," her mom said, voice muffled by her hands. "I need to call Mike. I just..."

"I'll do it," Georgia said, mostly because if she didn't do *something,* she would give in to the rage and grief, and her mom didn't need that.

Her mother's voice was a hoarse whisper of exhaustion. "Thank you."

———

THE SUNSET WAS CRUELLY BEAUTIFUL. IT LIT UP THE AUTUMN sky in a tapestry of golden orange, reds and purples while Georgia walked back and forth across the small strip of grass outside the hospital's western wing, listening to Larry's dad go through all the stages of grief on the other end of her cellphone.

"Larry asked us not to tell you, Mike," she said as gently as she could as he cussed and roared. "He didn't want you to worry. He was sure he would beat it." Her brother, an optimist until the end. Even when the doctors had given him his diagnosis and the grim chances for survival, he'd smiled at her and told her he'd beat the odds and not to worry.

"Fuck!" Mike groaned on the other end. *"This is my fault. He didn't think he could reach out to me because I've been so busy with Jeanette and the twins..."*

"It's no one's fault," she said, because despite Mike's shortcomings as a father, he loved her brother. And right now, loving Larry hurt something fierce. "You know how he is—always expects the best outcome of everything."

Mike coughed a broken sob. *"Fuck. This can't be happening, Georgia."*

"I know," she whispered. "But it is, and I think you should come see him."

"Of course. I... I'll be there within two hours."

———

THE SILENCE AFTER HE HUNG UP ECHOED THROUGH THE hollow place inside of her, the one that'd been empty since Larry's first diagnosis. She'd known, from that first day, despite her brother's complete belief he'd be all right... she'd known he wouldn't.

Numb, Georgia stared into the sun, stung by it's final flare as it sank below the horizon. The golden reflections on the city's skyscrapers dimmed and vanished, as if sucked away, leaving her alone in the creeping twilight.

"Got a light?"

Georgia jolted at the unexpected voice—she'd been too lost in her own misery to hear anyone approach. When she turned toward the speaker, another shock jerked through her chest, and she automatically took a half-step back before she caught herself.

"Sorry. Don't smoke," she muttered, trying to keep her eyes from the horns growing out of the stranger's pimply forehead.

"S'ok," he said, turning back toward the hospital. "Nasty habit anyway."

Georgia stared blindly at his tail swaying as he walked back toward the large building lit up brightly against the darkening sky. He was wearing scrubs, and she numbly wondered if he had to cut a hole in the pants for the tail to fit through. They didn't all have tails. She knew because it wasn't uncommon to find demons in places like hospitals or care homes. Any place with vulnerable people, really.

They'd always scared her. She'd called them trolls as a little girl as she'd screamed and pointed, but that'd only made them take notice of her. They'd stared at her, and even though she'd been young, she'd never forget that greedy look in their eyes as they watched her sob. As if her tears, her fear, excited them. It hadn't taken long before she learned to pretend she didn't see their horns or scales or claws.

She'd been in her late teens before she'd learned the adult word for what they were. And what they did.

"Hey!" the shout was out of her throat and past her lips before she could think to stop herself.

The demon turned to look at her over his shoulder. "Yeah?"

"I..." Her mouth was dry as she stared at him. Never in a million years had she thought she'd do this. But Larry was sick now, and in her gut she knew there wasn't anything she wouldn't do to try to stop her family from crumbling apart.

If he died, there wouldn't be anything left to live for anyway.

"I want to make a deal with you."

The horned man arched an eyebrow, slowly turning all the way back around to face her. His fully black eyes crept over her face. "A deal?"

Georgia quickly bobbed her head in a nod, before she could change her mind. Every instinct in her screamed to run at the calculating look in his slightly narrowed gaze. "That's what your kind does, isn't it? Make deals?"

A small smile with no warmth tugged on his lip. He crossed his arms over his chest and walked back toward her, every step slow and measured. "I suppose that depends. What kind am I?"

"Demon," she croaked, her throat tight as he stopped in front of her. "You're a demon. And I want to make a deal with you."

His eyes turned laser sharp then, head tilted back as he took her in from head to toe. "Well, well. And what do you have to trade?"

"My... my soul?" she whispered. "Isn't that your price?"

He cracked a grin then, wide and unpleasant, but thoroughly amused. "Not exactly the kind of business I'm in, darling."

"Oh." Georgia frowned, taken aback by this twist in the conversation. It wasn't that she was an expert on the subject, but all the religious scripture she'd found said demons fed on mortal souls. "I thought—isn't that why you hang around the hospital? To trade the souls of grieving relatives in exchange for their loved ones' lives?"

The demon snorted. "Nope. That's a few steps above my pay grade, I'm afraid."

"Then why do you work here?" she asked, confusion winning out over fear.

"Easy access to organs," he said with a shrug. "And juices. Eyeballs. That sorta thing. Plus, the benefits aren't bad."

Georgia blinked, every small hair on her body standing on end as horror crept back through the confusion. "O-oh. Okay. Nevermind." She made to push past him, but he brought a hand up to her arm, stopping her before she could.

"Don't flee, little mouse. Just because I don't want your soul doesn't mean we can't find another bargain."

She suppressed a shudder at his touch and forced herself to look up into his eyes. "What do you have in mind?"

"Well," he drawled, letting his gaze rest on her throat for a beat. "I like blood. And bile."

"You work in a hospital," she said. "Surely there's plenty of supply?"

"You'd think," he said with a grimace, finally letting go of her arm. She immediately took a step back, putting a foot's distance between them. "But as lax as they are with checking everyone gets buried with their liver, getting to the blood bank's a right nightmare. Every ounce is accounted for."

"Oh... right," she said, somewhat off kilter by his relaxed mention of harvesting organs from corpses. "So you want... to bite me?"

"I could," he said, flashing her that disturbing smile again. "But if I do, you ain't getting back up again, and that would put an end to my blood supply, now wouldn't it?"

"Uh...?"

The demon tossed his head in the direction of the hospital for her to follow, then began walking back toward the building again. "From what you were saying before, it sounds like someone you love is sick, and you want a bit of magic to make them all better, hmm?"

Georgia stumbled after him, her legs taking a millisecond to obey. "Yes. My brother."

"Well, darling, that sort of power doesn't come

easy. Or cheap." He shot her a meaningful look as they passed through the sliding doors, and the noises from the busy hospital intruded on the surreal conversation, surrounding them in an obscene cocoon of normality. "Tell me what room your brother is in and I'll bring a contract with me after my shift tonight. But a fair warning—once you sign it, there's no going back."

2

GEORGIA

Both her mother and Mike were asleep when the demon entered Larry's hospital room, sometime in the early hours of the morning. They sat by his bed, in the hospital's uncomfortable chairs, heads twisted uncomfortably to the side and their features drawn in troubled lines even after exhaustion had claimed them.

The night gave no respite when the person she loved the most in the world was drawing his last breaths.

Georgia forced her gaze from Larry's pale face as the door cracked open, revealing the demon. His black eyes immediately flicked to her brother, hunger evident in their depths.

"Don't even think about it," Georgia hissed, getting up and out of the chair as quietly as she could. They'd all earned their rest—and she didn't particularly want anyone to see whatever was about to happen.

The demon sighed impatiently, rolling his eyes as he dragged them from Larry to her. "Fine. Guess you'll have to do. Tastes so much better from the sick, though."

She grimaced, not willing to think too hard on the implications of what he'd said. "Be quiet—I don't want them waking up. Let's go into the hall."

The demon waved his hand, and dark... *something* left his fingertips, floating toward the sleeping trio. It swept around them like a thick fog, tendrils slipping into their nostrils, mouths and ears before it finally evaporated.

"There," the demon said, sending her horrified grimace a smirk. "They'll have a headache in the morning, but you and I can discuss our business undisturbed." He pulled up a piece of paper and presented it to her. "The contract."

She reached out and gingerly took the single sheet. The lettering was handwritten, with swoops and swirls that could have made any calligrapher green with envy. Georgia raised her eyebrows as she scanned over the words. The greasy demon didn't look like the kind of guy to care much for penmanship, but apparently he was.

"It says in exchange for my brother getting brought back to health, I will give ownership of my body, including but not limited to, my blood and vaginal secretions, to the demon Lewin?" she read from the page, grimacing at the mental pictures that painted.

"That would be me," the demon—Lewin—said, bowing his head in mock civility.

"I thought you just wanted my blood?" she said. "Why does it say you get ownership of my body?" *And vaginal secretions. Ugh.*

"Because, when you eventually die, I'm going to suck all that delicious bile straight from your gall bladder, rip open your stomach and lick the juices from your intestines," he said, slurping for emphasis. "Mmm-mh! Plus, nothing's quite as delicious as menstrual blood straight from the source. I do hope yours is chunky. Wait—don't tell me. It'll be a nice surprise."

Georgia choked back the nausea rising rapidly in her throat. "Ew, maybe learn to sugarcoat things. Jesus Christ."

"I would," he hummed, "but you're going to sign that piece of paper no matter what I tell ya. No human desperate enough to come to me offering her soul as the first bargaining chip has any other options left." He produced a pen and handed it to her. "You can sign on the dotted line."

He was right. If this had been for anything other than Larry's life, she'd have never talked to any of *them,* let alone revealed that she saw them for what they were. It didn't matter what he wanted to do to her— even if he decided to murder her the moment she signed, to drink the bile he was so enraptured by. Not so long as Larry lived.

Numbly, Georgia took the pen from his outstretched hand. It was an old-fashioned fountain pen, the kind you dip in ink. Only there wasn't any.

One glance at Lewin, and a particular aspect of the research she'd done on demons as a teenager, back when she finally realized she wasn't crazy, sprung to the forefront of her mind. A contract with a demon was always signed in blood.

Georgia poked the pointed tip of the fountain pen to her fingertip, breaking through the skin with a quick jab. Crimson blood pooled from the wound in a single droplet, only to be funneled up into the metal tip of the pen.

Breathing out quietly, she turned the now red tip to the paper.

Don't.

The word rang in her ears as clearly, as if someone had spoken it directly by her side. She startled, dropping the pen as she whipped around to see who'd snuck into the room without her noticing. But there was no one conscious but her and the demon.

Warily, Georgia bent to pick up the pen from the floor as she kept an eye on the demon. He was watching her intently, with bated breath, and she knew...

That voice, she'd heard that before. Warning her as a kid when she was about to scream at the horned creatures no one else seemed to be worried about.

Always it said the same: *Don't.*

Don't draw their attention.

Don't go near them.

Don't look them in the eye.

Don't.

Don't.

Don't.

When she'd listened, she had avoided their attention.

But this time, she couldn't obey the voice. Even if she knew the creature staring at her as if she were lunch had undoubtedly planned even worse things for her than what he'd admitted to.

Georgia shot a last, lingering look at Larry's pale, still figure before she scribbled her signature across the dotted line, finalizing the contract.

Lewin smiled slow and wide when she handed the piece of paper back to him. Before she could pull her hand back, he snatched her by the wrist and pulled her arm up, closing his lips around her wounded finger. His mouth was hot and dry, and her finger stung when he swiped his tongue over the pen-prick with a visible shudder of pleasure.

"My, you taste *delicious,* my dear," he rumbled when she managed to yank her finger from his mouth.

"Yeah, well, you don't get to taste before you uphold your end of the deal, remember?" she hissed, cradling her hand against her chest. Shivers of revulsion still prickled across her skin from the feel of his tongue.

"Sure," he said, giving her a nasty smile before he turned to the bed. "One cancer-free brother, coming right up. And then... then you and I are going to *enjoy* ourselves, little girl."

The dark fog from before gathered around his hands, sweeping over Larry's still figure. Nothing but the demon's panting breath and the slow beeping of the machines her brother was hooked up to disturbed the quiet of the hospital room for several minutes.

Finally, Lewin sagged against the bed with a curse, the dark fog vanishing. *"Shit."* He rubbed a hand against his forehead and turned to look at her. "It's too strong."

"No!" Georgia hissed, tears blurring her vision as impotent anger fizzled in her veins. *"No!* I signed your stupid contract! You heal him! *Now!"*

She didn't realize she'd gotten to her feet, nor that she'd charged at the monster, until his hand connected with her chest and he shoved her to the floor by the side of the bed.

"You really have a death wish, don't you?" he snarled, and though it wasn't the fog from before, something dark and *sinister* gathered around him, emphasizing the shadows under his eyes and the other-worldliness of his horns. "You know what? Fine. I was going to let you out of the contract, but if you *insist...*"

She frowned, unease creeping along her spine at the threatening tone. "You'll... you can save him after all?"

Lewin's thin lips turned up in a nasty smirk. "For you, I'll find a way."

3
GEORGIA

"Where are you taking me?"

She'd managed to keep her mounting fear under control as the sleazy demon drove her out of the city's center, all the way into the depths of the industrial quarter. But when he pulled the car to a stop deep in the midst of stacked shipping containers, by the side of a large, run-down warehouse with a broken neon-sign spelling out 'HELL', Georgia's bravery started to fade.

"What's eating your brother from the inside, we need more power than I've got," Lewin said, flicking two fingers at her to follow him as he got out of the car and began walking to a door on the side of the warehouse. "Jimmy will be able to source that. For a price."

Georgia bit her lip, every instinct in her body telling her not to trust the demon—but if Larry's salvation lay beyond the dingy metal walls of that warehouse... well, that's where she was going.

Lewin led her to the door and yanked it open, clamping a hand around her shoulder when a broken sob from within met them.

Georgia hesitated, frowning at the dimly lit room inside. It wasn't more than a small space walled off by flimsy plasterboards, but another demon sat behind a reception desk. He was about as sleazy-looking as her companion, with small horns poking out through the greasy strands barely covering his scalp.

Lewin shoved her through the door and slammed it shut behind them, never releasing his grip on her shoulder.

"You again?" the receptionist said, his lips flattening into a disapproving line. "You know Jimmy doesn't wanna see you here before you pay him back for the merchandise you damaged."

"Oh, he's gonna want to see me this time." Lewin flicked his eyes to Georgia for a brief moment before he lifted his chin at the other demon. "I'm here to pay my debt. In kind."

The receptionist turned his gaze to Georgia, acknowledging her presence for the first time with a quirk of his eyebrows. "Got a contract on her?"

"Yup. Ironclad."

The new demon sighed. "Fine. Go on through."

"Come along, darling," Lewin purred, but the sense

of foreboding in Georgia's stomach tightened to the point of pain.

More sobbing rang through the warehouse from multiple directions, along with unmistakably rhythmic slaps of flesh against flesh. The smell assaulting her nostrils was a mixture of blood, decay, and sex.

"What is this place?" she asked, even as that neon sign flashed in her memory. *Hell.* She had a sinking feeling that perhaps that was intended a bit more literally than she'd initially thought.

"Does it matter? You wanted your brother healed—this is where you'll find the cure to save him." There was nothing soothing about the look Lewin gave her, but... *Larry.*

Her heart gave an achy spasm as a flash of memories of his easy laugh flickered for her mind's eye. When Lewin pulled her along by his tight grip on her shoulder, she didn't resist.

They headed down a narrow, makeshift corridor flanked by five-by-eight cubicles on both sides. Each opening was covered with rough-spun fabric, but the sobs, grunts, and fleshy smacks from within ruined any semblance of privacy. About midway down the corridor, one of the curtains was only half-pulled, and what transpired inside confirmed, with all too much clarity, what the sounds and smells had already revealed.

A human woman was strapped to the wall of the tiny cubicle, her wrists secured over her head and her knees pulled up and out to the sides, leaving her spread open and unable to escape the monster in there with her.

He was big—much bigger than Lewin, with many more demonic features, his skin scaly and black, leathery wings flexing from his muscled back as he drove into the helpless woman, ignoring her babbling pleas for mercy.

Georgia dug her nails into her palms and forced herself to keep walking. Her stomach clenched with empathy as the woman's tormented voice was lost in the cacophony of human cries echoing from every cubicle they passed. Gross as Lewin's payment for her contract was, at least it wasn't that.

Perhaps... Perhaps when Larry was okay again, she could try to save them. Somehow. Alert the police. Even if they didn't see the demonic features of the males brutalizing the women trapped here, they would do something. They would have to.

They reached the end of the corridor and stopped in front of a closed door. Lewin drew in a deep breath, as if steadying himself, before he rapped his knuckles against it with his free hand.

It swung open two seconds later, and someone snarled, "What?" from within. A huge, burly demon, with features not unlike the one they'd just passed in that cubicle, took up most of the doorframe, his bumpy forehead locked in a glower. His eyes narrowed further when they landed on Lewin. "You again? You've gotta be shitting me."

Georgia let out an involuntary squeak at the monster's sudden closeness and made to scramble backwards, but Lewin's hold on her shoulder kept her in place.

"I'm here to see Jimmy. Got a trade for him," Lewin said. His Adam's apple bobbed under the newcomer's glare, but he raised his chin. "He's gonna want to take this meeting, Irral."

The bigger demon arched an eye-ridge before he took a half-step back. "It's your funeral."

Lewin crept sideways through the door, dragging Georgia along.

"Now, now. What do we have here?" a drawling, nasal voice sounded from inside the moment they stepped through. "Lewin the Grave-robber. I thought I made it perfectly clear what would happen if I saw you in my establishment again."

Georgia darted her gaze from the huge demon in the door toward the speaker—and clenched her jaw. There were two more monsters in the room. One was the approximate size and shape of Irral and stood casually, leaning against a closed door on the opposite side of the room. Another demon, more rotund than the others, sat behind a large mahogany desk far too opulent for the grimy warehouse. A pinstriped suit clung tightly to his body, the jacket gaping open between straining buttons as he leaned forward, his small, beady eyes fixed on Lewin. A thick gold chain completed the impression of a low-budget movie mafioso. Only the redness of his gaze and yellowed claws on his fingers gave away his true nature, but that cool, calculating look in his eyes made him no less terrifying than his two burlier companions.

"I know, I know. But I can pay this time, I swear," Lewin said. He forced Georgia forward with him, stopping only a few feet from the large desk. "I've got a contract you're gonna want a bite of, Jimmy."

"What?" Georgia turned to the demon by her side, that sense of foreboding that had pounded in her blood since she saw where he brought her turning to a dull throb low in her gut. "My contract is with you. You can't *share* me."

Jimmy's cold eyes finally moved to her, flicking over her for less than two seconds. "You bring me an untrained cunt? You broke one of my most prized girls, and you think I'll just, what, swap her out for whatever street whore you've picked up and we'll call it a day? Do you know how much money I've lost out on while she's been unable to fuck? How long it takes to break in a new girl?"

"This one's worth it," Lewin said. His fingers digging deeper into her arm were the only indication that he'd heard her protest. "She can see us. What we really are."

Jimmy froze, gaze whipping back to meet Georgia's. Excitement bloomed in it, along with unmistakable greed. "She can *what?*"

"It's true—she clocked me, no probs." Lewin

seemed a bit less panicked, since the big brute who'd been advancing on him had also turned to stare at Georgia. "Ask her."

Jimmy raised up from his chair, surprisingly nimble for his size, and waddled around the desk to them, those red eyes never leaving hers. When he stopped in front of her, he held out a hand and offered her a smile that held no warmth. "Come to me, my dear. Don't be afraid."

Georgia didn't move so much as an inch toward him. A shrill scream broke through the underlying cries and moans drifting into the makeshift office from the warehouse beyond, making her heart thump unevenly in her chest. *Don't be afraid*—said the creep who had God knew how many women tied down like sacrificial offerings for horny demons. Yeah, *hard* pass on getting any closer.

"This is not our deal," she said as evenly as she could muster, turning her attention back to the demon who still had his claws in her. "You said you only wanted my... fluids, and you'd heal Larry in return. I only signed your contract to save my brother—and it doesn't say shit about *selling* me."

"Don't tell me you signed a contract for nothing more than her fluids," Jimmy said, annoyance tainting his voice. He snapped his fingers. "Show me the paperwork."

"How dumb do you think I am?" Lewin muttered. He reached into his jacket with his free hand and produced the now slightly crumbled piece of paper she'd signed.

One of the large goons snatched it from him and took it to his boss—but his eyes stayed glued to Georgia.

Jimmy unfolded the contract, *tsk*ing as he smoothed the paper with his hand before skimming his red gaze over it. An unpleasant smile hiked up the corner of his mouth.

Georgia's stomach tightened.

"Unfortunately, my dear girl, it would seem good old Lewin tricked you. You'll find some of our kind have that nasty habit. You did indeed sell him your body. It's his to do with as he pleases," Jimmy said.

The tightening in her gut climbed up to her throat, squeezing her windpipe. "No. That's... That's only supposed to be after I die! You can't make me do this."

"Now now," Jimmy tooted. "It's not so bad. You like sex, don't you? Humans are usually so obsessed with it anyway, and if you are what he says you are... We'll treat you like a princess. Don't you want your brother healthy, hmm? Just look at Loyt here and tell me what you see." He gestured to the big demon, the one who hadn't opened the door for them.

Georgia hesitated, eyes flicking from Jimmy to Loyt. She'd sold herself in exchange for Larry's life without hesitating. But she'd thought... She'd thought it'd be a gross, monthly transaction with a creepy but not *too* terrifying demon. Not forced prostitution to an endless horde of nightmarish creatures.

Did it matter?

If she did this, Larry would live. If she didn't... He would die.

Since the day he'd been born, she'd known she'd protect her baby brother. No matter the cost.

She dug her nails into her palms and opened her mouth to describe the thick scales and brutish horns on the burly demon, but the same voice that had echoed in her head before she signed Lewin's contract rang through her like someone had struck a gong.

Don't. Don'tdon'tdon't. Georgina. Notthis. Don't.

Georgia blinked. Through the years, she'd come to think of that voice as her sixth sense. But it had only ever said the one word; don't. Never more. Never her name.

And never with such panicked urgency.

"I... Don't know what you mean," she whispered. "I see a man."

Jimmy sighed irritably. "Oh, you do, do you? Fine, if you don't want to cooperate, you certainly don't have to." He snapped his fingers, and darkness rose from his yellow claws in a slowly twisting plume.

Georgia gasped and shrank back on instinct, but Lewin still held onto her shoulder, keeping her in place.

Jimmy gave her a nasty smile, and then the plume of dark energy began to float toward her like a thick trail of smoke.

"What are you doing?" she wheezed, eyes round and not leaving what she was pretty sure was some sort of black magic.

"Not to worry, princess. If you are what old Lewin claims, you won't feel a thing," the demon pimp purred. "Of course, if you *aren't*... Well, then he gets to scrape his contracted whore off the floor in bits. And we'll have a nice little chat about how you'll pay what you owe me, won't we, Lewin?"

"She's the real deal," Lewin growled, his hold becoming tighter as Georgia bucked against him, panic clawing at her throat as the plume brushed against her skin.

It was like being touched by slimy, temperate tendrils. Georgia shuddered and fought harder against Lewin to escape its unpleasant caress, but it vanished as instantly as it'd appeared.

Gasps sounded from both the burly bodyguards, one of them croaking out, "It's true!"

"Oh, *my*." There was no disguising the lecherous glee in Jimmy's voice, nor the greed in his cold eyes roaming over her as if she were a particularly tasty piece of meat. "Consider your debts repaid in full, Lewin. It would seem you've managed to find me a Breeder."

4
GEORGIA

Breeder?

Georgia swallowed hard. Not exactly a classification she'd have loved on the best of days, but stuck in a demon brothel, the word twanged especially ominously down her spine.

"Look, I don't know what you think's going to happen here, but I can assure you I won't be *breeding* with anyone of you," Georgia snarled, somehow managing to sound a lot less terrified than she felt. "My contract was for *fluids*. With Lewin. Not some hell-beast pimp."

Lewin snorted behind her, finally releasing his hold on her arms so he could trail a nicotine-yellowed finger down her cheek. Goosebumps of revulsion broke out all along her skin. "Humans. So... *naïve*. A bit of desperation, and you're always ready to sign whatever gets put in front of you on blind faith alone."

Georgia cringed away from his touch, but before she could put distance between herself and the asshole demon who'd tricked her, one of the big guys—Loyt—stepped forward and shoved Lewin off her, nostrils flared with anger.

"You're not worthy of touching a Breeder," he growled. "Get out."

Lewin took a few steps back and raised his hands. "Calm down, man. If I was interested in that, I wouldn't have brought her around here, eh?" He flicked his gaze from Loyt to Jimmy, once he'd made sure the bodyguard wasn't pursuing him. "But, I mean, she *is* a Breeder. Surely, she's worth more than that whore I broke. It *was* an accident, after all."

Jimmy narrowed his eyes. "Really? You have the balls to bargain? You should count yourself lucky I don't have your head mounted on the wall." Then he sighed and made a gesture at one of the big goons. "But I suppose, with the understanding that no one hears so much as a *whisper* from you... Irral, get our friend here ten grand from the vault." He eyed Georgia. "And a ring for the girl. The sooner she gets broken in, the sooner her cunt will make us rich."

"You're all insane." The snarl in Georgia's voice wavered, breaking to a whisper. "You can't do this."

"Come now, princess," Jimmy said, his round face breaking in a smile that was possibly supposed to be warm but only made her skin crawl. "It's not gonna be worse than what old Lewin would have done with you.

Did he really convince you all he'd want in return was a sip of bodily fluids now and then?

"Do you want to know exactly what he did to one of my prized whores the last time I let him have a go at her while she was on her monthly? He *ate* her labia and sucked out her uterus as if it were an oyster. If Loyt hadn't gotten to her in time, he'd have eaten her whole reproductive system while she was still alive."

"Oh, my God." Bile rose violently up her esophagus, and she swallowed hard to keep it down.

"Nasty creatures, his kind," Jimmy continued, ignoring an indignant huff from Lewin. "I won't let anyone as, ah, *unrefined* near your precious cunt. Only demons who'll understand your worth and treat you right. Worship and sex—most humans bargain their souls to get what you have to *pay*. You'll see, it won't be so bad. Once you get used to it."

Despite the demon's attempts to reassure her, the echoed sobs and cries from the surrounding warehouse made her ball her hands into fists, her heart hammering out of rhythm in her chest. Every cell in her body screamed at her to flee as fast as her legs would carry her, but when she glanced at the door, it was blocked by Loyt's huge frame.

She couldn't escape. And if she tried... She looked back at Jimmy, suppressing a shudder of revulsion at the thought of what he might do to her if he decided playing nice wasn't working.

Perhaps... Perhaps if she let him believe her meek

and pliable, he'd lower his guard? Once he trusted her to have accepted her fate, she could find a way to escape. After she'd made sure her brother was healed.

"What about Larry?" Georgia whispered, her throat tight and dry. "You have to save him first. That's the bargain, right? You can't do anything to me until he's okay."

"Larry's the brother?" Jimmy glanced at Lewin.

Lewin nodded. "Yeah. Cancer. A particularly nasty one. Too strong for me to cure. Shouldn't be a problem for someone with your power."

The pimp hesitated for a brief moment, but then huffed and waved his hand. "Fine. Guess it'd be too much to ask for our golden goose to come without a few challenges." He nodded at Georgia, grabbing a pen and Lewin's wrinkled contract. "Once you're ringed, I'll take care of your brother, Breeder. It's what you wanted, isn't it? Or is he not worth a bit of time on your back, hmm?"

Georgia stared mutely at him as he added a few lines to the contract she'd signed, waving over Lewin to add his initials below the crimson words that sold her as a whore for demons.

She'd been seven years old when Larry was born, and from the moment she lay eyes on his squinty little face, she'd known it was her job to protect him. Always. And she had. Her mom had even trusted her with some of the night feedings, the diaper changes—and rocking him to sleep when he was fussy, because no one else could calm him as quickly as she could.

A few years later, when Mike left and their mother retreated to her bedroom to grieve, Georgia was the one to cook dinner and make sure there were clean clothes. Once she got her license, she took him to school and lacrosse practice, and when Mike got married and had kids with his new wife, she was the only one who got to see how much that hurt her baby brother. She'd rocked him like she'd done when he was a baby, and he'd told her she was all the family he needed.

If this creep of a demon gave her a way of saving his life... It shouldn't matter what she'd have to pay.

Irral returned moments later, a roll of bills in one hand and the other closed into a tight fist. He lobbed the bills at Lewin and handed whatever was in his other hand to Jimmy before he looked at her.

Georgia blinked. If she wasn't mistaken, there was reverence in his black eyes.

"Nice." Lewin flicked a thumb through the wad of cash and nodded at Jimmy. "See ya around, Jimmy. Breeder."

Georgia glared at him as he exited the room with a joyful whistle, but he didn't so much as glance her way. To him, she was truly nothing but a piece of meat to be bargained or... or *eaten.*

"What're you gonna do with her, boss?" Irral asked, and when she looked back at him, he was still staring at her as if she were some kind of prophet reborn.

Jimmy sighed and pushed away from the table, getting to his feet. "Well, she'll need to be ringed before we put her to work. A crying Breeder's gonna be a turnoff for some of the clientele."

"Boss... Are you sure you want to whore her?" Much to her astonishment, Loyt sounded more than a little reluctant. "She's supposed to be... sacred."

Sacred? Georgia looked at the big brute. The grim look on his demonic features made her heart skip a beat. If he thought she was *sacred*—

"Please. There's nothing *sacred* about Breeders. So they can push out horned babies, big whoop. Don't tell me you two knuckleheads are gonna be a problem just because her pussy smells good, hmm? You'd make shitty fathers anyway, so don't be getting any ideas with my merchandise." Jimmy gave them both a stern stare.

"Of course not," Irral said quickly.

And the sliver of hope that either bodyguard might help her escape turned to ash when Loyt shrugged and added, "Just thought you'd like to consider what'll happen if someone runs their mouth in the wrong place. But I'm sure you've got a plan for what to do if the Prince shows up after hearing a rumor that we're keeping a Breeder on the premises."

Jimmy scoffed. "The Prince is busy with the war. *If* he heard about her, he won't be hauling his ass off the battlefield to rescue one pathetic little Breeder. But he won't hear anything. I'll draw up a contract for anyone who wishes to buy a round on her. She's staying a secret—no one will be able to breathe a word of her existence without turning inside out. Now stop fretting like a couple of old maids and get her to the prep room. The sooner she gets done, the sooner she starts earning her keep."

"As you wish." Irral grabbed her above the elbow, his scaly hand like an iron band around her muscles. She flinched away from him on instinct, but Loyt crowded her in on the other side, blocking her off. He didn't touch her, but he didn't need to. His nearness was enough to remind her that she would not be able to run from this.

Not that she could, even if she'd had the chance. Not before Larry was okay.

Georgia didn't struggle as they pulled her through the door and into another room filled with file cabinets and what looked like a safe, then out another door and into a narrow corridor made up of stud walls. The sound of female cries still echoed from further back in the warehouse, but she pushed them to the background until all she could hear was her own harsh breathing and the rush of blood in her ears.

Whatever happened next, she would get through it. For Larry.

The demons only stopped after dragging her through a steel door and into a room clad in metal rather than drywall. Unlike the corridors and Jimmy's office, it had a ceiling, and when the door closed behind them, the sounds of sobbing women abruptly cut off.

"Get her on the bench," Jimmy ordered, moving from behind them toward the middle of the room, pausing next to what looked like a medical examination couch—complete with stirrups and buckled leather straps on both ends.

"You can't be serious." The protest left her on a wheezing exhale. Her lungs constricted painfully, making it hard to breathe. It didn't get any easier when she forced her eyes from the bench to the rest of the room. An array of devices hung on the wall and lay spread out on a wooden tabletop pushed up against the far corner. They looked like something out of a medieval dungeon. Of the especially awful variety.

"It'll be over soon," Irral murmured, the softness of his voice a sharp counterpoint to his grip on her arm. He pulled her forward, and when her legs refused to move on their own and she stumbled, lifted her with a grip on both her biceps and carried her the final few steps.

"No." The word escaped before she could fully form the denial in her mind. "I don't want this. Not... not this."

"I thought you wanted your brother to live?" There was a taunt in Jimmy's voice. He gestured to the two other demons, then turned to the table in the corner. "Besides, this is a great honor. Only my most valuable whores get ringed—and they have to work long and hard to earn it. *You*, my golden goose, get one from first fuck. Sure, there'll be a little pain now, a little humiliation, but I suspect you'll be grateful soon enough. Horny demons can get a little, shall we say, *enthusiastic.* I'm given to understand that bedding one can be rather unpleasant without a ring."

She did want Larry to live. More than anything.

But when Irral held her still so Loyt could pull off her jeans and underwear, and they then lifted her onto the bench, there was nothing she could do to keep back the tears.

She stared straight up into the ceiling, blurred by her tears, and the single lightbulb illuminating the room while they tied her wrists above her head and forced her legs wide. The stirrups pushed into her insteps as they restrained her ankles. When they tightened the leather straps around her thighs, she bit down on her cheek until she tasted blood.

For Larry. For Larry, for Larry, for Larry.

"Fuck, Jimmy, she's *crying*," Loyt growled. He reached for her just-bound wrist as if to undo the strap, but flexed his clawed digits above the leather instead. "This ain't right."

"Of course she's crying," Jimmy sighed. "She sold her cunt. Don't tell me you're growing a conscience, just because the little twat's a Breeder. The last whore you broke in sobbed like a baby while you were on her —didn't seem to give you any pause then, hmm?"

"Jimmy, come on, man." Irral made an agitated

gesture at her teary face. "We're not like you. We can't fucking help it. She's a *Breeder*. If she cries, we're fucking hardwired to stop it!"

"Satan's tits," Jimmy growled. He returned from the table, entering her field of vision as he stepped between her and Irral. "That's what I get for surrounding myself with primitive idiots. Get out. Go put your dicks in a bucket of ice water if your pea-sized brains need the blood supply. She'll be ringed and begging for it soon enough, and if you two breathe another protest, you won't get a single go on her. Understood? You want a taste of Breeder cunt, you get the *hell* out. *Now.*"

Both goons hesitated, their dark eyes darting from her to their boss. Finally, Loyt whispered, "You'll let us have her? Truly?"

Jimmy rolled his eyes with an exasperated sigh. "Of *course*. You know how I operate. You stay loyal, you get a share in the profits. But if you'd rather trade your yearly bonus for a one time lay with my little prize sow, then I won't stand in your way. *After* she's taken a few hundred paying customers, of course."

The two of them looked at each other, looked at her. There was a flicker of regret in both their gazes, but it wasn't strong enough. Without another word, they left.

That moment's hesitation should have filled her with some semblance of hope. If they didn't like her crying, perhaps they could be persuaded to help her escape. But it seemed whatever sense of discomfort they had in the face of her fear, it wasn't stronger than the desire to take their share of her. If they could be convinced to free her, it wouldn't be before they'd had their payment.

A few hundred customers. Would there even be anything but an empty shell left to save?

"Well. I'll grant they're not my cleverest subordinates, but they *are* loyal," Jimmy said. He gave her a smirk, as if they were sharing a joke. "It's possibly not surprising that's a rare thing in our world. I can put up with a few primitive instincts for that." His smirk turned sharper. "Ridiculous as they may be. It's not as if those two idiots would have had any clue what you are, if they hadn't been told. They can't smell you—it's all in those empty noggins of theirs."

"*Smell* me?" She wasn't entirely sure why she asked. She didn't want to know any more about their depraved customs, but he was holding something in one clawed hand that gleamed metallic. Any distraction from the horrors that were about to befall her was welcome.

Jimmy waved his empty hand in a dismissive gesture. "Awakened Breeders smell irresistible to male demons. It's part of the magic in a blinding mark. To amp up your natural pheromones and ensure you get mated frequently and produce plentiful offspring."

He saw her horrified expression and gave her a thin smile. "Don't worry—I'm not about to let anyone knock you up, little goose. And there will be no blinding mark either. Your pretty cunt's all the encouragement these idiots need to part with their coin—too much and they might start getting ideas about claiming themselves a mate. Then I'll have to kill them, and I'm down a customer... You see how that's bad for business, right?"

Georgia didn't answer.

"Well, best get on with it." He smiled a little wider, showing off small, yellowed fangs when his words made her squirm against her bindings. "Now, now. You've got *nothing* to worry about, little goose. I'm not gonna feed on you. It's just a small pinch."

Her racing heart didn't calm down at his syrupy tone, nor when he opened his hand to reveal what he'd picked up from the table: a wicked-looking metal clamp.

What on Earth—?

Her panicked confusion came to a sharp point when the demon stepped in between her spread thighs, that evil smirk growing. He reached out with his empty hand and trailed a claw up the inside of her leg, from her calf, up over the strap keeping her knees locked to the stirrups, and along her inner thigh. When he reached her groin, and she drew in a sharp breath and strained harder against the bindings, he paused.

"I know what you fear, Breeder," he murmured. "What you *all* fear. Will it comfort you to know that I have no interest in fucking you? True, many lowly demons think with their genitals, but sex has no appeal to me."

"You're a pimp." The words came unbidden, her

focus scattered between the crawling sensation of his touch and the evil-looking clamp in his hand.

Jimmy gave a low laugh. "Yes, I suppose I can see how that might be confusing. Do you know what my kind needs humans for? Why we make bargains and bind you in servitude?"

"You're evil," she said. It came out as more of a whisper than she'd meant.

He barked another laugh. "Perhaps. But, while I do admit that there is some amusement in torment for its own sake, mostly we need to feed. And that precious energy you all are stuffed so full of just so happens to be our primary food source."

"Our souls." She swallowed thickly and tried not to flinch when he drew his thick claw up over the seam of her closed labia and rested it against her hooded clit.

"Sometimes," he agreed, his gaze flicking from hers down to his claw resting intimately between her thighs. "Some demons do feed on souls. Nasty creatures—give all of us *quite* an unpleasant reputation. Most of us find other ways of extracting what we need from your pitiful flesh. Your good friend Lewin prefers fluids and organs. My tastes are more... refined."

A sharp sting right against the hood of her clit made her jerk hard—and immediately freeze when his claw scraped painfully over the very tip of her center of nerves.

"I take my nourishment from anguish... misery. Not so much *pain,* per se. Too crude." Without taking his eyes off her nether region, he ever so slowly moved his fingers along her trembling flesh, forcing the protective hood back to expose her clit. "What I crave is the bitterness of terror and regret. Right now, your fear for what I might do to your pretty cunt is *pouring* out of every orifice in your body... and most especially from that trembling hole between your legs.

"Females give so much more than males, because right here..." He squeezed his fingers together, trapping her clit and making her hiss with the pain of it. "Right here is where the richest source of human energy lies. No matter how we take it, no matter that we could choose to extract your life force in so many creative ways, *this* is what we want: your helpless little cunt. Lewin delights in sucking moon blood straight from the source, incubi feast on the pleasure they extract, others need torment and torture... I take my nourishment from the horror my whores feel while they are forced to take demonic cock for the rest of their miserable existence. So no, my golden goose, I won't rape you. I don't need to."

And with that, he pried open the clamp and brought it down on her bared clit, letting the metal squeeze tight before she'd fully processed his plan.

Pain exploded through her pelvis, bright and brutal.

Georgia screamed—screamed until her voice broke and bile filled her mouth and she gagged to keep from suffocating. Nothing had ever hurt like this, hurt so much she wanted to peel her own skin off to escape the torture of that wicked clamp biting down on her most sensitive bud.

But slowly, so, so slowly, the agony ebbed until it was a dull throb echoing through her body with the pulse drumming through her veins and she could finally breathe again.

"I know, it pinches a little."

Jimmy's voice, laced with false sympathy, made her force her eyes open. Her vision was blurry with tears, but the sight of him still standing between her forcefully spread thighs made bile rise in her throat again. The orange lightbulb illuminating the room cast his face in sinister shadows, emphasizing every demonic feature—and that cruel smirk.

"You're a disgusting pig." The words came unbidden, anger forced out from the agony of his torment, surpassing terror, if only for a moment.

His smirk thinned into a smile. Dark amusement sparked in his eyes. "Such *language*. But, you'll come around to thanking me. Eventually." He reached into the pocket of his pinstriped suit and pulled out a small circle of metal. "If I am to ring you, your clitoris needs to be good and swollen. And trust me, you want me to ring you. Or you should. Once it's fitted, one little-bitty twist and any reluctance you may or may not have about our gentlemen callers will just, *poof,* vanish. You'll even enjoy every last one of them."

Enjoy it? He thought there was any way a woman could *enjoy* being taken by a monster?

Her disbelief must have been written all over her face, because Jimmy chuckled and held up the ring, letting the low light gleam off it. "Have you ever been so thirsty, you'd do anything to quell it? So hungry, you'd eat dirt just to fill your belly? That's what this nifty little trinket will do for you. And yes, sure, it might *sound* like less of a gift than it does a curse, but let's just say there's a reason my more experienced whores will do anything to earn one of these. Everyone would like to enjoy their work, after all."

She didn't respond. The picture he was painting was too gruesome, any fire brought on by the pain withered to horror-flecked numbness.

The demon smirked at her silence. "Ready to finish this?"

He didn't wait for an answer. With a jerk of his hand, he yanked the clamp off her trapped flesh, not bothering to open it first.

If she'd thought the pain had been unbearable when he put it on her, it was nothing compared to the agony when her blood rushed back into her clit, forcing the sensitive pearl to swell.

She tried to scream, but all she could do was dry heave, her muscles locked too tight to thrash against the leather straps keeping her tied down for him. The dim room turned red at the corners, then fully black. And still, for an eternity, all that existed was the pain.

Mercifully, the come-down was faster. One second, her entire body was alight with agony—the next, waves of relief washed it away to a low throb of tender sensation.

Georgia sagged against the bench, breathing raggedly.

"No more. Please. No more," she gasped between gulps of air.

Cold metal touched her engorged flesh was the only response she got.

She managed to open her eyes just in time to see Jimmy slip the ring on her clit and *twist.*

"No!"

This time, the pain was accompanied by a sick wave of arousal.

It rushed through her trapped center of nerves, deep into her pelvis, and forced her body to contort in a pleasureless climax so brutal, her vision faded to black.

The last thing she felt before her mind finally snuffed out was numb relief she wouldn't be conscious for whatever torture still lay ahead.

5
GEORGIA

When she came to, she was alone in the room.

Disoriented, Georgia blinked against the dull light from the singular bulb, the memory of the past few hours slow to return.

The second it did, horror followed.

She jerked upright, a small burst of relief that leather straps no longer tied her to the bench doing little to calm her.

The room seemed undisturbed, save for a bucket next to the bench. It took her a moment to gather its purpose.

Great. But why would she be spared the humiliation of having to use a grimy plastic bucket as a toilet? It wasn't like the demon asshole who'd trapped her had held back on the indignities so far.

Her pants and underwear still lay carelessly tossed

on the floor by the foot-end, but when she swung her legs over the edge to get them, something rubbed against her clit, sending a shock of sensation through her.

The ring.

Georgia hadn't been very old when she'd realized that seeing monsters no one else could was upsetting to her mother, and so, she'd learned to hide her fear. She wouldn't scream when she saw the scaly demon driving the ice cream truck past her house that summer a couple of kids disappeared from the neighborhood, but she still lay awake at night, ever vigilant, in case he came to eat her and Larry, too.

It was only when she got older she realized that the demons roaming the world didn't always look to murder their victims.

Biting her lip to keep the tears at bay, Georgia reached down to carefully spread her labia.

And there it sat. A small band of silvery metal encircled her still red and swollen clit, forced free of the hood. Entirely bared and unprotected.

This is what we want, Jimmy had said. *Your helpless little cunt.*

Staring at what he'd done to her, she did feel helpless. Whether or not that ring worked like he'd claimed it would, it was concrete proof that when it came down to it, there was nothing she could do to stop these monsters from abusing her however they saw fit.

Up until now, her only protection against them had

been that they didn't know she could see them for what they were. She would never be able to hide from them again.

But this was the cost of Larry's life. She would pay it. And once he was safe... Somehow, she would find a way to escape. Whatever happened next, she wouldn't give up hope, and she would get through it.

She would.

Moving stiffly, Georgia climbed off the bench and grabbed for her clothes. The ring didn't hurt like it had when he'd placed it on her, but there was no escaping the physicality of its firm grasp nor the twinges of too-much sensation against her abused clit. Every step was a sharp reminder of what had been done to her. And what lay ahead.

———

WAITING FOR NEWS ON LARRY—AND WHAT CAME AFTER— was a special kind of torture. The metallic clank of the door handle made Georgia jerk upright, a bolt of adrenaline pulling her from her quiet misery.In the seconds from the click of the door handle moving to the door swinging open, panic squeezed her lungs. She wasn't ready for this. And what if...

What if they hadn't been able to save him, after all?

One of the big goons stepped through the door. Irral, she was pretty sure.

"Is my brother okay?" She jumped down from the

bench where she'd been sitting while she waited, forcing the question out despite her naked fear at the answer.

The demon grimaced, showing off sharp fangs. "Fuck your brother. Come with me, *now.*"

Georgia blinked. "What? No! That was the deal—you can't do anything to me until he's healed!"

He scoffed and stepped into the room, clawed hand outstretched to grab her. She shrank back from him, eyes widening when it dawned on her that she had no way of forcing these monsters to stick to the contract. They could tie her up in one of those awful booths, and there would be nothing she could do about it. How could she have been so stupid to trust they'd honor their word?

"Breeder." Irral's voice was a low growl, frustration mixing with impatience. But much to her surprise, he stopped his advance. "If you don't come with me, you'll spend the rest of eternity with your legs spread, wishing your brother had never been born. His death is nothing compared to what awaits you here. I promise you that."

"Are you..." She frowned when it dawned on her what he was doing. "You want to break me out of here? Now? Why? I thought—" She stopped as the memory of Jimmy telling Irral he'd get to have 'a go' with her flashed through her brain. How he'd seemed perfectly okay with her fate. "This is a trick? Is that it? You are going to lure me out of here so you can take what you want without your boss interfering?"

Irral bared his fangs in another grimace. "Of course not! You're a Breeder. I may be Jimmy's man, but what he's got planned for you... It isn't right. Your destiny is to birth us sons—not to lie bound on your back, servicing unworthy scum like a common whore."

"And being a broodmare is better?" She didn't try to keep the indignation, the horrified incredulity out of her voice.

"Yes." He didn't elaborate, but the look on his face as he stared at her made her swallow thickly. He might be a demon, he might be lying to her face for all she knew, but the tightness around his eyes suggested otherwise.

Georgia drew in a deep breath, trying to steady her reeling mind. She wanted to escape what Jimmy had in store for her more than almost anything. And no doubt, even if Irral planned to squirrel her away to *breed* her, escaping him would likely be easier than Jimmy. But...

"I can't go with you until I know Larry will be okay. Perhaps after—"

"Once he's been healed, I won't be able to get you out. The second the contract's complete, Jimmy owns you. There is no escaping him after that. So we go—*now*—or you will have to stay here. Forever." Irral held out his hand toward her, his frightening features softening into something like a plea. "Trust me when I tell you that no one is worth the fate that awaits your here, Breeder. Not even this brother of yours."

Her pulse throbbed in her throat as she stared at his offered hand. She couldn't choose her own life over her brother's. It felt... so wrong to even contemplate it. But the horror creeping up her spine at the demon's plea was hard to push down.

"Look, I am taking you to the Prince of Demons. He is the strongest of our kind on the Eastern Seaboard, and he will make sure you are protected. You can bargain with him for your sibling, if you must," Irral said, urgency coloring his words. "But you cannot stay here. *Come with me.*"

6

KESH

"There's a demon at the gates who insists on seeing you. Says it's urgent."

Kesh sighed deeply, pulling his attention from the war map he'd been trying to update with the latest news of their enemies' movements.

"More urgent than stopping the Europeans from taking Maine?" Kesh asked, his voice deceptively gentle.

Mallorn, accustomed to his lord's ways, took a slight step back, bringing him out of arm's reach. "I said you were busy. I more than hinted at what happened to the last underling who claimed an emergency and found you disagreed. He still insists."

Kesh growled, scrunching the map in his fist as irritation flared hotly. "Do these fools not realize the importance of what we're doing? How fucking close we are to annihilation? Why must they pester me with their petty squabbles? Who do I have to disembowel to get some peace?"

"Weight of the crown, I'm afraid," Mallon said, infuriatingly uncowed by his lord's anger. "He's waiting outside the throne room."

Kesh shot him a glare and straightened up. "Fine. Take five troops to Maine. Tell our warriors I'm sorry I can't help take down the invaders—I have a fucking contract dispute to settle, or whatever the hell it is this time."

The throne room still looked like the casino it had been up until recently. His men had done a decent job at taking out the gambling tables and slot machines, but the bar still remained along the eastern wall, and the stains of alcohol and stench of desperation weren't coming out of the carpet no matter how many times Mallorn had had it dry cleaned.

Kesh strode to the throne—an imposing chair bolted to the hastily constructed dais—and slung himself down, propping a foot on one armrest as he drummed his irritation into the other.

This was the part of the job he hated the most. If he'd known how much time he'd have to spend playing referee for minor demons bitching about someone screwing them over in contract negotiations, or listen to some lord or another wax poetic about how he thought the Kingdom should be run—or, stars forbid, try to curry favor with the prince—there was no way

Kesh would have helped his brother claim the Americas.

"Right. Send him in," he growled, motioning for the man guarding the door to open it.

The guard obeyed, pulling the painted-over glass door open with more pomp and circumstance than the situation required. Kesh swallowed his annoyance—the guy was doing his job. Ceremony was part of the illusion needed to claim a kingdom.

The man who entered looked like your standard low demon, more muscle than true power. Not exactly known for their interest in contracts. And one hundred percent not capable of having the sort of problems that'd be worthy of Kesh's attention.

"What do you want?" Kesh growled, staring holes through the demon's skull as he imagined hanging him from the rafters by his tongue.

"I... I bring you a gift, your Highness." The slight quake in his voice betrayed his unease at standing before the prince.

"A *gift?*" an outraged voice squawked. "What the hell do you mean, *a gift?*"

Kesh blinked, focusing on the human girl he'd barely noticed when the demon first entered. She was tall, for a human female, with unkempt dark hair, dark circles under her eyes and something between terror and fury plastered across her pale features.

"A gift?" he parroted, turning his attention back to

the demon. "You demand an audience with the Prince of Demons to give me a *human?* Have you lost your mind?"

"She's a Breeder, Highness," the demon said. "I wouldn't have disturbed you from your important work if she wasn't in desperate need of your protection."

Kesh blinked again, his gaze turning back to the female. "A Breeder?"

"Yes, my lord." The demon pushed the girl forward, despite her obvious reluctance. "I... found her. She sees us for what we are."

"And you didn't keep her?" Kesh arched an eyebrow, but kept his gaze on the girl, who was staring back at him, chin thrust out in defiance despite her wide eyes betraying her terror.

"N-no, my lord. That would be treason. I would never—"

Kesh silenced him with a raised hand. He knew the fucking laws—his brother had written them.

A Breeder.

He sent his Breeder sister-in-law a less than grateful thought. She might be the new queen, but she was also a gigantic pain in the ass. *And* the reason for the whole bloody war.

But of course, Selma was a Pure Breeder—the only human females capable of not only surviving sex with a demon lord, but also carrying his spawn. This sorry little thing might be exactly what he didn't need to deal with right now, but at least she'd be out of his hands soon enough.

If she even was a Breeder.

"If you consider me worthy, Your Highness, I would be most grateful to be considered among her suitors," the brawny demon said.

"I'm sure you would." Kesh sighed deeply and scrubbed a hand over his face, wishing his idiot brother hadn't rewritten the laws concerning Breeders, and motioned for her to step forward with a flick of two fingers. "Come on. Let's have a look, then."

The girl didn't move—only kept her blue eyes locked on him, the stubborn set of her chin wobbling.

Kesh narrowed his eyes at her disobedience. He leaned forward on the throne and ground through gritted teeth, "Come. Here. *Now.*"

She stumbled a step forward, as if jerked along by a chain, and Kesh leaned back, his smoldering temper calming ever so slightly.

The girl paused for a second, but the command in his gaze made her continue forward and up the dais, one hesitant step at a time until she stood in front of him. Her body shook ever so slightly as she stared at him, and her fear wafted against his nostrils, stirring a delicate sensation of unrest in his gut.

Ugh. Not a promising start.

Kesh pushed his foot off the armrest and reached for the girl. She might be taller than most human females, but she still only came to around eye-height with him when he was seated.

Her eyes went impossibly wider at the approach of his hand, and she tried to jerk away with a startled squeak, but she wasn't nearly fast enough. Kesh wrapped his fingers around her throat and brought her closer, ignoring her clawing to get out of his grip.

He pushed his index finger up, forcing the girl's head up and to the side, and buried his nose in her exposed neck.

Instantly, his senses were alight with a wash of scents, smells of other demons, hospitals. Human decay and chemicals clawed at his throat. But behind that...

Kesh closed his eyes and drew in another deep breath, his skin prickling with the sensation of her hair brushing against his face. Her fear was the strongest of the scents that belonged to her and not other pollutants she'd come across. It was thick and acrid and made him growl before he could stop himself.

She whimpered at the sound, and he huffed with irritation and breathed in again.

There was warmth underneath that fear. Something sultry and rich, tangled with something he couldn't quite put his finger on. Mindlessly, he sniffed her again, pulling her closer to his body to find the source of that enthralling scent.

She whimpered again and pushed against him, babbled some unimportant words of protest, and he smothered his annoyance at her resistance by wrapping her closer to his body, quelling her squirming with the strength of his arm around her back.

She was soft and warm against his chest, the press of her breasts and the small gasps of her breath sending fissures of excitement through his skin. He breathed her in, taking in greedy gulps, wishing he could wash away her terror so its scent wouldn't disrupt those beautiful notes underneath. It was disturbing, her fear—making unease spread from his gut to his blood, until all he could comprehend was how he needed her to be content.

"You're safe," he rumbled, his lips brushing over her skin and raising goosebumps along the slender column in his grip. Mindlessly, he loosened his grip on her throat, brushing his hand along her back to calm her.

The girl spluttered, outrage tingeing the sounds—and then, without warning, sharp pain bloomed through his arm.

Kesh jerked back, more from surprise than anything else, and blinked down at the little creature in his grasp. Her blunt teeth were still firmly lodged in his forearm from where she'd bitten him.

What...?

It was only then he realized what he'd done. He stared down at the woman in his arms in horror, sick dread clenching in his gut. He'd wrapped himself around her body like a fucking meat shield, the urge to protect and soothe still thundering in his blood, making his temples throb and his cock ache.

"*Shit,*" he muttered, pushing her off his lap hard enough to make her stumble a few steps backward, nearly tripping down the two steps of the dais.

Yeah. She was a Breeder, alright. One of the few human women capable of bearing a demon's offspring. And so fucking valuable, even the war would have to wait while he prepared her for a mate.

There'd been a time, before his brother took control of the Americas, when specialized Procurers would seek out and train these women, then auction them off to the highest bidder. But since Kain had met Selma, that was no longer how things were, because stars forbid anything be simple. His brother had literally gone to war with the previously reigning family to protect his mate—and by extension, the whole sub-race of sweet-scented little cunts she was part of.

These days, any potential Breeder was to be brought to the nearest lord, who would then be responsible for gentling the woman into her new life and finding a suitable mate for her.

And Prince or not—Kesh was the only lord within a fifty-mile radius.

He scrubbed his face with both hands, trying to steady himself from the onslaught of her scent as he gathered his thoughts. He'd have to ring and mark her, find some unlucky sod who'd be more than willing to spend the rest of eternity getting mind-fucked by her pheromones, somehow persuade her to allow a mating, and at the same time, while he was preoccupied with playing matchmaker not lose the entire fucking eastern coast to the European king.

He should have left his brother to rot in the old queen's prison.

Of course, then he'd have been responsible for Selma.

Kesh suppressed a shudder at the thought of claiming his brother's mate as his own and refocused on the current clusterfuck at hand.

The girl was huddled at the edge of the dais, seemingly too scared of him to try to run away, yet clearly not in any hurry to get closer either, and when he tore his gaze from her to address the sorry demon who'd brought him this nightmare, he found the rest of the throne room empty, save the guard.

"Where the fuck did he go?" he snarled at his guard, getting to his feet to take up pursuit. The Breeder stumbled another step back at the sudden movement, lost her balance—and fell down with a hard thump.

Without thought, Kesh took the stairs in one leap, kneeling by her side to cradle her head in his hand as he ensured she wasn't hurt.

"Don't touch me!" she hissed, cringing away from him. She pushed herself along the rug, scrambling to put distance between them.

"He left, your Highness," the guard said.

"I can fucking see that," Kesh growled, irritation flaring in his veins, both at the renewed smell of the Breeder's fear and his own inability to hunt down the demon who dropped her off. He had *questions*—but the girl was obviously not in a good state. And his first priority was to calm her down.

"Curse it all," he muttered, finally straightening up and taking a couple of steps back, putting enough space between himself and the girl to hopefully calm her down. If she was an unmarked Breeder, she'd be able to see his true form. Even if she'd been among demons before—which her scent suggested—he knew he would be frightening, his features much less human than most lowly demons'.

"Is she truly a Breeder, my lord?" the guard asked, the note of longing in his voice unmistakable. Kesh rolled his eyes—at least it'd be easy enough to find a man willing to mate her.

"Yes," he bit out. "And you will tell *no one*. Understand? We don't need the entire territory to be distracted."

"I would never," the man said, sounding more than a little aghast at the suggestion he might betray his prince.

Kesh sighed, shooting him a glance over his shoulder. He'd hand-picked every single man in his service. He knew they would never betray their loyalty to him.

"My lord..." the guard began.

"Once she is settled, I will put you on the list of potential suitors, Sefron," Kesh said, returning his focus to the girl still huddled on the floor. "Now, go. Bring food to my private residence." He wrinkled his nose as he looked the Breeder over, for the first time noticing how grimy she was. "And draw a bath, too."

"At once, my lord."

The sound of the doors closing behind Sefron echoed through the throne room, leaving Kesh alone with the Breeder.

7
GEORGIA

Georgia had seen a lot of demons in her life, but she'd never met one remotely as terrifying as the prince.

He was covered in reddish-black scales, black horns curving from his skull in an imposing arc, and his eyes were black as empty voids. But more than anything, it was the sheer *size* of him that had her struggling to control her panic.

He had to be more than eight feet tall with the muscular build to match, and the odd hum of *power* that seemed to vibrate off him made her hairs stand on end. It was like being in the presence of a nuclear bomb —with a temper.

Georgia stared mutely up at the giant demon, too terrified to move or get off the floor, but the prince didn't return her gaze. Muttering under his breath, he fished out a phone from his pocket and began... *texting?*

Georgia glanced at the device, startled by the sight of the modern gadget in the giant monster's huge hands. If he'd looked even slightly less menacing, it would have been an amusing juxtaposition.

This was supposed to be her savior? Georgia swallowed thickly as she watched the behemoth. The hairs on her body still stood on end from the sensation of his breath against her skin when he'd sniffed her. She had absolutely no doubt that if this monster decided to rape her, she'd not survive it.

The prince finished his text and shoved his phone back in his pocket before he finally rounded on her again.

She shrank back against the carpet on instinct when those void-like eyes landed on her, her breath hitching in her throat. "D-don't hurt me."

She didn't know why the ridiculous plea bubbled past her lips—he was a demon, and as far as she knew, hurting people was the entire purpose of their existence.

The prince arced both eye-ridges. "Don't *hurt* you?" He snorted, and she could have sworn exasperation flicked across his harrowing features. He opened his mouth as if to say more, but seemed to think better of it. With a deep sigh, he rubbed a clawed hand over his face and sank into a crouch several feet from where she was huddled. "You have nothing to fear, little one. Nothing bad will happen to you."

Georgia eyed him suspiciously. His voice had

changed pitch entirely, the gruff boom of it now sweetly cajoling. He sounded exactly like she did when trying to lure her mom's cat into his carrier for a vet visit.

"Then let me go," she said, tipping her chin up in an attempt to project strength she didn't feel.

He huffed another breath. "I would love to. But I can't. Thank your *friend* who dropped you off in my lap. I certainly plan to, if he ever has the bright idea to cross my path again." His voice had lost some of its dulcet tones to an acrid note.

Was he... *annoyed* at her presence? She blinked, the small burst of injustice that the giant monster who had her in his claws seemed inconvenienced at her plight gave way to a burst of wild hope.

"No one... No one has to know. I won't tell anyone, and I'm sure Irral is long gone."

The prince stared blankly at her for several seconds before he raised his hand to rub at the bridge of his nose. "No one has to know?" he parroted. "You don't know what you are, do you?"

Georgia hesitated, that uncomfortable word Jimmy and his bodyguards had called her echoing in her mind. There was no way she was saying that out loud. She didn't need the giant monster getting any ideas that she was on board with its implications.

"Right. Of course the prick didn't explain anything. Why would he, when he could just drop you off on my doorstep?" The demon drew in another deep breath.

"You see us for what we really are, yes? Horns, fangs, claws, et cetera?"

She nodded, eyes darting to the black, curved horns atop his head.

"Women who can see through our human disguise are rare. You're what we would call... *compatible*. We value your companionship immensely." He gave her a tight smile that did nothing to quell her unease. "And for that reason, it is my duty to protect you. There are those that would do you harm for what you are to us. So no. I cannot let you leave."

Right. *Companionship.* Georgia narrowed her eyes at the prince. Even if she hadn't experienced exactly what kind of *companionship* his kind was interested in, it was pretty obvious that he was glossing over some major details.

"I'll take my chances. I've managed on my own so far."

The demon's smile tightened until scary-looking fangs popped out from below his lips. If it was meant as a comforting gesture, it wholly missed the mark. "You've been lucky. You won't continue to be so. My men are loyal and will keep your presence in my domain a secret for as long as I request it. The scumbag who brought you to me? Less likely. And the *second* word gets out about you, darling, you'll be hunted down like a single rabbit by a pack of hungry jackals."

Georgia swallowed, instinctively cringing away from his menacing words. "I..." Her protest died before she'd voiced it. She knew exactly what Jimmy would do to her if he found her again. The demon prince was the singularly most terrifying creature she'd ever laid eyes on, and he was most definitely not being forthright about his plans for her, but... He might still be better than the alternative. Irral had certainly believed so, or he wouldn't have risked his superior's wrath to bring her here.

Defeat slumped her shoulders and pressed down on the knot of guilt and despair that had festered in her stomach since her mother had told her that Larry was dying. She had failed them both. And Mike. And for what? A more comfortable cage?

The tears came unbidden and without warning. Grief cracked through her esophagus and up her wind-pipe, releasing through her throat in loud, ugly sobs.

"What are you doing?" The demon croaked, the sound of alarm in his voice making it pitch. "Stop that!"

Through the tears blurring her vision, she saw his terrifying face pull into a look of pure panic. It seemed so completely out of place on his brutal features, she would have laughed if she'd been capable of feeling anything but heartbreak.

"Stop it!" His voice was a more appropriate, commanding boom this time, but it did nothing to quiet her sobs.

The demon growled under his breath, his fangs showing once more before he crossed the space between them and reached for her.

Georgia yelped, fear spiking through her sadness, but she didn't manage to flinch away before he dropped to his knees and bulky arms closed around her body and pulled her onto his lap.

Heat enveloped her from all sides, seeping through her clothes and sinking into her skin, making her panicked heartbeat stutter even as she pushed at his impossibly hard chest to escape the uninvited closeness to the monster. "Let me go!"

"Stop. Please, stop." The pleading note to his voice was wholly unexpected, as was the hesitant way his large hands brushed down her back, almost as if he was fighting some insurmountable compulsion to try to soothe her.

Georgia blinked, her hands stilling against his chest from pure shock. Was he... trying to *comfort* her?

She looked up at him through the blurry haze of tears—at his massive horns, his black eyes and monstrous face—and saw anguish on those terrifying features.

The prince exhaled a shaky breath, his dark gaze darting over her as if to ensure she was physically unharmed. "Don't cry. You're safe. I promise, little one. You won't be hurt. Please don't cry."

He *was*. For whatever unfathomable reason, the giant, horned monster was kneeling on the stained carpet of his own throne room, holding her like a child in an attempt to *comfort* her.

Her pain shouldn't have mattered to him. Heck, he

was a demon—he should have delighted in it. But as she stared at him through snot and tears, it was obvious that he, at the very least, desperately wanted her to stop crying. Why, she couldn't fathom, but the reluctance painted all over his demonic features as he tried to soothe her made it clear this wasn't a manipulation. No one was that good an actor—not even a demon prince.

Irral's words came back to her on a wave of desperation. He was the Prince of Demons. The strongest of his kind in the area—but a demon. She could attempt the bargain that had started her journey into this nightmare again.

"My brother is dying." The horrible words tumbled out of her mouth on a bubble of saliva, pulling a fresh wave of tears with them.

The demon blinked in what looked like a moment's confusion, but his face immediately broke in dismay at her renewed sobbing.

"Humans die all the time. It's nothing to be upset about," he said. Judging from the softness of his voice, she assumed he was still trying to soothe her, but the cruelty in those words did nothing to calm her anguish.

"He's nineteen! He's not supposed to die, not yet!" She hadn't meant to yell, but fury at the injustice of Larry's illness ignited at the demon's callousness. "You can save him. Can't you? You're a prince. You're strong enough?"

He stared at her for a long moment, his hands

stilling their stroking movements against her back as his features smoothed into stony blankness.

"If you want me to stop crying, if you... If you want me to accept this, you have to save him. I can't... I can't live if he dies." She set her wobbly chin and held his dark gaze, trying to force enough calm through her lungs to stop the grief still making her shake. "You have to."

The prince let out a slow breath, not breaking her stare. "I *have* to?"

Where softness had painted his deep voice before, ice had taken its place. Ice, and darkness.

Georgia only barely managed not to shrink away as a new wave of fear washed through her. Whatever mimic of empathy had been present in him before, it was gone now.

"Please," she croaked. "What you want from me... Companionship. I'll give it willingly, if you just... Save him."

"You're attempting a *bargain* with the Prince of Demons?" he said softly. "After I have offered you safe haven? My protection?"

"Isn't that what you do?" There was most definitely an unspoken warning in his silken voice, but for Larry... The prince was terrifying, but if he truly was as reluctant to harm her as he seemed, he was a better fate than the whorehouse. And he was right—if she fled his protection, she would only end up in the hands of Jimmy or someone like him. No matter what she did, she would end up as a *companion*. If she could save Larry by doing so, she might as well surrender voluntarily.

The demon gave her a hard look. Then he pushed her off his lap and rose up to his full height in an agile move, leaving her huddled alone at his feet and unexpectedly cold without the warmth of his embrace. "I rarely have the need to strike bargains with humans. What I want, I take."

She swallowed at the implication and silently prayed that his discomfort at her tears meant what she hoped it did. "If you want my compliance, you will save my brother. Do that... and I won't fight you. Just... don't hurt me. Please."

He was silent for a long moment. Then, finally, with a pull of his mouth, he nodded. "Fine. If that is your wish, then you shall have your bargain. I will not harm you, and I will save your brother. In return, you will submit yourself to whatever I require without a fight."

It sounded better than any deal she could have hoped for, but the dark look in those void-like eyes made her shudder. He looked... angry.

Not that his mood mattered. He would save Larry, and all she had to give up in return was her resistance to a fate she wouldn't be able to escape, regardless.

Gathering her leftover scraps of strength, she returned his dark gaze. "Then I, Georgia Moore, agree to your bargain, Prince of Demons."

8

KESH

The sun had crested the horizon when he drove them through the city in the quiet hours. Soon, the streets would once again be busy with humans going about their daily drum, oblivious to the creatures who ruled at night. This was the only time the city knew true quiet, once the drunks and thugs had gone home, and the ordinary citizens were only just starting to wake.

It was also the best time to avoid drawing attention from his own kind—something he desired even more than usual, considering the passenger he was carrying on the back of his bike.

In times of peace, he could accept that Breeders were a boon to their kind. Since their own females refused to give them sons, they needed the human women capable of bearing them heirs. But in times of war, the sweetly scented little cunts were nothing but distractions. One word of an unmated Breeder in his territory, and every one of his otherwise loyal warriors would be too busy proving himself the best choice to court her to protect his domain against their enemies.

Behind him, the girl pressed in against his back, and he cursed himself for not taking the time to source a car for the ride to the hospital where her sick brother waited for death.

As much as Kesh loathed her kind for how they fucked with otherwise dependable men's minds, he wasn't immune to her enchantments. The soft press of her body against his back had his cock at half-mast, his blood thrumming with eagerness to remove the clothes separating her soft skin from his.

How fucking undignified.

At least she wasn't crying anymore. The sense of pure panic that had gripped him by the throat at the sound and smell of her tears was still fresh in his recollection, his muscles still wound too tight from the complete clarity that if she didn't stop crying, he would die. Simply... cease to exist.

This insignificant human who'd been dumped on his doorstep—a female he had no desire to keep for any longer than he absolutely had to, let alone know—had almost dismantled him. In those moments her sobs had echoed through his throne room and straight into his gut, she'd held his entire, immortal existence by the throat.

And the second she'd realized as much? She'd used it to get her way.

Kesh bared his teeth, his cock softening partly in the presence of his anger. He knew what conniving bitches Breeders could be—though he was pretty sure they weren't even cognizant about their influence most of the time.

Georgia, though. Georgia had seen the weakness she'd stirred, and she'd struck.

A bargain. It was not a surprise—desperate humans had called upon his kind since the dawn of time, pouring out their deepest desires as if they'd summoned nothing more than a benevolent djinn. He had granted several such wishes in his lifetime. And he had collected his payment once it was done.

Not one of the miserable cretins had found their bargain worth it, in the end.

He hadn't made Georgia sign a contract—it would only complicate matters for whichever sorry fuck ended up claiming her, and he'd rather not have any evidence. He may not have forced her into a bargain, but he doubted his temperamental sister-in-law—his new queen—would approve, should she ever find out.

Besides, the only thing he needed from her was compliance for as long as she was under his care. This way, he wouldn't need to pamper and cajole the little bitch. He'd simply demand she submit to getting ringed, branded, and given away to some sorry fuck who would only be too happy to be enslaved by her cunt for the rest of eternity.

With a little luck, she'd be out of his hair by the end of the week.

Sure, it wasn't entirely in the spirit of the law that obligated lords to gentle new Breeders, but not losing his brother the entire East Coast ranked infinitely higher on his list of priorities than easing a Breeder into her new life. Especially a Breeder who was clearly not above purposely manipulating him with her cursed pheromones.

Georgia shifted behind him, her arms tightening around his waist for added security, and he swallowed a curse at the stutter in his chest as his dick surged with renewed want.

It was only pheromones. *Chemicals and instincts.* She was nothing but an irritating distraction from his duties, and soon, she'd be someone else's problem.

Oh, how he couldn't fucking wait.

———

THE HOSPITAL WAS MOSTLY QUIET——AS QUIET AS SUCH A HUB of human suffering ever got. A few scrubs-clad people gave him apprehensive looks as the Breeder led him through antiseptic-smelling hallways. As a lord, there was only so much Kesh could do to blend in with humans. He could take on the appearance of a mortal, sure, but his nearly eight-foot demonic frame couldn't entirely fit into normal human proportions, and there were places he stuck out like a beacon. The quiet of a hospital at dawn was definitely one of them, and the caregivers' natural urges to protect their patience flared at the sight of him.

However, Georgia's presence seemed to stop any protests at his presence. Possibly because, while he clearly did not belong there, she looked exactly like someone who did: small, weak, disheveled, and distressed.

"When did you last sleep?" he asked, the lines on her pale face drawing his attention.

"I..." She frowned, glancing at him before quickly turning her attention straight ahead again. She did that a lot—tried not to look at him. "Yesterday. I think. Time's... a little blurry. Anyway, it doesn't matter. I'll sleep once Larry's better."

He grunted. He shouldn't let her sleep until she'd been securely processed, now that their bargain meant he didn't have to spend time gentling her first.

But... She looked so damned weak. Like she was teetering on the edge, only pure desperation still keeping her upright.

Had she eaten? He'd spent enough time around humans to know they needed to feed frequently.

"It's here." Georgia interrupted his spiraling thoughts as she stopped in front of a closed door. She drew in a slow breath before she pushed the door open.

The room housed three sleeping humans—one

female and two males, one of whom was occupying the hospital bed. The other man and woman sat on each their side of the bed, sound asleep in uncomfortable-looking chairs. The brimstone touch of demonic magic hovered over the cloying scent of lingering death.

"The demon you were with was here?" he asked, keeping his voice low. It wasn't particularly strong magic—unsurprisingly. The goon who'd brought her to him wouldn't have had the power to do anything for a sick human. He was surprised he'd even tried.

"He said he wasn't strong enough." Her gaze didn't leave the male on the bed. "Please tell me you are. If he dies, I... Please."

Kesh shuddered at the whispered plea. It slid like a silky caress up his spine and into his chest, squeezing his lungs with the urge to soothe. To take away the pain so clear in her hoarse voice.

Her fucking pheromones again.

Kesh bared his teeth in a silent growl, taking a moment to force his brain back into control before he crossed the room and stopped by the bed.

The young man's breathing was shallow and uneven. It wouldn't be long before death claimed him.

Kesh placed a hand on his chest and, grunting with the effort, shoved his dark magic into the boy.

Strictly speaking, demonic magic wasn't particularly useful for healing—but as with all things in life, with enough power, most problems could be forced into submission. Including this kid's illness.

Cancerous cells had spread through his system like a network of underground fungi, and the damage was vast and went deep. Stronger than he'd ever seen before.

No wonder the third-rank demon who'd exploited her desperation hadn't been able to help.

Kesh gritted his teeth as he forced his power through the boy's spine, tensing his muscles to overload his magic enough to catch a spark. The flesh below his palm was like a dry sponge, sucking up every drop of power he poured in, and it took a long time before a flicker of energy moved along his backbone.

Slowly, so, *so* slowly, his magic chased away the shadow of death. In response, the young man's breathing turned deeper.

More and more power syphoned from Kesh's body to the boy's, driving back the disease with sheer force, until finally, there was not so much as the shadow of a tumor left.

Breathing in harsh pants, Kesh stepped away from the bed, propping himself up against the wall with a shaky hand. *Shit.* He hadn't anticipated how much of his energy it would take to cure the little prick.

"Is he...?" Georgia's voice ripped him from the haze of exhaustion as she cautiously stepped toward the bed as if frightened her mere approach would send the boy to his death. "Did you...?"

"He is healed," Kesh growled, irritation sparking at the roughened state of his voice. The last thing he needed was the girl to clock on to how weak he was right now. She'd already proven herself exceedingly skilled at manipulation when he'd had more strength to resist.

But Georgia didn't pay him any notice. Stumbling, she moved to the other side of the bed. "Larry," she whispered, touching her brother's pale face with a gentle hand. "Larry, wake up. Show me he's telling the truth. Please. I need you to wake up."

The kid's eyelids fluttered, his lips pulling into a sleepy smile at the sight of her. "Georgie? What time is it?"

She drew in a small breath, her hand against his face shaking as she stroked his cheek. "It's still early. How are you feeling, Lar?"

"Oh, you know, great," he said, voice dry as if delivering a well-rehearsed line of sarcasm. Then he frowned, his brows knitting. "Actually, I... I *do* feel good."

"How's the pain?" she asked.

The boy's frown deepened. "It's... it's gone. Did they give me new pain meds?"

The Breeder let out a little sob, her trembling fingers still caressing his face. "No, Lar. You're cured. You're gonna be alright."

"What? How is that even—?" Larry's voice died when his gaze landed on Kesh. He stared at him for a long while, then returned his focus to his sister. "Georgie... who's that?"

"He's no one," she said, smiling through tears. "No one that matters. All that's important right now is that you're okay."

No one that matters. Only the demon here to take her away as payment for a second lease on this sorry human's life.

"It's time to go." Kesh pushed off the wall and closed the distance to the Breeder, planting a large hand on her shoulder. She jolted at the contact, drawing in a shallow breath.

The boy in the bed jerked at his sister's reaction, pushing himself up as if he were thinking of coming to her rescue.

She must have thought so too, because she raised her hand to stave him off. "It's alright, Lar. I need to go."

"Go where?" Larry asked, his gaze darting back to Kesh. "Georgia, go where?"

"Away. For a little while." She smiled at him and let her palm fall from his face, catching his hand between hers without disturbing the tubing sticking out of it. "Please, Larry. Don't worry about me, okay? You have a whole life to live now, and I'll be alright. All I need is to know that you're happy and healthy."

Larry looked at her, his gaze flickering to Kesh for another glance before he returned his focus to his sister once more. "Who is he, Georgia?"

"He's a friend." She still smiled, though the scent of her tears was becoming strong enough to put Kesh on edge. Noises from beyond the closed door alerted him that the hospital was waking. He tightened his grip on her shoulder.

"*Now*, Breeder," he grunted.

She winced at the unspoken threat in his voice and nodded. "I'm coming. Bye, Lar. Take care of Mom, okay? And tell her not to worry about me. You both deserve to be happy, and I'll be okay, I promise."

"Georgia, no." Larry clamped down on her hand, strength he hadn't possessed in a long time keeping her by his side. "Is he... is he one of... of *them?* Are they... are they real? Is that why I'm better? What did you do? What did you give him?"

Georgia grimaced, stroking her brother's arm with her free hand, trying to calm him, but Kesh was out of patience.

He reached down and wrenched the mortal's hand off her, yanking her back from the bed. When the kid protested and tried to scramble off the bed to come to her aid, Kesh sent him backward with a push of energy.

"Your sister made a bargain to save your miserable life, kid. Don't waste her sacrifice by trying to play the hero now," he warned, giving the human a glare so dark it made Larry gasp with terror despite the human disguise he saw. "If you think to come looking for her, know that not only will I undo what I've done for you this morning, I will seek out every blood relation you have and break their bodies apart while you gasp for your last breath. The last thing you'll see before you meet your own death is their intestines pulled from their guts and their bones snapped and sucked for marrow, one by one. While they still scream. Understand?"

Neither of the two siblings said a word, but the sharp stench of fear hit his nostrils with all the confirmation he needed to know that his warning had been heard.

Without another look back to the bed, he pulled Georgia from her brother's grasp and out the door. Leaving her family behind for good.

9
GEORGIA

The demon didn't take them back to the refurbished casino where she'd first met him. Instead, he drove the roaring motorcycle through the early morning traffic toward a part of town she'd never been to before—a choice she'd made entirely on purpose.

Broken down old buildings shielded them from the pale sun's first rays, the stench of decay clinging to her skin when the prince kicked the bike to a stop.

Georgia released his waist the second it was safe to do so. As thankful as she'd been that he'd healed Larry, his growled threat as he pulled her from the room still echoed in her mind as a sharp reminder of what, exactly, her brother's savior was.

She cast a nervous look around at the bleak loca-tion. A figure sat huddled by a scratched doorway on their left, but otherwise there was no sign of life. "Where are we?"

The demon grunted but didn't answer, swinging off the bike and pulling her with him in the process. With a firm grasp on her arm, he started walking toward the door.

"W-what are you going to do with me?" she asked, fear prickling at her spine. The last time a demon had dragged her to a deserted-looking building, it'd been with the purpose of forcing her into prostitution. While Irral's comments had made it seem like this demon prince wouldn't want the same fate for her, she wasn't stupid. They called her a Breeder—there were only so many ways this could end up for her.

Once more, the giant monster by her side didn't answer her question, and she tried her best to not panic as he dragged her down a dingy hallway to a dimly lit staircase. She'd agreed to this, and he'd held up his end of the bargain. Larry was well. He'd have a good life.

Whatever the prince had planned for her, hopefully it would be marginally better than what her fate would have been if Jimmy the Pimp had been the one to fulfill her contract.

The staircase was littered with old fast-food wrappers, syringes, and all manner of dirt and grime of questionable origin. Blood and excrement smeared the walls, making Georgia gag as they climbed the stairs.

At the top, the demon turned left and opened a door

to a restroom in an even worse state than the stairwell. He pulled her inside, and she had to clasp a hand to her mouth and nose to avoid dry-heaving at the stench.

On the filthy floor lay two sleeping people. Or perhaps they were passed out. A syringe stuck out between the guy's toes, and what looked like a crack pipe dangled from the woman's fingers. She was smiling, though the only sign that she was still alive was the faint up and down movements of her chest.

Georgia's stomach clenched tight at the sight of them. Whatever had happened to these two that the only place they could find happiness was in this hellhole, she wished with all she was that she could take it away. Help them somehow.

The demon closed the door shut behind them and finally released his grip on her arm, turning to the man on the floor. With a snarl of disgust on his terrifying features, he plucked the syringe from the man's foot and lifted him up by the scruff of his neck, dangling him in front of his face. Eying him as if he were a piece of meat.

Sick dread rose as bile in Georgia's throat. They weren't here to help these two, that much was obvious.

"What are you going to do to him?" she croaked. "Please, don't... don't hurt him."

The monster didn't so much as turn to look at her. With his free hand, he grabbed the man's head and squeezed.

The crack as his skull broke sent Georgia forward with a lurch, bile spilling from her lips as she coughed and gagged. It was a mercy, really, because she didn't see what he did with the freed brain matter after that. The comments about Lewin's dietary habits were too fresh in her mind for even an ounce of morbid curiosity to make it through the horror.

She dry-heaved until the body of the now dead man, with scars so deep they'd driven him to this place, landed on the floor in front of her with a thunk. Through streams of tears, she saw the demon step over his limp corpse, moving toward the still comatose woman.

It was only the sickening knowledge of what he intended to do next that gave her the strength to stagger forward and throw herself over the woman's prone body.

"No! Don't!" Her voice was hoarse and harrowed, still raw from throwing up bile and the sheer terror shaking her body. It took all her strength to turn and look up at the frightening monster looming over them. His already horrifying features were pulled into a silent snarl at her interference. Dark liquid glistened on his lips.

"Move, Breeder." The command was quiet. A dark warning.

"Please. Please don't hurt her," Georgia whispered. "Please, oh God, you can't... please!"

His eyes narrowed. "I *can't?*"

She swallowed thickly, realizing the challenge he took from her words. And that she wouldn't win a battle of wills. Not with this beast. "Please."

The demon huffed a sigh—an irritated sound, but it gave her a surge of hope. He could have easily removed her and murdered this helpless woman if he wanted to, no matter how much Georgia protested. But so far, he hadn't.

"Your brother took a lot of my power. I need to refill. If not from this useless pile of flesh, then who, little Breeder?" He stared at her, the darkness of his eyes making her shiver as she clung to the passed-out woman underneath her. "Who would you like me to take the energy I need from? Give me a name. Who deserves to live less than this pitiful stain on humanity?"

Georgia breathed shallowly as the horror curdled in her stomach and turned inward. It hadn't so much as crossed her mind before—that there would be a cost to what she'd asked of him, beyond their agreement. That his power didn't come from nothing, that it would need replenishment. And that for a demon, that meant... *this.*

The challenge in his inhuman black eyes was clear. Someone was going to give him what he needed, and she had gotten in the way of his feeding. He knew she couldn't name someone to die. He likely read it on her soul as she huddled over this nameless woman whom no one would ever miss, if she just let him take what he wanted.

There was no winning, not with him. She felt it in the pit of her stomach as he stared her down, challenging her to either give up the woman she was currently protecting or naming someone more deserving of dying.

She was the reason he was here. She'd made the bargain with him, she was why he needed to refill.

"Me," she said softly. "Take your energy from me."

His brow ridges arched high on his scaly forehead, arms crossing over his massive chest. "You? Are you so much of a martyr that you'll throw your life away for anyone you stumble across? First your brother, and now this wretch?"

Georgia forced her throat to swallow the lump lodged there. She was gambling with true darkness; she understood that much as she stared into the voids of his eyes. Perhaps it was everything she'd already seen today, perhaps it was sheer exhaustion, or a full psychotic break, but she knew the only way to save this woman was to bank on the fact the prince seemed to want her not-dead. For now.

"You can take energy without killing. Right?" She remembered Jimmy's words about how demons went about obtaining human life force. How it could be done in so many horrible ways.

And how, for women, there was one universally preferred source.

She forced herself to remain silent as she waited for his answer. Rape at his hands would unquestionably lead to mutilation and death—he was just too big for any other outcome from a violent encounter.

But he wanted her alive. However he went about taking what he needed from her, she'd be better off than the poor woman in here with them. She clung to that thought as she stared up at the huge beast.

The horned monster drew in a deep breath as he stared down at her, seemingly evaluating her offer. Then he nodded once, but the dark look in those void-like eyes had her skin break into goosebumps. "If you are so determined to sacrifice yourself, fine. Stand."

He watched her impassively as she scrambled to get up from her prone position, arms never leaving his chest. Once she was on her feet, he nodded toward the door. "Move."

Shakily, she obeyed, feeling his looming presence behind her like a stalking beast as they made their way down the filthy stairs, out the door and all the way to his bike.

Only then did he move from behind her, straddling the vehicle before he turned to look at her over his shoulder. "On."

"Where are you taking me?" she asked, though she did as she was told, not wanting him to change his mind and return to the building and the unconscious woman in that awful bathroom.

"Home." Without another word, he kicked the bike into gear, the engine roaring to life between her thighs.

Georgia clung to his leather clad waist as he drove them through the city, the aching pulse in her heart reminding her that she would likely never see anything she could call home ever again.

10

KESH

There were many ways for demons to feed, few of them pleasant for the human providing the meal.

Kesh went over them all as he drove Georgia through the city to his private residence. He usually wasn't too particular about how he extracted the human life force he needed to sustain himself, but he couldn't exactly kill the girl to get his fix—which left out most of the more filling options.

I could terrorize her, he thought sourly as an image flickered for his mind's eye. One of her tear-stricken face when she'd protected that worthless female. Why she would care about some random human she didn't know, one who clearly didn't care much about herself, he couldn't understand. And to care enough to take a stand... Against *him.* It irritated him to the bone.

He'd known the girl for a few hours, and twice in

the span of that time, she'd sacrificed herself for the benefit of someone else. *Disgusting.*

I should make her think twice about throwing herself in harm's way for whatever pitiful human she comes across.

But as much as the thought of punishing her for her ridiculous inclination toward martyrdom appealed to him, realism shuddered through his lungs for every breath he took that tasted like the bitter notes of her fear.

The scent of her terror had been pulling at his instincts to soothe and *protect* since the abandoned building—especially frustrating since he was well aware her horror was about him, and any attempt at soothing it would only be met with more fear. He wouldn't be able to feed from her terror if every cell in his body was aching to calm her.

When he pulled up in front of his high-rise, he was still no closer to deciding how he would replenish his strength, but his circling thoughts changed course at the sight of the two guards stationed outside the entrance.

Shit.

"Don't so much as breathe until we're inside," he growled quietly over his shoulder before he switched off the ignition and got off the bike, pulling the girl in close against his body in the process. The smell of her fear intensified, but hopefully his own scent would drown out hers. If she'd been awakened, he would have no hope of his men being oblivious to the lush aroma of a Breeder, but until he got her ringed and marked, she would be much more difficult to clock.

Fortunate, since he wasn't ready to deal with the distraction her presence in his domain would cause, once his underlings knew a mate was in the process of being prepared.

"All is quiet, Your Highness," one of the guards—Greyer—greeted him. "No callers through the night."

Kesh nodded. "Good. Make sure no one disturbs me today. I don't care how big of a contract dispute they have. I don't even care if the Europeans are on my doorstep knocking, you got it? *No* disturbances."

The other guard slanted a look at Georgia, half-hidden in Kesh's armpit, and gave him a smirk. "Of course. I take it she is why Sefron came by with food a few hours ago? It's been a while—think feeding her will get her through alive?"

"Don't worry about her, Leopold," Kesh growled, the warning in his voice clear enough for his guard's smirk to whither. "You will tell *no one* of her presence here."

"Of course, Your Highness," Greyer said, his voice infinitely more formal than his partner's. Kesh had a vague thought that he really should make sure Leopold learned better manners too, but Georgia's increased trembling against him had his focus returning to her before he could make good on the notion.

Probably the word 'alive' had been too much for the Breeder's already frayed nerves.

With a final glare at his underlings, Kesh strode to the door, pulling Georgia with him. Her body was stiff against his, the scent of her fear burning the back of his throat, but he kept her secure in his grip until they were inside the empty, marble-clad lobby and the door closed shut behind them. Only then did he release her shoulders.

Georgia immediately stumbled several steps away from him. *"Alive?"* she hissed, confirming his assumptions.

"Our deal is that I don't harm you," he sighed, flicking two fingers at her in the direction of the elevator.

Despite the disgust on her face, she obeyed his unspoken command. "But the other women you drag home? You kill them when you're done raping them?"

Kesh arched his eye-ridges at her as he followed her in the elevator and hit the button for the top floor. "I rape them, do I?"

Red splotches appeared on her too-pale cheeks. "I assume the Prince of Demons doesn't haul girls into his lair to play chess."

Annoyance burned through his already paper-thin patience, and he leaned in over her, bracing an arm above her head to glare down at her. "The females I bring home see my human disguise, Breeder. They are more than willing."

His looming nearness did nothing to still her quivering, but she jutted out her chin in defiance. "You are a demon. I know what your kind does to women."

He wasn't sure why he bothered arguing. He really shouldn't give a shit that she thought him a rapist. With a dark glare at her, he pushed off the wall and shifted his focus to the display showing the incline in floors. She could believe what she wanted—he didn't need her to trust him. Not with the deal they'd made. All he needed was for her to obey his command to pick a mate, once he had prepared her with a blinding mark and selected a list of appropriate males she could choose from.

But first, he needed to fucking eat. Somehow. Why had he caved when she'd begged for him to take her energy instead? He needed more than he could take without harming whatever human he got his fix from, and the Breeder already looked like she was about to keel over.

Oh, right, yes. She'd cried.

When the elevator doors dinged open, Kesh grabbed her by the arm and pulled her through to his front door. She didn't object, but her tremor at his touch transferred up through his arm and into his chest. He stopped short on the threshold.

Sefron had been busy.

Kesh grimaced as the stench of the multiple bouquets of red roses littering every surface within view of the front door hit his nostrils. Growling a low curse, he ignored the floral assault on his otherwise sparse interior and continued through to the open-plan living space where the rarely used kitchen island was laden with trays upon trays of food. There were platters of fruit—three different kinds of melon, berries in all shades of red and purple, and bananas arranged upright in between them in obvious phallic reference. Oysters dripped with lemon and decorated with caviar, smoked salmon and pots of clotted cheese next to rolls of bread and seeded bagels, slices of beef, dripping butter and arranged on top of green leaves. And, at the end of the display, a three-layer chocolate cake decorated with dark frosting and glossy cherries. Kesh wasn't all that familiar with how much a human woman needed to sustain herself, but as far as he could tell, it looked... acceptable.

By his side, Georgia's eyes widened as she took in the offerings. "Are you... Are you going to share me?"

"Share you?" he growled, irritation still fizzing in his veins. "If I can get enough energy from you to make it through the day, it'll be a fucking miracle. If I shared you, you'd die. Now *eat.*"

Her mouth opened and closed once, something like relief flickering over her strained features before she looked back at the food, eyebrows rising. "So... no one else is coming? All this food... You had this prepared *just* for us?"

"For you. I don't care for human food." He released her arm and sank onto one of the bar stools by the island so he could rest his elbows on the counter.

"Then what do you—Oh." Her voice died off before she could finish the question, her skin turning impossibly paler. "Right. You eat *us*. How could I forget."

Kesh rolled his eyes at the tremor in her voice, even while his gut tightened with the ridiculous urge to coo at her until it went away. "Just fucking *eat*, Breeder. You need sustenance before I can take any energy from you. Unless you've changed your mind? I can easily go back for my original meal."

"No. Please. I haven't changed my mind," she croaked, quickly stumbling onto the stool next to him.

He watched her with an irritated scowl as she began to pluck first pieces of fruit, then a roll of bread, layering it with a thin slice of fish. She smelled like fear again, and the sweat, blood, and shit from where she'd knelt on the stained bathroom floor to stop him from killing the other woman.

She was terrified of him, and still, she obeyed his command at the threat to this nameless, faceless human who wouldn't have been missed by another soul. What a pointless self-sacrifice.

Disgusting.

"That's not enough." Kesh narrowed his eyes at the bread roll halfway to the Breeder's mouth. He may not know much about human nutrition, but he did know that a woman about to provide a demon lord with energy needed more sustenance than that wafery piece of smoked salmon could offer.

"What?" She froze, her arm spasming when he

reached forward. But he didn't touch her—only pushed the dish of yellow butter toward her with two fingers.

"You need more..." He flicked his wrist at the spread when the right word came to him, albeit belatedly. "Calories. Nutrients."

She eyed him dubiously, but even though she looked like she wanted to argue, she held her tongue. Slowly, she put the roll down, picked off the fish and began spreading a thin layer of butter on the bread.

"More," he demanded.

The Breeder huffed a breath through her nose. This time, her lips parted before she managed to rein in her protests, but a tightening of his eyes made her close them again.

"And more of that, too," he said, when butter glistened thickly on top of the roll and she placed the fish on top of it again.

She didn't look at him—just flattened her lips and picked up another slice of salmon.

"One more. And some of the... green stuff." He pointed at the vegetation scattered around the tray of salmon. Out of all the variations of human food, plants seemed the least appealing to him. There was no blood and no killing involved, which made it even more uninteresting than whatever else her kind used to fill their bellies. However, he had a vague sense that it was necessary for their survival. Something-something crop-failures and starvation.

Georgia shot him a look out the corner of her eyes

before she reached for the feathery foliage and a brightly colored slice of citrus. "Is it okay now?"

"It'll do."

She gave him another side-glance before carefully biting into the roll. He wasn't prepared for the suction in his gut when her eyelids fluttered shut and an involuntary moan of pleasure brushed past the mouthful of food.

Stars above. Kesh clutched at the edge of the countertop, his eyes trained on the Breeder's pink lips as she chewed and swallowed. Energy pulsed at the base of his spine, the urge to lick butter off the corner of her mouth as intense as it was bewildering.

"Again." The gruffness in his voice wasn't from anger this time, but Georgia jumped at the sound of it, her muscles twitching before she took another bite. She didn't moan with pleasure at the taste like before, not that it did anything to stop the throbbing in his cock at the sight of her taking in nourishment. Nourishment *he'd* provided.

When she finished the roll, he didn't wait for her to choose her next piece. He picked up three oysters, two slices of beef, and several pieces of cheese and put them on her plate. "Eat."

She bit her lip, blunt teeth digging into the pillowy flesh for a hesitant second before she picked up one of the caviar-covered shells.

He nearly came when her tongue darted out to lick

up the insides and a small hum escaped her at the taste of it.

Kesh didn't let her finish what was on her plate this time—he chose bits and pieces from the spread and put them in front of her, his own hunger inflaming his desire to keep feeding the Breeder under his care.

But some forty minutes later, when she was halfway through a large slice of chocolate cake, and before she'd even tasted the deep-red cherries atop it, Georgia put down her fork with a groan.

"You stopped," he said, the note of warning in his voice making the woman flinch.

"I'm full."

"You're not done." He narrowed his eyes at her. "You will eat what I have provided."

Her eyes darted over the still mostly full platters of food in front of them, widening slightly. "You want me to eat *all* of...?" She barked a sharp sound—a laugh with more than an edge of hysteria. "Feeding me until I rupture was *so* not the way I thought you'd kill me."

"I'm not going to harm you," he growled, as irritated that he had to repeat himself on the matter as he was that it was true. If simply killing her had been an option, it would have been a far simpler solution to the problem her presence presented. "I'm nourishing you. So *eat.*"

The Breeder hid her face in her hands. She drew in a few shaky breaths and rubbed her fingertips against her forehead. "I'm full. If you force me to eat anymore, I'm going to be sick. Unless you plan on going full *Seven,* you have to let me stop."

Kesh bared his teeth, frustration nearly drowning out the single note of worry at that word. Feeding her too much could make her *sick?* Why was that even a thing? A demon could be sated, sure, but sick from consuming too much nourishment? No. If they were *this* fragile, how humans had managed to overpopulate the planet was a fucking mystery.

"Fine." It came out as a snarl he almost regretted when the Breeder jumped in response, and her already fear-heavy scent spiked in his nostrils. "Come."

Georgia hesitated for several seconds, but when he held out an arm and gave her a pointed look, she seemed to finally remember the consequences of disobedience. She followed him out of the room without a word.

———

FOR A DEMON PRINCE, KESH DIDN'T HAVE MANY indulgences. As the lord of his area, he had his pick of hunting grounds, and the taxes his not-so-loyal subjects paid for his patronage afforded him enough wealth to rival the deep coffers of European nobility. He'd never seen much appeal in hunting for sport, nor in most of the human luxuries his riches could buy. Except for maybe *one* thing.

His bedroom was large but sparsely decorated,

because the focus of the room was the floor-to-ceiling wall of windows offering an undisturbed view of the city's rooftops and the large expanse of the sky above. And in front of it, a large copper tub stood on a dais cut from white marble.

Sefron had set it up as requested and added several sprinkles of pink rose petals and a circle of candles that had long since burned down.

Kesh smothered an eyeroll and crossed the floor to dip a finger into the tub. Cold. *Great.* Just another wonderful consequence of being forced to take a several-hours detour to that cursed hospital.

He eyed the Breeder, who seemed too transfixed by his large bed to notice his attention, and weighed his options. She smelled like sweat and fear and hospital—scents he usually didn't mind in a meal—but on her, it was messing with his stupid instincts to the point that he might start fucking *cooing* at her again at any moment.

However, his energy was so low, he didn't know how much longer he could hold out without eating, and he still wasn't entirely sure how he'd go about extracting energy from her without permanently harming her. He'd more or less decided on feeding off her negative emotions—something he knew would barely do as a snack on the best of days—and if he waited for as long as it'd take to refill the large tub and bathe the woman, he wouldn't be able to guarantee that he'd be able to stop in time.

Fuck. He'd just have to count himself lucky that if he did end up cooing like a moron, none of his underlings were around to witness it.

Kesh drew in a deep breath, steeling his resolve before he turned fully around to face the Breeder, mouth partway open to tell her she'd have to wait until after he fed to get clean. Only no sound managed to escape his suddenly desert-dry throat.

On the crisp linen sheets covering his large bed lay a dirty, crumbled shirt and a plain cotton bra, both of which had been covering the Breeder only moments ago. Now, though, she was bare from the waist up, peachy pink nipples tight in the cool air of his bedroom and creamy skin glowing in the sun shining through the floor-to-ceiling windows.

What.... the shit?

Before he managed more than a grunt of surprise, Georgia hooked her thumbs in her trousers and pushed, letting the fabric drop to the floor.

There wasn't a power in the universe great enough to force his gaze from the magnetic pull of that hallowed triangle of dark hair between her tightly clasped thighs.

"Okay." Her voice was barely more than a whisper. "I'm... I'm ready."

11

KESH

Kesh swallowed thickly, attempting to get his too-thick tongue to shape words—any words—but the distraction of her bared vulva was making it hard to think. The hair there was darker than the silky strands on her head, and lush enough to hide the valley below.

He moved without thought, blind urgency driving him toward her. He wasn't aware he'd crossed the floor until Georgia's sharp inhale finally broke the spell.

He flicked his eyes from her pussy to her face, frowning at the look on her pretty features. The blood had drained from her skin, and her eyes widened with the same terror he smelled in her scent—but the set of her jaw was pure, steely resolve.

Drawing in a deep breath, the girl backed up a step until the edge of his bed hit the backs of her knees. She kept her gaze locked on his as she climbed onto the mattress—and spread her legs.

The rushing of blood in his ears drowned out any and all sound for several seconds.

"What are you doing?" It came out like a growl.

"You need... to eat. Right? This is how...?" A deep blush spread from her chest up her neck to her cheeks in scarlet blotches, and she closed her thighs partway. "Oh, God, is this not... is this not what you meant? I'm so sorry, I—"

He gave her a stare laced with enough darkness to silence her mid-sentence.

She thought he intended to take his nourishment from her cunt.

He wasn't entirely unfamiliar with that approach to energy extraction, though usually when he was so desperate for release he sought out human women for company, he didn't waste time feeding on them. He wasn't an incubus—he could get much more satisfying meals with more... bloody methods.

However, over the years, a few women *had* left his bed weakened from more than multiple orgasms. And, when his hunger had been too great to control, some hadn't left at all.

But what he'd said to her in the elevator was true: though he'd happily slaughter her entire species if the need arose, taking a female against her will? *Never.*

The thought of forcing a scared Breeder under his

care to spread her thighs hadn't so much as crossed his mind.

His dick gave an achy throb, urging him to release whatever flimsy morals had made him ignore the most obvious of solutions. She had offered herself in exchange for the worthless, faceless human she'd made him spare, and she'd stripped naked, climbed on his bed and opened her legs for him unprompted. She was hardly *unwilling*. At least not in the strictest sense of the word.

He let his gaze slide from her pussy up her body, lingering on her breasts for a heartbeat before he finally met her eyes again. "I can feed from you there."

"Oh." She looked like she was going to say something else, but only her slightly panting breath escaped her parted lips.

Kesh drew a long, slow inhalation, focusing his lust-hazed mind. She'd offered her cunt willingly, and taking her energy from there was about the only way he wouldn't hurt her in the process—but he wasn't oblivious to the heavy throb in his eager cock, nor what would happen if he lost control during this particular meal.

She was a Breeder—every pheromone in her cursed body was crafted to lure him in, and if he surrendered to that pull... She would die. Horrifically. But it was either this or somehow extract her energy while knowingly hurting her. How was he supposed to feed on her terror when his entire body ached to soothe her?

He bared his teeth, frustration making his skin itch, and looked back up at her.

Her blue eyes were wide with fear, yet that willful tilt to her chin remained.

He would never be able to hurt her.

The knowledge lodged itself firmly in his skull, solidifying with his every breath as he stared into her scared eyes. Even now, starving and so hard he barely had enough blood supply left to think, he knew into the marrow of his bone that—with this woman?—he would break himself into atoms to avoid causing her harm. *Fuck.*

"Close your eyes." His attempt at softness died on the gravel in his throat.

Georgia darted a startled look at him, pink lips parting in what was likely going to be a *'why?'* But one glance at his demonic features, and the Breeder seemed to clock on.

"Okay." Her trembling whisper went straight to his dick, and he gritted his teeth around a deep breath when she closed her eyes and laid her head back on the pillow. Surrendering to him.

She was so... *vulnerable.* Naked and scared, with lines of exhaustion drawn on her pale features.

He pushed down the rush of possessiveness bubbling up from his gut in response, forcing his mind to clear of the stupid instincts clamoring up from the depths of his primordial makeup. Right now, she was a meal—nothing more.

The weight of his knee on the mattress made her suck in a superficial breath, and when he climbed all the way up and rested a hand on each side of her shoulders, she stopped breathing all together.

"I'm not gonna hurt you," he heard himself say. "And when you wake up again, all will be well. Okay?"

A delicate frown marred her forehead, and he didn't have to breathe in her scent to know that, after seeing how he went about feeding earlier that morning, after knowing exactly what he was, she didn't believe his reassurances.

She still managed to force out a nearly inaudible, "Okay."

Kesh kept his gaze firmly on her face as he shifted on the bed, the graze of a peaked nipple against his forearm enough of a reminder that he needed his full focus to get them through this with her life and his dignity still intact. She smelled... too good, and even a featherlight brush of her skin against his sent shockwaves of need through his exhausted body.

Focusing on keeping his breaths slow and even, he knelt back up on the bed and let his hand slide up one of her legs. She stiffened at his touch, but didn't resist when he grabbed her by the back of her knee and spread her open.

"Blackened stars!" He was only half aware of the snarled outburst, hands clamping onto the Breeder's thighs in response to her small squeak at the threatening sound.

How? How did she *smell* like this? His entire being was alight with the scent of her.

Dazed, he slid off the bed and pulled her to the end of it in the same motion, snarling a warning when she tried to resist his hands spreading her thighs wider. She thought to deny him? Sought to cut him off from the source of everything there was? *No.*

Without preamble, Kesh buried his face in her pussy and inhaled.

Heady musk so intense he could barely take it rolled over his tongue and down his throat. Eyes clenched against the onslaught to his senses, he slipped his hands from her thighs to her soft labia and spread her open, pressed his nose against her warm flesh and breathed her in again. And again. Every mouthful of her scent shot lightning through his veins, almost painful in its blissful addictiveness.

He opened his mouth on instinct, driven by the hard need for *more,* and pushed his tongue between her soft folds.

Heady, tangy flavor filled his mouth and pulled a groan from deep in his chest. If he'd thought her scent was addictive, the taste of her nearly short-circuited his already flagging brain.

He sought the source of it on instinct alone and teased his tongue around her tight and reluctant entrance. She gave him a few hesitant drops of her essence, but it was far from enough. He wanted to *bathe* in her—drink her up until she had no more left to give.

Her flesh parted more willingly as he moved up her pussy, seeking the center of her pleasure.

"Shit!" The Breeder's gasped cry came the second his lips brushed her clit. She jumped and tensed her thighs, but he easily kept her spread open with the bulk of his arms.

What was that?

Frowning, Kesh flicked his tongue over her clit, ignoring Georgia's mewl of protest. *No.* Surely it couldn't be?

He jerked his head back and swallowed a curse. Between her parted folds, a band of gleaming metal encircled her small nub.

"Someone... Someone *ringed* you?" Anger throbbed through his heated blood, forcing enough of his focus from his desperate need that he managed to pull his gaze from her pussy to her face. Her unmarred face.

A Breeder's ring, meant to help her future mate secure her willingness until she settled into her new life by his side, was always given to a woman at the same time as her blinding mark. *Always.* The implication that Georgia had hers while still retaining her ability to see their true forms... Someone had had her in their grasp, had known what she was... and they had inflicted terror upon her. Purposely.

The fog of lust waned, replace by his fury. He pulled further back, darkened gaze sweeping over the Breeder's prone form. She might be tall for a human woman, but compared to his massive bulk, she was only slight. Delicate.

It would be so very easy to simply... break her.

He'd had human women in his bed before, but they'd been thrumming with lust for him, blind to his true form and eager for pleasure.

Georgia stared at him with nothing but fear in her round eyes.

"I can't do this." He moved his hands from the softness between her legs and pushed off the bed, rising to his feet.

"W-what do you mean?" she croaked, scrambling to push up on her elbows.

For a moment, his vision blurred at the edges. *Fuck,* he needed to feed. He hadn't been this drained in years.

Kesh flicked a couple of fingers in the direction of her naked body before he turned, intent on the exit. "Deal's off. Go to sleep. The building is secure, and I will be back soon."

"Wait." Her voice rang through the room, surprising him with its strength.

He looked at her over his shoulder, eye-ridges raising with impatience. "What?"

"Don't go. Please. Please, don't." She knelt up on the bed, chin wobbling once before she steeled her jaw.

"I have to *eat.*" It came out as a snarl. "*Now.*"

"Take what you need from me," she begged. "I don't understand what happened. Please, you promised. Don't hurt anyone. Feed from me."

He bared his teeth, fury pounding in his temples. Fury that he wasn't ignoring her, fury that he wasn't already out the door in search of a meal. *Fucking Breeders and their sorcery.*

"I would be hurting *you*," he snarled.

"No. No, you wouldn't." She forced her lips to quirk up—not quite into a smile, but not a grimace either. "You promised you wouldn't, and I... I believe you. Please. Take it from me. Not... Not someone innocent."

He scoffed at the ridiculousness in her statement. "Someone *innocent?* You think that worthless piece of scum you saved is *innocent?* As compared to who, *you?* Tell me, Breeder, who have you hurt to get your next high? Who have you stolen from, beaten up, *killed* for your own gain?"

She blinked, the idea that every human didn't possess a base level of goodness clearly new to her. New, and unacceptable. "I... It doesn't matter, okay? I am... willing. And I will survive. They won't. Right?"

He didn't answer, but he didn't need to. She took his silence as the confirmation it was.

Swallowing, she held out a trembling hand. "Come back. Please."

She might as well have jerked on a chain wrapped tight around his throat. He wasn't fully aware of having crossed the bedroom floor to her, until her soft hand wrapped around his forearm, forcing crackles of sensations along his skin despite the fabric covering it.

"You won't hurt me," she said again, more conviction in her voice this time. A blush crept up her throat and heated her cheeks, and she lowered her eyelashes. "And... it felt... nice. What you were doing. It won't be like when... I was... was ringed. It's okay. Please. Let me feed you, like you did for me."

Some faraway part of him knew he should deny her—that he should find the will to resist her spell spoken in pleading tones—but he didn't have the strength. Perhaps if he'd been at full power, if his vision wasn't dancing from the need to refuel, and her sweet scent didn't linger on his tongue, he would have stood a chance.

Hazy images of butter glistening on her lips and her throat bobbing around morsels of food flickered for his mind's eye. He reached for her without thought, wrapping one hand around her jaw and cheek in blind search of the feel of her.

Her breath stuttered in her throat, but she didn't flinch away. Simply looked up at him with blue eyes more full of wariness than outright fear now. He didn't have the brainpower left to ponder the change, not this time. He needed her energy. Now.

Her body yielded for his, allowing him to guide her to her back. There was no resistance in her thighs when he pushed them apart this time, only a tremble in her muscles as he slid to the floor at the end of the bed and used his thumbs to expose her ringed clit once more.

Her scent enveloped him as fully as before,

sweeping away whatever lingering hesitance might have remained in his swiftly fogging mind.

Fuck, she smelled like... Woman, and sex, and *life.*

He groaned and leaned in, sucking her clit between his lips on instinct alone.

Georgia hissed at the contact, her thighs clamping around his head in instinctive protest.

Too sensitive. He eased off, kissing the soft skin around the center of her nerves instead, until her thighs slowly relaxed again. The hood of her clit had been pushed back with the fastening of the ring, leaving her pearl permanently exposed. He'd never given much thought to how a Breeding ring affected a woman when it wasn't activated, but the sound of Georgia's shallow breaths and the tremble in her muscles at his proximity to her unprotected nub made a thread of regret worm through his chest. Even without twisting the wicked device and inflicting its dark magic on her, her pleasure would always be forced to some degree.

Kesh ghosted his bottom lip over the tip of her clit, gentler than he'd ever touched a woman there before. She still jumped at the contact, but he didn't stop this time. Slowly, he moved his mouth against her tender spot, breathing in her blissful scent and ghosting his warm breath over her riled nerve endings before finding it with his tongue.

"Shi-it!" Her squeal was quickly accompanied by slim fingers weaving through his hair and then yanking on the strands with surprising force.

He didn't let her pull him off, but obliged her enough to shift his attention to the pink flesh around and below, lapping at her folds until her grip eased. Then he returned his focus to her clit, licking it twice before he took mercy on her once again to rub his nose at her labia.

Her scent grew stronger, and when he flicked his tongue down to that hallowed entrance to taste her again, her intoxicating essence flowed over his taste-buds much more freely than before.

Fuck, why did she *taste* like this?

Need crackled through his veins like lightning, blinding him. When he returned to her clit, it was with far more ferociousness.

"Shit! Shit! *Shit!*" Her high-pitched chanting sounded like it came through water, and the burn in the roots of his hair only fueled his urge for more. He lashed her little nub until she begged him to *stop, please stop,* then closed his lips around it and sucked it while she sobbed and writhed and squeezed her thighs around his neck. But her frantic bucking was rhythmic and her scent bloomed all around him, speaking another truth entirely.

When her pleas for mercy faded to throaty moans, he released her no-longer straining thighs and reached for his cock to alleviate some of the throbbing pressure. The squeeze of muscles around his aching length made him groan.

"Don't stop!" There was nothing meek about the

Breeder's shriek, and he let out a surprised snort—which was quickly cut off when Georgia wound her legs around his neck and grabbed onto his horns with more strength than she should reasonably have had left, yanking his face back into her pussy. "Fuck, come on, come *on!* I'm so close!"

Any amusement he had at the sudden change in her demeanor died in the roaring fire scorching his veins and incinerating any coherent thought. Snarling like a beast, he closed his mouth on her clit and sucked it in hard, deep pulls.

"Yes! Holy shit, *yes!*" The Breeder's cries sang through his burning blood as she ground herself against his face, clutching at his horns for dear life until *finally*—

"*Yes!*"

Kesh felt her release like a thunderclap shattering through his bones and deep into his pelvis. Wetness gushed from her entrance, but he kept sucking her clit until her fingers slackened around his horns and her moans turned to whimpers of overstimulation. Only then did he move his mouth to her trembling opening to drink her.

He didn't need to suck her there—her energy came willingly, flowing smoothly over his tongue, mixed with the tangy flavor of her pleasure.

Stars, she tasted so fucking *good.* Rich. *Strong.*

Entirely addictive.

He drank deep, lost to the rush of her energy filling

him from within until he could barely contain it. Yet still, he drank, groaning with greed and eternally desperate for more. For everything she had to give.

Too soon, the rhythmic pulse of her life force slowed.

Kesh moaned a protest, somehow managing to rein in the last vestiges of his willpower until he found the strength to pull away.

His entire being thrummed with power, and he had to brace against the edge of the bed for a few moments until his head stopped spinning from the overload. *Blackened stars,* how could one single pussy give so *much?*

He looked up at the Breeder and found her still sprawled on the bed. Entirely motionless.

For a second, sick fear clawed at his esophagus, but it eased when her chest rose with a slow breath. He'd stopped in time.

He pushed to his feet to put distance between himself and the girl, but found it impossible to pull his gaze from her. His hunger had been sated, but every cell in his body still throbbed with need.

She lay on his bed, unconscious and entirely vulnerable, and the sight of her made his cock ache.

If she'd been a regular woman, he would have given in.

It had been a long time since he allowed himself to fuck a human female. The dark magic emanating from every cell in his body was impossible to contain while he penetrated a tight little cunt. Demon or not, it was extraordinarily unappealing to climax into a gory pile of blood and ashes, and that was all that would be left of any woman who suffered a lord's penetration.

But right now? The need for her was so painful, every cell in his body screamed for him to give in. To sate himself deep inside of her, consequences be damned.

Kesh stared at the glistening cunt splayed open between the little Breeder's still-spread thighs, knowing that if it hadn't been his most sacred duty to ensure her survival, she would have died in his bed tonight.

It wasn't often he envied his brother the woman who'd birthed him his son.

Only the rarest few humans could withstand a lord's magic, and his brother, King Kain, had risked everything for his mate. Truth be told, the little bitch was a mouthy, conniving nightmare that really needed to be kept in her place—but at least Kain got to fuck her as much as he pleased. And right then, for the very first time, Kesh was beginning to understand how that might be worth the many, *many* sacrifices his brother had made for her.

Georgia didn't move as he pulled out his aching cock and climbed onto the bed to lie atop her. He pushed himself up on one elbow, ensuring he didn't crush her, and brought his free hand to his thick cock. Growling at the touch, he squeezed it tight and lowered his hips, pressing the bloated head of his meat to her still-softened entrance.

Zings of rapture made him arc into her, but the small mouth of her sex ensured he didn't push inside. Instead, he pulled his hips back through his own grip, thrusting forward with a hard jerk that had his head pressed against her pink entrance once more. Again and again he fucked his own hand, growling with pleasure every time she kissed his crown.

It took only moments, and then he was *there*.

Kesh snarled his release out, clutching at her breast and his own dick as he spurted his semen against her pussy, smearing the pearly strands up and down between her lips until he had nothing left to give.

Only then did he find the will to pull away, panting harshly as he stared at the still passed-out Breeder.

So vulnerable, and yet...

And yet, the clenching in his gut as he took in her sleeping form and his semen clinging to her skin reminded him all too brutally that this little thing had the power to bring even the most powerful of his kind to their knees.

12

GEORGIA

It took Georgia a moment to remember where she was, once the dark nothingness of dreamless sleep finally released its hold on her.

Her tongue stuck to the roof of her mouth as she stared blearily up at rose-gold streaks of sunlight playing across the white-painted ceiling. Sunset.

Had she slept the whole day?

Georgia sucked in a breath when the memory of last night fought its way through the brain fog and arrived at the forefront of her mind with a sharp snap.

The demons.

Larry!

She scrambled upright, the jelly-like state of her muscles nearly sending her sprawling before she managed to force them into compliance.

Larry was... Larry was going to be okay.

Something akin to relief washed through her body, even as the memory of how, exactly, her brother had been healed nestled into the pit of her gut.

The demon prince had saved his life, and in return...

Georgia breathed deeply, fighting back the rising panic threatening to take her over. It could have been a lot worse. She could have woken tied up in that awful brothel.

The prince had only...

She flushed hotly at the exact memory of how the Prince of Demons had gone about extracting her energy. She had a vague memory of grabbing onto his horns and riding his face like some sex-crazed porn star.

It had to have been the compilation of stress and horror. But unlike what Jimmy the pimp had planned for her, the prince had taken what he needed without violating her.

Well... almost.

Grimacing, Georgia poked at the unmistakable white residue crusting all over her nether parts and inner thighs. She didn't remember him jerking off on her, but clearly, he had.

She supposed it was fair enough, considering the mind-blowing orgasm he'd given *her*. Christ.

Thankfully, he was nowhere to be seen. The bedroom was entirely free from any reminders of her savior-slash-captor, save for a pitcher of water on the nightstand, still cool when she greedily swallowed down a full glass. As if someone had refilled it every so often in anticipation of her waking.

Georgia pushed down a shudder at the thought of the demon watching her as she slept, crawled to the side of the bed and staggered to the floor. She nearly lost her balance when her legs were forced to carry her weight, and she quickly bent to support herself on the bed.

Damn. So this was what it felt like to have a demon suck your energy.

The word 'suck' flashed through her brain, and flames heated her cheeks again. She'd been so scared and horrified after watching him crack that poor guy's skull like an egg. And yet, when he'd pressed his lips to her nether region, all her terror and trauma from the past eighteen or so hours had simply... melted away.

And then he'd made her come so hard she'd *fainted.*

Too bad he was a murdering creature of nightmare, or this whole companion business might have had its silver linings.

"You're losing it, Georgie," she muttered, grimacing as she finally forced her body fully upright. Nothing *hurt,* per se, but she had no strength left in her muscles —as if someone had sucked it right out of her.

There was that word again. *Suck.*

Choosing to focus on more urgent matters, she forced her mind from the prince and his, ah, *dinner pref-erences,* and looked around for a bathroom.

Apart from massive bi-fold doors leading out to

what looked like a full-length balcony running the length of the bedroom and beyond, three closed doors led from the room.

The first she recognized from when the prince had brought her into the room that morning. The second proved to be a sparsely filled closet, but the third opened up to reveal an entirely utilitarian bathroom clad in gray concrete and glass.

It wasn't that she'd had a lot of time to ponder what kind of luxuries a demon prince might indulge in, but so far, this one seemed remarkably ascetic in his tastes.

She supposed she should just be grateful there was a toilet available at all. If he didn't eat human food, then what did he even need one for? For whatever human women he dragged home to... not-rape?

Georgia finished up and cast another look around the sparse room. A glass screen shielded the massive walk-in shower, and on the counter by the sink lay two incredibly soft-looking white towels.

He'd smeared her with cum. Surely he wouldn't mind her grabbing a shower?

Before she could think too hard on what the monstrous demon might do if he did, in fact, mind her using his shower, she stepped around the glass screen and turned the tap.

The spray of warm water against her skin was bliss.

Georgia let out an involuntary hum of pleasure, but quickly had to lock her knees when the soothing heat made her already jellied muscles give up their last remaining ability to function.

"Shit." She leaned heavily against the gray wall and tried to cling on with her fingers, but it did little to slow the inevitable. Her feet skidded out from underneath her, and she hit the wet floor with an undignified grunt.

"Ow." It came out as a pitiful whimper. Georgia blinked up at the spray, still pelting her with warm water, but she didn't manage to ponder how she was going to get upright again before the door exploded inward with a dull *boom,* and fractured wood smacked against the glass and clattered to the floor.

"Breeder!" A giant monster stood in the splintered opening, his sudden appearance making Georgia squeak before her brain managed to remind her that this was the demon who'd saved her brother.

The prince's dark gaze landed on her, eyes widening before he leapt into the shower with a curse.

"Are you hurt? What happened?" he demanded as he crouched down above her, shielding her from most of the spray with his wide torso.

"I f-fell," she croaked, the startling outline of his curved horns doing little to calm her frantic heartrate.

One large, clawed hand cupped the back of her head, pillowing her against the hard floor. "Where does it hurt?"

Georgia blinked. The concern coloring his deep voice was such a startling contrast to his monstrous appearance, it took her a moment to respond. "It... doesn't, really. I just banged my hip a bit."

He let out a low rumble, and then slid his other hand down her wet skin to her hip. The squeeze of his fingers on her flesh was gentle and didn't aggravate the small hurt from her fall—but it did make her very aware that she was entirely naked and sprawled out underneath a giant demon who insisted on calling her *Breeder*. Goosebumps broke out across her body, peaking her nipples in the process, as her brain flashed another reminder of the morning's depravities.

"Uh... I'm okay."

The prince exhaled deeply, eyes roaming over her body as if to confirm her claim. When his gaze lingered at the apex of her thighs, she crossed her legs on instinct, hands flying down to cover herself.

"Don't be ridiculous," the demon growled, disgust lacing his voice. Without waiting for a response, he scooped her into his arms and stood, hitting the knob for the shower with an elbow to turn it off.

Georgia blinked up at him, almost as startled that the giant monster cradled her so gently as she was at the uninvited closeness while she was butt naked. "I don't need you to carry me. Please, I just want to finish my shower."

"You need to feed," he rumbled. "You've been out for a day and a half—that's much too long for a human to go without nourishment."

"A day and a half?" She'd never slept that long before.

"I took too much of your energy." His voice pitched lower, and if she hadn't known better, she'd have thought he sounded almost... embarrassed. The idea of an embarrassed demon nearly made her snort out loud, but before she could, the prince stalked out of the shower cubicle and placed her on her feet by the sink, and she was swiftly distracted by having to stay upright.

"Can you stand?" A frown drew down his eye-ridges.

"I'm fine." 'Fine' was definitely a stretch, but she wasn't about to admit that out loud and risk getting picked up like a kitten again. Not before she could wrap a towel around herself, at least.

The prince looked less than convinced, but much to her relief, he took a step back toward the door.

"I will be back with clothes," he said, somehow managing to make it sound like a threat.

She had just managed to secure a towel around herself when he returned with a handful of flowing, plum-colored fabric clutched in one hand.

"You're still wet." He looked her up and down, the displeasure in his voice painted on his harrowing features, too. "Dry yourself, before you get sick."

Georgia opened and closed her mouth once. Judging from how he'd tried to force-feed her, and apparently thought she'd catch a cold from a shower, the demon prince didn't know much about humans and their needs. However, as disturbing as it had been to wake up smeared in demon seed, she much, *much* preferred it to the alternative. If he'd refrained from penetrating her because he thought her so fragile she might get sick from a bit of water, well... She wasn't about to argue.

"Okay." She grabbed another fluffy towel and bent to wrap it around her hair. Only the motion made the world tilt and her vision to turn white.

"*Shit.*" Strong arms hoisted her back upright, and when her sight returned, the prince was hovering above her, his hands still bracing her shoulders.

"Oops." She grimaced at the lingering lightheadedness. Seemed he wasn't entirely wrong about how frail she was, at least not at the minute.

His monstrous features locked in a deep frown, and the worry on them was intense enough to show through his scary appearance. Without a word, he snatched the towel from her and began drying her hair.

Every stroke of fabric through her wet strands was gentle, like a caress. When he reached her face, he dabbed the towel against her cheeks and forehead carefully, and drew it down the back of her neck to dry behind her ears.

Georgia blinked at his care. He was treating her like she was made from spun glass. This nearly eight-foot monster, who'd murdered a man in front of her with no remorse, was being gentler with her than anyone before him.

He sank to a knee in front of her to dry her shoulders, collarbones, arms. Warm fingers wrapped around her wrist and brushed over her palm, setting her skin alight with a weird, tingling sensation before he methodically dried each of her individual fingers, then reached for her other hand. The black-red scales covering his large fingers were surprisingly soft, though the visual contrast between them and her smooth, pale skin was startling.

"Do you have kids?" She blurted the question before she could stop herself, because an insane image of the giant brute packing lunches and singing lullabies flashed through her hazy brain. Possibly because his gentleness reminded her of how her mother had cared for Larry, before Mike left.

The demon paused with her hand in his. Even through the towel, his body heat warmed her skin. "No." He flashed her a look she couldn't decipher— probably stunned disbelief she would ask him that. "Do you?"

"No. Just my brother."

He exhaled a soft breath, but only returned his focus to drying her off.

Georgia frowned as she stared at his horned head. "Would it have mattered? If I did?"

"You mean, would I have let you go?" His tone was oddly flat, but she was quickly distracted from the oddity of that when he brushed the towel back up to her breasts. Her nipples tightened at the first touch of the fabric, and she drew in a sharp breath when he cupped them to dry underneath. Images from their time in his bed flashed uninvited through her mind—of his head between her legs and the feeling of his horns in her hands.

"Your life before you came to me doesn't matter. No, Breeder, a human child would not circumvent your fate. Nothing will." He released her breasts and swiped the towel lower, drying her sides and stomach without so much as glancing up at her.

She knew those words should be chilling—and they were. He was a merciless killer, a monster of nightmares, and while he hadn't spelled out what he wanted with her, there wasn't a lot of subtlety in the way he kept calling her 'Breeder'. She would need to figure out how to escape his clutches once she had enough strength to do so—and preferably before he got over the apparent belief that she was too fragile for the necessary activities needed to implant his hell-spawn.

However, with her head already swimming and his warm hands reminding her of how much pleasure this particular monstrous nightmare could inflict, it was hard to keep a firm grasp on anything but the way her skin heated the further south that towel traveled.

There's something seriously wrong with you, Georgina.

But he was so gentle, and she was so... So incredibly

tired of being scared all the time. She'd spent her life fearing the demons and what they might do if she fell into their claws. And now she had, and it had nearly ended up worse than she had ever imagined, even in the darkest of moments. The Prince of Demons was the most terrifying creature she'd ever seen, but right now, when she allowed the dizziness to swallow her fears for just a few seconds...

He reached the apex of her thighs and, pausing only for a fraction of a second, rubbed the towel through her pubic hair.

Georgia exhaled sharply as every nerve ending below her navel came alive.

The demon grunted at the sound, and she had the wild thought that he, too, was remembering how he'd sucked her energy.

When his nostrils flared and a shudder went through his powerful body, her heart slammed into overdrive. Every lewd image of his feeding rushed through her brain, and instead of filling her with horror, it sent a rush of blood to her pelvis. Her clit throbbed with her rapid pulse, the metal confines around the sensitive nub making her feel every drum of it deep into her bones.

For a long, agonizing moment, neither of them moved.

The prince inhaled again, deeper, and a soft sound she wasn't sure he even realized he was making rumbled out of his chest. And then the towel was on her mound again, the pressure firmer this time, and right against her clit.

"*Ooh.*" She was only half aware of the moan escaping her, all her focus snapping to the sensation of *touch* at the center of her being. She didn't realize she'd spread her thighs for him until the pressure shifted and the soft towel rubbed deep through her cleft, all the way to her entrance.

And again. He swept back, applying pressure to her clit and tugging gently at the metal ring there until her toes curled, then rubbed through her spread labia to her opening, pushing against it for just a moment before he repeated the whole thing over again. And again.

Fuck, why did it feel so good? Her exhausted muscles did their best to rally as the promise of release tightened low in her abdomen with every pass of that wicked towel. She needed this, *God,* she needed it. *Just a bit more pressure, just—just a bit more.*

Mindlessly, she pressed back against the prince's hand, too desperate for the pleasure he was rubbing into her throbbing clit to pay her shaking legs any mind. A mistake she only realized when her jellied thigh muscles decided enough was enough and gave out.

Georgia yelped and flailed for purchase, fingers grabbing onto the prince's horns at the same moment as strong hands tightened on her hamstrings, keeping her from falling on her ass.

"Crap." It was a low mutter, and when she glanced down, dark frustration was painted over the demon's harrowing features. He eased her weight back onto her feet and released his grip on her, moving away. Clearly intending to stop the depravities before they went any further.

She didn't pause to think. Growling with the need to fucking *come,* she yanked him back by the horns and forced his mouth to her clit.

13

KESH

He'd had every intention of finishing the drying of the near-unconscious woman and getting her fed. Really, he had. Even as his cock throbbed and the sweet scent of her sacred core made it hard to think about anything other than how she'd cried out in pleasure when he brought her to climax before.

Ensuring her survival was his primary duty, after all.

However, there was no force in the fucking universe strong enough to break through the roar in his blood when the meek little Breeder *growled* at being separated from his touch and then used his horns to guide his face right into her pussy for more.

Her smell enveloped him, musky and strong and full of *need*. The world faded to black, until there was nothing left but the scent of *her,* and the pounding of his own pulse setting every cell in his preternatural body aflame.

He didn't hear his own snarl, didn't register her yelp when he sucked her clit into his mouth, ring and all. He was barely aware of wrapping his arms around her when she swayed under the onslaught, didn't feel the hard tiles under his knees as he half pushed, half carried her to the countertop next to the sink. His entire being was focused on the smell of her pussy, on the mind-breaking *taste* of it.

Her cries of pleasure rang through his body like a bell, honing his mouth to the exact way she needed it, until her grip on his horns turned savage and her thighs tightened around the sides of his neck in a vice.

"Yes, yes, *yes! Fuck!*" She arched off the counter with a snarl that sounded anything but human. Her climax followed on a flood of her intoxicating flavor, and he groaned at the prickle of her energy teasing his tastebuds.

She offered her life essence so willingly, as if it were not the most precious thing she possessed. Kesh licked at her still trembling entrance and rubbed his nose against her clit while she slowly came down, ensuring he didn't take so much as a drop of her energy.

Finally, some long moments later, her thighs relaxed around his neck and her hands slipped off his horns.

Slowly, he regained awareness of their surroundings. And of his responsibilities.

Shit. Dread coiled in his gut, and though it did nothing to ease his throbbing cock, it did allow his brain a modicum of control.

He pulled away from the Breeder's tantalizing little pussy and eased her legs off his shoulders so he could rise to his feet and survey the damages.

She was slumped on the counter, panting for air and with a rosy hue to her cheeks, but he saw the exhaustion in her glazed eyes and trembling muscles.

Shit, shit, shit. She was a Breeder—a *ringed* Breeder. Even without activating the nefarious little device, she couldn't be held responsible for succumbing to basic needs. But he could, and he should have refused her, no matter how desperately she'd rubbed herself against him, and no matter how every cell in his body burned to give her what she craved.

"Do you... Need me to...?" The Breeder made a vague gesture toward his straining dick without looking at his crotch, the color in her cheeks deepening until her entire face was a vivid red. "Um... Help *you?*"

Did she just...? Kesh froze. He stared mutely at her for five full seconds—long enough for the roar of blood in his ears to ease and his brain to regain control. "What I need you to do is *eat,* Breeder. So if you're quite done sating your primitive urges, perhaps you will allow me to ensure you don't keel over and die?"

She winced at his sharpness—or perhaps at the words themselves—but it seemed to have done the trick. No further offers of pleasure followed. Which was fortunate, because he could still feel the ghost of her grip on his horns, and just the thought of her hands on his dick sent a shiver up his spine that threatened to shatter what little self-control he'd managed to scrape together.

Kesh bent to grab the dress he'd discarded on the floor when she'd been about to keel over from the strain of drying herself.

She didn't complain at the crumbled state of the expensive silk fabric, nor did she resist when he pulled it over her head to mercifully hide her naked skin from his tormented gaze.

She did, however, frown as she looked down at herself. "Are we going somewhere?"

"The only place you're going is to the kitchen, Breeder," he snapped, reaching out to pull her into his arms.

She stiffened at the closeness—and he didn't bother to smother an eyeroll. For someone who'd just ridden his face, she seemed awfully inconsistent with her fear of him.

She smelled like woman, the scent of her release teasing at his nostrils as he hoisted her off the ground and held her against his chest. Despite her stiffness, only the faintest waft of fear made it through.

Kesh glanced down and caught her staring at him with wariness, those blue eyes of hers darting from his to his horns.

Wariness — from a Breeder who saw his true face.

He'd been there the first time his sister-in-law saw his brother's demon form. That Georgia was merely stiff in his arms, rather than screaming and fighting to get free, was no small feat.

Perhaps she was going to be less of a hassle than he'd initially feared. Selma, his brother's mate, had caused him no end of trouble, up to and including having to conquer the entire fucking continent to keep her safe. But of course, the now-queen was a Pure Breeder, one of the exceedingly rare humans able to withstand a lord's magic and conceive his child. Her presence in their world was always going to cause an upheaval. A normal Breeder—like the one currently in his arms—though uncommon and of utmost importance for their survival, would not throw their entire power structure into disarray. And if she proved this tame while still able to see his demonic features? Once he gave her the blinding mark that would allow her to see his men's human disguises rather than their true faces, she might even be willing to mate with one of them, rather than reluctantly submitting as their bargain demanded. With a little luck, she'd be out of his hair in no time, a boon to his territory as she birthed new warriors, rather than the annoying distraction she currently presented.

A point further cemented when, out of fucking nowhere, a seething stab of anger spiked through his chest at the thought of her hands around another man's horns as she guided his mouth to her sacred core.

Fucking Breeders. One taste of her cursed little pussy and his instincts already rebelled at the thought of giving her to another.

Yeah, the sooner she was someone else's problem, the better. But before he could ship her off to do her duty with whichever of his men she ended up choosing, there was work to be done. The shame of handing off a Breeder in Georgia's current condition would be more than even a lord's reputation could withstand.

Suppressing a growl of annoyance, Kesh carried her through to the living area and deposited her on the barstool by the kitchen island. "Eat."

"Um… You do remember I'm not a horse, right?" The girl looked across the spread of food, eyebrows raised. "This is way too much. And it'll spoil within a few days in the fridge."

Irritation that she dared criticize his offering made him sit down on the chair next to her with enough force to make her jolt. Growling, he grabbed a pear and held it to her lips. *"Eat."*

Startled, Georgia darted a glance at his face, but the glare he gave her was thankfully enough to make her comply without further complaints.

Parting her plump lips around the piece of fruit, she bit down—and immediately hummed with pleasure.

Kesh swallowed a groan at the responding throb in his cock, still painfully hard from the bathroom ordeal, and when she darted her tongue out to lick at the juices trickling down her chin, his stomach clenched.

Blackened stars, what was it about watching this girl eat?

Leaving her to handle the pear on her own, Kesh leaned back before his already riled testosterone made him throw the cursed woman on the banquet to feast on *her.* Again.

Fuck.

Georgia, seemingly oblivious to his torment, finished with the fruit and turned her attention to the rest of the spread. When a flaky-crusted tart caught her gaze, her eyes widened. "Is that... Did you *make* a quiche?"

Something in her voice made him want to say yes. How absolutely ridiculous. He was the prince of demons. Of-fucking-course he wasn't spending his time *making* the food he supplied for her. "No."

She grimaced at his growled answer, and a tightening at his tailbone made him grit out, "Why?"

"Oh, just, it looks homemade." Hesitating for a second, she grabbed a bagel and some cream cheese.

Kesh stared from the quiche to her knife, smearing dairy over the bread. The tightening in his tailbone rose higher. "Is what I have provided not *satisfying,* Breeder?" he demanded.

She jolted, eyes darting to his. "O-of course. I'm sorry. I didn't mean to insult you. This is wonderful."

Great. And there was the smell of her fear again, clawing at his brain to make her *happy.* Furious with his own idiotic instincts as much as her for sparking them, he glared at her until she reached for the quiche with mildly shaking hands, cut a piece and ate it.

"It's really good," she lied. "Thank you."

Kesh closed his eyes, tempering his urge to coo at her until she calmed down again. "One thing you should know, Georgia—you can't lie to a demon. We can smell it on you."

It wasn't entirely true. Yes, an awakened Breeder who attempted to lie gave off a distinct scent, but Georgia had yet to receive the mark that would temper her resistance to their magic. Sure, if he buried his nose in her neck, his powers were strong enough he'd be able to scent her deceit, but mostly, the lie was written all over her face.

Georgia blanched. "I'm not—it isn't bad. I like it."

He arced an eyebrow.

"I just... really like homemade baked goods, especially quiches and pumpkin pies. I'm sorry, I didn't mean to imply this isn't good. It is! More than good. No one's ever made me a brunch spread like this, and I mean—you're a demon. You don't even eat food. Expecting you to bake was silly. I'm sorry. I'm still a little out of it, after..." She swallowed nervously, cheeks flushing a delicious pink as she quickly looked down at her plate. "Anyway, I'm pretty sure it's a lot better than what that asshole Jimmy gives women to eat."

Kesh rested his elbows on the countertop and pinched the bridge of his nose. He knew a Jimmy—a slimy demon who ran a popular brothel down in the industrial quarter. As good a reminder as any that he needed to pay the guy a visit and discuss his unfortunate decision to put a contract on a Breeder. Yet another distraction from the war he *should* be focusing on. "That the guy who tried to whore you?"

"Y-yeah."

"Place called Hell?"

She darted another look at him. "You... go there?"

"You mean, do I fuck chained-up whores on my days off?" The memory of how she'd assumed he brought women home to rape them made his stomach tighten with an unreasonable sense of injustice. He knew several of his men frequented 'Hell' on a regular basis—and he'd occasionally bought them a night there as a reward for diligent service. Georgia assuming he bedded prostitutes himself wasn't that outlandish. Still. Her barely concealed horror at the idea prodded at his stupidly flaring instincts. A fact he didn't appreciate.

"I-I'm sorry." By his side, Georgia shrank into her seat, the scent of her fear intensifying. "I didn't mean to imply—"

"I swear on the fucking sun, if you apologize one more time—" Kesh cut himself off, as stunned by his growled outburst as her wide eyes suggested she was. Meekness and subservience were treasured qualities in a Breeder. Georgia defaulting to ridiculous apologies to placate him shouldn't grind against every nerve in his body—if anything, *that* is what should make him hard, not watching her bite into a piece of fucking fruit. By all the dead stars in the sky, this girl was going to be the death of him.

"I'm s—"

"*No.*" Narrowing his eyes, he pointed at her plate. "Just eat. Once you've regained your strength, we begin your training."

14
GEORGIA

raining.

Not the least ominous sounding word when coming from an enormous demon who insisted on calling her *Breeder.*

Georgia picked at her breakfast, not in any rush to find out exactly what the brutish prince meant by that. It only served to irritate him more.

"Eat."

She jolted at the snarled command, daring a look at the demon by her side. He was glaring down at her as if her very existence offended him on a personal level, arms folded across his massive chest. Despite his anger at her apologies, she had the distinct impression he was still offended by her lack of enthusiasm for the damn quiche.

"I'm eating, I'm eating." She stabbed a piece of scrambled egg on her fork and popped it in her mouth with what she hoped was suitable appreciation. But when she put the fork down next to her plate while she chewed, the prince picked it back up, wrangled another forkful of egg, and, without ceremony, brought it to her mouth.

"Wh—" Georgia's surprised protest broke off on a cough when he shoved the fork between her lips. She barely managed to chew before he forced another mouthful in. And another. Crisp slices of bacon followed the eggs, and then several olives, a buttered blueberry muffin, and a handful of grapes that he pushed against her lips one at a time, gaze heating when her tongue flicked against his fingertips.

The demon prince clearly had a feeding kink.

Great. Just great.

But still, it beat Jimmy. By a *wide* margin. At least for now.

Georgia slanted a glance up at the demon's burning eyes as she chewed on yet another grape. His attempt at shaming her for offering to repay him the favor in the bathroom aside, his interest in her was obvious. She wasn't here to do his laundry and vacuum his floors, and once whatever hellish *training* he had planned was complete, she doubted he'd hold himself back like he had up until now.

So she allowed him to feed her far past what was comfortable, keen on delaying the inevitable for as long as possible. Only when her stomach ached and the grape he pressed to her mouth made bile rise in her throat, did she finally put a shaky hand on his wrist.

"I can't eat anymore."

The prince frowned down at her. "You've hardly touched your food."

Georgia glanced at the table and let out a weak laugh. "You've not dealt with humans much before, have you?"

"I've dealt with plenty."

"Well, I don't think you ever got around to feeding them. We have limits, you know? Physical restrictions? Less-but-more-frequently works better, if you're not actively trying to rupture our stomachs." She put a hand to her belly and groaned, regretting not stopping him sooner. Unless whatever *training* he had in mind consisted of a long nap while she digested the absurd quantities of breakfast he'd made her eat, being so full she could hardly move was unlikely to make the experience any more enjoyable.

The prince only frowned at her, clearly not convinced. "How are your energy levels?"

"Um..." Despite the urge for a nap, surprisingly good. Somewhere during the ridiculous breakfast, her muscles had stopped trembling, and she no longer felt like a mild gust of wind might make her collapse.

Georgia glanced up at the prince and briefly considering telling him she was still too weak for whatever horrors he had planned, but quickly remembered that apparently he could *smell* her lies. As much as she wasn't looking forward to his *training,* pissing him off by lying first probably wasn't going to improve the experience. "Better. Thank you."

"Alright. Let's go." He got to his feet and flicked two fingers at her. When she obeyed, he began walking back down the hallway. Toward the bedroom.

The hope she'd harbored that his *training* would consist of sit-ups and cardio, already practically non-existent, hit the floorboards.

Kesh shouldered his way through the doorway and gestured with a nod of his chin. "Get on the bed."

Georgia drew in a shaky breath and glanced from the bedding still tousled from when she'd gotten up this morning to the giant demon. "Um... what... what are you going to do?"

"First, I'll mark you. Then I'll train you."

How delightfully nondescript.

She grimaced. "Will it... hurt?"

He huffed a breath through his nose. "If you were worried about pain, perhaps you should have asked this before you sold yourself for that useless brother of yours."

Unexpected anger flared hotly in her gut, suppressing some of her anxiety. "He's not *useless.* He's kind and good-hearted and he didn't deserve to die. I'd sacrifice myself a thousand times over for him."

"Then what do you care if there's pain?" There was a taunt to the prince's voice, but also... something else. Irritation? Anger? It made her skin prick with primal awareness, her anxiety pushing to the forefront again at the sound of it.

"If he's worth your body, your *life,* then surely he must be worth some pain, hmm? A bit of humiliation." The prince snapped his fingers. "So get. On. The. Bed."

He was right. Even when she'd thought she sold her body so Lewin could harvest her juices, she hadn't expected a pleasant experience. This dark monster might be a better fate than the brothel she'd been facing before one of Jimmy's goons grew a conscience, but he was still the Prince of Demons. Even if he'd been surprisingly gentle with her so far, she wouldn't soon forget how he'd crushed that poor man's skull to replenish his own energy. By comparison, a little pain and humiliation wasn't the end of the world.

Steeling herself, Georgia climbed onto the bed and lay down on her back. He hadn't asked her to strip out of the silky dress, but the flowy garment wasn't much help in protecting her modesty. The skirt bunched up around her thighs, and she felt the sear of the demon's gaze on her skin as he moved closer.

Whatever *branding* meant, he'd healed Larry. It was worth it.

"You're shaking." His deep voice didn't betray any emotion, and when she cut her eyes up to his terrifying face, the expression on it was impassive.

Georgia clutched her hands in the bedding, trying to anchor her trembling muscles. "Sorry."

The demon blew out a breath and sank down on the

foot-end of the bed, a single fingertip skimming over her bare ankle. "Are you always so *sorry*, little lamb? When you lay down your life for another, when you don't do what you're told... When you tremble and fear for your pretty little cunt, the first thing that comes to mind for you is to apologize?"

His heated touch traveled higher up her shin, rendering her tongue dry and her skin pebbled with nervous goosebumps. His voice was soft, but there was a quiet, lethal quality to it that set her on edge as much as his touch and the ominously lacking explanation of what he was planning on doing to her.

"I... we made a deal. You kept your end of the bargain, and I promised... compliance," she whispered, squeezing her eyes shut when his hand moved to her knee and warm anticipation spread up her thighs. Perhaps if her body didn't remember the two times he'd touched her there already, it would have been nothing but dread. But even as her mind turned over the words 'branding' and 'training' with frantic repetition, the slow slide of his hand, ever upward, sent a thrill of excitement along her skin. The utter and complete mortification made her clutch harder at the sheets. He was a prince among the darkest monsters to haunt the Earth—and his merest touch made her clit swell against its metal confines, eager for pleasure that should have disgusted her.

Only it didn't.

Deep down, she knew that even his demonic face

would do nothing to tamp the increasing burn in her blood as his fingers finally reached the hem of her skirt and pushed up underneath it—but so long as she kept her eyes shut, she wouldn't have to acknowledge it.

Something is seriously wrong with you, Georgie.

"Oh!" The first stroke of his knuckle over her lower lips sent a lightning bolt up her spine that had her breath exploding out of her chest.

A deep, rich growl vibrated through the air, pebbling her nipples.

"You're wet." There was more than a hint of accusation in the Prince's voice—but not nearly enough to drown out the heat. It crawled up her thighs and sank into the bones of her pelvis, cementing the shameful truth of his words.

"S-sorry."

He huffed an irritated sound and then rubbed his thumb up the length of her slit to find her exposed clit. When he brushed the pad over the sensitive flesh, the crackle of sensation—too sharp, too intense—made her jerk and suck in a sharp breath.

The prince pinned her in place with a large, heavy hand pressed firmly to her abdomen, low enough to not agitate her still-full belly. "Oh, no. You promised *compliance*, remember? So you will *comply*."

His snarled command shouldn't have made her pussy clench—it really, *really* shouldn't.

Her body didn't give a single fuck.

The next brush of his thumb over her clit was still

much too intense, but behind the screaming of nerves, something dark and needy rose. She was entirely help-less, entirely at his mercy—forced to take the stimula-tion to her exposed little clit, no matter how much it might hurt. That thought should have filled her with terror—and it did—but not nearly enough to drown out the tidal wave of lust that rose from the deepest parts of her mind in response.

"Oh my God! Harder! Please—*please,* more!"

15
KESH

More.

The word rang in his ears as the needy little Breeder spread her thighs wide and arched up into his touch, even as she squirmed under his hand to escape the direct stimulation.

He'd left the kitchen with more steely determination than any enthusiasm for what he'd have to do to the girl. His tongue still pricked with the taste of her earlier climax, and his cock seemed to be in a state of permanent erection. But the dark undertow of need the cursed little thing provoked was underlined with the increasing scent of her fear and the knowledge that if he didn't keep his magic in check during her branding, he would kill her.

She was the first Breeder to grace his territory since his family had assumed power in the Americas, and if he accidentally killed the girl before he could finish preparing her for one of his men, there was every chance it'd cause enough uproar throughout the territory to give the Europeans the edge they'd need to win the war.

In the good old days, she'd have been given to a procurer, who'd blind and ring her before she realized what was going on, then ship her off to auction where she'd learn to take a demon's cock soon enough. But no. Queen Selma had declared their age-old customs *barbaric,* and somehow that meant it was now his job to put a brand on this woman and train her body to enjoy a demon's anatomy, without accidentally murdering her with his too-powerful magic along the way.

"More!"

The sharpness of the command jerked Kesh out of his stupor. He stared at the Breeder's face for one long moment, the tight grimace on her features as she rode up against his fingers making blood pound in his temples and rush in his ears. The meek little human who'd cowered at the foot of his dais and apologized for everything short of breathing was gone, replaced by the wanton woman who'd grabbed onto his horns and forced his mouth to her pussy, despite being so weak she could barely stand.

"Look at you," he snarled, frustration lacing through the gravel of his voice, even as he pressed his thumb in harder against her pulsing clit, obeying her demand. "What a pretty little whore you make. Are you wet from knowing you can't escape? Is that it? The big, bad monster has you pinned and there's nothing you can do but submit that needy little pussy to every dirty thing I can do?"

The Breeder moaned brokenly, shame coloring her cheeks, but the rush of liquid trickling from her opening showed the truth: yes, that was exactly why she was wet for him.

As a demon, Kesh was plenty familiar with humanity's dark desires, but the knowledge that the soft-spoken, fragile little female, who reeked of fear whenever she looked at him, got off on forced submission —*that* he hadn't expected.

Predictably, it went straight to his dick.

"*Shit.*" Electricity crackled up his spine as the scent of her need penetrated his nostrils and sank deep into his lungs, filling his very being until there was nothing left but *her*. His cock throbbed painfully in the confines of his pants, and his body *ached* to settle on top of her, to feel her smooth skin, *taste* it—

He was barely conscious of moving until Georgia's fearful gasp brought him back from the brink. He looked down at her, splayed on her back beneath him, eyes no longer squeezed shut but opened wide as she stared back up at him. He had her wrists pinned above her head, and his pelvis rested heavily on top of hers, forcing his clothed but aching cock hard against her pussy and ringed clit.

Fuck, that look of terror on her pretty face did nothing to stop every dark instinct clamoring to force his way inside her body and to hell with the conse-quences. But the sick thread of dread it sparked in the deepest parts of his conscience was enough to rein in his all-consuming need for her cunt.

Breathing heavily, he released her wrists and shifted some of his weight from her pelvis to his arms. "You okay?"

Georgia's blue eyes widened even further, as if she couldn't quite believe he'd asked. "I... y-yeah."

How was he meant to do this? He couldn't fucking *think* with the maddening scent of her arousal in his nose.

"You're going to be the fucking death of me."

"I-I'm sorry."

Another fucking apology. He bared his teeth at her, and instantly regretted it when the bitter taste of fear intensified on his tongue and she shrank deeper into the mattress.

Aaaand there went his gut, clenching with regret. Great. Fucking great.

"I'm not going to hurt you," he murmured, voice softened despite his urge to scream with frustration at the clashing roil of instincts warring somewhere south of his ribcage. *Fucking. Breeders.*

"What... what *are* you going to do?" Her voice was tiny and pulled on his maddening urge to coddle and coo like an overgrown mother hen. "You say you're going to brand me... and... *train* me. I don't know what that means."

They'd made a deal. He'd spent a great deal of power on healing her useless brother in return for her cooperation. The main reason he'd agreed was so he wouldn't have to do *this*—coddle and *explain* and take his time when he had none to give. But as she lay beneath him, her bewitching scent thick in his nostrils and that scared look on her pretty face—the one that pulled on everything primal and stupid in him—he realized he'd been a fool to make that bargain. His experiences with his infuriating sister-in-law should have taught him that one breath of a Breeder's manipulative pheromones would make him bend over backwards to ensure they had whatever they wanted. He'd thought Georgia would be different, that the fact she wasn't a Pure Breeder would help him keep his mind focused. But clearly, that wasn't how this was going to go.

With a deep—*deep*—sigh, Kesh pushed himself up to kneel between her splayed thighs. One glimpse of her flushed pussy and bared clit and he made sure to yank the silk skirt down to cover her before he lost his ability to focus again. "All Breeders are given a blinding mark—a brand. It takes away your ability to see through our human disguises. We find that it makes it easier for a woman to accept a mating and settle into her new life."

She blinked up at him. "So I'd... see what others see when they look at you? Just a regular human?"

"Yes."

She frowned, eyes darting to his horns for a long moment before she asked, "Um... so... why are we...?"

"Why am I getting you off?"

Georgia flushed a deep red, and he rolled his eyes. Considering she'd been begging him for *more* only minutes ago, embarrassment at stating the obvious was pretty fucking ridiculous. *Humans.*

"Your innate resistance to our magic is at its weakest during a climax. For the brand to take, you need to come. Hard."

"Oh." Her blue eyes flicked briefly to his mouth, and he knew exactly where her mind went—to the bathroom where he'd pushed her up against the vanity and sucked her clit to orgasm. Heat coiled low in his abdomen in response, and when she looked up at his eyes and blushed even deeper, it took all his willpower not to push her dress back up and wrap his lips around her clit.

"So..." She hesitated for a moment, then seemingly found her courage. "Why aren't you...?"

His face darkened. "Because, Breeder, your pussy is fucking crack, and if I lose control for even a second, my magic will enter you and you will die. Horrifically."

"Oh." She paled, knees curling up to close his direct access to her hallowed core, survival instincts finally kicking in.

"Yes. Oh." He rubbed the bridge of his nose. "This is such a fucking nightmare."

Slowly, she sat up, eyeing him cautiously. "And we

can't just... pretend you never met me and send me on my way...?"

His hard stare made the red flush return to her cheeks.

"Right, okay, yeah, that was probably... a bit optimistic," she muttered. "But then what? I don't want to die. Does this... this brand really need to happen?"

Kesh sighed, pinching the bridge of his nose. "You tell me. Look at my face, Breeder. Can you see yourself settling into domestic bliss with a man whose mere features make you quiver with fear? Could you nurse children who look like this?"

Georgia's eyes roamed over his face. As expected, the truth was written all over her features.

"Yeah. Didn't think so," he growled, inexplicably irritated with her natural fear of his appearance. "So yes, Breeder. I need to brand you."

A short moment's silence fell between them as Kesh tried to figure out how the hell he was supposed to get this girl branded. It was interrupted when Georgia quietly asked, "I'm supposed to birth your... children?"

He scoffed. "No, not mine. As I said, if my magic enters you, you will die. But yes, you will birth your future mate's children. You are a Breeder, after all—this is your job."

Horror slashed across her face. "What... what will you do to... to my babies?"

Kesh stared at her. "What do you mean, 'what will we do?' Your mate will protect them, just as he will you.

Bringing our sons to adulthood is one of our most sacred obligations." He frowned when it dawned why she looked at him with such horror. "You thought we'd *eat* our own children??"

"Well, I... You're demons. I don't know what your drive for parental care is like," she protested, a mix of shame and defensiveness replacing the look of horror on her pretty face.

He leaned in close, staring hard into her eyes. "It's *strong*, Breeder. As is our drive to protect our mates. Bargaining your body to demons was foolish, but one thing you do not have to fear for is the safety of you or your babies. Ever."

"Oh..."

She looked like she was about to say more, but the sound of his apartment's front door slamming open pulled Kesh's attention with a hard yank.

16

KESH

He got to his feet, adrenaline rushing through his body in an instant as every cell kicked into protective mode, but before he could take a step a familiar voice called out, "Your Highness! You're needed urgently!"

Growling at the interruption, Kesh pulled the bedroom door open, lingering adrenaline making him slam it into the wall hard enough to make the Breeder jump on the bed. Immediately outside, his second in command stopped abruptly, a harried look on his face. Marks of battle covered his leather armor.

"Mallorn? Why aren't you in Maine?" Kesh growled.

The other demon drew in a deep breath, familiar with his prince's temper. "Prince Kesh, you're needed in Maine. Our troops are getting overrun. The Europeans brought two lords. They're too strong for Lord Aran to fight back on his own."

"Son of a bitch!" Kesh snarled. "How the fuck did they manage that without anyone noticing?"

"We're not sure yet, but we need you there. Now."

Kesh glared at his second, every battle-hardened instinct in his body throbbing to fly at the threat to the borders. But... He hesitated, glancing over his shoulder at Georgia, who stared at him wide-eyed from the bed.

"Kesh, come on," Mallorn said, voice impatient as he dropped the formalities. "Find yourself some pussy in Maine to celebrate with, once we've beaten back the Eurotrash. We don't have time for you to get off first!"

"She's not here to get me off—the girl's an unmarked Breeder, Mallorn," Kesh growled. "I can't very well leave her here unguarded."

"Shit. Really?" Mallorn's eyes widened, some of the urgency on his features swiftly replaced by excitement. "I could—"

Kesh leveled him with a flat stare. "No."

"Well then, you'll just have to bring her with you."

Kesh narrowed his eyes. "You're kidding."

"Look, she's a Breeder, and you're the lord responsible for her. We both know she can't be unguarded, so unless you'll assign a guard to her you trust more than me, you'll have to take her with you. But whatever you choose, make it swift—our men are dying up in Maine."

"You know very well there's no one I trust more than you," Kesh growled. "And I don't trust you as far as I can throw you around an unmated Breeder. Shit." He turned back to Georgia, eyes narrowing in frustration. Why? Why did she have to show up in his territory? Why not the next state over, where she could have been some other lord's problem. "Alright." He snapped his fingers at the girl. "Get up. You're coming with me."

———

THE HELICOPTER RIDE TO MAINE HAD HIS NERVOUS SYSTEM ON edge; the whir of the blades and the knowledge that he was heading into battle with a Breeder in tow only added to his stress. He glared at the wide-eyed Georgia, wishing her into unexistence with every fiber of his being. Her scent in his nostrils spoke with all clarity of her fright at being hauled into a helicopter with two demons, and his entire being throbbed with the need to coo and soothe her. An urge he thankfully managed to keep at bay behind gritted teeth—he really didn't need to add Mallorn's mocking to his current state of agitation.

"Once we get there, you'll stay in the helicopter. I'll shield it with my magic, and you'll be safe. Do. Not. Leave. Understood? If you do, you'll be without the protection of my magic. And trust me, Georgia—you don't want that." He leaned forward, imposing the threat with his darkest glare. "Do you understand?"

She nodded, eyes impossibly wider, and he settled back in his seat, ignoring the side-eye from his second.

They landed in a clearing in the woods, just outside the coastal village where the Europeans had made their landing and launched their assault, the sounds and stench of battle thick in the air. Plumes of black magic rose from the battlefield, and Kesh felt the familiar sensation of battle lust threatening to descend. He turned to Georgia, who was thankfully still sitting in the helicopter, eyes still wide and head turned in the direction of the fight. At least she was obedient, unlike his sister-in-law. Thank the stars for small favors.

"Stay. No matter what—stay," he ordered, giving her a glare for good measure. Then he let his magic spill out, encapsulating the helicopter in a safe cocoon of protection before he turned to Mallorn. "Let's go."

The battle was a mess. Despite Maine's Lord Aran and his men joining the battle, it seemed the Europeans had already managed to establish a stronghold on their shores. And their lords... Kesh sensed them before he saw them, their combined power lighting up like a beacon. How they'd managed to keep themselves hidden and gain the advantage with a surprise attack he hadn't a clue. Whoever they were, they were strong, and they had his men on their asses.

"Fuck," he growled, taking in the scene. "Alright. Let's get these bastards off our shores."

"My pleasure, Your Highness," Mallorn growled, a vicious look on his face.

Kesh charged onto the battlefield, dark magic swirling high into the sky before crashing down in the middle of enemy lines, throwing ten enemy warriors violently into the air and scattering body parts in every direction.

"The prince!" he heard one of his men call over the battle, relief in his gruff voice. "The prince is here!"

"Here he comes, to save the daaay," Mallorn hummed under his breath, a sly grin on his lips as he twirled his axe, easily decapitating an enemy demon without falling behind.

"Shut up," Kesh growled, scanning the battlefield for Lord Aran. Mallorn had been his friend and second in command long before he'd gained his royal title, and as loyal as the lesser demon was, he also wasn't the least bit impressed with his old friend's new status. A trait Kesh normally appreciated—when he wasn't, in fact, there to save the fucking day. "Where the fuck is Aran?"

"There." Mallorn pointed with his axe. Up on a hill, pinned between the two enemy lords's foul magic, a large, vaguely familiar demon knelt in the mud surrounded by mutilated corpses, his own magic barely a crackle in the air around him. The centuries-old Lord of Maine, brought to his knees.

"What the shit?" Mallorn muttered by Kesh's side. "What the hell is going on? Even two to one, Aran is fucking powerful as shit. He should have been able to hold out for days."

"I guess I'll ask him if we manage to save his ass," Kesh growled, unsheathing his sword as he focused on the nearest of the two enemy lords. "Let's go."

17
GEORGIA

Stay, he'd said.

Georgia wasn't entirely sure why the big, scary demon prince had felt it necessary to remind her not to leave the safety of the helicopter and go wandering around this close to an honest-to-god demonic war, complete with giant swords and plumes of magic. She was perfectly fine hiding in the metal carcass of the chopper, thank you very much!

From her vantage point inside the aircraft, she had enough of a view of the battle to know it was no place for a human. A thought she tried not to dwell too hard on, considering the many houses off in the distance. Hopefully the citizens of the little fishing village they'd landed in had all managed to flee.

Shaking, she pressed her back against the wall of the helicopter and wrapped her arms around her knees, trying to ignore the screams and growls and clashes of metal outside.

All she had to do was stay put. Either Prince Kesh would win this nightmarish battle and come fly her back, or... Or he wouldn't, and she could try to sneak off in the aftermath and hopefully escape back to a world where she could pretend she didn't see demons, and no one called her 'Breeder'.

A loud crash from the distance made her jump, and she peered out the window, heart in her throat.

On a hill in the distance, four larger-than-average demons were locked in battle, dark magic blazing around them. Through the sparks and plumes of darkness, she recognized the prince's huge form swinging his sword at one of the other burly demons, while firing dark magic at a second. From the looks of it, he was trying to protect the fourth demon on the ground.

A twinge of something tight and uncomfortable in her gut made her pull her eyes from him.

Not my circus, not my monkeys. In fact, if the prince happened to get killed, all the better for her and her chances of escaping the lifetime as a broodmare she'd signed up for in exchange for Larry's recovery.

Determined, she flicked her gaze to another part of the battlefield, where two groups of smaller demons were fighting each other. She had no clue which side was which—apparently demons didn't believe in color-coordinated uniforms. She also didn't have the faintest idea why European demons were trying to invade Maine. Were demons just late on the whole War of Independence?

Georgia cast another look back toward the houses. How the winning demons planned on keeping the humans unaware of a full-scale battle was beyond her, but she'd seen them weave their filthy magic around people's minds enough times to know they were capable of distorting reality for the majority of the population. Judging from the immense power cracking through the air from the hilltop where the prince was currently fighting, he'd be strong enough to make an entire town getting leveled to the ground seem like a gas leak or whatever.

"Mama!"

What... the hell was that?!

"Mama!"

Heart in her throat, Georgia scrambled off her seat and rushed over to stick her head out of the helicopter's open door, drawn by what sounded all too much like a small child crying. And there, in the middle of the battlefield, between warring demons and magical explosions, stood a little girl. A *human* girl.

Everything inside Georgia went tight and cold.

"Oh my God! Oh my God, no!" Without thought, she hurled herself out of the helicopter and ran.

By some miracle, she made it to the kid without getting blown to pieces or losing her head to a wayward axe swing. She didn't pause for a second—simply scooped up the girl, turned around, and began running back toward the helicopter.

"It's okay, honey, don't worry. Let's get you out of here," she gasped as she ran, trying to settle the child on her hip to carry her weight. The girl looked to be maybe six or seven, small enough to carry but not light enough to do so at a full sprint without significant strain.

Small, slim arms wrapped around her neck, and Georgia felt the girl's tears soak through her dress. "Mama!"

"I know, honey, I know," she panted, trying to keep her eyes on the fight around them as she ran. "We'll find her, I promise. But first, we've gotta get you safe, okay?"

Out of nowhere, a demon's massive body landed right in front of her, the monster grunting as his shoulder impacted with the ground. Georgia shrieked and came to a skidding halt, clutching the girl in her arms tighter. *Shit, shit, shit!*

He looked up at her, eyes widening in shock. "Breeder?! What the fuck are you doing out here in the open?" Then his eyes moved to a point behind her, his gruesome—and vaguely familiar—face pulling into a fierce snarl as he leapt to his feet, axe raised high.

Georgia screamed again and stumbled backward, twisting on instinct to shield the child in her arms with her own body—but the demon's axe wasn't aimed at her. A resounding clang of metal above her head shot through her nervous system like a bullet.

"Down!" the vaguely familiar demon growled as he moved forward, shoving her to the ground with one hand before swinging his axe again.

This time, Georgia saw who he swung at. A massive, scary-looking monster with wings and large fangs thrust his sword at her rescuer, the blade cleaving through the space her head had just been occupying seconds ago.

Clutching the child to her chest, she desperately looked for a way to get out of reach of the two fighting demons, but the only available escape route was blocked by more combatants. Trying her best to stay in control of her wildly beating heart, she held the girl to her chest with one arm as she used the other to scramble backward in search of a safe way out. "Hold on tight, baby," she whispered breathlessly to the child sobbing inconsolably against her. "We'll make it, I prom—"

A heavy thunk cut her off mid-sentence as the winged demon's head landed on the ground right in front of her, his glassy eyes staring her right in the face.

The girl screamed loudly and buried her face in her neck, and it was all Georgia could do not to join her.

"Holy shit," she croaked.

A large, clawed hand closed around her shoulder and yanked her to her feet.

"Get in the helicopter," her savior growled.

Georgia stared at him, mouth agape. "W-what?"

"Get in the fucking helicopter, Breeder! Let's go!" Without releasing his grip on her shoulder, he began pulling her across the battlefield, his other hand on his axe as he dragged her along with him.

It took Georgia several terrified seconds before she recognized Prince Kesh's second in command. "M-Mallorn?" Despite his presence in their helicopter on the ride over, the blood and gore covering him had rendered him almost irrecognizable.

He spared her a glance over his shoulder, eyes softening a smidge as he took in her terror. "Yes. Lucky for you." Then, as if he only then noticed the kid clinging to her neck, he frowned. "What the hell is that? Put that down right this instant!"

Georgia stared at him, wide-eyed. "What? No!"

"No?"

"No! She's just a child! I can't leave her in the middle of a battlefield! She'll get hurt!"

The demon's frown deepened. "It's just a human spawnling. There are literally millions of them. One less won't hurt. Now put it down so I can get you back to safety—you don't know what sort of diseases it carries."

"She's not an 'it'!" Georgia snapped, clutching the girl tighter. "She's a little girl, she's terrified, and she needs me. I'm not leaving her!"

"Breeder, I don't have time for this!" Mallorn

snarled. "Your life is infinitely more valuable than a human's." He grabbed the girl by the arm, trying to pry her off.

"Let go of her!" Georgia kicked him in the shin with as much force as she could possibly muster and twisted, shielding the now screaming girl from the demon's grip with her own body.

Mallorn cursed, his eyes narrowing as he reached for her again. "You stubborn little— I'm trying to protect you!"

"Don't you dare touch her!" Georgia snarled, tears burning in her eyes.

Beside them, a patch of dirt exploded with the impact of dark magic, showering them in a rain of soil and soot.

"Fuck!" Mallorn spun around, ready to defend them if need be, but the explosion seemed to have been caused by a stray burst of magic aimed at another demon.

"I want my mama!" the girl wailed, making Georgia wince as her voice made her eardrums ache.

"I know, baby," Georgia murmured, rubbing the girl's back as she scanned for a way out.

Mallorn spun back around to her, grabbing her shoulder with a less than pleased look. "Fine. If you come with me, you can keep the thing. For now. Just don't expect the prince to be as lenient when he finds out you left the helicopter for the brat." Without another word, he began dragging her through the field, back toward the safety of the shielded helicopter.

Georgia stumbled after him, trying to keep up with the demon's long strides. "Wait! Wait, please, I need to find her mom!"

Mallorn's only response was to tighten his grip on her shoulder as he kept walking toward the helicopter.

"We'll find her later," Georgia whispered to the girl, realizing she wasn't going to win another battle of wills with the pissed-off demon right now. "I promise."

Back at the helicopter, Mallorn didn't release her arm until she was all the way inside. He pointed his axe at her, nostrils flared. "If you move so much as a muscle before Prince Kesh is back, I will personally lop off the spawnling's head and eat her in front of you. Do you understand?"

"Oh, my God," Georgia croaked, nausea filling her gut at the brutal threat. "Don't hurt her. I'll stay. Please."

The demon's eyes softened at her terror, and he let out a deep sigh. "Look... It brings me no pleasure to scare you, Breeder, but you have no idea what would happen if you got yourself killed out here. The loss of your life... it would be a tragedy in itself, but the repercussions for the kingdom... If the prince gets a Breeder killed, there'll be an uproar and we'll lose all support. So, as much as it pains me, my pretty, I'll do what it takes to make sure you stay put." He gave the child in her arms a hard look.

Georgia gulped and held the girl tighter. "Okay. You made your point. I won't leave again."

"Good." He gave her a lingering look, then jumped back out of the helicopter. "It'll be much easier to court you without having to traumatize you first."

18

GEORGIA

The second the demon disappeared out of view of the helicopter, the child in Georgia's arms stopped trembling and looked up. "Is the mean man gone?"

Georgia gave her a small smile. "Yes, honey. The mean man's gone for now. But don't worry, I won't let anyone hurt you. I'm Georgia. Can you tell me your name?"

"Suzanne." She looked up at Georgia with big hazel eyes. "You saved me. I was so scared, but you saved me."

"Of course I did," Georgia said softly, brushing her long hair gently. "And once all those big, scary men are done fighting, we're going to find your mama, okay? Can you tell me her name?"

Suzanne blinked up at her. "Mama."

Sighing internally, Georgia smiled gently. "Okay, honey. How about your daddy? Or the street you live on?"

"There's a swing in our front yard," Suzanne said brightly. Then she reached into the pocket of her dress and held out her clenched little fist to Georgia. "Here."

Slightly surprised by the change in the girl's focus, from crying for her mother to handing out pocket treasures, Georgia accepted the stone placed in her palm. It was a semi-opaque, milky-white crystal, roughly palm-sized and polished to a smooth oval shape. A faint glow seemed to emanate from within it.

"Oh, wow... That's so pretty, sweetheart. Where did you get this? Don't you want to keep it?" The stone felt warm in her hand, and she could almost make herself believe she felt a faint pulse from it against her skin.

Suzanne shook her head firmly and reached out to close Georgia's fingers around the gem with surprising strength, her voice taking on an odd, grown-up tone. "It was meant for you, Georgia."

"That's so sweet of you, but I'm sure whoever gave this to you would want you to keep..." Georgia's voice trailed off as the kid's bottom lip began to tremble, her already large eyes growing wider and sadder.

"It's for you. Don't you like it?" Suzanne sniffled, tears seemingly summoned out of thin air threatening to spill down her cheeks.

"No, no, of course I do. I love it," Georgia hurriedly

said, slipping the odd stone into her pocket to placate the traumatized child. It looked way too valuable for a child to be handing out to strangers, but hopefully she could discreetly slip it back to her mother, if they managed to find the woman alive. *When. When* they found her. "Thank you so much—it's so sweet of you to give it to me."

Mollified, Suzanne cuddled up closer against her.

Georgia sighed softly and held the girl against her chest, automatically rocking her gently on her lap. The feeling of her in her arms reminded her of holding Larry like this when he was small. She'd still been a kid herself, but the memory of that overpowering love she'd felt for her brother since the day he was born made her smile softly into Suzanne's dirty-blonde hair. All this—the fear, the demons... the prospect of birthing demon offspring? It was all worth it because, thanks to Prince Kesh, Larry got to live a full life. And she'd make sure Suzanne did, too. As much as she could, after witnessing something as traumatizing as a demonic battle horde descending upon her sleepy town.

"I'm so sorry you had to see all this," she whispered to the girl snuggling against her, as she ran her fingers soothingly through her hair. "You must have been so scared. But don't worry, we'll find your mama, and everything will be alright."

Georgia knew she shouldn't be making promises

she wasn't sure she could keep, but the weight of the trusting child nestled against her made iron will rise along her spine. Whatever it took, she would make things alright for this girl. Demons had ruled her nightmares since she was younger than Suzanne—she wasn't about to let them ruin this little girl's life, too.

She sat in silence with her arms around Suzanne for what felt like hours. The sounds of battle quieted to eerie silence, broken only by rough shouts now and then.

The slow, even breathing from the little girl on her lap made her assume she'd fallen asleep from the trauma weighing on her young mind, but when she suddenly popped her head up, her wide, fearful eyes were alert and free from the drowsiness of sleep.

"Don't let him hurt me."

Georgia frowned at the pleading tone, tightening her arms with the instinct to protect the small child. "Don't let who hurt you, baby?"

Before Suzanne could respond, the sound of heavy footfalls reached them from outside the helicopter. Georgia stiffened, twisting her head toward the window just in time to see the horned prince rip open the door and jump in.

He looked pissed.

Covered in blood and soot and *chunks* Georgia had no desire to study closer, he glared down at her clutching Suzanne tight. Even with the huge sword sheathed on his back, he still looked every ounce the demon warrior, and she couldn't fault Suzanne for whimpering with fear and pressing closer into Georgia's embrace, despite the girl not being able to see his monstrous features.

"What. Is. That?" He pointed at Suzanne's cowering form. "I told you not to leave the fucking helicopter! Where did *that* come from?!"

"She can't find her mother," Georgia said, twisting her body to shield the girl from the prince's angry stare. "I couldn't leave her out there—she would have gotten hurt."

Kesh's black eyes widened with outrage. "And so you thought disobeying my orders and putting yourself at risk was the smart thing to do? Don't answer that. Of course you did. You haven't seen a wretch you wouldn't martyr yourself for in a second, have you?" He scrubbed a large, clawed hand over his face. "I don't have the fucking energy for this. Get rid of her—I need to get you home before you leap in front of a train to save a rat."

"I can't just leave her. She's too young—I need to find her mother." Despite the waver in her voice in the face of the prince's clear agitation, she set her chin in defiance. "Is it safe out? I'll be quick. You can wait here—"

The metallic clang as Kesh's meaty hand slammed against the side of the helicopter made both her and Suzanne jump, and she clamped her jaw shut.

"Are you *insane?* Do you not understand that I would rather fucking die than see you hurt, you insufferable human! No, you don't get to fuck off on your own, like some idiot with a death wish! Now get rid of the girl, or I will do it for you."

The prince's anger was a near-tangible thing, the scent of aggression in the air thick on her tongue. Every instinct in her screamed to cower and obey, before his fury became violent. But she couldn't do that. Not when a small, defenseless child needed her. "Please. I... I can't leave her before I've found her mother." She covered Suzanne's ears. "Please, Kesh. I... I'll make you another bargain. Just don't make me leave her to die."

The prince narrowed his eyes to slits. "You'll make me another bargain?" he repeated, something akin to disgust in his voice. "And what do you have left to sell, little one? I already own you. That's the problem with sacrificing a piece of yourself every time your heart bleeds. Very swiftly, you run out of assets to trade."

Georgia swallowed thickly, the truth of his words making her gut tighten. "I..." She paused. He was right. For Larry, she'd bargained her body first, then her compliance. For the nameless woman in the abandoned building, she'd traded her energy. She opened her mouth to offer him the same for Suzanne, but his angry glare made her think better of it. She'd have to offer him something he couldn't get elsewhere. Something he couldn't just demand from her, either. Something he needed but would never think to ask for.

She looked up at him, at his battle-worn armor and streaks of dirt and blood littering his scaly skin. The idea struck like lightning—preposterous and obscene, but… if there was one thing a prince of demons wouldn't think to ask for…

"I'll take care of you," she whispered.

"Excuse me?"

"I'll take care of you," she repeated, more conviction in her voice now that he hadn't immediately dismissed it. "You've fought. You're injured. Tired. When we return to your home, I'll take care of you. I'll bathe you, dress your wounds if they need it… Help you relax. And if you need to consume more energy, well…"

The prince stared silently at her, his expression unreadable, and her gut tightened with panic, certain he'd deny her request.

"If you make me leave her alone and defenseless, I'll never forgive you."

She wasn't sure what part of her had the audacity to snarl a toothless threat at the monster—possibly wherever blind desperation was stored—but it made Kesh arch an eye-ridge.

"You'll never *forgive* me?" he repeated slowly, as if he couldn't quite comprehend the ridiculousness of her threat.

Despair wormed its way through Georgia's desperate fury at his disregard for a child's life, but pleading had gotten her nowhere. She clung to her anger, jaw set tightly as she glared back at him. "Never," she echoed.

Kesh held her gaze for another uneasy heartbeat.

Then he huffed what could have been a laugh but entirely lacked the mirth and jumped back out of the helicopter. "Fine. Get the girl. But, little Breeder, once she's been deposited with her own kind, I'm gonna collect on your bargain. And I don't think you'll enjoy it."

19
KESH

orgiveness.

He'd made *a lot* of bargains with humans over the years. Not *one* had ever had the audacity to try to trade him their forgiveness, as if a demon would have even the slightest interest in such a ridiculous concept.

And yet...

He glared at the Breeder out of the corner of his eye as she walked by his side, the little spawnling on her hip. The creature was too heavy for Georgia to carry comfortably, but she refused to let it walk across the crumbling sidewalks on its own perfectly functioning legs.

He didn't care about her forgiveness. She wasn't his and would be out of his hair soon enough, off to breed some other unlucky bastard sons. He had no need to make her sweet on him.

But...

An image of Georgia flooded his mind. One of her clutching the child protectively, in defiance of his demand to abandon her. He clenched his hand to tamp down the roil of emotion attempting to force its way up his esophagus.

She will be a ferocious mother.

She was going to be the kind of mother who'd move heaven and earth for her children. And as much as it infuriated him that she kept fucking sacrificing herself for anyone and anything that crossed her path, in that one moment, when she'd looked up at him with fearful defiance, she reminded him of what he'd never had.

He forced down the ache of unwanted memories. Georgia was a Breeder, like his mother had been, but if he started confabulating the two, this wouldn't end well. Not for him, not for her, and certainly not for the kingdom his brother needed him to focus on defending.

"How much farther?" he growled. Not that Georgia could answer—she had as little knowledge of the location of the child's home as he did, but annoyance at this ridiculous venture of returning the spawnling to her parents was far better than letting himself get dragged under by thoughts of his mother. There was every chance the kid's mother was one of the humans who didn't make it through the stray blasts that hit the populated areas. And then what? He highly-fucking-doubted Miss 'Can't-Abandon-A-Child' was going to accept the reality that this kid was a lost cause. And he was *not* bringing home a human child to raise as a fucking pet. Not fucking happening.

He glared at the small girl, anger already boiling at the thought of the fuss Georgia was going to kick up if the kid's mother was dead. Why couldn't she just have perished on the battlefield? What kind of human child survives a demon battle *just* long enough to make his life difficult? He'd never been fond of human spawn anyway, but this particular child made his fingers itch with violence. She had her face buried in Georgia's shoulder, refusing to meet his gaze, but there was something about her that just... made him want to snap her frail little neck.

Only the thought of having to deal with Georgia's inevitable meltdown, were he to follow that urge, made him clench his hands by his sides, tempering the impulse.

"Do any of these houses look familiar, baby?" Georgia cooed at the child on her hip.

The girl twisted her neck to look at the houses. After a moment's contemplation, she pointed a finger at the yellow-painted door of a relatively unscathed home. "That one."

"Oh, that's wonderful! Your mama's gonna be so happy to see you!" Georgia chirped, relief plain in her voice as she immediately changed direction to head up the garden path.

"Wait." He clasped a hand to her shoulder and pulled her and the child behind him. "There's enough magic restraints on this village to make humans... unstable. I don't want you face to face with one before I can ensure they're not a threat."

"What do you mean 'magic restraints'?" she asked, and only then did he realize he'd justified his actions to her, clearly giving her the impression she could ask fucking questions. *Fuck's sake.*

He briefly considered telling her to pipe down and just follow orders, but he really couldn't be arsed with the inevitable flood of guilt and other squishy, uncomfortable emotions he knew she'd cause with that frightened-yet-stubborn look he'd already learned to loathe. Fucking Breeders.

"Lord Aran had the wherewithal to cloak the village in restraining magic before the battle began. It keeps the humans docile and mostly unaware of what's going on around them, so we don't suddenly have the human military attempting to intervene, or clips of magic spreading on the Internet. It's standard procedure when we have to break our human disguise on a larger scale."

"Oh." She gave him an uncertain look as she instinctively clutched the child closer. "And Suzanne... Is she also under this influence?"

He eyed the spawnling, who still had her face buried against Georgia's shoulder, refusing to look at him. "Yes. But it wouldn't hurt to give her an extra dose, seeing how she was apparently wandering around in the middle of the battlefield."

Despite his reluctance to touch the grimy kid, he reached out to press two fingers to her temple, to ensure his magic laser-focused on her feeble little mind. But Georgia took a half-step back, mouth already open to protest.

"I'm not going to harm her," he growled, irritable and ready to be done with this whole farce. "What do you think is best for her—mild confusion and a long nap, or the risk of *real* memories surfacing in a couple of days, causing a lifetime of trauma?" He didn't give a shit if the kid had a psychological breakdown, but judging from Georgia's softened stance, presenting it as being in the child's best interest did the trick.

Human religion spoke a lot of the sins that could lead them astray: Greed. Lust. Envy. And sure, more than one hapless human had signed a bargain with him over the years, motivated by mortal sin. But their *real* weakness? The easiest thing to exploit?

A tender heart.

No doubt Georgia had been manipulated and exploited for hers plenty before she ever met him.

"Let's get you back to your mama," Georgia whispered softly to the child clutching onto her for dear life. Then she nodded to Kesh.

The kid stiffened noticeably when his fingers connected with her temple. A wave of revulsion ran through him, and a snarl curved his lip, but the look of hesitant trust on Georgia's face made him reluctantly temper it down. Ignoring the urge to unleash a blast of dark magic strong enough to splinter the pitiful thing's skull, he sent a single thread into her brain, carefully calibrated not to cause harm.

A strange, slimy sensation crawled up his fingers and into his arm, but Suzanne went instantly lax. Out cold.

"Is she okay?" Georgia asked anxiously.

"I already told you she would be," he growled, irritable from the lingering buzz of discomfort in his fingertips. Without another word, he stalked up to the front door and gave it a hard rap of his knuckles.

A moment later, a woman opened the door. Her eyes were glazed with the effect of Aran's magic. She stared dumbly up at him, mouth half agape. Thankfully docile.

"We found your child." He took a half-step to the side, allowing Georgia to come forward with the sleeping Suzanne in her arms. "Take better care not to lose her again."

"My child?" the woman repeated slowly. "I don't have a child."

Georgia gave him an alarmed look. "How can she not remember her child?" she whispered, tightening her arms around the sleeping girl. "We can't leave Suzanne with a woman who's so drugged on magic she can't even remember her own daughter."

Kesh narrowed his eyes at her, already sensing where this was headed. "She's not a fucking pet. You're not keeping her," he growled under his breath. Forcing down the disgust at touching the child, he reached out and easily plucked her from Georgia's arms before shoving her into her mother's. The woman automatically held the sleeping girl against her, blinking stupidly up at Kesh.

"That's your daughter. Her name's Suzanne. You will care for her and make sure she doesn't wander off again." He followed the command with a push of magic.

The woman looked down at the child, surprise and delight weaving through dazed confusion. "Suzanne, where have you been? Come, baby, let's get you to bed." Without another look at either Kesh or Georgia, she turned around and disappeared into her home, the sleeping girl safe in her arms.

"There." Kesh placed a hand on Georgia's shoulder. The sensation of her body under his palm sent a buzz of pleasure through his skin, washing away the remnants of disgust from touching Suzanne. "The kid is with her mother. My end of the bargain has been fulfilled. And now, little Breeder... Now it's your turn to keep yours.

20

GEORGIA

The ride back to Prince Kesh's penthouse was tense.

The knowledge that she would be performing her end of the bargain once they landed had tension knotting in her stomach, not helped by the hard glare the prince had given her before he focused his attention on piloting the helicopter.

Thankfully, the loud thrumming from the machine made conversation impossible, so she didn't have to begin buttering him up just yet—nor talk with his second in command.

Mallorn hadn't stopped staring at her since they returned to the helicopter, his expression something between reverence and an uncomfortable dose of raw lust. All in all, Georgia was more than happy to spend the helicopter ride with nothing but machine noises filling the silence.

. . .

WHEN THE PRINCE PUT THE HELICOPTER DOWN ON THE ROOF of his penthouse, darkness had long since fallen, and Georgia's stomach was twisting with hunger—a feat she hadn't thought possible only this morning, when the demon lord had force-fed her until she was full to bursting.

The moment Kesh cut the helicopter's engine, a particularly loud rumble made Georgia press a hand to her stomach.

"You're hungry," Mallorn said, with an urgency suggesting this was the greatest crisis ever to arise in his lifetime. He got to his feet and placed a clawed hand on her arm, which made her tense on instinct. "Come, little one. Let me feed you."

"Mallorn." The prince's snarl rumbled through the air, low and threatening.

"When did she last eat?" Mallorn countered, an air of outrage to his voice as if forgetting to feed the human during an honest-to-god battle was entirely unacceptable. "Humans are frail, especially the females. They need nourishment several times a day."

Kesh's eyes widened at his subordinate's challenge, then narrowed. Mallorn must have been able to see the impending storm coming too, because he quickly softened his tone. "Look, you have a war to win and a territory to run. It's understandable that details like feeding the Breeder will slip your mind from time to time. Let me take over her care. I'm much more accustomed to human companions than you."

"No!" The word was out of her mouth before she could process why the thought of being alone with Mallorn seemed infinitely more terrifying than being under the prince's dubious care. They were both monsters—it shouldn't matter which of them was in charge of her, because both scenarios were nightmarish.

Mallorn gave her a wounded look that was almost comical on his demonic features, and a twinge of guilt weaved its way through her gut.

"I—I'm sorry, I—"

"Enough!" The prince gave her a glare that made her mouth clamp shut before she could finish her stuttered apology. Seemingly content with her swift obedience, he turned his glare to Mallorn. "The Breeder is mine to care for. *Mine.* Get your hand off her, and don't ever challenge me on this matter again."

Mallorn's face stiffened, and from the tension in the air, Georgia got the distinct impression something significant had just shifted between the two males.

"As you command, my prince," Mallorn said stiffly, bowing his head as he took a step back, removing his hand from her arm.

"Brief my brother on what transpired in Maine, and make sure our men are taken care of. I will debrief them tomorrow, once I've had a chance to talk with Kain myself." Shifting his attention to her, Kesh flicked two fingers—a command to come to him. As if she were a dog. "Let's go, Breeder. You need to eat—and then, you have a bargain to fulfill."

Georgia stepped toward him, managing not to wince when he put an oversized hand on her shoulder and began steering her toward the stairs leading from the roof of the building to his penthouse below. As the door closed behind them, she glanced back over her shoulder. Mallorn still stood by the helicopter, watching them with burning eyes. His hands were clenched into fists by his sides.

———

THE PRINCE DIDN'T FORCE-FEED HER THIS TIME. NOT THAT IT made the experience of eating under his watchful glare particularly more pleasant.

It wasn't that he'd displayed a delightful temperament up until now, but he seemed in a worse mood than ever as he stared at her eating the leftovers from that morning. Nostrils flaring when she swallowed a bite, sharp claws drumming dangerously against the countertop when she took breaks, but he stayed silent. Silent and broody.

"So... why did the European demons attack a fishing village in Maine...?" she finally asked, when she couldn't take the looming silence any longer.

Kesh's glare turned even darker, which she hadn't thought was possible, and she instantly wished she'd stayed quiet. But much to her surprise, after a moment, he said, "Their crown prince attempted to steal my brother's mate. He had to make sure she'd be safe, so he killed the European prince and took control of the Americas from them. They were... displeased. They've been poking at our defenses ever since, looking for weaknesses. It won't be long before they launch an all-out war." He gave her another look through narrowed eyes. "Which is what I should be focusing on. Not babysitting *you*."

Georgia didn't point out that she'd be happy to get out of his hair if he wanted to release her from their bargain—she'd tried that once before, and right now seemed to very much not be the right time to push that point.

"I... guess I can understand why that would be frustrating," she said instead.

Kesh raised an eyebrow at her. "You're not apologizing? That's a first."

She blinked. "Um... I'm sorr—"

He interrupted her with a curl of his lip, showing a hint of fangs. "No. Don't you fucking dare. Why does it take so little for you to prostrate yourself?"

"I thought you wanted me to..." She trailed off, heat rising in her cheeks as his stare made her think about his question. "I... I don't know," she admitted softly. "I just don't like upsetting people."

"You're a doormat," he said, voice cold and dismissive. "You've spent your life making yourself as small and inoffensive as possible, and what has that gotten you? Nothing. Less than nothing."

"You don't know me or my life," she protested, a hint of anger worming its way through her innate fear of the demon.

"Oh, but I do," he huffed, a disgusted look on his harrowing face. "You were the quiet girl growing up, always doing what was expected of you, but never claiming the spotlight when you excelled at anything, right? Wouldn't want anyone to think you were too proud, or thought yourself better than them. And you were praised for it, weren't you? Little Georgia, always putting others first. So self-sacrificing. Such a saint. Such a *nice girl*.

"And here you are, fully grown, and you still haven't fucking clocked on that while you were busy putting yourself last, everyone else put you last as well. I don't have to know your life to know that you're so used to being taken advantage of, you wouldn't feel safe unless you were somehow sacrificing for others."

"You don't..." Georgia opened her mouth to rebut his harsh characterization of her with another assertion that he didn't know her or her life, but her voice died as his words sank deep underneath her skin, burrowing into the most vulnerable parts. Memories flooded through her mind—going without dinner now and then as a young teen, when Mom was struggling as a single parent and there wasn't money to put food on the table for everyone. Mom had to have energy to work, and Larry was a growing boy. So she'd gone to bed hungry. Sacrificing her GPA to work more hours as an older teen, so she could contribute to the household. Walking to work for months, because Mom suggested the single mother living next door needed the rundown old beater she'd managed to scrape and save for more than Georgia did herself. Not taking that art scholarship to an out-of-state college, because that would have left Mom and Larry to fend for themselves.

Memory after memory flickered through her brain. She'd never questioned it—the habit of stepping aside for others who might have more need—and she couldn't deny the stab in her gut at the prince's derisive tone as he called her a *nice girl.*

"Well, excuse me for being a good person," she finally huffed. "I'm sure the concept is alien to a demon, but it's a basic, vital part of humanity. We can't all be self-absorbed assholes. I was raised this way. I've done nothing the rest of my family wouldn't do in a heartbeat, and I almost pity you that you'll never know what it's like to have people you would do anything for."

Kesh only snorted at her defensive tone. "Oh, I'm sure your people would definitely sacrifice themselves for you if only they got a chance... But wait! Why were *you* the one bargaining your body to save your brother's life? Why didn't he seek one of us out? Why didn't his mother? His father?"

Two hot spots bloomed on her cheeks with anger at

his persistence. "Because I'm the only one who can see you. They don't know you exist."

"No?" The prince raised his eyebrows in mock surprise. "So when you were a little girl and cried whenever you saw a monster, what would they do?"

"They'd..." She hesitated, the heat in her cheeks intensifying. "I was a child. What were they supposed to think? That demons were real, but their daughter was the only one who could see them?"

"So they dismissed us as figments of your imagination?"

"Of course they did. Like I'm sure most sane parents would," she snapped. She wasn't aware she'd wrapped her arms around herself until she saw the demon's dark gaze dip to take in the protective gesture.

"And when you grew older and still saw us...? They had you speak to a psychiatrist? Like most sane parents would?"

The way his dark eyes taunted her, she knew he already knew the answer to that. She just glared at him.

"Well?" he pushed. Forcing her to say the words.

"No." It came out like a soft whisper—not at all as assertive and unbothered as she could have wished.

"Tell me, then. What did your supportive family do? You know, the people who would sacrifice for you, just like you have for them."

"We didn't have that kind of money. And Larry was still little and needed a lot of attention."

"Georgia," he interrupted her, voice sharpening as

he crossed his arms over his chest and speared her with a look that made her lungs tighten. "What happened when you told them you were still seeing monsters?"

"I... had a new P.E. teacher. A demon. He was... mean. Scary. I told my mom I didn't want to go to class. She asked why. I told her he was a monster." She exhaled softly as the echo of terror from that moment reverberated through her. "She... didn't have the capacity to deal with it. She and Larry's dad were going through a rough patch, and..."

"What happened, Georgia?" Kesh repeated, his voice as commanding as before, if perhaps a fraction softer.

Why was this so hard to say? She understood why her mom hadn't been able to deal with it. And it was so long ago. So why did admitting out loud what had happened when she went to her mother for help still hurt? "She... told me I was too old to believe in boogeymen. And that she didn't have the energy to deal with my drama. That if I didn't like P.E. to eat less candy and start jogging. And to never bother her with it again."

"And let me guess—you never did?" he asked. He spoke more softly than before, but something in those dark eyes made the hair at the back of her neck stand on end.

Wordlessly, she shook her head, eyes lowering from the intensity of his stare. Her skin prickled, something numb and unpleasant stirring in her gut at the opening of old wounds. Mom had done the best she could with what she had. Georgia knew that.

But it still hurt to remember.

"How old were you?"

"Eight," she said softly.

Silence fell between them. Though she didn't look up, she could still feel his eyes on her. Feel the judgment in them.

"She really trained you well, didn't she?" he said quietly. Disgust laced every word. "Taught you that your pain and fear mean nothing if they get in the way of her convenience. Or, let me guess, in the way of her Golden Child? I think you know, deep down, that even if she'd believed in our existence, she wouldn't have sacrificed herself for your brother's life. She'd have expected you to do it. Just like you've been trained to do."

"That's not true!" Georgia glared up at him, anger and hurt giving her the strength to meet his disturbing eyes again. "She gave up everything for me and Larry. She wasn't perfect, but at least she stuck around. That's a hell of a lot better than what my dad did. And why do you even care? What is my upbringing to you? Didn't you say you had a war to focus on, rather than the massive inconvenience that is me?"

The prince huffed what could have been a mirthless laugh, one corner of his sinful lips curving up a fraction of an inch. "You're right. I don't care. Keep being a doormat, Breeder. It'll only make you easier to control for whichever demon claims you in the end." He got to his feet and flicked two fingers at her—his command to follow.

"Where are we going?" God, how she wished her voice didn't wobble.

Kesh glanced at her before he began walking out of the kitchen. Toward the bedroom.

"You sold yourself for a stranger, Breeder. You know where we're going."

She did. Nails digging into her palms, she followed him. Whatever humiliations he had in store for her, she'd chosen this willingly. For Suzanne.

At least there was some comfort in that.

21

KESH

Georgia practically crept into the bedroom after him, silent and cowed.

He was a demon—finding a human's pain points was as natural as breathing, and the satisfaction of forcing the Breeder to finally face the reality of her spineless existence should have given him nothing but pleasure.

Instead, seeing her this...*pitiful*... made his skin itch and his pulse drum in his temples.

Kesh glared at her as he rubbed his forehead, trying to ease the unpleasant sensation. What the fuck was he doing? Accepting a bargain from a fucking Breeder that would have her, what, servicing him like a common whore? Neither of them had spelled out exactly how she'd be paying for the time and effort he'd expended on the human spawnling, but he knew how a woman could help a male *relax*.

It was one thing to take her energy, though if Mallorn ever found out, he didn't doubt his Second would have further things to say about the Breeder staying in his care. It was quite another to take pleasure from her for base gratification. He had to get his shit together before he ruined any chance of her training to take, despite how desperate his stupid instincts were for her attentions.

"Get out."

The Breeder jolted at his growled command, nervous eyes flashing up to his. "W-what?"

"Get. Out," he repeated, emphasizing each syllable. "I'm releasing you from this idiotic bargain. I don't need you to *take care* of me. Go rest in the living room— I'll come get you when I've talked to the king about the events in Maine, and then we'll get you branded before you sleep so we can continue your training tomorrow." And then mated off at the earliest possibility. He didn't say the last part out loud.

Georgia blinked, body jerking with the instinct to obey his command. But as she placed a hand on the doorknob, she turned to look back up at him, and a flash of reluctant determination settled in her eyes. "No."

"No?" he repeated, eye-ridged arching.

"We... we made a bargain." She drew in a deep breath and set her shoulders before releasing the doorknob, stepping back toward him. "You kept your end. I am going to keep mine."

He gave her an incredulous stare. "I don't think you quite understand, Breeder. I am rescinding our bargain. Do you know how often a demon will do this?"

"I'm guessing rather rarely," she said, cheeks flushing. "I'm not trying to be ungrateful; it's just..."

"It's just *what?*" He narrowed his eyes at her. A demon didn't voluntarily give up a bargain 'rather rarely'. It was 'never'. And yet this infuriating human girl chose *this* moment to challenge him? "Is it that you *want* to get on your knees for me?"

Her blush deepened. "No. I just... if I don't keep my end, then you're unlikely to make another bargain with me in the future. And it's been made very clear that bargaining is the only way I get any say or agency with you or any other demon. So please... let me... let me take care of you. I'll make it worth your while. I promise."

Kesh bared his teeth, frustration making a low snarl rumble out of his throat. Georgia's eyes widened in response, her muscles tensing as if she were fighting the urge to flee. But she stayed put.

"Please."

Please. Why did that word make his gut clench? He looked at her, at that soft mouth and the innate vulnerability in her eyes. She'd never be able to hide that, not from him or anyone else. So she wanted agency. It was not a surprise—every human woman who discovered the horrible twist of fate that allowed her to be bred by demons would eventually become desperate for any kind of say over her own life. Her body.

His mother had too.

"Fine." He turned his back and began undoing the straps of his armor, angry at the soft, aching thing twisting in his chest. "Do what you want."

Her steps were hesitant, and when she stopped behind him, she didn't move again for a long moment. He felt her presence like the sun on his back, heating his skin.

Finally, gentle hands skimmed over his back before grasping for the straps on his armor located there. Her fingers brushed against his scales as she began working on the leather and buckles, and his breath caught in his throat.

"Tell me about your brother and his mate," she said, voice as soft as her hands as she pulled off his shoulder guards and began working on his chest plate.

"Why?"

"You said your brother went to war with the European demons for his mate. He must love her." A small silence. "I... didn't know you could. Love a human."

Kesh scoffed. "That a demon fights to keep what is his doesn't mean what he feels is *love,* Breeder. Once we claim a mate, we're consumed with possessive urges. It's primal, on a level far more fundamental than you have any hope of comprehending."

"So... he doesn't? Love her?"

"I didn't say that," he sighed, annoyance rising at the mere memory of how absolutely, ridiculously soft his brother got around his mate. "Love is... complicated for my kind. It would be better if you didn't expect such a human thing from your mating."

"Why?" She finished undoing the straps on his back, moving to his front to lift off his breastplate. Her scent hit his nostrils, tinged with smoke and blood from the battlefield, but still woven through with the warm, gentle touch of female.

The memory of his mother returned unbidden, tightening his sternum.

Not again.

"Because if you go to your mate believing you will eventually be loved like a human man would grow to love you, you will not have the resilience to survive the truth of being mated to a demon. We are possessive creatures, Georgia. Dominating. All-consuming. That is what your attempts to bargain have bought you—eternity as a monster's most coveted possession.

"If you accept your fate for what it is, you will find a way to face it. Perhaps you might even experience moments of joy. I am told some Breeders come to love their offspring."

"*Some?*" she asked, glancing up at him before she began working on the straps for his wrist guards. "*Some* of your women come to love their children?"

He gazed down at her bent head, his sternum squeezing again. "Yes. Some. In the past... Not every Breeder recovered from the trauma sustained during her procuring process. Which is why the new queen decreed that we first train you, in preparation for your new life."

"I suppose... that makes sense," Georgia said, frowning at his wrist guards. "And..."

"And?" he pressed when she hesitated, irritated that he found himself interested in her thoughts on the matter.

"And... well, I didn't really understand why you've been bothering with being... careful. We made a bargain. You could just make me do whatever it is you need me to do, but... you haven't. Not really." She gave his left wristguard a tug, pulling the leather off, then focused on his right without looking back up. "So I guess... Thank you. For trying not to traumatize me. The other demon, the one who... ringed me, he... Well, he fed on terror."

Kesh grunted at the reminder of the slimeball who'd tried to pimp her. He reached down, grasped her chin between his fingers and tugged, forcing her to meet his eyes. "You won't be given to a man who will abuse you. I swear it."

He didn't know why he felt the need to reassure her. She didn't need him to—as unenthusiastic about her fate as she was, she also seemed resigned to it. Not like his sister-in-law at first. Or his mother.

Blue eyes searched his. Looking for a trick. Or maybe she was looking for the why, too.

Curses, she had beautiful eyes. Deep. Gentle. And with a curiosity that defied her otherwise meek nature.

She saw through his disguise, knew what he was, and still... She searched his gaze with interest, as if something about him fascinated her. Like he was a puzzle she couldn't piece together.

He'd killed in front of her. Fed from her. Told her he would make sure she spent her life being bred by monsters. Why did she look at him like this?

"Is your mother like me? A... Breeder?"

The question appeared in the air between them like a rolling fog, unexpected, sudden. All-encompassing. It sank into his lungs, clung to his skin, and thickened the air, and for a long, awful moment, all he could see was a lifeless body slumped on a thick, Persian rug. The smell of blood clinging to his palate; not exciting this time, not arousing. Terrible. World-ending.

"Kesh?"

The sound of his name snapped him out of it. He inhaled sharply as the present came back into focus, and the only scent that filled his nostrils was *hers*.

"She's a Breeder?" Georgia said again, the question mark perfunctory. His silence had already confirmed it, and from the empathy now in her eyes, her curious gaze had found something he'd rather not acknowledge was still there.

"Yes." He dropped his hand from her chin and stepped back, pulling his arm out of reach. "She was. Draw me a bath. I smell like Eurotrash." Without another look at the Breeder, he pulled off his arm guard, then began working on the other.

Hesitating, she asked, "Was? She died?"

"Yes, she died. She took her own life because no amount of gilding could make her accept her cage. Which is why, Georgia, I tell you to abandon your human notions of what your life is supposed to look like. If you accept the reality of what awaits you, and if I make sure you aren't mated to a monster as brutal as my father, perhaps you won't slice your wrists just to escape. That is my job. That is my responsibility. And yes, that is why I am *careful* with you. Why a whole fucking *war* has to be put on the back burner so that I may prepare you to spread your legs without fear.

"You are incredibly valuable—we need your womb to strengthen our numbers, or we are fucked. The Europeans, the gods... If we don't have the men to fight them, we will be exterminated." Angry, with only a diffuse sense of why, he finally managed to wrest the last arm guard off and tossed it on the floor. "Now do you have any more questions before you fulfill the bargain you were so keen to strike? Please, don't hold back;. I'm fucking *dying* to sate your inane curiosity."

Only silence answered him. When he shot her a glare, she averted her gaze and finally moved toward the bathtub. Cowed by his burst of temper.

Good.

He stared at her back, silently daring her to turn around and continue testing her luck, but she didn't. She pulled a stool to the side of the tub and kept her focus on the rising water, not daring to so much as look at him.

Why was she so fucking meek when it came to fighting her own battles? She'd run onto a *battlefield* to save that spawnling. She hadn't hesitated to defy him then. But herself? There was no fire to be found when it came to protecting her own interests.

A fine quality in a Breeder—biological instincts to protect younglings; trained subservience to a dominating force. She'd make one of his men a perfect mate.

There was no reason whatsoever for the guilt-laced frustration simmering in his gut at the sight of her cowed posture.

Breeders and their fucking pheromones.

Determined to push down the idiotic response his wiring had to her, he kicked off his steel-enforced boots and pulled off his leather pants, intent on the bathtub. She wanted to fulfill their deal so she could convince herself she'd be allowed to bargain herself, yet again, some other time? Fine. He wasn't about to feel fucking guilty for it.

"There's a sponge, soap, and oils in the bathroom."

"Right, I'll just get—Oh, what the *fuck,* what... *What is that?!*"

The Breeder's sudden, and borderline-hysterical, screech sent a wave of adrenaline through his body as his biology prepared to defend the terrified female. But when he jerked his head up to see what had scared her, her eyes were glued to his crotch.

22

GEORGIA

Frowning, the demon prince looked down at himself. "That's my dick."

"That is *not* a... a penis!" Georgia sputtered, withdrawing several steps as she stared at the monstrosity between his powerful thighs.

From the smooth, blackish-red scales covering his body, a dark, tubular mass of flesh hung from where his man-parts *should* have been. But *that?* There was absolutely no way something that thick and... *ridged* was supposed to be used to make love. Even for a huge demon, that was going too far!

"Don't tell me you're a damn virgin," the asshole demon said, having the audacity to sound exasperated. "Yes, it's a dick. Would you like to get better acquainted, or can I get in the fucking tub?"

Georgia took another swift step backward, unable to look away from the ridiculous thing. It twitched at her attention. "No! No, get in the tub!" Jerking her attention away, she swiveled on her heel and darted for the bathroom.

Relief flooded through her when, only a moment later, the sound of water sloshing indicated that the prince had climbed into the bath. *Thank God.*

She rested a hand on the vanity, trying to collect herself. She'd been thankful for his insistence that she wouldn't survive sex with him before, even if she hadn't fully understood why. Now, however, she was infinitely more grateful he didn't have plans to put that medieval torture device inside her.

But... did all demons have members like that? With her newfound knowledge of their reproductive organs, repeatedly being called a 'Breeder' painted an even grimmer picture of what was already an uncomfortable moniker.

Surely, they couldn't all be like that? It would injure a human woman to take that, possibly even kill her. Lesser demons had to be more... reasonable. Probably not pleasant, but... manageable. Yes. That had to be the case.

An echo of the tormented cries of the poor women forced to serve in the demon whorehouse made her shudder and force her focus to gathering the bath supplies. At least she'd been spared that fate. There would only be one monster using her, not a legion.

The prince was in the tub when she returned to the bedroom, resting against the back of it. His long horns curved up behind him, obsidian black and strong. They were oddly beautiful in their animalistic quality and almost managed to make the sharper, scaled protrusions along his shoulders look natural—as if every jagged edge and rough texture on his body was perfectly blended to compliment his hulking frame.

Gathering her courage, she stepped up to the tub and pulled the nearby wooden stool to its side so she could sit. He'd given her the choice to back out of the bargain. She'd insisted because, so long as he held her fate in his hands, she needed a way to be able to sway him. Which meant keeping him open to the possibility of future bargains.

Which, in turn, meant making sure she gave him something he couldn't easily get somewhere else.

Georgia dipped the sponge into the warm water by the demon's side, then brought it to his wide shoulders, squeezing it out over the scales to wet his skin. When she dipped it again, she rubbed soap into the sponge, then began gently lathering his shoulder with soothing circles.

A low, involuntary groan rumbled out of the beast's chest.

She dipped the sponge in the water again before returning to his shoulder, this time washing off the soap. He exhaled, low and deep. Strong muscles softened ever so slightly under her touch.

Georgia glanced up at his face, half expecting his usual glare, but he had his unsettling black eyes closed, long eyelashes fanning his cheeks. She bit her lip to keep the small smirk there in check and kept her attention on bathing him. Turned out, not even big, grumpy demon lords could resist the magic of a sponge bath. From the way small tremors crossed his stark features now and then, he hadn't expected her plan to bring him comfort to be quite this effective.

It was oddly... Endearing wasn't the right word. Demons weren't capable of being *endearing*. But there was something surprisingly... almost sweet about seeing a hulking, battle-hardened monster-like the prince relax under her touch.

Carefully, she washed the dried blood and dirt off his face, then turned to his long, matted hair.

The long, low rumble that escaped him when she dug her fingertips into his scalp had her unable to hold back a giggle.

Kesh cracked an eyelid, lips flattening disapprovingly. "What do you find so funny, Breeder?"

"Nothing," she said, hastily reining the amusement back in, but the damage had been done.

His eyebrows pulled down in a frown, and she sensed his shoulders tensing.

That wouldn't do. Not if she wanted him to realize just how beneficial bargaining with her could be for him, too.

Georgia speared her fingertips through his hair again and gently scraped her nails along his scalp as she massaged the shampoo deeper.

"Mmm... damn it all." This time, it was a full moan. "What kind of fucking witchcraft is this?"

"It's okay to enjoy touch," she said softly, making sure to keep her fingers rubbing the same, enticing patterns through his strands. "To relax. I couldn't hurt you even if I wanted to. The battle is over. You won. Let go of all that responsibility for a little while and let me take care of you."

Kesh grumbled something under his breath, but his shoulders relaxed, and he sank deeper into the tub, eyes closing again.

"That's it," she murmured, keeping up the scalp massage until the prince had melted fully into the bath, his head leaning back against the rim, eyes closed. Throat bared. Vulnerable.

Well, as vulnerable as a huge, battle-hardened monster got. She was pretty sure she'd need to be hiding a very sharp machete up her sleeve to be able to do any damage to the prince, even in this state. But the sentiment was there.

"You don't allow anyone to see you like this very often, do you?" she asked, still keeping her voice low and soothing to avoid riling him up again.

"Of course not. At the best of times, demons tend to slice the throats of anyone standing in their way to power, if given the chance. I'm a prince, and we're at war." Despite his terse words, his tone was almost drugged from relaxation.

"I bet your cortisol levels are sky high," she said,

frowning when she realized she didn't know if demonic biology had human stress hormones. "Or… is that a good thing for you? Since some of you feed on misery…?"

Kesh scoffed, but didn't deign to give her an answer.

Choosing to refocus on keeping him relaxed, she pushed her curiosity aside and scooped up a pail of water to pour over the prince's head, making sure not to get any in his eyes. He released a soft exhale, and another when she ran her fingers through his strands to help rinse out the shampoo. It took five pails to get his hair clean—it was thick and long, and felt lush to the touch, if a little rough with enough split ends to suggest he didn't take any care of it.

There hadn't been any conditioner among the supplies in the bathroom, but a woman could improvise.

She popped the cork on the body oil and began massaging it into his lengths. The parched hair sucked it up in seconds.

"I thought royals were supposed to be pampered," she mused.

Kesh snorted. "I'm sure the Europeans have plenty of little human servants enthralled for this purpose. We've been a bit too busy trying to survive to really establish the appropriate life of luxury just yet."

"You don't seem… keen. On the whole prince-thing," she said as she moved the stool so she could resume washing his body. There were sprays of blood all over his chest, and she had to scrub a little harder with the sponge to get it off. He didn't complain at the treatment, but his black eyes opened to watch her while she worked.

"It's a responsibility I didn't ask for."

"But also power, I imagine? You said demons will slice the throats of anyone in their way to get to power."

He tilted his head, his gaze turning sharper. "They will. And I cut the heads off many a man to get my brother on the throne. Power is... a double-edged sword. A necessary evil, if you will. Even you, little mouse... You strive for power over me, with your bargains and your gentle touches. Hoping to influence me to give you agency. You don't have the strength to physically subjugate me, so you use other means. Your touch. Your scent. Even the timbre of your voice.

"We all need power, and we all have to face the consequences once we get it. For me, it's the responsibility of the lives lost to this war. For you... Well, let's hope you don't succeed in your quest for power, little Breeder. For both our sakes."

There was no mistaking the smolder in his black eyes.

Georgia grimaced and quickly lowered her gaze to his chest, refocusing on scrubbing the blood off his scaled skin. The blood and dirt were thick in the water, and she reached down to pull out the plug, making sure not to look further down as the tub emptied.

Power. If he thought servicing a male strong enough to crush her with a flex of his hands, while hoping he wouldn't lose control and brutally rape her to death was *power,* then he really didn't understand what it was like to be small and helpless. Not that he would. No. Someone as strong and physically dominant as the demon prince would never know what it was like to be truly powerless.

She refilled the tub, then dipped the sponge to his abs. They tensed under her touch.

"Does it not feel good here?" she asked, darting a look up at his face.

The intensified smolder in his eyes when she caught his gaze was all the answer he gave her, but it was plenty.

"Oh…" She cleared her throat, wishing she couldn't feel the blood pool hotly in her cheeks. "Sorry." She made to pull her hand away, to move on to washing his legs instead, but a large, clawed hand grabbed her by the wrist before she could clear the waterline. Keeping her gaze locked in his, the demon pulled her hand lower down, until the sponge made contact with something rigid and *huge.*

"You missed a spot."

The growl in his voice made something clench low in her gut. Terror. Had to be terror.

"I…" She trailed off, biting her lip. She'd known what she was offering when she made her bargain for

Suzanne. That he had a horrifying dick didn't change what he valued in her.

Wordlessly, she relaxed her arm and let him guide the sponge down the full length of him.

He shuddered at the caress, another low growl escaping his throat before he released her wrist and leaned back. Black eyes still locked in hers.

Slowly, she rubbed the sponge back up the length of his cock, then down again, moving around the thick column of flesh to wash every part.

He shuddered in response, clawed hands tightening around the rim of the tub. When she gave the head a gentle stroke of the sponge, he bit his bottom lip and tilted his head back, a soft groan rumbling through his massive body.

Power.

The word rang through her mind again as she looked up at the monster so entirely enthralled by her touch, even muted by the sponge. Perhaps.... Perhaps he hadn't been entirely wrong, after all. There was a strange rush of power at having this hulking monster of a male trembling with a simple touch. A dark dichotomy between her life ending in his hands if she broke through his ability to control himself, and the knowledge that perhaps she *could* push the Prince of Demons to his breaking point. She had that power.

Slowly, carefully, she rubbed the sponge along his cock—up and down, up and down. He hissed every time she brushed against those scary-looking ridges along the rim of the head, as if they were so sensitive he could barely stand it.

Curiosity finally won out. Georgia dipped her gaze to the thick column of flesh rising from between his powerful thighs. It was an angry red, aggressively textured, and just... absurd. Gently, she traced a finger along the coronal ridges, drawing a full-body tremble from the demon.

"They're... softer than I thought they'd be," she murmured, emboldened by finally having some semblance of control. "Cartilage? Not bone."

"Yes." His voice was a low, raspy rumble. "It's for dominance, not injury."

"But you would still kill me if we...?" She put the sponge aside and pressed a fingertip into the valley between two ridges, testing the flexibility in the tissue. Despite the uneven texture of his skin, it was still silky soft under her touch.

Kesh growled at the pressure, eyes narrowing—but he didn't stop her from continuing. "Yes. I would. But not because of the ridges. I'm a lord. My magic is... potent. When I couple with a female, I can't hold it back, and a human woman can't withstand its untempered touch within her. You would rip apart from the inside, leaving nothing but a pile of guts and ashes."

Georgia froze, her attention shifting abruptly to his face at the mention of 'guts and ashes'. "Um... How do you...? Has that... happened before?"

"It has." His lip quirked at the look of horror

spreading across her face. "Barbaric, isn't it? Tell me, Breeder, what are you imagining right now? My roar of pleasure as my unwilling victim dies beneath me? The terror and agony for her before I finally snuffed her life?"

That was exactly what she was picturing. Suddenly having zero interest in touching his dick, she pulled her hand away. "Is that not... accurate?"

"Does it matter? You're a Breeder—no matter how many times you sell your body to me, I'll never desecrate it. You're too valuable to end your life screaming on my cock."

"Of course it matters." Despite the terror clenching her esophagus, a spark of anger rose at the thought of what he'd done. "You seem incapable of understanding that I care about other people. And... and if you did that... if you..."

"If I raped someone? *Multiple* someones? Would that be worse than what you already know me to be? You've been on your knees before, begging me to spare a woman's life." He stared her down, something almost like accusation in his black eyes. As if her horror... *offended* him.

Georgia set her jaw and shifted her weight on the stool, away from him. "Yes."

"Why?"

"Because there isn't a max level of awful you can reach! That man you killed... at least it was to feed yourself. But to hear that you've raped women? Knowing they'd die horribly? You're no better than the asshole who wanted to sell me in his brothel!" She wasn't sure why that realization stung like a betrayal. She'd known him to be a monster from first sight, and when he'd killed that poor guy in the bathroom and tried to kill the woman, too, she'd seen exactly how he saw humans: as resources to use. And still, somehow, she'd still felt... not safe with him. But not truly terrified, either. Not like she had at the brothel, because... Because she'd believed him when he'd said he didn't rape the women he took to his home, and she'd nurtured a sheer, desperate hope that he wasn't all the way evil. That, however bleak the circumstances, he was proof that her future mate might also be capable of some decency.

He let out a laugh, low and bitter. "Oh, so there are gradients? If I need sustenance, your squishy little Breeder heart can find forgiveness for my atrocities, but if my cravings are for pleasure, for comfort, you'd judge me for indulging?"

"Yes!" she spat. "One is for survival, the other... the other you could *ask* a woman to give. Or does it have to be forced for you to enjoy it?"

Kesh exhaled slowly, his eyes locked with hers, smoldering with desire again—as if her anger excited the beast within him. "No. It doesn't. But I don't have to ask, either, do I, Breeder? Not when I have a mouthy little female at hand who so eagerly traded her services for the night."

"I suppose desperation to save a child's life is what a rapey monster would class as 'eagerness'," she bit.

A snarl ripped from the prince's throat. He stood, so abruptly the water sloshed over the edge of the tub, and yanked her up by an iron grip on her arms.

Georgia yipped, terror overriding her anger as he lifted her into the tub and then off her feet, bringing her all the way up to his face. She struggled against his hold, pushing against his massive chest, but he didn't so much as flinch.

His lip peeled back from his teeth, revealing his sharp fangs, and the look of utter *fury* in those black vortex eyes shot tendrils of ice to her tailbone. "You want to be a martyr, Breeder? You want me to play the role of the big, bad monster foaming at the mouth to violate you? *Fine.* I'll make you the victim you so desperately want to be."

23
KESH

Fury pounded in his temples as he waded out of the tub and carried the Breeder by her arms to the bed. She screamed when he tossed her on it, and scrambled backward when he knelt on the foot end, towering over her. She didn't get far. He grabbed her by the ankles and yanked, sending her onto her back. She kicked to free herself, but her strength was no match for his. One vicious rip of fabric, and her body was bared to him, long, creamy legs leading up to the tuft of hair covering the apex he yearned to devour. He inhaled deeply on instinct, desperate for the tang of her —but along with warm pussy, what filled his lungs was acrid terror and despair.

A bright memory filled his mind on the heels of that uniquely devastating scent, and his breath caught in his lungs as anguish flooded his body: His mother. Curled up on her marital bed. Weeping.

His father's semen seeping from her.

Her hiss at him to stay away when he, with childish panic, tried to comfort her, tried to glue back together the center of his universe.

Don't touch me! You're all the same.

He'd been five when he'd learned that entire being was nothing but darkness and destruction.

"...Kesh?" The gentlest whisper, followed by a soft touch to his arm. He jerked at the contact, his focus zeroing in on the Breeder before him. Concern mixed with her fear, her stupid, kind heart drawing her to him despite how all he wanted was to ruin her. Like his mother had been ruined.

"Stay away from me!" he snarled, recoiling from her.

Her innocent, blue eyes widened, but instead of obeying his command, she shifted up on her knees so she could lean further toward him.

"You're crying." It was a simple statement, the wonderment in her voice penetrating deep into his chest. She reached for him again, her delicate fingers trying to encircle his wrist like weighted shackles on his soul. As much as he wanted to put distance between them before his darkness consumed her, he found himself unable to move.

Before he could break through the stupor of her declaration, Georgia reached for his face with her free hand, smoothing away the tears from his cheek with a soft brush of her thumb. "What's wrong?"

Every fiber of his being wanted to snarl at her, to tell her he wasn't fucking *crying*—that the Prince of Demons didn't *cry*. To make her pay for this weakness her presence forced out of him.

But her touch on his skin flooded his body with longing. And deep, dark, soul-crushing despair.

He couldn't breathe. Couldn't think. He could only feel.

Deep, ugly sobs tore through his body, forced up from so deep, horror and bile singed his taste buds. There was no stopping it, no willing it away. Pain flooded out of him, visceral and raw, and there was nothing he could do to hide it from the woman who'd unwittingly ripped him open by her mere existence.

Slim arms wrapped around his body, embracing him in softness and warmth. "Shh. It's okay. It's gonna be okay."

She was *hugging* him. The sensation was so absurd, so violatingly intimate, it should have made him push her away on instinct. Instead, his arms wound around her body of their own accord, pulling her tighter to his chest as he buried his face in her dark hair.

Stars. Oh, fucking *stars.* He inhaled shakily, his sobs quieting as her scent filled his nostrils. The horrible ache in his chest eased with every breath, comfort vibrating through his nerve endings as she gently stroked his back and... *hummed.*

Another flash of his mother made him shudder in Georgia's embrace. She'd hugged him, too. Twice.

When he was very little. But she'd been the one to cry, then, and there had been no soothing touches and no soft humming, either. And when he'd tried to hug her back, she'd pushed him away.

He clutched harder at the small Breeder in his arms, desperation born from weakness making him ensure she couldn't push him away, too.

Georgia only hugged him tighter in response.

It took a long while for his roiling emotions to ebb enough for him to soften his grip on her, finally remembering how fragile she was. If he'd bruised her with his need...

She pulled her head back from him as he released her, blue eyes searching his. "Are you okay?"

He nodded once, too emotionally drained to feel the embarrassment and horror he knew should fill him after this pathetic display of vulnerability. The Prince of Demons—*crying*. In the arms of a Breeder under his care, no less. "Did I hurt you?"

"No." She reached up and brushed her fingers over his brow ridge, achingly gently. He didn't have the strength to pull away. "Tell me what happened just now."

"I can't." His voice came out like a broken whisper —so far from his usual gruffness he barely recognized it.

"You can," she insisted. Permission, not a demand. "Whatever this is... I'll listen. You shouldn't carry something so painful alone."

Kesh stared into her eyes. There was nothing but gentleness and empathy there. He was the monster who kept her from her family and loved ones, who'd killed in front of her. Had threatened her. And still... this fragile little human offered him only kindness, when she could so easily take his weakness and use it. Stars knew she had every right to.

"You remind me of my mother." The words left his throat before he could stop them.

"What happened to her?"

His face twisted with pain, but before he could pull back, could protect the most vulnerable parts of himself, she cupped his cheek and the warmth of her spread through his nervous system like the morning sun.

"She killed herself." He fixed her with his gaze; only her blue eyes locked with his made the words possible to say. "She was... She never took to my father, or her role as a Breeder. She had a human family before she was taken. A husband and an infant daughter. But she was captured. Put to auction. My father, who wanted offspring, purchased her. She hated him. Hated the violations and how the ring made her beg for it." He paused, his voice softening. "And she hated me and my brother, when we came along.

"My father... I think he tried his best. But his best still had her caged in a life she didn't want, and she longed for her real family, begged for them... And eventually, she grew desperate enough to threaten."

"What did she threaten?" Georgia asked softly when he trailed off.

The memory still ached, even if it'd since been buried by pain far more all-encompassing. He exhaled, pushing on. "To kill me and Kain. She told him if he didn't let her go back to her real family, she would kill his sons. His. Not theirs. Not hers. I hadn't realized until then that she didn't see us as her children."

Georgia blinked. "She... she said that in front of you? How old were you?"

"Five." He sighed softly. "By that point she'd been my father's prisoner for ten years. There wasn't much of her spirit left. I think she tried to love my brother and me. When we were very little. But though we looked human to her, thanks to her blinding mark... there was no hiding the fact that we were my father's spawn."

"What happened then? After she threatened your life?"

Her question was as gentle as her touch, but it still cut through his chest like a molten knife. But there was no putting the genie back in the bottle, not now.

"My father did what he had to—a threat to his heirs was the one thing he couldn't let slide. He twisted her ring. Forced her to submit to ease the torment. Took her until the ring was sated, and she sobbed for mercy. And then he did it again. And again. And again. Until her mind snapped, and she finally became docile." His voice was devoid of emotion, numbness spreading through his veins to allow him to recall the events that had ruined his family.

The horror he couldn't feel reflected back at him from Georgia's blue eyes. She opened her mouth to say something, but no words came out.

"She slit her wrists the second she was left alone," he continued, a grimace that looked like a smile but wasn't pulling at his lips. "My dad thought he'd finally tamed her. He thought he'd made her into the mate and mother she was always meant to be. All he did was break the final shreds of her spirit."

The Breeder stared up at him in silence for several long moments, glistening tears shining from her lashes. Finally, she wrapped her arms around his torso and hugged him tight, like she had while he'd cried. Her cheek pressed into his chest, warm and wet against his scales. "I'm so sorry," she whispered, sorrow choking her words.

"You have such a tender heart," he murmured, staring down at the little female clutching him as if she wanted to absorb the pain from his body into her own. For once, there was no venom in the words, only mild bewilderment. "How... how can you feel anything but revulsion?"

"Humans are complicated that way," she said, her voice muffled by his chest. "I can be revolted at what your father did, and still ache for the trauma you went through. Demon or not, that's... No child should see what you did."

"I am my father's son. What horrors he has committed, I am more than capable of inflicting as well. You had no misgivings about my nature moments ago." He didn't understand the clenching in his gut as he spoke, nor why he bothered. Her embrace felt so good —like a balm, like a beacon of light in the darkness. He didn't want her to let go, not now, not ever. He *needed* this, needed *her*. But if she realized what he truly was, what he was capable of, she wouldn't hold him like this. She couldn't.

"You're a demon; a monster," she said, and it shouldn't have hurt—it was a truth that had never concerned him before—but in this vulnerable moment, in Georgia's soft voice, it stung like a dagger wound. His muscles stiffened, but before he could put distance between them, she continued, "But that doesn't mean you're evil, does it?" She peered up at him, searching his eyes for the answer. "You are capable of love and loyalty to your family. You hurt for the loss of your mother. And... you can't bring yourself to violate me, no matter how often you threaten it. You could never do that to a woman—not with what happened to your mother. Not with how deep that wound still is."

"I've killed plenty of women," he said, the admission a warning growl, anger at how desperately he wanted her to not think him *evil,* despite what he knew to be true rumbling through his chest. "Some have died when I lost control of my base desires and fucked them, despite knowing what my magic would do to them. My mother's death does not make me *noble,* Georgia."

"No," she said, still looking into his eyes, still holding him. "It doesn't. But... it has given you empathy, I think. And whatever else you are, so long as you have the ability to feel for someone else... you can't be truly evil."

He chuffed through his nose, the sound meant to be derisive, but it came out soft. "What does it matter to you if I am evil or not? You still despise my very nature —and you will still be made to surrender to a lifetime subjugated to my kind."

She smiled. It was barely more than a weak twitch of her lips, but it still lit up her face and penetrated through his ribcage. "Perhaps. But subjugation to a demon who won't violate and abuse me is infinitely less terrifying than the alternative."

"I won't be the one to mate you, Georgia. It will be one of my men." He had known this from the moment she was brought into his throne room, trembling and weak. There was no reason for lead to sink heavily into his gut as he reminded them both of this indisputable fact.

"No, it won't be you. But you won't give me to someone who will hurt me, either. And who knows? Maybe he will even be capable of love." She looked at him with that soft smile, the expression in her pretty eyes suggesting her future mate's potential to love her should somehow be a comfort to them both.

It wasn't.

24
GEORGIA

Georgia had always tried to stay as far away from the demons she saw as she could. Regardless, she'd been painfully aware of their dark nature and tendency toward violence and degradation. Her P.E. teacher, with the horns and the tendency toward sadistic, public humiliation, was a mild example of what she knew them capable of.

To now be faced with the reality that they could feel remorse? Empathy? It was... startling.

She looked up at the big monster on the bed with her, his demonic features softened with remnants of grief. Once upon a time, he'd been a little kid who loved his mom. And he'd lost her in the worst way imaginable. She'd never thought she could feel sorrow for a demon's misfortune, but her gut still clenched from the raw pain he'd been unable to hide from her.

And still... it wasn't just empathy for his loss that

filled her. It was staggering relief, too. She had sold herself to the monsters to save Larry, and she'd expected the price for her brother's life to be a lifetime of misery. But if they were capable of love... Of *tears*... Then there was a chance, however small, that her future might not be as grim as she'd dreaded since signing Lewin's contract.

Even if she would still need to do some things she'd rather not.

"We should continue." She held out a hand, her fingers wrapping around Kesh's clawed digits when he reached for her on autopilot.

"Continue?" he repeated, eye ridges rising in question at her sudden change of topic.

"You look exhausted. Let me... Let me nourish you. Our bargain..." She trailed off, feeling guilty for reiterating how she was offering him comfort purely to fulfill her end of their arrangement.

Kesh shook his head, a humorless smile pulling at the corner of his mouth. "No." He drew a deep breath, releasing her hand as he climbed off the bed. "You've given enough. Our bargain is fulfilled, little Breeder. Get some rest. I'll have to mark you tomorrow, but for now... Just rest."

"Wait."

They both froze at the sound of her soft plea. She stared up at him, her pulse picking up. Was she really going to offer...? But one look up into his black eyes, still softer than she'd ever known they could be, and the nervous energy fizzing along her spine dispersed to a tolerable prickle.

"Wait," she repeated, a little more strength to her voice this time. "You need... Please. Let me take care of you."

He frowned, the expression severe on his harrowing features, but for the first time it didn't cause unease to clench at her esophagus. For a long moment, silence stretched between them. Then he exhaled a shaky breath and knelt back down on the bed.

"You're sure?"

She nodded, teeth digging into her lower lip as she fought the shyness threatening to rise. He'd had his face between her thighs three times already. With a beast like the demon prince, there was no room for bashfulness.

Which was perhaps the one good thing about him; the second she nodded her consent, there was no awkwardness nor hesitation—nothing but hunger in his eyes as he moved forward and captured her mouth in his.

"Mm-*h.*" He swallowed her surprised moan as scorching heat traveled from his kiss all the way down her chest and stomach to center right in her clit with a throb of excitement. Large, clawed hands cupped the back of her head and her lower back as he eased her down on the bed without ever breaking the kiss.

Her legs parted for balance, and he settled down between them as if he belonged there, forcing a stretch along her inner thighs as she spread to embrace his wide body. Heat bloomed everywhere his scaled skin grated roughly against hers, but that was nothing compared to the hard press on the full length of her abdomen as he put his weight on her and his absurd cock pressed down.

A glimmer of fear tried to worm its way to her brain, but before her adrenaline could respond, Kesh's tongue plunged into her mouth, and anxiety was replaced with another rush of heat.

Gods, why did it feel so good? The demon's kiss was edged with gasoline and lit matches—danger distilled into scent. But every cell in her body bloomed awake, heat curling in her abdomen for every stroke of his tongue over hers.

She'd never been kissed like this; like nothing else mattered to this male than the taste of her. He groaned into her mouth, filling her airways with his demonic scent and her head with the pounding of her own blood. Every part of her lit up, as if her very biology was tuned to his need on a primal level.

Of their own accord, Georgia's arms wrapped around his wide torso as she let herself melt into him.

"Blackened stars," he groaned, pulling back from her lips to place scorching kisses along her jaw, down the column of her throat. The heat in her blood turned to champagne fizz with every press of his lips against her skin, inching lower and lower. When he kissed his way down her breastbone, she didn't think;

moaning with need she hadn't known she possessed before the first night in his bed, she speared her fingers through his hair and pulled him to one achingly tight nipple.

Kesh obeyed her unspoken demand. Warm, wet heat closed around the needy little bud, the flick of a tongue following. When he sucked, her groan of pleasure mixed with his.

"More!" The demand rasped out of her throat, pulled by the aching throb in her clit for every suck on her nipples. *Shit,* he made her feel so fucking *needy.* Like every nerve in her body was strung too tight, and the only way to relief was through him. "Please, Kesh, I need—*oooh!*"

Her desperate cry cut off on a moan when he pushed one large hand between them, thumb landing on her ringed clit as he turned his mouth to her other breast. Deep, rhythmic suckles echoed down the length of her body and back up her spine with every strum over her center of nerves, until there was nothing left but wet, clenching need. Without thought, she grasped onto his horns and pushed, trying to guide his mouth downward.

"I love how desperate you are for me," he rasped against her, scorching lips nipping at the skin covering her belly as he let her steer his head down. When he finally reached her pussy, his breath hitched, and a growl rumbled out of his throat. "Fuck, you smell so fucking good. Do you want to come? Is that why that needy little pussy is soaking for me, hmm? You want me to feast on your helpless little clit?"

Georgia nodded frantically, giving his horns a hard tug to try and guide him down to her throbbing clit. "Yes, yes, please, that! I need that!"

Snarling, he roughly parted her labia and, without further warning, buried his mouth in her pussy.

"Ah!" Her cry as shocks of sensations rocked through her pelvis and down her thighs was overlaid by his rich growl.

"Fuck!"

Feast, he'd said. It was exactly what he did. His hungry mouth moved against her spread pussy, lips sliding over wet flesh and encircling her throbbing clit. When he began to suck, she saw stars.

"Fuck, goddamn, yes! Don't stop, don't stop!" Her frantic cries were breathy and desperate as she clung to his horns and rode his face with wild abandon. All sense of modesty and fear wiped away by the all-consuming need to come for him. It took only moments before the fire ate through her last resistance, and her climax thundered through her.

"Kesh!" His name spilled from her lips, her hands yanking his face deeper into her pussy by her grip on his horns as her thighs clamped shut around his neck. "Mmmhyes!"

He groaned in response, lips easing off her spent clit as he kissed his way down her seam to her entrance.

Greedy, wet sounds followed as he licked up the liquid proof of her orgasm.

Georgia lay in a haze of fading pleasure, fingers softening on his horns. Relaxation flooded her muscles in a lazy wave, allowing him to easily lap up her energy as he drank her. It was a curious sensation, feeling the trickle of life essence leave her body. Calming. Pleasurable, even. She eased her thigh's grip on his neck, but he wrapped his arms around them before they could slip off his shoulders and anchored his hands on her ass, keeping her legs wrapped around him.

He was such a juxtaposition. Georgia looked down at him through hooded lids—at the creature of nightmares who called her 'Breeder'; a ruler among demons who was in the process of drinking her very life force... and felt only pleasurable calm, and a startling thread of affection. Every inch of him was monstrous—from the horns and scales, to his foul temper and murderous tendencies. But he'd let her see his vulnerable parts— and she would never be able to look at him like nothing but a monster again. Whatever else he was, he would always be the man who'd cried in her arms over the loss of his mother.

The creature who gave her pleasure beyond anything she'd known to be possible.

As if drawn by her thoughts, Kesh broke his mouth's connection to her core, easing off with a reluctant groan, followed by several kisses to her pussy.

"You don't need anymore energy? I think I have

more to give—I'm not anywhere near as tired as last time." Also, she wasn't ready for the pleasure to end, or for his walls to come back up.

The prince gave a soft groan of reluctance, but raised back up with a final kiss to her swollen pussy. "Don't tempt me, little one. I could feast on you for days."

"That doesn't sound like the *worst* way to spend time with a demon," she quipped, earning her a throaty chuckle from the big male.

"I like you like this. Unafraid." His voice was unexpectedly soft, and the way he looked at her then—black eyes full of adoration; worship... Her stomach tightened with a flutter, but her chest warmed and eased. No one had ever looked at her like *that*. Like she was the center of the universe.

"I like me like this, too," she whispered, unable to take her eyes off his. Unwilling to.

Kesh made a soft sound at the back of his throat and leaned in, as if pulled by a string. His lips crashed against hers, still fiery with need, but when his hands swept up to cup her face, it was with aching gentleness.

"I think... it's your turn," she gasped between his scalding kisses.

"My turn?" he rumbled, tongue flicking in between her lips to stroke against hers.

"To come." She pulled away from his kiss and, drawing in a breath to find her courage, reached for the intimidating column of flesh she'd tried her best to ignore up until then.

25

KESH

Raw sensation flared up his length as Georgia's slim fingers wrapped around his aching cock. His breath hitched as he stared from her hand, barely making it more than halfway around, to her blue eyes darkened with desire. For him.

"You're so fucking beautiful." The words were out of his throat before he could stop them, rough with sincerity. Vulnerable. But she'd already seen him at his most exposed, his weakest. What did it matter that she knew how utterly breathtaking he found her right now? There was no hiding the depths of his yearning for her, not with how fully her scent and taste and sounds filled him up from the inside out.

A faint flush spread across her cheeks. "Thank you."

He cocked a grin. "Really? You happily ride my face like a little slut, but being told you're beautiful is what makes you blush?"

Her face turned raspberry pink, and she made to pull away, severing the blissful connection between her fingers and his cock. He quickly wrapped his hand around hers, returning her grip where it belonged, and bent down to nuzzle at her ear.

"Don't. I like it when you let go. Your hands on my horns when you're horny for a come is the best fucking feeling in the world. Never be embarrassed for taking what you need. Or for knowing how absolutely, devastatingly gorgeous you are." He nipped at her earlobe, delighting in her responding shudder.

"I've never been called beautiful before," she said, pulling back to dart her gaze up to his. As if searching his eyes for any trace of dishonesty. He knew she found nothing but burning truth there. Her blush spread down her chest, and her nipples tightened in instinctive response to his blatant desire.

"Then the humans you've been around are blind and stupid. I could look at you for hours and never grow bored. Learn every freckle. Every curve." He slid his hand up and cupped a breast, thumb brushing over the hard nipple peaking it.

Her blunt teeth dug into her bottom lip at his caress, a soft little exhale making his cock throb in her grasp. The movement drew her attention back down to it. When she gave it a squeeze, he was the one to gasp.

"You have no idea how good that feels," he rasped. "I would trade every ounce of my power right now, if it meant I could be inside you."

A small smile curved her mouth, his needy declaration apparently as amusing as it was flattering. "Well... maybe we can do something that feels almost as good." And then, the little vixen bent down and put her mouth on the smooth head of his cock, tongue teasing over the opening.

"Sh-*it!*" Lightning fired through every nerve ending in his pelvis, momentarily weakening his leg muscles enough to send him backwards. He caught his weight on his hands and let out a shuddering breath as Georgia shot him a shit-eating grin before giving the sensitive opening a full, deep lick.

"Fucking *stars,* you little—!" His snarl sounded like a threat, claws shredding his bedding as he clenched his fists in his sheets. It was anything but. His cock throbbed for every teasing swipe of her tongue, the warm, wet sensation of her mouth driving him mad with need for *more.* And yet, he stayed perfectly still, every muscle in his body tight with restraint to ensure he didn't do anything that would make her stop the exquisite torture.

She grew bolder. Her other hand joined the first, wrapping more firmly around his shaft as her tongue darted down to tease at the cartilage ridges riding the circumference of his corona. His gaze was locked on her face, taking in every flutter of her eyelashes as his taste washed over her senses, and when she fit as much of his head in her mouth as she could and sucked, a crooning sound he hadn't known he could produce escaped his throat.

"That's it. Fuck, that feels...!" He clenched his fists harder around the already ruined sheets, head dropping back as his world narrowed in to nothing but the deep, pulsing pleasure building at the base of his pelvis. Soft, wet sounds filled the bedroom and mixed with his panting breath. Her mouth didn't open nearly wide enough to take him in, but the burning frustration at not being inside her tight heat only heightened the waves of arousal coursing through his body.

When she began simultaneously massaging his length with both hands, he lost what little restraint he'd had left.

"Georgia... Georgia...!" Her name spilled from his tongue like a prayer, his entire focus on the wave of pleasure building, building... "Oh, stars!" *Release.*

His entire body gave in to her, his climax thundering through him so powerfully, he only just managed to push her mouth off his cock before his dark magic flooded out of him on jets of semen.

Mind spinning, he pulled her into his arms to brush kisses to her mouth, her jaw, her ear, making her giggle as his panting breath tickled her skin. Finally, as the euphoria settled down to deep satisfaction, he pressed his forehead to hers and simply enjoyed the feeling of her.

"You fit so perfectly in my arms." The words were out of his throat before they'd even registered in his brain. Only when her pretty face broke into a surprised smile did he realize what he'd said. The implication of it.

Fuck.

"So all males really do become putty from a blowjob, huh? Even big, scary demon princes," she teased.

"Something like that," he rumbled, pulling back just enough to peer down at her. She looked... happy. Playful, even. Completely at ease in his embrace in this one, perfect moment.

He needed to end it. Now. Before this soft, intimate feeling took root and he entirely forgot that she would never be his. Couldn't be.

But, *fuck,* she really did fit perfectly in his arms.

Soft fingers trailed up his chest, pulling an involuntary purr from him and ruining any ability he might have had to release her from his embrace.

Georgia chuckled, low and soft. "I like that sound. It's cute." She looked up at him, curiosity in her eyes as they darted over his face and up to his horns. "What does your human disguise look like? Do you really look... like a normal man? I can't picture it. You're so... huge. And... demon-y."

A wry smile pulled on his lips at her description of him as 'huge' and 'demon-y'. "I do. A little... big, though, even as a man. It's difficult to fit my body into human proportions. Sometimes more sensitive people get a little uneasy around me, but I mostly pass. When I brand you, you'll see for yourself."

"Ah, yes. The branding-thing." She bit her lip, and fuck, why did she look absolutely irresistible doing it? "Um, you said it needed to happen when I was... coming, right? So how come you didn't do it just now...?"

"I was a little busy enjoying the taste of your pussy and making sure I didn't take too much of your life force," he said, the memory of having his face between her thighs waking his cock with a twitch of interest.

"Ah. That makes sense. I appreciate you waiting and not accidentally murdering me." Her tone was dry, but a delicious blush colored her cheeks rosy, betraying a lingering shyness, despite her growing trust in him.

"But now that I've eaten..." His hands slid down to her ass, grabbing it firmly and pulling her pelvis tighter to his. Her still-wet labia split for his cock. He rocked her forward, dragging his hard flesh through her slit to catch on her ringed clit. She gasped and jerked, but he held firm, grinding her down harder. "What do you say, little Breeder? Want another come?"

26

GEORGIA

Perhaps she should have been ashamed of how her pussy clenched at the prince's offer to get her off. Instead, she felt nothing but hot excitement down low in her belly when his monstrous cock rubbed against her clit.

"It won't hurt? The branding?"

"There's a sting as the magic sears into your skin." He kissed the side of her neck. "But you'll be too busy writhing in pleasure to care. I promise."

Her breath hitched as his lips traveled down the tendon to her clavicle, his hands on her ass still rocking her back and forth along his hardness. "Yeah? Women are usually too busy coming for you to notice you *searing* them?" She tried for sarcasm. It came out breathy.

"You're my first Breeder," he murmured against her skin. "But yes, you will be. You'll come like the dirty little slut we both know you want to be, and once it's done, there'll be no more fear when you look at me." He punctuated the statement with a wet suck against her throat. Georgia groaned, her thoughts scattering to the wind. Mindlessly, she wound her fingers around his horns and guided his mouth to her breasts. He followed willingly, and when his hot lips closed around the first nipple and he sucked it deeply, she began grinding down on his cock on her own. The ridges, though scary to look at, proved perfect to rub her clit against.

"Mmh, God!" she mewled when her clit caught on one of the rounded spikes, shooting sharp pleasure up her spine.

"You really shouldn't invoke a deity while riding on a demon's cock," Kesh growled hotly. He squeezed her ass tightly and pulled her down harder against the protrusion, forcing a delicious ache through her clit. "I'm inclined to take offense."

"Sorry!" she gasped, back arching to take some of the pressure off her tender bud. "Just an expression. Don't stop, please, don't stop!"

Another growl, and then she was on her back on the bed, blinking up at the ceiling. Half a second later, the prince's monstrous face, crowned by those imposing horns, came into view, hovering above her. "It seems I was mistaken—you don't fear me at all, even in this form, do you? Not when you're desperate to come. Then all that matters is how I make your pussy sing."

"I thought you liked me like this," she panted,

trying to grind against the knee he placed up high between her thighs.

"I fucking love you like this," Kesh growled, black eyes sweeping down her body with enough heat to flame her skin. "It's how you were meant to be, Georgia. Unafraid. High on sex. Demanding pleasure." He moved his knee away before she could press down on it, but when she whined in protest, he pressed two fingers either side of her clit ring and tugged on it. Sharp bliss rocked through her pelvis, too intense but all the more addictive for it.

"Shit, that's—!" Her words snuffed out in Kesh's mouth as he pressed his lips to hers and kissed her deeply, never ceasing his fingers' rhythmic movements. It didn't take long before her pussy tightened in preparation for orgasm.

The demon pulled back an inch, leaving her panting for breath and moaning with every tug on her clit. "I want you to come nice and hard for me, Georgia. Can you do that? Come until your pussy hurts and you've got nothing more to give? That's what I need, beautiful. Every ounce of your pleasure."

She nodded feverishly. "Yes, just... I need.... Can you...?"

"Tell me what you want, Georgia," he rasped, lips brushing over hers, his breath tickling her skin. "Don't ever be ashamed of demanding what you need."

"Your fingers... inside," she gasped, biting her lip

hard when he settled his thumb on the tip of her exposed clit. "F-fuck, that's...!"

Kesh hissed out a breath, his gaze darkening as he eased his thumb's touch to a maddeningly light brush. "You need penetration, gorgeous? Of course you do. Only good girls are satisfied by playing with their clits, and that's not what you are, is it?"

"N-no," she gasped, bucking up against his hand, willing to say anything to get him to increase the pressure. "I'm not a good girl. Oh, *please*...!"

"Then what are you, Georgia?" he growled, not allowing her the friction she so desperately needed. "Tell me what you are, and I'll give you what you need."

"I'm a slut!" Her voice rang through the bedroom, a desperate keen. "A slut who needs your fingers inside her. Please!"

"That's right. And dirty little sluts get what they ask for." Still massaging her clit with the thumb of his left hand, he lifted the middle and index fingers from his right hand to his mouth and bit off the sharp claws adorning them.

Her entire body thrummed, heat pooling between her legs as he brought his fingers back down to lightly stroke up and down her labia, teasing her open.

"Inside!" she demanded, need roughening her voice to a growl.

A dark smirk pulled at his lip. "As you command, little Breeder." Light pressure, followed by the exquisite sensation of one thick finger penetrating deep. Immediately, another finger followed, stretching her perfectly. Georgia mewled and arched her pelvis up on instinct, coaxing him to go further, press harder.

He obeyed instantaneously, filling her deliciously. When he began stroking them in and out, any last vestiges of control abandoned her entirely.

"Ohshit!" Her moan mixed with his harsh snarl as her pussy fluttered and squeezed on his digits, every rapid thrust bringing her closer and closer to the edge. "Don't stop, don't stop...!"

"Do you have any idea how good it feels to have you squeezing me like this? What I would give to be inside you?" he rasped, voice filled with dark desperation. *"Stars,* you're so fucking perfect! Come for me, beautiful. Come for me before I lose myself and kill you."

Alarm zinged up her spine at the warning, but when her eyes met his, her pussy pulsed hotly, the fear only adding to the thrill of it. His gaze burned with lust, every ounce of his attention fixated on her. She'd never been wanted this much, this intensely. The threat that he might lose control and push that horrific cock inside her made her clit throb, her body riding high on the adrenaline.

"I'm—I'm close! Harder, please, harder!" She bucked up against his touch, thigh muscles tightening as her body was swept away on the rising tide.

Kesh smoothly switched hands, forcing his right thumb to her clit without ever stopping the perfect, maddening stimulation, and pressed his left hand to her forehead. "Squeeze my fingers, gorgeous. Make me feel that perfect little pussy come undone."

There was no stopping it. He pumped her hard three more times, and then—

"Ah! Kesh!" Every muscle in her body tightened to the point of snapping as her orgasm roared through her pelvis, heat and pleasure and relief making her cry out wordlessly.

Without warning, fire seared through her forehead where his palm was pressed to her skin. She gasped in shock, but another wave of pleasure from her orgasm softened the pain enough to make it tolerable. Dark magic flared from his hand, burned her forehead, and sank into her mind.

"K-Kesh." She looked up at him in an instinctive need for reassurance, but her vision blurred and faded, distorting his face.

"Relax, beautiful, it's just the magic settling in. You're okay. I'd never harm you," he said, voice raw as he moved his hand from her forehead to her cheek, cupping it with a gentleness that entirely contrasted his size and strength. "I couldn't, even if I wanted to. And I don't. Not now, not ever." He bent, his mouth finding hers with an urgency that made warmth prickle down her body.

She parted her lips on instinct, still pleasure-drunk from the fading waves of her climax. His kiss was deep and needy, and she moaned softly into his mouth, surrendering.

There was no more pain, just relief as her consciousness slowly gave way.

"I would sell my soul for you if I had one," he whispered against her lips before pulling back.

The last thing she saw before unconsciousness took her was the blurred outline of his monstrous features morphing into an achingly beautiful man, his dark eyes haunted with regret.

27
KESH

He hadn't meant to fall asleep. He'd simply intended to make sure Georgia was comfortable and settled, and the mark branded on her forehead wasn't causing her any pain. But in her unconscious state, she'd pressed herself into his arms as if instinctively needing his protective embrace, and nuzzled her head up underneath his chin where she fit perfectly. As if she were made for him.

When he woke the next morning, she was still nestled against him, fast asleep. Entirely safe in his presence.

"Fuck," he murmured, peering down at her peaceful face. Traitorous gentleness fluttered through his chest. *Not good. Not good at all.*

Last night was a fucking disaster. *I would sell my soul for you if I had one.* What the fuck was he thinking? Oh, that's right. He wasn't. It had been all soft, icky *feelings* and pitiful need.

"You're going to be the death of me," he rumbled, quietly enough not to wake the little female as he carefully extricated himself from underneath her.

She whined softly in protest at the loss of his body heat, but thankfully slept on.

"I know." He gently brushed a knuckle over her cheek, then tucked the duvet tightly around her, ensuring she was still warm and secure. She settled down with a rebellious murmur that made his lips pull into a reluctant half-smile. He felt the loss of her body against his as keenly as she did. She'd slept on his chest, pressed against his heart, and he wanted nothing more than to slip back under the covers and return her to where she belonged.

Only she very much did *not* belong in his embrace. His instincts were spinning out of control because he'd let her cursed scent and his own weakness take the lead, instead of focusing on doing his duty, and nothing else.

"*Fuck.*" Kesh forced his gaze from the sleeping woman and quietly moved to his closet to find fresh clothes. After dressing himself, he got out one of the dresses he'd purchased for Georgia when she first came into his care. The garment was made from black silk, picked specifically for the way it would flow around her body and feel like a luxurious caress. He'd only bought her dresses; nothing else. Though September, it wasn't yet cold enough to worry about keeping her warm with thicker clothing, and a Breeder didn't need undergarments.

Silently cursing himself when his thoughts strayed further down the path of Georgia's sweet little pussy so easily available under the flowing skirt of the black dress, he laid out the garment and quickly exited the bedroom before his stupid instincts got the better of him. Again.

———

TO KESH'S DISPLEASURE, WHEN HIS CALL TO HIS BROTHER connected to the video call, Kain's face wasn't the only one that appeared on the wall-mounted screen. His bossy little mate was by his side, and before she opened her mouth, Kesh already knew why the opinionated queen had decided to join them. At least she was holding their squirming son in her arms, too. He'd softened *a little* toward his difficult sister-in-law since she'd given birth to his nephew.

"Kain. Selma. How are you both? And Kamaran?"

"We're great," Selma said, cutting Kain off before he could respond. "You found a woman? A Seer?"

"I found a Breeder, yes." His tone was pointed. He knew she wasn't fond of the Breeder moniker, but the claim that her kind had been Seers before demons realized they could carry their spawn had been made by a goddess. If she hadn't mind-fucked his brother with her damned pheromones, Kain would have disabused his mate of the notion that anything a goddess said carried any value, but the king was entirely too soft when it came to Selma. "Or rather, one of my subjects found her and brought her to me."

"Is she alright? Where is she?"

"She's fine. She's been ringed and marked, and she's currently sleeping." Kesh looked to his brother, hoping against hope he'd rein in his mate. "Kain, I called to discuss the situation in Maine. Perhaps we can return to the Breeder at another time?"

"Mallorn briefed me last night. A Breeder showing up in your territory is exciting news and will be good for morale amongst your men. Something we can sorely use," Kain pointed out.

Selma gave him an annoyed side-glare. "Really? She's a person, you know, not just a morale-boosting prize for your warriors to fight over. And may I remind you, as a future demon's mate, she's *my* subject, not yours."

Kain smiled, a ridiculous, soft expression flickering in his eyes as he stroked a thumb over her cheek. "I'm aware, little one. Which is why this woman is currently safe with Kesh and not being processed for auction. The changes you've made to Breeders' lives aren't diminished by how desperate our men are to find a mate to worship, hmm?"

Selma leveled him with a flat stare. "So we're calling it 'worship' now? You know, what you horny bastards consider *worship,* the rest of us call marathon sexing. Which is fun and all, so long as you've not been traumatized by your would-be admirer first." She sighed with resignation, then returned her focus to Kesh. "How *is* she, Kesh? Is she still scared? Does she miss her family? Do you need me to make a visit and try to reassure her?"

Some of his irritation eased at the genuine concern in his sister-in-law's eyes. As annoying as her iron will could be, the fact that she was taking her responsibility to Breeders—and Georgia in particular—seriously enough to offer to travel to him with the single purpose of reassuring his ward, made a measure of gratitude toward her bloom in his chest.

"She is still a little on edge about the whole situation, but she's settling in remarkably well." He sighed softly, his gaze flickering to Kamaran in her arms. As often happened when he saw his nephew, he couldn't help thinking that. If things had gone differently, Kam would have been his son. He was grateful they'd managed to save his brother, and he hadn't had to take Selma as his mate after all, but the thought still popped up now and then.

"At this point, it would not be worth the risk for you to travel. But I promise to inform you if that changes, my queen."

Selma chuffed, arching an amused brow. "Listen to him, trying to keep his sister-in-law at bay with honorifics."

"If the girl is settling in, it would be best to wait with a visit until I can prepare for your travels better," Kain rumbled. His arm snaked around his mate's shoulder, pulling her tight to his body. "If the Europeans ever get a hold of you. Or Kam…"

"I know, I know," she sighed, rolling her eyes even as she allowed him to plaster her against his ribs as his instincts took over at the thought of losing her. Normally, Kesh would have been rolling his eyes right along with her, but this time, unbidden, his thoughts went to Maine, and the acid shock of terror he'd felt when Mallorn had let him know Georgia had been on the fucking battlefield. At risk of imminent death. And that was *before…*

He cut off his thoughts, not willing to bring back the flutter of soft, idiotic *feelings* that had bloomed during last night with her. Not now, not in front of these two.

"Speaking of the Europeans… We nearly lost Maine, and Aran along with it. I don't know what the fuck happened. Aran is one of the oldest lords in the Northeast, and even at two to one, he should have had the edge. Or at the very least not been on his literal knees within a day." Kesh crossed his arms, a frown pulling down his brows as he recalled the absolute disaster he'd arrived to. "And even more baffling is—they fell within hours once I arrived. They seemed relatively inexperienced in battle. Aran should have been able to handle them on his own."

On the screen, Kain and Selma exchanged a look. "What?"

Selma glanced at Kain one more time before she said, "I felt... something. Yesterday. Through my Stone of Power. Something I haven't before."

A sense of unease crept up Kesh's spine. The three Stones of Power had been in the European royal family's possession for more than a millennium—powerful tools they'd employed to keep the gods from gaining the upper hand in the Eternal Battle. And to secure their right to rule.

Selma's gaining control of one of the stones was a large part of how Kain had been able to gather the American lords under his banners and break away from European rule. But the knowledge that such immense power was in the hands of a fragile little Breeder still filled Kesh with unease.

"What *kind* of something?" he asked.

"It's hard to describe. It was a vibration of sorts. A swelling of energy. With what you're saying about what happened in Maine, I have to wonder if—" Her train of thought was cut off when Kam began fussing. "Shh, little man. You've just been fed. Are you really hungry again?"

"You're wondering if the European lords had a Stone of Power with them?" Kain prompted, his brows furrowing.

"We didn't find one on either lord's corpse after the battle," Kesh murmured, his focus slipping when

Selma, without any hint of shyness, pulled out a breast and popped the nipple in her baby's mouth.

Something dark and needy curled in his lower abdomen.

Kain cleared his throat, breaking his single-minded focus. The moment he looked back up, he caught sight of Kain's glare.

A touched of heat brushed Kesh's cheeks, and he grimaced, shooting his brother an apologetic look. He had no interest in delving into why, but the sight of a woman nursing? Fuck, it got him every time.

Unbidden, a hazy image of Georgia flickered through his mind. Swollen breasts. A baby in her arms. Milk leaking from her ripened nipples...

Nope. Not going down that *fucking path.*

With a command of will, he forced his mind back to the matter at hand. "An outside source of power would explain their ability to subdue Aran so swiftly. But whatever it was, they must have lost it when I arrived. Outside of a Stone of Power, I don't know of anything that could have boosted their strength like I saw, but... Who the fuck loses one of those in the middle of a battle?"

Kain sighed deeply and rubbed the bridge of his nose. "I'm going to send Kirigan up to Maine to speak with Aran. Search the area. If anyone knows how to locate some obscure power source, it's our father."

"It would also be nice to not have him hovering for

a few days," Selma muttered, focus still on her nursing baby.

"He's still...?" Kesh trailed off, not sure how to describe the mad demon's behavior after his daughter-in-law gave birth to his grandchild. 'Disturbing' didn't really cover it.

"Yep. Even follows me to the freakin' bathroom if Kain's out of the house for so much as five minutes." Selma shifted her grip on Kam, grimacing slightly at the weight of him. Kain spotted her discomfort immediately.

"Go get settled while you finish nursing him, little one. I'll finish up here and be with you in a minute." He bent to kiss her forehead and rub a knuckle over his son's cheek. The expression in his eyes was so achingly tender, Kesh looked away, uncomfortable.

Selma leaned into her mate's touch for a moment, then nodded. "I'll see you in a bit then." She looked back up at the screen and nodded at Kesh. "Please take good care of the Seer. With everything going on, I don't want the importance of her wellbeing pushed aside."

"I promise, she's my first priority." Reluctantly, in the beginning, but now? Putting Georgia above every-thing, even the war, felt... worryingly natural.

Both brothers watched in silence as Selma left. Only when the door closed behind her did Kain turn back to the screen.

"There is another matter concerning the Breeder we need to discuss."

Kesh frowned. "My Breeder?"

The words 'my Breeder' hung in the air between them for a beat. Sick dread settled somewhere below his ribs as the unintended implication reflected off Kain's face.

"What do we need to discuss regarding my ward?" he corrected, irritation rippling over his skin. It seemed he was fucking incapable of keeping it together, just because.. what? She reminded him of his fucking mother? Even for a demon, that was messed up.

Kain cleared his throat. "Mallorn's report last night was... worrying."

In a flash, irritation was replaced with a hot spike of anger. "Worrying? Don't fucking tell me he was whining to *you* about how I'm handling Georgia."

"He wasn't *whining*, Kesh. He was agitated. I understand your inclination to keep the presence of an unmated Breeder in your territory quiet, considering the clusterfuck of a war we're in, but I'm telling you, you're gonna lose control of your men if you don't allow them to start the courting process soon. We can't afford to lose any of them, let alone a warrior as loyal as Mallorn."

Anger faded to dread. He remembered the seething resentment in his old friend's eyes when Kesh had commanded him to release his hold on Georgia. He'd been too preoccupied with his own roiling aggression, thanks to her presence, to worry about his Second's.

Could he truly lose his most trusted warrior over her? His friend?

Kesh looked up at the screen. At his brother. The man who'd slaughtered the old crown prince and split the continents with war, all to keep his mate.

Kain was right.

If anything would break his men's loyalty, it would be this.

He pushed away the hollow feeling in his chest, forcing his focus to the priority: the war. His men. His duty as their prince. "I understand. I will send out the official invitation to her courting tomorrow. She should be mated within the week."

28

KIRIGAN

A beep from his phone alerted him to movement from the west wing of his estate, where his son and daughter-in-law had gone to have their video call with Kesh. When he glanced at the screen, he saw Selma walking down the corridor with Kamaran in her arms. Unescorted.

The darkness in his gut tightened. He was moving before he'd decided to, crystal glass clanking as he roughly placed his bourbon on the table and headed out the library door.

He intercepted her before she reached the cozy lounge she favored. Her eyes widened slightly at his sudden appearance, her grip on the baby tightening a little, but her scent no longer soured with fear at the sight of him, like it had in the beginning. "Kirigan…"

"Kain let you leave his side? Without a guard?" he interrupted.

The Breeder sighed, rolling her eyes. "Yes. Seeing as I'm his queen, not his prisoner." She stepped to the side to get around him and continued to the lounge she'd claimed after she and Kain moved in.

Kirigan followed her, taking a seat on the window ledge as she got comfortable on the sofa and began nursing her baby. Despite the lack of fear in her scent these days, he knew she found his companionship... unpleasant. He didn't have the capacity or the inclination to care.

They settled into tense silence, broken only by the small suckling sounds from his grandson.

Kirigan stared out the window, trying to ignore the sound. It cut like tiny shards of glass through his nervous system, and the darkness in him snarled to wring the little creature's neck. End the sounds, and the agony of the memories they brought from when his own sons were young. He exhaled slowly, deeply, letting the madness wash through him. There was no point fighting it; he'd given up on that folly decades ago.

A small hiss from the Breeder brought him back with a sharp twinge. He snapped his head around just in time to see her yanking Kamaran from her breast to rub at her nipple, eyebrows locked in a displeased frown as she glared at her baby.

"He *bit* you?" He only noticed his clenched fists, his furious voice, and the dark well of magic pouring out of him when he saw Selma's eyes widen in shock, followed by a protective bubble of light erupting around her. With a force of will, he tempered the madness down. Only when he was sure it was back under control did he say, "My apologies. You and your child are safe. I promise."

His daughter-in-law took a long, hard look at him before she lowered her magic barrier. "What the hell was *that?*"

"Nothing. It was nothing." He turned back to the window, staring blindly out at the tapestry of autumnal foliage lighting up the grounds. It wasn't 'nothing'. But if he confessed to her, or to Kain, exactly *what* it was, they would leave. Which would make them more vulnerable to the Europeans. His estate was the safest place for them, and so they would stay. He'd control the madness, even if it broke him to pieces. He had to.

"He shouldn't hurt you. You're his mother. He owes you everything. More than everything."

"He's a baby. And I think he's teething. It's normal." With another cautious look his way, Selma placed his grandson at her other breast. He heard her mutter, "But if you bite me again, you little asshole, I'm gonna start bottle feeding you," under her breath.

She was nothing like his mate had been.

It should fill him with relief, should allow the belief that she would never be driven to take her life in order to escape to settle into his broken mind. Diligently, he'd watched her on the cameras he'd installed since she and Kain moved into his home, looking for any sign that she was fading like his Janette had, and he'd found none. By all accounts, she was a doting mother, fulfilled by her life by his son's side. She even took him eagerly when they coupled, sometimes initiating the intimacy, without activation of her clitoral ring.

Yet still... the idea that one day she might realize the horror of her situation, and then his firstborn would experience what it was like to lose his mate? It kept him on edge, alert to her every movement. In some ways it was a relief—to feel a brush of fear again, instead of the decades of nothing but dark, maddening despair.

Kain joined them shortly after. He went to his Breeder immediately, ensuring she was well, as instinct dictated he do.

"Did Kesh say anything else about the Seer?" Selma asked her mate while he fussed around with the pillows behind her.

"Only to confirm that he would invite her suitors and begin the official courting process." The hesitancy in Kain's voice pulled Kirigan's attention from the window.

"What aren't you saying?" Selma asked, eyes narrowed. She'd heard it, too.

Kain sighed. "Nothing. Just... I don't know. Kesh seemed..."

"Kesh seemed what?" Kirigan snapped. Something clawed from the darkness—icy foreboding.

"He seemed... somewhat reluctant to call for her courting. I spoke with his Second last night—Mallorn was agitated at the territorial behavior he claims Kesh is exhibiting over the girl. The last thing we need right now is for Kesh to lose control of his closest allies due to this woman. I'm sure it's nothing, though. Just testosterone and instincts running high in the presence of an unmated Breeder. Things will settle once she has selected a mate."

"And what if it's not nothing?" Selma said softly. "You know how he is—pretends he has no interest in women, but deep down..."

"Even if that were the case, this girl's not a Pure-Breeder. He can't lay claim to her." Kain's brow creased in a frown. "Not that it would necessarily stop him from wanting to, but he is too honorable to risk everything for a woman he can't have. No matter what his instincts may or may not want."

Selma only looked at him. Nothing was said, but Kain's face still crumbled with frustration. "Fuck! This is the *worst* fucking timing!"

"I'll go see him," Selma said. "I know you don't want me and Kam traveling unless we need to right now, but if you've got even the slightest hunch that something's amiss with Kesh and this woman, I need to make sure she's going to be okay."

Kain opened his mouth to protest, but he didn't get the chance.

"No. I'll go." Kirigan pushed off the window ledge, already headed for the door.

"Kirigan, it's *my* responsibil—"

"Your responsibility, little queen, is to stay alive. It is *my* responsibility to ensure my son is not getting twisted up in instincts that will ruin him and the Breeder under his care," he interrupted her, tone soft but brokering no argument.

"I need you to go to Maine first," Kain said. The gratitude in his eyes for the diversion was not missed. He didn't like telling his mate no—a sentiment Kirigan understood well. Now. They both knew the consequences of making a woman realize she had no agency over her life. Or body.

"Maine? What for?"

"The disturbance I felt in my Stone of Power—it may be connected to the attack in Maine that Kesh thwarted," Selma said. "According to Kesh, the two lords that led the assault were much stronger than they reasonably should have been. If the Europeans have brought one of their remaining Stones of Power to our shores, we need to know. Urgently."

"There's no one strong enough to pick up a magical imprint like that, no one I'd trust not to attempt to take that power source for their own gain—except you." Kain sighed, pinching the bridge of his nose. "And if it wasn't a Stone of Power, then we still need to know *what* it was, and what happened to it, so we can work out if the Europeans have access to more of them. We nearly lost Maine in this assault, despite Aran being one of the strongest lords on the Eastern Seaboard."

The crown was a heavy weight on his eldest son.

He'd known it would be, since before he claimed it. Kirigan glanced back at his daughter-in-law, still cradling his grandson to her breast. She seemed to truly love her demon child. And her demon mate. One day, she would realize the truth. The despair would set in. Hopefully, when that day came, she would be stronger than his sons' mother. And if not... he would be there to ensure she couldn't leave this world, and take his eldest's sanity with her. His duty to his family's survival wasn't a light in the dark recesses of his madness, but it was the only thing he had left.

Stopping the Europeans from breaking them came before the foreboding clawing at the back of his skull, urging him to go to Kesh and the Breeder under his care.

With a silent nod, he strode out of the room, his focus turning to finding and securing the power source their enemies had attempted to use in their quest to bring down his family.

29
GEORGIA

Once again, she awoke alone in the prince's bed. Yet unlike last time, it didn't fill her with relief. *That*, however, filled her with dread.

Her memory of last night was fuzzy at the edges, but several things stood out in crystal clear definition. Such as the demon's tortured expression when his self-control started to fray, and the understanding that if it'd snapped, her life would have ended.

There should be nothing but relief at his absence this morning.

Least of all disappointment.

"You are *so* messed up, Georgie," she muttered, scrubbing both hands over her face as she pushed her legs over the edge of the bed.

There wasn't any lingering wooziness when she got into the shower this time, nor did she feel wobbly at the knees like she had the last time he sucked her energy. Apparently, fighting an army of demons didn't drain his power nearly as much as healing a single human did.

He'd laid out clean clothes for her. Another silky dress, black this time. Georgia ran her fingers over the soft material, luxuriating in the feel of it. Less than twenty-four hours ago, she would have thought a demon incapable of caring for another living being. But last night...

Last night, he'd let her see a glimmer of humanity she'd considered an impossibility before. And he'd said... such achingly tender things to her.

She hadn't expected to find anything but hardship and misery in his hands, but after last night, one thing was abundantly clear in her mind: no one had ever made her feel like the Prince of Demons had last night. Like her life, her pleasure, was the most important thing in the world.

He wasn't what she'd thought he was. Not entirely. There was gentleness behind his ruthless nature. Brutality and a flippant attitude toward the value of life, yes, but he wasn't cruel for the sake of it.

Especially not with her.

A rush of unbidden pleasure filled her when she recalled what he'd whispered as her conscience checked out.

I'd sell my soul for you if I had one.

Words spoken in passion, no doubt, but in that

moment, he'd meant them. She'd felt the truth of them sink into the core of her being.

It was funny, in a way. She'd never considered demons capable of containing a *soul.* But after last night? The way he'd cried in her arms over the traumatic loss of his mother? She could have sworn she saw his soul in the voids of his pained eyes. Felt it hum in tune with her own as he worshipped her body.

But he would know better than she about such matters. He was a demon, after all. Even if he didn't trade in souls, she had no doubt he had a far better grasp on the subject than she.

She slipped on the black dress and sighed with pleasure as the silk wrapped around her body in a soft caress. Perhaps he didn't have a human soul, but he knew how to care for a woman and make her feel safe. She couldn't name a single human friend or boyfriend she'd had over the years who'd cared enough to treat her like the Prince of Demons did: like she was precious to him.

An uncomfortable stab spiked below her ribs when she thought that her mom had never made her feel particularly precious, either. Kesh's derisive words about how she'd been trained to put everyone ahead of herself from a young age came back, dampening the bloom of warmth in her chest.

It'd been easier to ignore the jab when she'd thought him nothing but a monster, incapable of understanding complex emotion like familial love. But a man who cried for the loss of a mother who'd hated him knew the pain of rejection on an intimate level.

It had always been about Larry. Georgia'd never questioned it, because she loved him more than anything, too. It'd seemed natural that his needs came first.

But why had it been so natural for her mom?

And the time before he was born... Her memory from that time was fuzzier, but no matter how hard she tried to recall it, she couldn't remember ever feeling like she was first. Not to herself, either.

It was only now, after Kesh challenged her, that she even paused to consider that perhaps that wasn't so natural after all.

She brushed her hands over the silky dress again. They were trembling a little. She clenched them until the wave of sadness eased.

Since Lewin sold her contract to Jimmy the Pimp, she'd thought her life forfeit—sacrificed so that Larry could live. Kesh had shown her that while she would be serving demons for the rest of her life, it didn't mean her life was over. Not with him.

It had only been a few days, and she had already learned more about herself in his company than she had for the past decade. Her gaze caught on the rumbled bedsheets, and a faint blush heated her face. Most notably that she was the kind of woman who'd ride a demon's face to orgasm.

But as embarrassing as it was to remember grabbing his horns and pulling his head between her legs, she couldn't deny how powerful she'd felt in those moments. How good it'd been to release all her fear and anxiety, to fully and completely focus on nothing but her own pleasure.

On cue, a pang traveled up her pelvis from her trapped clit swelling against its confines at the memory of Kesh's tongue. Another thing she was learning about herself under his care: he wasn't wrong when he'd called her a needy little slut—something that should have felt degrading, but didn't. One upside to demons: a woman taking charge of her needs was a point of pride, not shame. He'd only made her feel beautiful and infinitely desired.

She glanced at the reflection in the large double windows. The woman staring back at her was not the same person who'd been dragged into his makeshift throne room only days ago. The ethereal dress, bare feet, and shimmering silver mark on her forehead where he'd branded her weren't the only differences from what she'd known herself to be. Her spine was straighter now, her chin held higher.

For the first time in her life, she had the indisputable knowledge that, whatever came next, she was strong enough.

Even in the midst of demons, she could thrive.

———

THE APARTMENT WAS QUIET WHEN SHE LEFT THE BEDROOM, but in the absence of the demon prince was an honest-to-God, silver-domed plate of food waiting for her in the kitchen. A handwritten piece of card leaning against the dome simply read 'Eat. All of it.' in swooping letters.

"Alright then," she mumbled, taking a seat at the kitchen island. While she wasn't weak from his energy sucking this time, her stomach did make insistent noises about needing to refuel.

Under the silver dome lay five pieces of toast, a large chunk of glossy, yellow butter, a tub of jam, slices of smoked salmon decorated with lush fronds of dill, four poached eggs, and roasted cherry tomatoes still on the vine. All arranged around a perfectly rare T-bone steak.

Georgia snorted a laugh at the huge chunk of red meat residing in the midst of the more expected break-fast items. She was 90% sure he'd researched human eating habits while she slept and tried his best to follow whatever guidelines he'd found—but then also been a demon about it and apparently found the lack of meat unacceptable.

At least he'd scaled the amount down from the twenty-person buffet. Granted, there was still enough food to feed five very hungry bodybuilders, but it was several steps in the right direction.

So far as weird demon habits, his wild overestimate of how much a human could eat was kind of... cute.

Now that she was relatively certain he wasn't fattening her up to eat, anyway.

The food was delicious—though she didn't touch the still-mooing steak—but she stopped long before the overfilled plate was even halfway empty, pleasantly full. She covered the leftovers with the silver dome and took them to the fridge—but paused when she saw what was already in there. The entire thing was stuffed to the gills with some sort of huge, bumpy-skinned, crookneck-looking squashes in bright orange.

"What the...?" What in the world did a demon who didn't eat need with *that* many squashes?

The answer came as she pulled a few out to make room for her leftovers. She found several sticks of butter and bottles of cream shoved in the back, too, and when she turned to place the squash on the counter, because she couldn't fit them all back in the fridge, a printed-out recipe for pumpkin pie drew her attention.

Was he...?

She wasn't prepared for the flush of warmth that spread all the way from the tips of her toes to the roots of her hair as realization set in. He'd not only remembered her throwaway comment that she really liked homemade pumpkin pie, he'd also found a recipe and gone shopping for it. Or, likely, sent someone shopping for it. But the thoughtfulness was all his.

The amusement at the mental image of the huge demon trying his hand at baking scattered when she heard the front door open and heavy footsteps announce the prince's return, but she was still smiling when she turned to greet him.

Instead of the expected monster, a tall, black-haired human man rounded the corner, and for a split second, she froze in confusion. Then she remembered what had happened last night, before she'd sunk into unconscious sleep—how the demon had transformed, morphing into a handsome man with deep, regretful eyes.

She gave him a cautious once-over. He was shorter than he'd been, and not as wide, but still... absolutely huge. Almost as if there was too much mass to fit into human proportions. His eyes were still black, but the sclera was visible around the irises now. "Kesh?"

"Yes, little one." He walked over to her, cupped her cheek, and tipped her head up, those black eyes zeroing in on the silvery mark on her forehead. "How do you feel? Any pain?"

"No, I'm fine."

He rumbled an approving noise, then ghosted the tips of his fingers over her new brand, as if to make sure everything was in order. The touch sent a shudder through her, a tingling sensation crawling down her skin. Not entirely unpleasant.

She stared up at him, trying to mentally align his smooth skin and handsome features with the monster she'd come to know. There was an echo of recognition in the angles of his face, but it was his eyes that allowed the softness of familiarity to settle in her muscles. She gave him a small smile. "I think I'm gonna miss the horns."

"Hmm. Have you eaten?" His eyes flickered to the squashes she'd not been able to fit back into the fridge, a small frown marring his forehead. Choosing not to answer her quip about his horns.

"Yeah. Thanks for breakfast." She quirked a grin at him. "Listen, the ingredients in the fridge? Are you going to bake me a pumpkin pie? I didn't think you cooked?"

To her amusement, a touch of pink tinged his cheeks. "Yes, well, you made it clear you want your baked goods homemade. If it will make you eat, I'm sure I can figure out how to mix ingredients together following a set of simple, written instructions." His voice was stiff, some of the insult toward the supposed simplicity of baking lost in the embarrassment at doing something as adorable as trying to make her favorite food from scratch.

"Well, at least you have enough squash available to try a time or two," she teased. "Y'know, seeing how spoiling me with homemade pie is seemingly as important as that war you keep telling me I'm getting in the way of..."

His cheeks turned redder, a disapproving frown pulling his brows down in a way that didn't seem nearly as intimidating now that he didn't look like a huge, horned beast, and she couldn't help it. The intimacy of last night came back, mixing with the sweetness of his intention of learning to bake for her. It filled her from the inside with warmth, and before she realized what she was doing, she'd raised up on her tiptoes and pressed her mouth to his in a soft kiss.

His eyes widened at the unexpected contact, but then fluttered closed. Strong arms wrapped around her waist as he bent his head to deepen the kiss.

Pleasure sparked down her chest and up her spine, heat thundering in her veins. His tongue slipped past her lips, stroking deep into the cavern of her mouth.

Georgia groaned, low and deep, her entire body lighting up from within. She fisted her hands in his shirt, surrendering fully to the sweet rush. A rush that only intensified when he ran his large hands down her back, to her ass, and lifted her up on the counter. Her knees parted willingly for his hips, excitement fizzing through her veins and burrowing deep into her pelvis.

Without thought, she reached for his belt.

He groaned into her mouth at the first brush of her fingers over the front of his pants, the sound vibrating through her, tightening her nipples.

Panting, she pulled back from their kiss, needing a smidge of brain power to undo the button, excitement making her fingers tremble.

"Georgia."

"Shh. I'm gonna make you feel as good as you made me last night," she purred, before returning to the button and zip.

"Georgia. Stop." Large hands closed around hers, hindering her attempts at opening his pants.

She froze, darting her eyes up to meet his in abject confusion. The expression in his dark gaze shocked the horniness from her brain more effectively than a bucket of ice water: cold. Detached. No shred of the warm need she'd felt in his kiss only seconds ago. Nor the aching tenderness she'd seen last night.

"I have told you time and again: I am not your mate, nor will I ever be. You have been branded now, and you are responding favorably to sexual contact—there is no need to waste time on further physical connection between us." He pushed away from the kitchen counter, turning his back on her. "I will arrange for your courting, starting tomorrow. I expect you to pick a mate from among my men before the end of the week."

30

KIRIGAN

"And these European lords... you're certain they were too young to wield the power you experienced?"

Lord Aran huffed an unamused snort. "Yes, Kirigan. I'm certain. It was Eidelsward, out of Switzerland, and Rihncurr from... one of the Nordic countries. I forget which. Both less than a century old. From powerful families, to be sure, but it should have taken me less than a day to beat them back to the Old World. Instead, I was on my knees, minutes from obliteration, when your son came to save my ass. However humiliating it was to need rescue from your kid, who's barely out of fucking diapers, I am grateful. Your bloodline proves strong. I suspect our old monarchs would have been uncomfortable with your family, even if your son hadn't taken control of the Americas."

Kirigan bent his head in acknowledgement of the

compliment, then turned his gaze to the bay below. Lord Aran's home was an imposing estate atop a high cliff overlooking the Atlantic—chosen for its strategic location more than its beauty. "My sons are a source of much pride."

"Deservedly." He chuckled dryly. "My only complaint is the mate your eldest picked. Our new queen is a boon to our cause, no doubt, but that... light of hers... It's caused quite some furor in many of our homes. My own Yiyun has become... discontent. Questions our way of life and has even taken to refusing me access to her body now and then. All because she sees our queen wield power, she's somehow gotten it in her head she should have access to agency as well. I hear from my mated men that this phenomenon isn't entirely uncommon."

"And when she refuses you, you don't force her?" Kirigan gave the other lord a curious look.

Aran grimaced. "No. I can't stand it when she gets angry with me. I tried giving her a firm hand early on. She... didn't take too kindly to it." He sighed, rubbing two fingers over his brow. "I know I should put her in her place, that it's the best thing for her, but..."

"Do you love her?"

Aran blinked. "What kind of question is that?" he rumbled, his tone turning defensive.

Kirigan exhaled softly and turned his attention back to the crashing waves below. "I suppose it doesn't matter. Love or not, if you break her spirit, you'll suffer tenfold the damage you inflict on her. Mate bonds are... tricky... that way. If I were you, Aran, I would find a way to bring her the light she covets. A powerful woman brings far more pleasure than a broken one."

"The lords you fought. When exactly did you feel their assault lessen?"

"Moments before Prince Kesh reached me. No doubt they were distracted by his arrival." If Aran was unbalanced by the change in topic, he didn't show it. Likely, he was only too relieved to change the conversation from his discontented mate.

"And did you notice anything... odd at that time?"

Aran chuffed a mirthless laugh. "Odd? Outside my life force ebbing away? No, Kirigan. I was somewhat preoccupied with not dying, while also attempting to limit human casualties. As much as that was possible. We had just enough warning before the battle to glamour most of the village where the enemy landed, but some slipped through the cracks, and there was damage to several buildings. It was a pain in the ass to build the coverup after, with most of our magic reserves entirely depleted."

Kirigan frowned. "Some slipped through the cracks?"

"Some of my men reported seeing a human woman and child in the middle of the battlefield towards the end."

"Were they killed?"

Aran chuffed another breath. "Apparently not.

Reportedly the prince's Second broke off mid-fight to pull them away."

"Odd."

"I suppose. In the grand scheme of things, a man pumped up on testosterone seeing a pretty face and getting distracted doesn't really register against the current scale of the clusterfuck we've got going on with the Europeans."

The darkness clawed at the back of Kirigan's skull. Something about that explanation was... off. He didn't share his misgivings with the other lord. "Thank you for your recount of the events, Lord Aran. Your staunch defense of our borders has proven invaluable in this instance, and will undoubtedly do so again before the war is over. The king will not forget your loyalty. And neither will I."

A pleased look crossed Aran's features. However much of a toll the attack had taken on his resources, he was an old demon known for his acumen on the battle-field as well as in politics. Having shown his loyalty to the new king in a significant way, early on in Kain's reign, would be a boon to him and his heirs for centuries to come. "The European crown prince defiled our most sacred law by attempting to claim another lord's mate. So far as I'm concerned, their entire conti-nent can burn. Anything else I can do to support the king, don't hesitate to let me know."

———

The large field next to the sleepy fishing village still bore marks from the battle. Scorch marks carved grooves deep into the earth, and most of the grass had been singed by magic and trampled by boots. Several buildings from the village itself had been leveled to the ground, though the humans had removed most of the rubble by now. A freak power grid explosion was the explanation that had been magically enforced on the population.

Humans were easily manipulated.

Kirigan glanced at the video feed on his phone. His daughter-in-law was curled up on the sofa, once again nursing his grandson. Smiling. A couple of taps, and the feed showed Kain in the conference room with three of his top commanders. It had been harder to get around his son's vigilance than it had Selma's, but neither of them had noticed the hidden video cameras covering every inch of the estate. Despite their being installed for Selma's safety, Kirigan had no doubt both would have objections, should they ever discover how closely he watched her. So he made sure they didn't.

Temporarily comforted by the knowledge that she was safe and not showing signs of despondence, he shoved his phone back in his pocket and concentrated on the task at hand: finding out what had happened here—something that had been covert not only to the human population, but the demon combatants as well.

He started on the hill where Aran had fought the two European lords. Pressing his palm to the ground, he let his magic penetrate deep and wide, searching for the echo of the battle. Images rushed through his mind immediately; the combined power of three demon lords throbbed through his own magic, but even that was overwhelmed by the blinding light rushing through his skull.

"Shit." Kirigan pulled his hand from the ground, severing the connection to the echo as he blinked to regain his magical vision. There had been a Stone of Power employed in this battle, alright. That Aran had survived long enough for Kesh to save him had been a miracle. Or, more likely, suggested the wielders had been unfamiliar with the relic, and unable to use it to its full potential.

Kirigan probed the ground with his magic again, more cautiously this time. The echo flowed through him once more, the Stone of Power still overpowering everything else. Until suddenly—it didn't. From one moment to the next, it was simply... gone.

He frowned and pulled back the echo. Released it again, and again, until finally—*there.* A touch of something *other*, right as the Stone of Power vanished from the echo. It was only there for a half-second, but it was enough. He honed in, forced his magic to focus to a pinpoint, until—

A shudder of revulsion crawled up his spine when the echo grasped onto the fragment long enough to reveal its origin.

Divine.

A god's power.

A god had been here. A god had plucked the Stone of Power from its wielders, in the middle of battle, and no one had so much as noticed.

Sick dread settled in his gut as he pulled his focus back to the present.

They'd all known it would be only been a matter of time before the gods took advantage of the internal war raging within demon ranks. It was an inevitability they'd expected. Planned for.

But this?

Somewhere out there, a god now had possession of one of the three most powerful demonic relics on Earth.

There was no preparing for the consequences of a god wielding a Stone of Power against them, no way to predict the outcome. The only certainty was that the biggest threat to his family's life was now the holder of this stone.

31
GEORGIA

"*I expect you to pick a mate from among my men before the end of the week.*"

There were a lot of emotions that statement should have evoked—anger and fear being chief among them. *Hurt* should not have made the list, and yet hurt was what she felt most keenly, in a way that had her fighting back tears of rejection.

Stupid. What had she expected—that his gentleness had meant anything? He'd needed her to lower her guard so he could *train* her to accept a demon lover, and he'd manipulated her, like the demon he was. He'd told her from the start what would happen—what was expected of her.

And still. She'd let herself soften. Let him lull her into a fantasy that there was a real connection between them. That he genuinely cared about her, beyond his fucked-up responsibility to turn her into a compliant womb for another demon.

Knowing the mistake was entirely on her end did nothing to soothe the ache. She'd been so desperate for comfort amidst the horrors of her new reality, she'd thought she'd found human connection. With a monster.

More fool her.

She was grateful Kesh spent most of the day out of the apartment. Not looking at him made it easier to come to terms with her own idiocy. To accept reality. And this morning, when he laid out a pretty blue silk dress for her and told her she would be officially introduced to the men he had selected as her suitors, she didn't object. She dressed in silence, ate in silence, and followed him out of his apartment and into a waiting car. In silence.

The prince, for his part, seemed unfazed by her compliance. She supposed he would be expecting it, given how she'd been successfully *trained* for her new life as a demon's prospective mate. He exchanged a few words with the driver—instructions on which route to take—and then leaned back in the seat next to her, staring straight ahead.

"How will this be done?" she asked, finally breaking the silence. "Is there a process, or do I just... eeny-meeny-miny-moe?"

"Don't be absurd. This is your lifemate—you will never make a more important choice. Each man will court you for the week, and you will select the one you find most compatible." His tone was stiff.

Georgia blew out an exasperated breath. "They're all demons. I'm guessing 'won't eat brain matter in front of me' is as high a bar as I'm gonna hope for."

If her dig about the time she saw him eat a guy went through, he pretended it didn't.

"Out of the thousands of demons in my territory who would kill to claim you, I have handpicked five worthy of the honor. Each is a formidable warrior capable of protecting you and your offspring, should the need ever arise. They are also honorable men, who will treat you well. Beyond that, you should pick a mate whose temperament and interests best suit your preferences."

"*Interests?* What interests do demons have outside sex, war, and human misery?" She looked up at him, irritation fizzing in her veins, but he didn't so much as glance her way.

"I'm sure your five suitors will be more than happy to discuss this at length. Ellon, make sure you stop directly in front of the entrance. I don't want the Breeder outside for a second longer than necessary." The last part was directed at the driver.

Breeder. So she was back to that dehumanizing moniker. Splendid.

They pulled up next to the converted casino where Irral had taken her to seek the prince's protection. That night, there'd only been a couple of demons outside, and one guarding the inner doors. Today, however, at least twelve big, burly men were hovering outside the double doors. Demons, she suspected, though she couldn't see through their human disguise anymore, courtesy of her new brand.

Kesh got out of the backseat, then walked around to her side and held the door open for her. When she slid out, he put an arm around her. From the way he was scanning their surroundings as he walked her to the door, it was clear it was a protective gesture, not an affectionate one. It still made a traitorous part of her belly flutter—and then clench as she remembered how she'd been foolish enough to believe his care had been genuine. That he'd cared beyond his so-called duties.

A shift went through the demon by her side and seemed to transfer through the waiting guards in a wave as he led her through them to the double doors. Kesh clenched her harder to his side, fingers digging in at her waist as every single man's eyes snapped to her. To her surprise, concern was painted on each of their faces. One even took a step forward, brow knotted. "Breeder—"

"She's fine," Kesh snapped, cutting him off. His grip on her waist tightened. "Your duty is to her physical safety. Get back in line and keep the entrance secure."

The guard looked like he wanted to protest, but he obeyed the prince. She felt his eyes on her back, along with the rest of them, until the doors finally closed behind them.

The moment they were alone, Kesh turned toward her. Strong fingers tipped her chin upward, and then she was staring into his black eyes for the first time since he'd rejected her. Concern warred with agitation in their depths.

"You're sad. Why?"

"I'm not—"

"I can smell it on you. We all can. Your brand enhances the physical manifestation of your emotions. I can't take you into a room of five suitors while you reek of..." He trailed off, exhaling a long, deep breath. Steadying himself. "My instincts are screaming to burn whatever has upset you to the ground. If rivals are within sight... it'll be them."

"*Rivals?* How can they be *rivals?* You're not a suitor —you've made that plenty clear." She almost managed to keep the hurt out of her voice.

He exhaled again, brows drawing down in confusion. "That's why you're sad? Because I can't court you?"

"No," she bit out, pulling away from his grasp on her chin. "I'm *upset* because you act like you care, and the reality is, you don't. I'm a job for you. An obligation. And that's fine and all—but I'm human. It's upsetting when someone behaves like a... a friend, then when you start to... trust him... he reminds you, with all possible clarity, that you're just a piece of property to be given away."

"You would've preferred if I'd treated you like a slave? A prisoner?"

Georgia glared up at his stupid, handsome, traitorous face, a refreshing wave of anger washing away any lingering hurt. "You know what? I think I would," she hissed. And then, before he could stop her, she spun around on her heel, pushed open the doors to the inner hall open where five demons were waiting to court her, and marched through.

32
KESH

Kesh clenched his hands and forced a deep breath through his lungs before he followed the Breeder into the throne room. The sharp smell of her anger was better than the anguish of her sadness, but it riled his nervous system and put him more on edge than he'd have liked to be when heading into a room full of other males. Especially, as it turned out, when the five of them turned as one upon Georgia's entrance, and the eagerness in their eyes as they stared at her made jealousy and protectiveness flare hotly in his gut.

He reacted before his brain kicked in, placing a firm hand on the angry woman's shoulder to pull her back close. *Fuck's sake,* these idiotic instincts were going to drive him fucking nuts.

Kesh ignored Georgia's indignant sputtering at

being manhandled back into place, kept a firm grip on her shoulder, and marched her up toward his throne.

The five men sank to their knees as they passed, but though the subservient greeting might have been for him, their eyes were on Georgia.

He tamped down the ridiculous anger that they dared look at her with such blatant desire, scaled the dais, and unceremoniously lifted the Breeder onto his lap. She was stiff and unwilling against him, her anger still sharp in his nostrils, but it did nothing to still the rush of blood to his groin when her round ass settled over his cock. She shot him a withering look over her shoulder when it instantly rose to nudge at her from below.

"What was that about no further sexual contact being necessary?" she hissed.

To his irritation, heat touched his cheeks at her quiet sarcasm. Having exactly zero desire to argue with her in front of his men, he shifted her to one side, settling her on his thigh instead, and refocused on his men.

"Welcome to the first official courting event for Georgia Moore. Each of you has been carefully selected for your ability to care for and protect a Breeder. Should Georgia select you as her mate, you will be expected to surrender any and all obligations that may impede your ability to prioritize her and her future offsprings' well-being. If you are unable or unwilling to do so, speak now."

As expected, only silence met him.

"Very well. We will proceed. Mallorn, approach, if you will."

His Second got up and approached, eagerness painted all over his features. When he reached the dais, he bowed smoothly. "Breeder. It's my utmost honor to formally announce my courtship. I am Mallorn, Second in Command to the Prince of Demons. I have slain many an enemy on the battlefield, and I would prove a fierce mate, capable of defending you in any situation. Any sons I sire are bound to grow into strong warriors in their own right, destined for great honor. If you choose me, I will make it my life's mission to provide you with loyal and attentive companionship, and bestow upon you the joys of motherhood as frequently as possible."

A few years ago, Kesh would have considered his friend's bid for the Breeder's hand a strong opening statement. That was before he'd met his sister-in-law and learned that not all human females were reasonable. Judging from the way Georgia was squinting at his Second, whatever meek compliance she'd seemed capable of when she first landed on his doorstep, she wasn't planning on employing it today.

"Mallorn? I met you in Maine?"

Mallorn smiled, the smugness that he had the advantage of prior interactions with her radiating off him. "Yes, sweet girl. I protected you in Maine. I am pleased you remember me, though I know I must look very different to you now that you've been marked."

"It's hard to forget the monster who threatened to kill an innocent child in front of me," she said, eyes narrowed as she stared Mallorn down.

Mallorn's face dropped. "I-I wouldn't have," he stammered. "Please, sweet one, I had to say what I did to make sure you were safe. I hated that I scared you, but in that moment, your safety was paramount. Please, give me another chance to prove my worthiness, I implore you."

There was a small thread of malicious glee winding through Kesh's chest as his Second's smugness vanished in the blink of an eye, only to be replaced with blind panic. It was swiftly becoming evident that, despite their agreement, Georgia wasn't planning on being nice today. Kesh's traitorous instincts boiled under the surface, determined that she was his, despite the impossibility in that, and thrilled to see her put a would-be rival in his place.

Besides, a little spine looked good on her.

Ignoring how he really shouldn't encourage behavior that might hinder a swift mate selection, he curled his hand possessively around her hip, squeezing gently.

Georgia didn't pay him any mind. Her blue eyes were still spearing into Mallorn.

"Right. Another chance. Tell me then, have you ever been to Hell?"

Mallorn blinked at the odd topic change. "Er... can you be more specific, sweetness?"

"The brothel. Have you been? Have you... used its services?"

"I... have not. But I assure you, I know how to please a human woman—" Mallorn's slightly frantic attempt at wooing Georgia died when she silenced him with a casual wave of her hand befitting of a queen of old.

"Thanks. You can step back. Next."

"Sweetness—" Mallorn protested, entirely stunned by the rude dismissal, but Georgia had already shifted her attention to the next demon eagerly approaching.

"And who are you then?"

"My lady, I am Alliancef. Commander of the Third Regiment. At your service."

"What, no declaration of undying loyalty and a million babies?"

Stars, he enjoyed her ruthless side. Kesh squeezed her hip tighter, anchoring himself in the feel of her as Alliancef opened and closed his mouth a couple of times, struggling to find an appropriate response. "You're being a bitch," he murmured in her ear, unable to keep the amusement out of his voice. "Do you get off on making fierce warriors cry?"

Georgia ignored him.

"My sweet lady Georgia, I will give you as many children as you desire," Alliancef finally managed. "And I will be a loyal mate, putting you before my own life. I swear it, on my honor."

"And Hell? Are you a customer?" Georgia asked, her voice turning deceptively sweet.

Alliancef, the great oaf, smiled confidently. "I have frequently visited that fine establishment over the years, honing my skills in the art of pleasure. Trust that I am well-versed in satisfying a woman. And, of course, once mated, I would restrict my desires to your sweet flesh."

"Thank you for your time," Georgia said, still smiling sweetly before turning her attention to the next kneeling warrior.

Alliancef, though clearly having hoped for more of her time, shot Mallorn a smug look as he stepped back in line.

Kesh silently questioned how the otherwise strategic commander could be this thick.

Brestafan, one of the most notable warriors under him, also eagerly confirmed his frequent exploitations in Hell, and was treated to that same, deceptively sweet smile. Kesh was starting to think all his men would eliminate themselves from the gene pool due to stupidity, but Sefron—the guard who'd been on duty the night Georgia was dragged to his throne, shaking and traumatized from her brief captivity in the brothel, smoothly denied stepping foot in there outside 'official business'. An absolute lie, of course.

He shot Bestafan and Alliancef a side-glance as he stepped back, allowing the final suitor to approach.

"Hello, Georgia. It's a pleasure to meet you. I'm Ed,"

the dark-haired demon said, his voice a deep whiskey rasp.

Georgia arched an eyebrow. "Ed? That's not very... demony."

Ed offered her a half-smile. "My father allowed my human mother to name me. He theorized it would help her bond with me more easily. She called me Edward, after her brother."

For the first time, the Breeder in his lap showed a hint of genuine interest. "And did it? Help her bond?"

"It's hard to say, but she does tell me I look like my uncle did. Do you have siblings? My parents only had me, but my mother's bond with her brother was something special."

Kesh could sense the softening in Georgia's posture against him and shot Ed a begrudgingly impressed look. There was a zero percent chance the casual question about her brother was a coincidence. Unlike the other suitors, Ed hadn't been picked for his valor won on the battlefield. As the prince's Master of Spies, his home was in the shadows, among secrets and whispers. No doubt he'd learned all there was to know about the Breeder before arriving to court her.

"I have a younger brother," Georgia said quietly. "Larry."

"You love him very much." It wasn't a question, confirming Kesh's suspicions.

Georgia nodded. "He's the most important person in the world to me. You said your mother's bond with your uncle *was* very special. Did something happen to him?"

"Time, I'm afraid. She and my father mated in 1890. Her brother passed from old age in 1953." Ed noticed her surprised expression as the math sank in and smiled wryly. "I take it no one's explained that demons don't age like humans do—and that this extends to our mates, once the bond is in place?"

"No. They haven't." Georgia shot Kesh a look over her shoulder before returning her focus to Ed. "So everyone I love will die, and I will remain behind?"

The slight tremor in her voice caused a pang of something unpleasantly close to guilt to tighten Kesh's gut, but before he could think of a response that wouldn't just further upset her, Ed stepped in.

"Not everyone, Georgia. You will have a mate and, fate willing, children. My mother mourned her human family's passing, but the pain has dulled with time. She is content with my father's love now—and mine, of course, when I visit."

"Your father's love? I was told demons don't love. At least, not as humans do." Another pointed glance over her shoulder.

Ed gave her a half-smile, his gaze darting to Kesh before returning to her. "Hmm. Perhaps not as easily as humans, no. But when we do, we love fiercely. His Majesty, King Kain, has certainly proven as much. As has my father. Pick your mate wisely, and you will know love unlike any you could have found among your own kind."

He was playing her like a fiddle. Kesh's begrudging respect for his Master of Spies turned acid with annoyance as he felt the change in Georgia—how she leaned forward a little, relaxed her posture... and fell right under the sly bastard's spell. Was she really this dumb? This hungry for a fairytale romance? The little scaredy cat who'd cowered on the dais in front of him, entirely aware of how treacherous his kind was... A few pretty words and empty promises and she was ready to ride off into the sunset with another demon.

"You haven't asked Ed for his preferences in whores," Kesh said, barely managing to keep the irritation out of his voice.

"I find rape abhorrent. I don't use women for pleasure," Ed said softly, his eyes fixed on Georgia's. "Nor for breeding. I'm looking for a life partner who will fill my heart the way my mother has fulfilled my father, not a pampered slave."

"Excuse me!" Alliancef protested, the dismay on his features suggesting he was finally clocking on to the trap he and Brestafan'd wandered into. "No one is *raping* anyone. I treat my whores well—"

"As do I!" Brestafan interrupted, glaring daggers at Ed. "Only a scoundrel would leave a woman unsatisfied, whether or not payment is involved."

"Oh, and you think a woman would want to fuck you if she wasn't chained down?" Mallorn jumped in, gleeful at the realization he'd answered correctly after all.

Kesh pinched the bridge of his nose as his throne room devolved into loud bickering among his five otherwise rational men. "For fuck's sake! Will you be quiet? Georgia, have you made a decision of which of your suitors you would like to see at the next courting session?"

Silence spread like nuclear fallout, the five men turning back toward her as one. The hope in their eyes was frankly pitiful. Fucking Breeders, with their ability to turn powerful men into simpering idiots in the blink of an eye.

"I have," Georgia said, straightening on his lap. "Mallorn. Sefron. And Ed. I would like the chance to get to know you better—if you're interested."

Another cacophony of noise broke out as the three chosen cheerfully assured her they were more than interested, while Brestafan and Alliencef protested loudly and begged her to reconsider.

"Enough." Kesh silenced the lot of them with another glare. "The girl's made her choice. Thank you for your time. Alliancef, Brestafan, I will consider you again the next time a Breeder arrives in my territory. For now, return to your duties. The rest of you, I will send word of the next time and date for you to court Georgia. Until then, we have a war that needs attention. You're dismissed."

Quiet muttering spread among them—even the

chosen three, who clearly were hoping to spend more time with the Breeder—but they all bowed stiffly for him and finally left, shooting Georgia longing glances as they went.

When the double doors finally closed behind them, Kesh leaned back on his throne, eyes closing with annoyance at the whole fucking production. "Say what you will about our old customs, but the auctions were infinitely more dignified than this mess."

"I'm sure you'd have just *loved* to sell me off like a sex toy and get on with your precious war," Georgia bit, moving to scoot off his lap. The sharpness in her tone made it plenty clear she was still angry with him.

He curled his hand around her hip on instinct, keeping her seated on his thigh even as hot anger flamed through his irritation. She thought that little of him? That he'd *enjoy* seeing her terrified and subjugated underneath whichever brute had the finances and strength to win her? After what he'd told her about his mother? He could still feel the ghost of her embrace from when she'd held him while he cried, making slimy tendrils of betrayal crawl up his spine.

"Listen here, you little brat—"

"*Brat?!*"

Georgia's outraged hiss was cut off when the doors to the throne room banged open again. She tensed at the sight of the man who strode across the threshold and walked toward the dais without being invited, her body instinctively pressing back against Kesh for protection. As if she could sense the danger he represented even with her blinding mark in place.

Kesh wrapped his arm around her midriff and pulled her to his chest before addressing the newcomer.

"Father," he said, practiced calm in his voice. "I wasn't expecting you. What brings you here?" Without so much as a fucking text as a heads up.

"Her." Kirigan speared the girl on Kesh's lap with his unsettling eyes, and an urgent sense of alarm rushed up from his gut. Kesh only just managed to twist his body around to shield Georgia, before his father's powerful magic slammed into them both.

33
KESH

His magic defenses flooded out a millisecond too late, making his body take the full impact of his father's attack. A deep ache rattled through his bones, but Georgia's agonized cry made the pain fade to nothing on a rush of fear so deep, he could barely breathe.

"Georgia! No, no, no!"

"She's fine." His father's calm voice didn't suggest he'd just attacked his own son unprovoked. "Only a divine creature would be harmed from that kind of magic."

Kesh ignored him and carefully cupped Georgia's face, tilting it up to his. "Tell me where it hurts, sweet one."

She gasped up at him, eyes wide and shocked, searching his for reassurance, for protection. "My...

bones. All of them. B-but it's fading. I think... I think I'm okay."

He searched her gaze, verifying she was telling the truth before carefully standing up to place her on his throne... and then, he turned to his father.

"*You.*" Every cell in his body itched with violence. "Have you entirely lost what little was left of your mind? You come into my domain and *attack* me? While a Breeder is under my care? Do you have a death wish? If you weren't my father, I would smear the walls with your blood! Explain yourself!"

"I didn't attack *you*—I attacked *her*. It was your choice to put yourself in harm's way. I had to make sure you hadn't been bespelled by a goddess."

Kirigan's exasperated tone did little to calm Kesh's fury. He clenched his fists until his knuckles cracked. "Explain. Better."

"I've just come from Lord Aran, who said a woman and a child were seen on the battlefield—and that your Second dragged them off. And then I arrive here to find this female perched on your lap. Exactly as a manipulative goddess would be, were she undercover and trying to gain influence with demon royalty. I had to make sure you were not being poisoned."

"Why the *fuck* would a goddess have been on the battlefield in Maine? And why on Earth would I have brought her home, rather than slit her filthy throat? You think I can't recognize a divine cretin when I see one?"

"You wouldn't have recognized this one. As for why

she was there... I will explain, once we are in private. This matter is urgent, but it is not for the Breeder's ears."

Every molecule of Kesh's being resisted the idea of bringing the man who'd just attacked Georgia to his home, but they were at war. If his father said a matter concerning a goddess was urgent, then there was no way around it. Gritting his teeth, he said, "I can't leave the Breeder with my men—she's still unmated. Follow us to my apartment—we can talk privately there, while she is safe in another room."

———

HE LEFT GEORGIA IN THE BEDROOM, WITH ORDERS TO *STAY*.

She gave him an annoyed look and muttered something about not being a pet as he closed the bedroom door behind him.

It bothered him—that she was irritated with him. Instincts he could do nothing about prickled at his spine, urging him to *fix it*. Ridiculous, of course. There was nothing to fix. He wasn't to be her mate; it wasn't his job to keep her happy. And yet, his stupid, primitive wiring kept his mind preoccupied with thoughts of how to please her... make her sweet on him.

Frustration oozed off him as he entered the living room where his father waited. "Out with it, then. Why did you think the Breeder was divine?"

Kirigan arched an eyebrow at his insolent tone, but

thankfully didn't call him out. He wasn't in the mood to be put in his place by his insane but immensely powerful sire.

"There were signs of divine presence during your battle with the Europeans in Maine. But... hidden. Expertly so. One of them was there."

Kesh sucked in a breath. He knew better than to question his father on matters concerning magic. The ancient demon was one of the utmost experts on the matter, not only in the Americas, but in the world. The thought of a goddess having been so close, without Kesh so much as sensing it? *Unsettling* was too mild a word.

"Why? What was her purpose? To make us rip into each other? We don't exactly need divine intervention for this war."

"To steal a Stone of Power. The Europeans had one with them. I felt its echo, along with the faintest trace of a god's presence as it vanished off the battlefield. To pull that off, whoever they are must be... very old. Powerful. And sly. Aran mentioned his men seeing your Second drag a human woman with a child off the battlefield... hence my assumption about the girl on your lap." Kirigan leveled him with an emotionless yet somehow entirely judgmental look. "I didn't anticipate you bringing a Breeder into battle."

Heat touched Kesh's ears, his brow pulling down with a sense of defensiveness. "There was no other choice. I couldn't leave her behind. Aran needed urgent assistance, or we would have lost his entire territory, and there wasn't time to get another lord to look after her. She was *supposed* to stay out of danger, behind magical wards."

"Your sister-in-law should have prepared you for the fact that Breeders aren't always meek and compliant." Kirigan's gaze slid toward the hallway and the closed bedroom door. An unsettling intensity flickered through his black eyes. "Why *did* she enter the battlefield? Does she possess the light?"

"No. She's not Pure." Kesh took a half-step to the side, blocking his father's view of the door shielding Georgia. "She's just a soft-hearted Breeder, who saw a wayward spawnling on the field and decided to put her own life at risk for an insignificant human's. Which would be the child Aran mentioned. She clung to that thing like she'd birthed it herself, so Mallorn had to rescue them both."

Kirigan's gaze narrowed, returning to Kesh's. "What happened to the child? After it was rescued?"

Irritation bubbled up Kesh's spine, partly from being grilled on the less-than-ideal decisions he'd had to make in a less-than-ideal situation, and partly from the reminder of how thoroughly he'd been manipulated by Georgia and his ridiculous instincts to please her. "I took it back to its mother. Can we perhaps return to the slightly more important issue of a fucking *god* having stolen a Stone of Power right from under our noses? What kind of havoc can they wreak with that? Because I assume we're all thoroughly fucked."

"I'm not certain. The three stones are forged with ancient, demonic magic. A divine creature would run into some trouble wielding one, I would imagine. However, for them to risk the theft, they most certainly will have a plan to use it. Whatever *havoc* they're planning, it will be bad." Kirigan paused. "You say you took the child back to its mother? And there were no... irregularities in the handover?"

What was everyone's obsession with that fucking girl? First Georgia, and now his father. Who, he knew all too well, didn't possess a protective bone in his body when it came to human children. "No. Except from us nearly losing the entire fucking Eastern Seaboard to a concealed Stone of Power—which is apparently now in some god's hands—and me having to bring a Breeder to a battle with the Europeans because Kain can't tell Selma 'no' which made it somehow my responsibility to play matchmaker to a wayward female, everything went smoothly."

"And she is proving... troublesome, is what I understand from your brother?"

It was unlike Kirigan to display any kind of tact. Which meant Kain would have passed on Mallorn's aggravating presumptions about Georgia, and any territorial instincts Kesh may or may not be displaying for her.

He narrowed his eyes in annoyance. "No more than

any Breeder would, given the circumstances. Once I've dealt with... a minor complication... and she's picked a mate, I'll be able to return my full focus to the war. Whatever else you may have heard stems from my men's growing agitation with the presence of an unmated Breeder, nothing more."

"Minor complication?" Kirigan raised an eyebrow in interest.

"The kind it would be better if her suitors didn't know too much about. She sold her body to a demon, ended up in a brothel... And the contract's technically still active. Not much more than a bump in the road, once I... *convince*... the demon who owns her that it would be in his best interest to surrender his claim willingly. But I can't bring her back to the brothel now that her presence in my territory is known, and I can't leave her here while I go deal with him, for the same reasons I couldn't leave to handle the Maine situation without her."

"So leave her with me."

Kesh blinked. "With you?"

"You think I might forcefully try to claim the girl the moment you turn your back, like your men?" Despite Kirigan's dispassionate tone, he still managed to make the idea sound as preposterous as it was.

Heat touched Kesh's ears. "No." Only a moment's hesitation there. "But your behavior with Selma these days is... a little concerning. Georgia is my responsibility. If something were to happen to her, especially at the hands of my own father... The ripple effects would be enough to take down our entire family."

Kirigan's eyebrow arched higher. "My behavior with Selma is cause for concern?"

Kesh sighed irritably, wishing his brother was the one to have this conversation, not him. "You follow her to the bathroom. That's not normal. You know that, right? And you... hover. To a disturbing degree. I'm frankly surprised to see you here, this far away from her and the baby."

A shadow passed over his father's eyes, and for a second, dread clutched at Kesh's gut. If he'd pushed him too far—

"I *hover* because, if she dies, Kesh... so does your brother." The words came out stilted; like they were too sharp to comfortably pass through his throat. "Women are... delicate, after giving birth. To a degree neither you nor Kain can fully comprehend. I am only here because no one else can be. But while I am, utilize me. If taking care of this *complication* will mean the girl can be mated and you can return your full focus to the war sooner, then trust me to guard her while you are away. She is not Selma; my... instincts... won't be on edge with her. And we need your attention on the kingdom, especially now that the gods are getting involved."

A long moment of silence passed between them. It was, perhaps, the closest his father had come to acknowledging how much their mother had hated them, and the shadowy talons raking at his guts in response were acid.

It didn't matter. She was long dead, and he'd known the truth since he was young.

Kesh forced a slow, even breath through his lungs, forcing his focus to what did matter. "Very well. I will leave Georgia under your care while I deal with the lowlife who owns her contract. I will be back shortly." He paused, giving his father a firm look. "But keep your distance. I don't want her traumatized."

34
GEORGIA

The sound of the front door slamming shut made Georgia perk up.

Finally.

It'd become very swiftly clear to her that the lunatic attacking her out of nowhere was Kesh's father—which hadn't made the situation any less tense. For the rest of her life, she would remember the tight clenching low in her gut as the big, brutish demon prince cried in her arms while he divulged the horrors his father had committed, and the devastation they'd led to.

She hadn't anticipated ever seeing him in the flesh, and now that she had, she was glad the experience was over. Even without shooting black magic at her and accusing her of being a goddess, of all things, it'd been obvious that there was something not-right about him. He'd *looked* like a human to her, in the same way that Kesh did now she'd been marked—slightly too big, ever-so-slightly *off*—but even so, his eyes had given away what even Kesh's recounts from his childhood couldn't quite capture: something fundamental was broken inside him.

Georgia shuddered at the memory of those black eyes, so similar yet so entirely different to Kesh's, and then resolutely pushed it aside. Whatever was wrong with him, it wasn't her problem. In a week or two, she would likely never see the demon prince again, let alone his unhinged dad. And that was absolutely fine. *More* than fine.

She pushed open the door and walked through the hallway into the living space. Kesh stood staring out the floor-to-ceiling windows, his back to her, black hair tumbling over his shoulders.

"Well, you weren't kidding. Your dad's certifiably insane. I've never been called a goddess before, but blasting magic at me seems like a *wild* overreaction. I see where you get your charming temperament fro—" Her snarky voice died on a wheeze when the demon by the window turned toward her, and dark, dead eyes pierced her to her soul.

"You feel comfortable mouthing off to my son? And *he* feels comfortable enough with you to touch on my... instabilities?" Kirigan looked at her with what *seemed* like nothing but polite interest. Georgia still took several steps back toward the hallway, her mouth turning dry with abject horror at her mistake.

"How very... interesting." Those awful eyes swept

up the length of her body, as if investigating a new puzzle piece for where it might fit.

"Where... where's Kesh?" she managed to croak.

"Out." He didn't take his gaze off her. "He will be back soon."

Kesh just *left* her with him? Alone?

Georgia fidgeted under the disturbed demon's intense stare, feeling heat flood her cheeks and her pulse thud unevenly in her throat. Kesh wouldn't have left her if he'd believed his father a threat to her—that much she felt certain of, despite everything else. Yet her instincts screamed at her that this creature was far more dangerous than any of her demons she'd encountered.

"Um... I'll... wait for him in there, then..." She backtracked until the bedroom door hit her ass, fumbled with the knob until the door swung open, and quickly stepped inside. Then she slammed it shut and turned the lock.

"Jesus Christ." It came out in a hoarse whisper. She shuddered and rubbed at her arms, trying to settle the sudden flush of goosebumps.

"I never did understand why humans really went so hard for *him* in particular. I mean, I know his PR campaign was flawless, but... there are so many other, far more interesting deities to worship. Don't you think?"

Georgia yipped at the unexpected voice and spun

around. On the bed, wearing a clean white dress, her feet bare and legs crossed at the ankles, sat Suzanne.

"Wh- How—*what??*" *Complete confusion.* This—this made no sense. Did Kesh bring her here? No, that would be ridiculous. He'd made it plenty clear he'd seen the girl as a stain to be scraped off his boot as swiftly as possible.

Did she follow them back from Maine?

No, even more ridiculous—and even if she somehow had, it didn't explain how she'd made it through Kesh's guards and up to the penthouse floor.

"Don't be scared. I'm not here to hurt you."

Georgia blinked at the scrap of a girl. "*Hurt* me? Honey, how did you get here? Does your mother know where you are?"

Pearling laughter cut her off. "Oh, Georgia... Your kind really *are* the gentlest souls humanity has to offer." Suzanne waved a hand. Golden light shimmered off her slim figure, and suddenly, a grown woman sat on the bed in her stead. "I apologize for deceiving you, dear one. I needed to tap into your protective instincts in a bit of a rush up in Maine. And seem as non-threatening as possible to the big brute you've been saddled with."

Acid shock replaced confusion, followed by a wave of fear.

Kesh's terrifying father was right—there *had* been a goddess on the battlefield.

"What do you want from me?" Georgia had seen plenty of demons in her life. A *goddess*, however? That was a first. Instinctively, she backed up and fumbled for the doorknob. A soft prickling in her fingers as she connected with the metal made her glance over her shoulder. The door shimmered in the same golden light that had turned Suzanne from a sweet, non-threatening child into a full-ass goddess.

"It's just a little... camouflage. That demon out there has quite the nasty reputation. Trust me, neither of us wants him aware of my presence." Suzanne shuddered. "And you really don't have to look so scared, Georgia. I'm not here to hurt you. I'm here to help. Come, have a seat. Let's have a little... girl chat." She patted the bed.

"Help?" Cautiously, Georgia peeled herself off the door and approached the goddess. She *looked* sincere, her facial expression friendly and open. And if there was even a chance... "Help *how?* Can you... can you get me out of this... Breeder situation?"

Suzanne sighed softly, her soft lips tilting with a hint of regret. "Unfortunately not. The *Breeder situation* was negotiated many centuries ago—it's not in my power to undo it. But I *can* help you get a bit more say in what happens going forward. To you, and the world around you. Is that of some interest?"

Considering her life had been written off as a broodmare? "Yes. Yes, that has... some interest." Georgia cautiously sat on the spot Suzanne indicated. "But as I understand it... well, I'm pretty much trapped. I signed a contract... this, being allowed to pick my own... er, husband, I guess… is pretty much best-case scenario. Right?"

Suzanne rolled her eyes. "Oh, I bet the brutes genuinely believe that's a real win for one of their helpless little Breeder slaves. No offense. Even after their new queen demonstrated what kind of power you contain, they still can't *quite* wrap their meaty heads around you being more than a womb to exploit."

Georgia blinked. "I'm sorry… power? What *power* am I supposed to contain? And… what exactly is it you can do to help me? And why do you want to? What's in it for you?" It felt borderline disrespectful to ask that of a freaking *goddess,* but considering the circumstances, it felt prudent. "And also, what was the whole Maine-charade about? If you didn't want Kesh to know your identity, why come here?"

"Ah, yes… All fair questions." Suzanne smiled, her eyes crinkling at the corners, but there was a sharpness in them. "Your power, darling, is what draws the demon scum to you like flies to honey. It's the light you carry—their darkness craves it on a primordial level."

"My light? I don't carry any light. At most, I carry a depressive gray. There's nothing special about me—outside of being able to see through demonic disguises. Well… I could. I can't anymore, not after this thing." Georgia touched a hand to her forehead. "And, supposedly, the whole… breeding thing."

Suzanne let out another pealing laugh. "Oh, sweet girl… Yes, outside of being one of the rarest creatures on the planet, there's nothing special about you. Your light, Georgia, is what makes you feel others' pain. Makes you do whatever you can to help them not hurt anymore. It's what made you run into the middle of a battlefield to save a helpless child. But it's more than that—it's magic in its purest form.

"For centuries, it was believed the ability to use it had been lost with the agreement to tie your fates to the demons. It hasn't. The queen proved as much. You are powerful, Georgia. More than you know. You just have to learn to unlock it."

Georgia rubbed at her temples, where a headache was threatening to form. "Okay… let me get this straight… You're saying I have *magic?* As in… make things levitate, heal illness, blow things up *magic?*"

Suzanne's lips curled up in an amused smile. "Yes… depending on application."

"…And that I don't currently have access to it, because… *someone* agreed to turn me… and people like me… into demon broodmares?"

"Simplified, but yes, in its essence."

"But now *you* have the key to unlock my 'potential' and turn me into a light-blasting badass?" Georgia lowered her fingers from her temples and stared at the goddess by her side. "Do you know what a pyramid scheme is? Because you very much sound like you're trying to recruit me for one of those."

The goddess's smile turned into a mischievous grin. "You're a little sassy, aren't you? Good for you. And you're not *entirely* wrong, of course. Helping you isn't an altruistic endeavor. The demons have always been... problematic. It's in their nature. They fight divinity on primitive instinct alone. But with the new king's mating, some of us have seen a... let's call it a spark in the darkness.

"You see, he loved his mate so much, he went against the evil core within his very nature to set her free. And with that one act of true love, he reawakened the magic we all thought lost."

Georgia blinked. "So... Okay, you're saying the king —Kesh's brother?—loved his wife so much, she can now do magic? That's... cool. But I'm not sure what that has to do with me?"

"You're like her, Georgia. You have that same spark just waiting to be ignited. And here you are, under the protection of the brother to the first demon in history to choose love over possession... Fate weaves her web rather obviously sometimes, don't you think?"

"Wait... wait, wait, *wait*." Georgia stared at the smug-looking goddess. "Are you trying to insinuate I need to mate *Kesh?*"

"Well, him or his father, yes." Suzanne smiled brightly. "That bloodline... Fate has touched their lineage. Whichever one claims you will be fine."

"Whoa, hold up." Georgia pushed down the wave of nausea at the suggestion of being 'claimed' by Kesh's scary father. "Even if we ignore for a second that he'd apparently kill me if he... you know. I don't love him.

And he certainly doesn't love me, either. Whatever happened to give the queen her powers, that's not... that's not something that will happen for me. I'm not like her—at all. I'm just..."

"A sad gray mouse?" Suzanne finished off for her, eyebrow arched sardonically. "A helpless little victim, content with bowing your neck and taking whatever scraps your demon overlords decide to throw at you?"

Heat flooded Georgia's cheeks. The mocking words echoed Kesh's opinion of her uncomfortably. Refreshing anger rushed through her veins. "That's real easy to say, but it's not like I can just wave my hands and be something I'm not. He says I'd *die* from being 'loved' by a demon lord.

"And again—*I don't love him.* I can't just start loving a demon who's treating me like an inconvenience that needs to be pawned off because it suits some random goddess's schemes. Which, by the way, you still haven't explained. Why do you care what demon takes me in the end? And why should *I* care about *your* plans? It sounds an awful lot like you want to use me just as much as the demons do. How are you any better? At least they gave me my brother's life in return."

"Oh, I don't think you have any idea what you are, little firecracker. But you will. All you need is a little... push." Suzanne gave her a wicked grin, her eyes lighting up with an otherworldly glow as she leaned in.

Some of Georgia's anger withered, unease creeping up her spine. "Wait, what are you—hey! Stop that!" Her voice rose to a sharp squeak as the goddess without delay pushed her down onto the mattress and slipped a hand underneath her skirt. Slim fingers brushed against her sex, then slipped up between her folds, violating and intimate. She kicked out, but it was too late. The goddess found the metal ring encircling her clit—and twisted.

Sharp, painful fire shot through her pelvis, forcing a cry from her throat as the dark magic in the ring sank deep into her flesh. And then... then came the awful, all-consuming *need*.

"Sorry about that. Had to be done, though." Suzanne stood back up and brushed off her fingers.

"What... what did you do?" Georgia's voice was a horrified rasp. Every molecule in her body throbbed painfully, her vision turning hazy at the corners. Her trapped clit swelled against the metal, angry and raw, and oh, *God*... she needed...

"I just gave Fate a little push. Sometimes, a drop of chaos is needed to get things moving in the right direction. Let's see if one of the demon lords can't help you awaken your power after all." With a cheerful wink, she snapped her fingers, letting the golden shimmer barricading the door fall, before vanishing into thin air, leaving Georgia alone to writhe on the bed.

There was no more coherent thought; no more of anything.

Only the burning, all-consuming need eating her body alive.

35
KESH

ell. Such a contrite name for a brothel servicing demons, and yet, it managed to encapsulate the atmosphere perfectly.

The smell of sex and tears was heavy in the air as Kesh pushed his way through the door of Jimmy's establishment, the groan of the hinges momentarily drowning out the female cries from within and the wet slapping of flesh on flesh.

A minor demon sat behind a desk in the makeshift reception area. He looked up, a service-minded smile on his face that quickly morphed into abject horror.

"Your Highness!" He got to his feet so fast, his chair fell backward with a loud clang. "T-this is such an honor! W-what can I do for you, my lord?"

"I'm here for Jimmy." Kesh didn't spare him a second glance. He strode past the desk and toward the main office, through an doorway hung with blue curtains which separated the narrow hallway from the four-by-eight rooms containing chained-up women, several in the process of being used by Hell's clientele.

He'd been here once prior, before he became a prince. Not as a client, but to settle a contract dispute on a girl. He hadn't thought much of it at the time—it'd been a minor annoyance in his busy schedule, nothing more. Now, though, as he passed stall after stall, the thought that Georgia almost ended up here made the tormented cries of females speared on demon cocks cause bile to rise in his throat. She'd been foolish, bargaining herself for her brother, and she had only narrowly escaped her fate. If the goon who'd brought her to him hadn't rescued her, he'd never even have realized she existed. Wouldn't have known to come save her.

Anger bubbled in his veins and thrummed in his temples as he pushed past the stalls to the door at the end. He wasn't going to knock, but before he could kick it in, the door opened, revealing the same goon who'd brought Georgia to him.

He was missing an eye, but the good one widened in shock at Kesh's appearance.

"Y-your Highness," he stammered, swiftly stepping aside. "Jimmy, it's—"

"Prince Kesh!" The heavy-set demon in a pin-striped suit at the desk inside got to his feet with surprising agility, a servile smile plastered on his punchable face. "What an incredible honor! Loyt, fetch the bottle of 1973 sherry from the vault. The one flavored with divine tears."

Another demon of the same stature as the man who'd brought him Georgia—also with a missing eye—moved toward a back door.

"I'm not here for a social call." Kesh didn't so much as glance at the two goons, his gaze locked on the pimp's as he ordered, "Get out and stay out. This is a private matter."

They obeyed without a second's hesitation, not waiting for confirmation from their boss.

Jimmy hid his obvious annoyance with another smile. "A lowly businessman has a private matter with the Prince of Demons? I am most flattered, my lord, but I am uncertain to what this matter could possibly pertain?"

"Don't try me," Kesh growled. "I don't have patience for your bullshit. You tried to whore a Breeder. A *Breeder*. I should cut your head off and mount it as a warning to anyone else who ever gets the idea that they can desecrate our most sacred, most valuable assets!"

The pimp's smile tightened. "I'm sure I don't know what yo—*ghh!*" His attempt to feign ignorance was cut off with a wet gargle when Kesh snatched him by the throat and squeezed. Snarling, he lifted the heavy demon up by his neck and brought him to within an inch of his face.

"I specifically recall telling you I have no patience for bullshit. Lie to me one more time, and you will spend the next three months having your ass whored far more brutally than anything that's ever been done to any of your human sex dolls' cunts. Do you understand me?"

Jimmy managed another gargling sound, but from the look of panic in his beady eyes, it was a rattle of confirmation.

Fighting back the urge to squeeze just a little harder and snap the miserable fuck's neck, Kesh released his grip with a warning growl.

Jimmy stumbled backwards, clutching at his throat. He fell against the desk, gasping for air.

"You not only tried to whore the Breeder—you took out a contract on her." Despite the fury and murder-lust pounding in his veins, Kesh kept his voice low and even. The threat in it was still clear. "You know the punishment for harming a Breeder is death—slow, painful death."

"My lord, she wasn't harmed," Jimmy wheezed. "The girl was desperate. She bargained herself before my associate even knew what she was. I swear to you, it was my intent that she be treated most respectfully and live a life of luxury and pleasure. I even ringed her, at great expense! Now, did I... circumvent the rules by accepting her into my employ? One could argue as much, but I never intended *harm* to befall the precious little—"

"Enough!" Dark power erupted out of Kesh's palms, shattering the table beneath the other demon. He stumbled backwards, but managed to stay on his feet, sweat beading on his forehead as Kesh stalked forward and snatched him by the throat again. Instead of pressing on his windpipe this time, he dug his claws into his sweaty neck flesh, drawing acid-green blood. "Every word out of your mouth makes me want to feed you your own teeth!"

"A-apologies, my lord," Jimmy rasped, but despite the subservient tone, Kesh saw the calculating expression in his eyes. "How can I atone? Surely, there is something I can offer the Prince of Demons in return for his mercy. Or, I suspect, I would already be dead, no...?"

Kesh narrowed his eyes to slits, his claws digging in a little deeper. Jimmy winced but kept quiet. The shrewd fuck knew how to play the game all too well. "Her contract. As you are well aware, unless she's the one killing you, her contract will simply pass to your beneficiary upon your death. So I will make you a onetime offer: resolve her contract immediately, and you will survive your punishment. Resist, and you will die screaming as your own men fuck your entrails out of your bloodied, gaping asshole, and I will make your beneficiary the same offer. Do we have an agreement?"

"Your Highness drives a convincing bargain," Jimmy rasped. "Ah, may I enquire as to what my punishment will be if—*when*—I comply? Surely, full cooperation will grant some leniency—?"

"You will live. That is all you need to know." Kesh

released him from his grip once more and folded his arms across his chest, his magic billowing around him, itching for violence. The cries from the whores still rang through the warehouse, making the image of Georgia strapped down in one of the claustrophobic booths dance for his inner eye. He may have to let the pimp live, for now, but his punishment... Kesh was going to enjoy it.

"Right... right." Jimmy rubbed at his neck, his acid blood coloring his fingers. "I'll fetch the contract now."

"You do that." Kesh watched with narrowed eyes as he scarpered into the adjoining back room.

"It'll just be a moment!" Jimmy called out from the backroom. The sounds of a filing cabinet getting yanked open and frantically rifled through followed.

The sharp sound of his phone's ringtone made Kesh momentarily shift his focus from the pimp. He frowned when his father's number showed on the display.

What in the world...? He never ca—

Icy dread shot through his veins when he realized that the only reason his father had for calling him was if there was a problem with... with Georgia!

"What?" he snapped the second his thumb swiped over the answer-button. "Is she alright?"

"There's been an attack. The goddess from Maine. She was here. She touched the Breeder—"

Everything inside Kesh went tight. Painful. There was nothing in existence but fear so powerful he didn't know how he would be able to breathe. But he did. For her.

"I'm coming."

Letting contract be contract, Kesh stormed out of Jimmy's office, out of Hell, his only thought that if Georgia was hurt, nothing would matter ever again.

36

KESH

It was obvious when he arrived at his apartment tower that his men were oblivious to any divine attack. They jerked to attention when he pulled up on his motorbike, threw it on the curb, and ran toward the entrance. Toward Georgia.

"Your Highness, what—?"

"Call Mallorn," Kesh snarled as he stormed past the guards. "Tell him to get here immediately." Whatever that goddess had done to Georgia, she would pay. He needed his Second by his side to ensure she didn't escape the city while he tended to the Breeder

He burst out of the elevator and into his front hall three minutes later, heart in his throat. "Georgia! Georgia!"

A muffled scream sounded from deeper in the apartment, followed by a heavy thud, and then nails clawing frantically at wood. He skidded around the corner—and found his father sitting on the floor in front of his bedroom, leaning heavily against the closed door. Another thud vibrated the wood against his back.

"What on Earth are you—?"

"Kesh! Kesh, help me! Oh God, please, help me!"

His voice died when Georgia's desperate cries made it through the closed door his father was physically barricading. "What are you doing? Get out of the way, she needs help!" He stepped forward, intent on the door, but his father's magic gripped him, holding him in place.

"Wait—"

Absolute fury exploded in his brain. For the first time in his life, there was no fear at the thought of confronting his father, no concern about pushing him too far. All he registered was that the other demon was trying to stop him from coming to Georgia's aid. A *roar* ripped from his throat, and black, dense power exploded out of his body.

Kirigan's magic hold on him shattered like glass, the blast wave blowing through the door behind him and knocking him out of the way.

Georgia, who'd been behind the door, stumbled backwards and landed heavily on her ass with a cry. Her dress was torn to shreds, her hair wild, and her skin flushed pink.

"Shit!" Kesh leapt over his father and crouched by her side, carefully cradling her head as he eased her back upright. "Where does it hurt, little one?"

"Kesh—she resisted my magic. I tried to contain her with magic, but she shrugged off my bindings as if they were nothing. She's Pure."

"What?" He'd barely registered his father's caution when Georgia dug her nails into his arms—and her scent hit him square in the nostrils.

Heat.

"Please... please, it hurts, I need you!"

Her voice was raspy and raw from screaming, but still perfectly modulated to hit every primitive, male part of his brain. Her eyes were hazy, her blunt nails drawing white lines on his skin as she clawed at him to get closer. And her *smell...*

He buried his nose in her neck and inhaled, all thoughts of a goddess and danger and war vanishing in the fog of lust roaring up from his pelvis and digging deep into his brain stem.

"Shh, I'm here. I'll make it stop hurting now." His voice was a coo.

Georgia mewled in response, unshed tears of relief shining in her beautiful blue eyes. "You'll make it stop?"

"I will," he promised, thumb stroking her cheek. He got to his feet and lifted her into his arms with ease, and carried her to the bed.

She got to her knees the second he put her down, cheek pressed to the mattress, ass up. "Please...!"

"Good girl." Kesh pushed up her tattered silk skirt and cupped her smoldering pussy from behind. Her pulse drummed against his palm, heavy and fast, the rhythm transferring to his own, aching cock. She whined at his touch and pressed down to rub herself against his fingers. Thick, viscous liquid pooled in his palm, the scent of cunt and heat so heavy in the air his vision blurred.

"Kesh!" Her whine turned sharp, the demand clear as she pushed herself back on his hand, rhythmically rubbing against it.

"I know—I've got you, love." Freeing his cock from the painful confines of his zip, he knelt up behind her and pushed her further forward, greedy eyes raking over the hot, pulsing flesh of her upturned pussy.

Her labia were thick and swollen, bright pink amidst dark, matted pubic hair, and eagerly revealing her tiny opening twitching with every rapid beat of her heart. And there, like a shimmering jewel, was the perpetrator of her desperate state; the vicious metal band around her clit cruelly twisted so tightly, the sensitive pearl had turned nearly purple and thrice its natural size.

A snarl ripped from his throat at the sight of her abuse, but it sounded like it came through water—from another plane of existence, where he was capable of rage. Here, now—all he knew was that hot, aching need to sate his female's torment.

Drawn in by the need to soothe, he bent down, buried his face in her wet pussy, and carefully sucked her clit in between his lips.

Georgia yipped, her entire body shuddering in

response. More liquid rushed from her core, the scent filling his nostrils.

Stars above. His entire being was already laser-focused on her desperate need, but the flood of her pheromones directly into his nose short-circuited his brain entirely. Groaning, he sucked her clit as gently as he could while she whined and rode his face, entirely focused on the dark magic's demand for orgasm, despite how painful the stimulation had to be.

When she finally came, it was with a cry and another gush of liquid that coated his face and made stars dance for his eyes.

"Kesh... Kesh, please..." Still panting from her release, she looked at him over her shoulder as he straightened back up, and the naked plea in her eyes clenched his heart as much as it made his dick throb. "I need you inside."

"I need to be inside you, too, love," he rumbled, wiping her liquids off his face before grabbing her hips. Her flesh felt perfect in his hands, as if she were made to fit in his grip.

Georgia keened as if in agreement, and arched her back, thrusting that perfect, swollen pussy up in renewed invitation.

"Shit, you're so tight," he groaned, spreading her entrance with his thumbs, testing its give. Even if he'd been capable of going slow with the scent of her heat melting his brain, this would still be painful for her.

"I don't want to hurt you," he rasped, gaze trained

on that glistening opening spreading with the pull of his thumbs. "Fuck, Georgia, you need to be trained for this, learn to open…"

"I don't care! Just fucking… fuck me! Right fucking now!"

He let out a surprised grunt at her furious snarl. Gone was the meek, subservient Breeder pleading for relief, replaced in the blink of an eye with a wild female with fire in her eyes and blunt teeth bared in threat.

Snarling, she tried to spin around, fingers curled as if they were claws, undoubtedly to rip at him. He kept his grip on her hips and yanked hard, sending her face first back into the mattress.

"You want it to hurt?" he snarled. "Let me prepare you—"

Dull pain from where her foot impacted with his knee cut him off.

"I don't need preparation! Are you fucking slow? I need your dick! Inside me! Right fucking now! I don't care if it hurts, I don't care if it splits me in two! *Fuck. Me!*" She tried to kick him again, and when he released her hips to grab her ankles, she thrashed like a wild animal, spitting and snarling in her efforts to turn around and rip him to shreds.

He'd never been so turned on in his entire, miserable existence.

Snarling, Kesh threw himself down on top of her, pinning her to the mattress with his weight. "Lie still! You want to be fucked? I'll fuck you until you plead for me to stop. Is that what you want? Is that what you need?"

"Yes! Yes, fuck, that's what I need!" Her soft, sweat-slickened body pressed up against him, warm and perfect and desperately trying to angle her ass to capture his cock between her straining thighs. "Kesh, I need you to make it hurt! I need you to fuck me until it stops!" Her efforts finally paid off, and she managed to trap his dick at the apex of her thighs. She let out a high-pitched keening and pressed back *hard.*

"Fuck!" Kesh grabbed her by the hips, stilling her attempt at splitting herself open on his cock, even though all he wanted to do was to follow through. His entire being pulsed in rhythm with that wet little opening pressing against the head of his cock, eagerly trying to swallow the tip, and it took everything he had—every memory of her vulnerable and frightened cowering on the floor for him to not give in and penetrate her with reckless abandon.

It wasn't helped by her whining, pleading sobs for him to *'just do it!'*

"Shh. Breathe, love. A nice, deep one for me," he rumbled, stroking her bucking hips with his thumbs while ensuring she couldn't push back further.

Georgia obeyed shakily, compelled by the rough dominance in his voice. Once she exhaled, Kesh pushed forward, pressing his thick cock head to her trembling opening.

"Ah!" Despite the twang of pain in her voice, the

horny little Breeder arched her back in an effort to help him in, pushing back against his force.

"Calm down, relax your pelvis. That's it, good girl." Her opening softened against him, her muscles relaxing just enough to let him press his head in to the rim, his ridges catching against her taut sheath.

"Ah, *shit!*" Her voice pitched to a whine, her body stiffening underneath him as the physical reality of submitting to a demon lord set in.

"You're okay. I've got you, love. Just breathe." Kesh drew in a deep, steadying breath too, forcing his mind from the first kiss of her wet inners to the tightness of her opening; the care he had to exert to enter her without damage. Georgia had yet to birth a child, and he hadn't had the chance to prepare her the way she would have been prepared, had this been her mating night.

"There's gonna be more pressure now, and then you'll feel my ridges. It'll hurt at first, but I promise, I won't go deeper until you're ready. Okay?"

Another whine, this time pleading. If she hadn't had her ring twisted, he may have been fooled into thinking she was begging for mercy, but the way she kept her ass pressed back against him showed the truth. She was pleading for him to just do it already.

"I know. But I'm not gonna rip you apart no matter how much you beg, so just *breathe.* Relax your pelvic floor. That's it, good girl... *fuck!* Breathe..." Anchoring himself with his grip on her hips, Kesh slowly pushed inward, timing the movement with her deep exhale. At the end of her breath, he eased off, only to increase the pressure when she exhaled again.

For five, agonizingly slow breaths, he slowly coaxed her pussy wider... wider... until *finally*—

"*Shit!* Fucking *stars!*" Wet, tight heat snapped shut around his full cock head, squeezing hard on his ridges. Blinding light sliced through his brain, brilliant and all-consuming. It was only Georgia's pained scream that kept him from following through on the instincts urging him to slam in to the hilt, to bury himself in the source of life itself.

"Breathe, *breathe!*" He growled the mantra as much to himself as to her, forcing air littered with her pheromones deep into his lungs.

"H-hurts! I want more!" she whined, body trembling in his grip, as if she didn't know whether to press harder back against him, or crawl forward to escape.

"I know, I know... I want more, too. Fuck, you feel so good," Kesh moaned, pressing his face into her wild hair. He wasn't going to be able to hold back for much longer. Every frantic pulse of her wet flesh against his sensitive ridges clawed at his fraying self-control, thoughts of finally uniting his flesh with hers pounding in his brain.

But his little female needed him to ease her into full submission.

Groaning, he reached beneath her and found her swollen clit with his thumb.

"Ah!" She yelped and jumped at the first brush of contact, but quickly pressed her mound to his palm in search of more stimulation.

"Yes, yes... Oh, God...!"

Anger itched at the edges of his conscience at her continual tendency to invoke divinity, but instead of punishing her pussy for it like every throbbing urge screamed to do, he channeled it into iron control of every movement, ensuring he didn't break her.

Slowly, firmly, he massaged her metal-encircled nub of nerves, forcing her focus to the intense sensation of stimulation and away from the hard pressure of his cock head inside her.

She mewled beneath him; groaned and panted—and soon, her pussy's death grip softened ever so slightly. Enough that he could finally push deeper.

"Fuck!" His roar overlaid hers as sharp sensation fired through his ridges and shaft. Everything was wet, tight, almost painful bliss. Mindlessly, he pushed against her pussy's resistance, slowly but mercilessly pressing his hips to her ass. Conquering her completely.

Through the roar of blood in his ears, he heard Georgia scream.

"Georgia... Oh, fuck, Georgia... Tell me you want this... Please, fuck, tell me... tell me you need me." There was no power in this world strong enough to make him pull out. All he could do, all he could offer his little female, was to use the last vestiges of his crumbling willpower to hold himself perfectly still inside her while he rubbed her clit and allowed her channel to get used to his presence.

"Kesh! Kesh!" The frantic sound of her whines shuddered through him, but she kept her ass glued to his pelvis, her rapid heartbeat echoing from her pussy and into his cock from their joining with every circle he rubbed on her clit.

And then, finally, like the most beautiful music, came his redemption:

"I need you! I want you! Don't stop! Please, don't stop!"

He let out a groan from the depths of his being, relief shuddering through every cell—and then burning to ash as he finally released the all-consuming fire of need.

The first thrust was painful for them both, and yet, nothing had ever felt as perfect.

Her cry raked goosebumps down his back. He buried his face in her sweaty hair and pulled her to his chest with one arm. "I won't hurt you. Trust me. Please, trust me. I need you so much. So fucking much. You're mine." The words spilled from his lips like a prayer, barely registering in his consciousness. In those moments, he was nothing but instinct and need.

He thrust again, and she took him. Encompassed every inch, every aching, needy molecule. And again. And again. Her cries turned throaty, her pussy's painful grip easing a little more for him each time his cock head kissed her cervix. Her body was adjusting to him—molding itself to fit him, to take him.

Primal satisfaction rushed through him, making him clutch her harder. Even her body knew the undeniable truth: she was his. Only his.

"Don't stop, don't stop!"

As if he could have, even if he'd wanted to.

"You need it harder? You want me to fuck that greedy pussy raw?" His voice was rough, deep—clawing its way up from the most primitive parts of his being. He raised up high on his knees to grasp her hips.

Her immediate response was to arch her back in wanton submission that drew fire up his spine. "Yes! Fuck yes, harder! Please, I need you harder! *Don't. Stop!*"

"I'll give you harder, my love. I'll give you everything you need—whether you want it or not." He dug his fingers dug deep into her flesh, ensuring she couldn't get away—and then, finally, he unleashed.

Georgia's screams pierced through his snarls of pleasure and the wet, continuous thwacking of his hips pounding against her ass and stretched labia. There was no holding back, no mercy—just the tight, blissful squeeze of his female's pussy learning to take him exactly like it was made to do.

She bucked in his grasp, cursed his name into the ground, and beat her fists against the mattress, but there was no escape.

Not that she wanted to escape, not truly. As much as she protested, as much as she fought him like the fierce little warrior he knew she was meant to be, her pussy remained upturned, swallowing him eagerly all the way to the root over, and over, and over again.

He lost all sense of time; all sense of anything that wasn't her—them. The only sense of moments passing came when her pussy began to convulse around him, and he knew it was it.

With a roar, he pushed her face into the mattress, raised up on his hands above her, and put the full force of his weight into his thrust.

She keened in desperation, but it wasn't from pain. A lesser woman would have shattered her pelvis, but Georgia was anything but frail. She was a Breeder, *his* Breeder, and she could take him. All of him.

"Kesh! Kesh, I'm gonna...!"

She clenched on his cock so hard he saw stars.

"F-fuck!" The curse shuddered out of his throat, and he barely managed to keep upright. When her pussy erupted in a series of wet spasms, and her keens turned to a sultry cry of release, there was nothing more he could do.

Pleasure erupted out of him in a hot spray.

His destructive magic followed suit, bursting into her with violence he could do nothing to stem.

"NO! NO, what have you done?!"

37
KESH

Dark magic slammed into his body, tearing him out of pure bliss as the power of it pushed him off Georgia's trembling body. Leaving her vulnerable and exposed.

A roar ripped from his throat as fury beyond comprehension slammed shut over his mind.

Mallorn stood in the broken-down doorway, horror and anger painted all over his face. Magic still sparked from his hands. "You *fucked* her! You could have killed her! Are you out of your mind, you piece of shit? That's *my* future mate! *Mine!*"

Another blast of power erupted out of his Second, but this time, it didn't make impact.

All that registered in Kesh's mind was that this male was trying to take Georgia from him. With force.

His fury exploded.

There was a mighty *boom*. Magic blacked out the air,

walls crumbled with a groaning screech as the building itself shook in its foundations.

Georgia screamed.

Fear shot through his fury, bright and horrific, turning murderous intent to single-minded focus.

"Georgia! I'm here, love. I'm here!" He stumbled forward through the slowly waning darkness, drawn to her like he'd been attached by a leash. She lay crumbled on the floor, curled around herself, black soot streaking her naked back and hips.

Kesh fell to his knees by her side and gathered her into his arms, protecting her body with his own. "Are you hurt? Tell me you're unharmed!"

"I... I think so," she stammered, voice hoarse; weak. Her hands found his arms, clinging. Instinctively seeking his protection.

Clutching her closer, he got to his feet, magic billowing around him in a protective cape.

The ceiling was gone. As were the walls. His entire apartment was one open wound, bare to the sky. Only a hastily erected magic shield kept the howling wind from tearing through the space.

His father, the creator of said shield, was crouched next to Mallorn—also contained in a swath of magic. Blood seeped from his Second's nostrils and fury blazed in his eyes.

"It seems we have a little... misunderstanding on our hands." The calmness in Kirigan's voice belied the situation entirely. "The girl is Pure. She belongs to a lord."

Pure.

Shock washed through Kesh's entire system. He stared down at Georgia safely nestled in his arms—at her naked body, and the semen still trickling from her flushed opening.

His father had called her Pure before her pheromones hit, and Kesh'd lost all sense—but he'd barely registered it at the time.

Had he truly known? Before he took her? That she wouldn't die from his need?

Horror that had nothing to do with Mallorn's attack turned his inners to ice.

"Pure?" Mallorn spat. "She's Pure, and you still dangled her in front of all your men—in front of *me*—to, what? Rally the troops? Ensure my loyalty? All the while, you kept her here, locked in your bedroom... for yourself?! What was the fucking plan, *your Highness?* Make her fall for you, make her *choose* you, so you wouldn't have to offer her to auction for the other lords?"

Mallorn's rage was like a storm of gnats biting at the edges of his focus. But he barely registered the words, the accusations. All he was capable of was the sharp cold spreading through his blood with every heavy thud of his heart.

"Get out." His voice came out shaky—unhinged. "Get out of my sight. I will deal with you later."

His Second's eyes widened, the rage turning molten, but Kesh had no capacity to care. He turned his gaze back to the woman in his arms, shifting his grip on her trembling body so he could turn her face toward him with a finger.

Her blue eyes were wide with alarm and her lips quivered.

A flash of every harsh thrust into her body lit up in his brain and shivered through his body. He'd been brutal with her. She'd begged for it, pleaded, but only because her ring had been activated.

He'd done to her what his father did to his mother.

The ice in his blood reached his heart.

He looked back toward the other two demons. Mallorn was gone, but Kirigan remained, still shielding the remnants of his penthouse from the wind with his magic.

"We need to move to the lower floors, get Georgia out of the open. Then discuss... what comes next." Without waiting for confirmation, he marched toward the stairway leading to the lower floors. They passed the open void of the elevator shaft, now sans carrier, Georgia clinging to him instinctively. Instincts seeking him for protection, despite what he'd done to her. His gut felt hollow as he carried her down five floors, making sure the structure above them wasn't compromised before he brought her into the empty space made up of steel and concrete.

He'd purposely kept the floors beneath his penthouse barren and unoccupied, making them easier to patrol and keep clear of hostile forces. It hadn't been enough to keep Georgia safe.

"What happened?" He turned to his father, still clutching Georgia tight to his chest. *"How* did this happen? I left you in charge of her safety, and you let a *goddess* near her?"

"She must have accessed the bedroom from the balcony and somehow blocked her magic's trace upon entering. I only noticed its lingering vibration once I entered the bedroom to investigate her screams." Kirigan calmly unbuttoned his shirt and held it toward Georgia. "Did she say anything to you, before the attack, dear one?"

Georgia accepted the shirt with trembling fingers. Kesh put her down to help her into it, frowning when she flinched at the cold concrete under her feet.

"Y-yea. She said... Fate needed a push. That..." She frowned, hands stilling before she could pull the shirt over her shoulders.

Kesh grabbed it from her hands, buttoning it around her trembling body, before lifting her back into her arms and off the cold floor. "What else did she say, Georgia?"

"T-that I have magic, but it needs to be unlocked, like the queen's was. And that..." Her blue eyes flashed up to his, large and uncertain. "That I needed to mate you or... or your father. She didn't care which. I think that's why she... She wanted either one of you to lose control and..."

"Claim you," Kirigan finished her sentence when she trailed off, his brows knitting into a frown. "So she knew you were Pure. But why would she want us mated? Why would she want your magic unlocked when it would only be used to strengthen our side?"

"She didn't say. She just..." Her bottom lip quivered at the memory of the violation. "I can't believe I risked my life to save her, and she was just... just..."

Under normal circumstances, Kesh would have been all too happy to point out that that's what happened when she let her stupid, soft heart overtake reason and self-preservation, but he couldn't. Not now, not with his semen still crusted on her nether lips and the knowledge of what she'd been through, at his hands, fresh in his mind. He gripped her body tighter to still his hands from trembling and forced his mind to focus on something actionable. Something that didn't make him feel like he might shatter into a thousand pieces if he thought about it for a single second longer.

"We need Kain here. And Selma—she's far more versed in the treacherous ways of goddesses."

Kirigan's disturbing eyes rested on his face for a long moment. Kesh got the uncomfortable feeling his father saw every petty, possessive urge he was doing his hardest to pretend wasn't there, but thankfully, he didn't comment on whatever he found. Instead, he said, "I already called them. They're on their way."

38

GEORGIA

Possibly the prospect of meeting the demon king and queen, whilst wearing nothing but an oversized button-down and with semen still coating her inner thighs, should have preoccupied Georgia's immediate thoughts.

However, nothing really penetrated through the fog of sheer shock and physical exhaustion as she sat in Kesh's arms like an overgrown toddler.

Her body still shuddered with the remnants of orgasm, and she still felt the echo of him in her aching pussy.

Georgia looked up at the demon prince, searching for... something. Even just a moment of connection. What they'd shared... there were no words. It had been brutal, violent even... and so intensely intimate, a part of her had transformed underneath him. Become something else, something new. She felt raw and vulnerable, and everything in her ached for his comfort; for a moment to look into his eyes and see the shift between them acknowledged.

He'd called her *love*.

He'd called her *his*.

She felt it in the core of her being. She was his now. Something had happened in those brutal moments beneath him, something irreversible. She was his, because... because there was no way she could have come out of that experience and been anything else.

But was he hers, too?

He refused to look her in the eyes, though he held her so close the heat of his skin radiated into her body, promising her protection, promising affection.

Mine.

She knew she was his, because she knew why he wasn't looking at her. Could feel his pain and fear like they were her own.

He didn't see a willing woman in his arms. He saw his mother's broken shadow.

"Kesh," she said softly, trying to get him to just... look at her. To reach him.

Only a slight tightening of his grip on her body indicated he'd so much as heard her. He didn't look down at her, didn't connect his gaze to hers.

Didn't give her the reassurance she needed.

Her heart sank, but she didn't push him. There

would be time for that later, when they were alone. She wouldn't force him to open up and talk this through now, in front of his father—the monster responsible for his scars. Instead, she placed her palm over his heart in a soothing gesture, and rested her head against his shoulder. He might be lost in the darkness, but she wasn't. What they'd just shared... There was no changing the outcome. Closing her eyes, she nuzzled her face in against his meaty shoulder. *Mine.*

Strong fingers stroked through her hair, almost as if he could sense her possessive thoughts. Perhaps he could. Georgia sighed softly and allowed the sensation of his fingertips against her scalp to soothe her reeling mind. Yes. Everything would be okay. They just needed to talk, and once he had met with his brother, and his scary father left, they would.

———

THE DEMON KING WAS EVERYTHING SHE COULD HAVE expected. He was as huge as Kesh, with auburn hair and the identical strong jaw and nose as both his father and brother—and he had the same air of too much mass compressed into his already overwhelming, human form, too. Even the scowl on his face as he entered the empty space under Kesh's penthouse was identical to his brother's.

The queen of demons was a different story.

"Hi! Georgia, right? I'm Selma. Oh, you poor thing, did he shred your clothes? Honestly, Kesh, if you were gonna go all caveman on the poor woman's dress, at least have the decency not to blow up her wardrobe." The small, round, very human woman shifted the baby in her arms, to better give Kesh a disapproving look, before she switched her attention back to Georgia.

"How are you hanging in there? Do you need some demon-free time? We can step out for a minute if you need, just the two of us."

Before Georgia could so much as open her mouth, iron bands clenched around her body as Kesh clutched her tighter to his chest. "She will be going *nowhere* without me." There was enough of a growl in his voice that the king's eyes narrowed, and he took a half-step forward, shielding his mate and baby. "Watch how you talk to your queen." His tone was low and rough, the edge of a threat unmistakable.

Kesh's lip curled up in response, but Kirigan stepped in between them.

"Boys. Now is not the time. We have urgent matters to discuss, and no time for posturing. The girl is unharmed, Selma, and separating her from Kesh right now is bound to end in violence. Give him some time to calm, and you will be able to check on her if she so wishes. For now, I need everyone to focus on the real threat: a goddess made her way past our defenses and into Kesh's *home.* Undetected. Which means she is old, and she is strong—and she has taken an interest in our family.

"I hope I don't need to tell you how serious this is. Nothing good comes from divine interference, and we can ill afford to fight a battle on two fronts."

"Well… what did she want? Do we know?" Selma asked, frowning. "I know you've got that whole demons-versus-gods thing going on, but they aren't all entirely awful. Just like not all demons are. Perhaps we can, I dunno, figure out a way to work *with* her?"

All three demons present gave her a look that suggested she was off her rocker. King Kain looked gently concerned, Kesh like she had just suggested the Earth was flat, and Kirigan simply sighed, exasperated.

"My love, she is a goddess. She wants nothing but our destruction. You know this. Bealith isn't representative of gods—she only helped you because she sees you as her subject," Kain said, his gentle tone suggesting he was trying to make a particularly fragile mental patient see reason.

"Only the desperate strike bargains with gods, Selma," Kirigan said, his voice patient but firm. "They are no different than demons when it comes to trickery and deceit. And this one has already proven as much. She violated Georgia to make either Kesh or I frenzied enough to claim her. Supposedly to activate her powers, like Kain did for you. We need to figure out why she would want more power concentrated in our family

—and we need to figure out where she has taken the Stone of Power she stole, and what she intends to do with it. She is not a potential ally—she is a threat."

Selma gave a small shudder, seemingly as creeped out as Georgia at the thought of Kirigan claiming her, but kept her cool. "Right. So she wants us to have more power? That doesn't sound like a potential ally to you? I'm not saying her reasons are going to be savory, and I'm absolutely not saying what she did to Georgia is acceptable. I'm saying we might have a singular goal aligned, and it would be stupid not to consider if we can use this as an advantage against the Europeans."

"Selma..." Kirigan paused, and Georgia could almost swear a flicker of something other than disturbing nothingness passed through his dark eyes. Something that looked almost... pained. "This girl is the first Pure Breeder to have been discovered since your auction. Before you, it was my late wife—who was the first in over thirty years. You are *rare*, dear one. So valuable, two continents are at war for the rights to you.

"If Kesh or I *had* put a claiming mark on this girl, it would mean the past three Pure Breeders in existence. across the entirety of the globe, would have belonged to our bloodline—and this time, we would have taken her illegitimately. Kain's claim to the throne would crumble in a matter of days. Even our staunchest supporters would abandon us.

"Whoever this goddess is, she is not our ally. If her plan had succeeded, our bloodline would likely end before Georgia's powers had a chance to awaken. If they would at all. Our first move needs to be securing the girl from further interference, and then we need to uncover this goddess's identity, location... and motives."

Selma sighed. "I'll try to contact Bealith—see if she is willing to share any information on this goddess."

"Wait... wait, what do you mean I'd be Kesh's 'illegitimately'?" The words were out of Georgia's mouth before she could stop them.

They all turned to look at her—the queen, the king, and the monster who'd sired him. She felt the full weight of their attention, and the full vulnerability of her own undressed state, but this was all wrong. What they were saying, the implications... Her gut felt tight with mounting foreboding, and despite her attempt to keep her voice calm, it still quavered. "I was told I get to choose. How can it be illegitimate if I pick?"

There was a moment's silence, the tension in her gut only increasing.

"She's right," the queen said. A brief but genuine smile flickered over her features. "If she chooses Kesh, that is her right."

"Selma, it's not that simple," the king said, his voice soft. "The law that allows Breeders to choose their own mates has only been accepted for regular Breeders—not Pure ones. You know how difficult it was to get support for it. Attempting to convince the lords that the third Pure Breeder in a row should go to our family, simply because she chooses to, is going to cause a riot. Especially because Kesh has had unrestricted access to her while thinking she was a regular Breeder. It would be argued that he's used this time to influence her affections."

Selma pinched her lips. "What do you suggest, then? That we tear her away from him? That we allow the lords to treat her like a piece of meat for auction, just because it's *inconvenient* for our politics that she picked your brother? You would never have allowed that to happen to me—yet you expect Kesh to allow it? And Georgia to submit to it? In the end, no matter how you look at it, her choice is all that matters."

A glimmer of relief threaded through Georgia's chest, softening the tightness there ever so slightly. The queen was on her side. They'd find a way—

"You're wrong." Kesh's voice was so soft, she barely felt the rumble of it where she was pressed against his chest. "It's not her choice. It's mine."

"Excuse me?" Selma asked, but her voice drowned in the thundering of blood in Georgia's ears as she looked up at Kesh and saw the distant, cold expression in his eyes. She knew what he was gonna say before the words came, and gut-wrenching pain twisted her heart.

"Kesh... Kesh, no. Please, look at me, please—" She reached for his cheek to turn his face toward her, to make him look at her—make him remember what she knew they'd both felt when he took her, but he didn't budge. He looked straight ahead, at his brother, not so much as acknowledging her panicked attempts at reaching him. There was only cold indifference in his voice when he said, "I am not mating this Breeder. Nothing is more important than our family's survival. She will pick her mate among the lords who support us. That is my choice."

39
GEORGIA

"Kesh..."

His name fell from her lips one final time, but the constriction of her throat made it sound like barely more than a whisper.

He ignored it, as he had her other attempts at reaching him, and turned his attention to his brother. "My Second knows of the Breeder's Pure status. If this information hasn't spread already, it's only a matter of time before it will. We need to regroup and prepare to send out invitations to her courting as soon as possible if we are to avoid a revolt. I suggest we move to my official premises and proceed. The sooner this is handled, the better for everyone."

Horrible, cold numbness sank deep into her chest.

This was really it. Everything she'd felt, that all-encompassing connection, truly meant nothing to him. Or, at least, less than his duty to his family.

She supposed she shouldn't have expected anything different. He'd made it clear from the beginning that his priority was to ship her off to some other demon as soon as possible, so he could return to what truly mattered to him: his war, and his family's survival.

She'd been naïve to think that moment between them meant the same for him as it did for her. The cold numbness spread through her whole body. He was a demon. What did she expect? He was a demon; any sense of humanity she'd seen during their time together would never measure up to the truth of his nature. And she... she'd allowed herself to believe that there was more to him, more to their so-called *connection* than the simple fact that he and all his kind saw her as a womb to breed, because... because he was the first person since Larry to ever treat her like she mattered.

The humiliating truth made her close her eyes, the sound of Kesh's family turning to a wordless murmur behind the rushing of blood in her ears. How pitiful, how disgustingly weak she was to have pinned hopes of *love* on the Prince of Demons.

The air felt too thick to breathe, his strong arms around her body like iron bands restricting her lungs.

"Put me down."

Kesh ignored her—they all did. They were discussing how to host this 'courting', this ritual to pretend she had semblance of choice in the matter.

"Put me *down!"* Anger, refreshing amidst the icy numbness, washed through her. This time, her voice projected loud enough that he couldn't ignore her.

Kesh's eyes flicked down briefly, but didn't connect with hers. "No. The floor is cold, and you have no shoes." His tone was calm but vaguely irritated. Like she was a persistent child demanding sweets before dinner.

"I don't care. Put me down *right now."* Her skin crawled, the sensation of his warmth against her no longer soothing, but violating—a reminder of a betrayal she had no right to feel. "Put me down, put me down, *put. Me. Down!"*

"Kesh—" There was a hint of warning in the queen's voice, but he ignored her, as he did Georgia.

"So it is decided? We will send for the lords this evening, and the courting will begin tomorrow aftern —" His voice died when Georgia's hand impacted with the side of his head with as much force as she could muster. Finally, his black eyes met hers.

"Put me *down,* Kesh. I don't want you to touch me— ever again." There was more malice in her voice than she'd ever contained in her life.

His jaw worked once. Twice. Something flared in his gaze, angry and raw, and for just a moment, she thought she saw just a sliver of regret. Her heart gave a spasm, somewhere past the rage, but then his expression smoothed into cold indifference and the fizzle of hope withered before it ever fully sprouted.

Silently, he let her slide to the concrete floor. Immediately, icy cold bit into the soles of her naked feet, and for a split second, she wished she was back in his arms. Then he turned his back on her, as if she didn't exist, and stalked out of the empty space, leaving her behind with his family.

Yes. What she'd felt underneath him, in his arms... even when she'd held him while he cried over the loss of his mother—to her human heart, those had been moments of connection had been so profound, it felt like it'd changed something in the very makeup of her DNA. To a demon, however... To a demon, they'd meant nothing.

She meant nothing.

———

KESH'S OFFICIAL PREMISES—AKA THE CONVERTED CASINO that housed his throne room—were in wild disarray all throughout the night.

From the room on the second floor where she'd been sequestered, Georgia watched men—she assumed demons, but thanks to her brand she couldn't know for certain—drag chairs and tables and enormous flower decorations out of an unending caravan of trucks and into the throne room below. It seemed the 'courting' of a so-called Pure Breeder required more pomp and circumstance than the ones who couldn't survive a demon lord's penetration.

Sometime in the early morning hours, when the exhaustion finally won out over misery and she managed to doze off, a large but not ridiculous plate of breakfast and a beautiful red gown appeared in her room. She woke up to the scent of bacon, and the dress draped across the dressing room chair.

It looked as expensive as any of the beautiful dresses Kesh provided for her during her time under his care, but on closer inspection, the fabric was stiff and heavy, with thousands of shimmering diamonds covering the bodice and rippling down the full skirt. He hadn't picked this one—his selections had always been silky and butter-soft, beautiful but made for a comfortable skin feel first and foremost.

Whoever had selected the red gown had considered how to make her appear striking and regal, but not how it would feel to wear such a dress.

Georgia slid her fingers over the stiff fabric. It was no doubt as expensive as the jewels covering it, but to hold up the heft of the gown it had to be rigid. She didn't mind—once upon a time, as a little girl, she would have given her left arm to wear such an extravagant dress. With what lay ahead in her life, she really should try to find the silver linings where she could. What did it matter that her already broken heart twinged at the knowledge that Kesh hadn't cared enough to choose the dress she would wear to her courting ceremony? He'd made it plenty clear it was an inconvenient event he needed over with as soon as possible, so he could return his focus to what mattered to him: his men, his territory, and his family.

Her morose thoughts were interrupted by a soft knock on the door. The queen entered, sans baby.

"Hey. I just wanted to check up on you. I know it's all... a lot right now."

Georgia shrugged, turning away from the dress. "It's been a lot for a while now. This is just... an extra helping of the crap-cake."

Selma sighed softly. "I'm... I'm truly sorry, Georgia. I keep trying to stop this... vile custom of using us as something to be owned, but as much power as I have now... I am not more powerful than the primordial need they have to possess."

"It's not your fault. I guess... it could be worse. Kesh said something about you changing the customs they used to have."

Selma gave a humorless laugh. "Yeah... they used to auction us. We got dragged naked into an arena surrounded by demons who then bid on us. Whoever offered the most money, while also being able to win a fight against the other competitors, would get to fuck us right there, in front of everyone, then haul us off to birth children.

"Giving you some semblance of choice in who you mate... It's not enough, but it's... a starting point."

Georgia shuddered at the far-too-vivid description. "It's... It's more than I thought I'd get. It will have to be enough."

The queen's chocolate eyes studied her for a long moment. "Do you love him?"

There was no point in asking who she meant. Georgia exhaled a slow, steadying breath and shook her head. "How could I? I'm just... I'm just an inconvenience to him. And he's... cruel, and brutal... a cold-blooded killer. No, I don't love him, I just..." She trailed off, unsure how to finish that sentence. When she dared a glance at the queen, the other woman's face was drawn in gentle empathy.

"There was a time I didn't think I could ever love a demon. They are... all those things. Monsters. But they are more than that—so much more. And there is no shame in loving them."

"It doesn't really matter whether I do or not. He's made his choice. At least I get to make mine today, too." Georgia managed a half-smile. "No one marries a demon and expects happily ever after. But it's comforting to know that it is at least... a possibility, of sorts."

Selma bit her lip, nodding as she let her gaze slide over the red gown. "There was... something else I wanted to discuss with you. The goddess who came to Kesh's penthouse, did she... give you anything? Before she activated your ring?"

Georgia frowned at the change of subject. "Give me something? No. Why, what would she have given me?"

Selma reached into her pocket and pulled out a

palm-sized, smooth, and dully glowing stone. A shock of recognition ran up Georgia's spine at the sight of it.

"Nothing like this?"

"W-what is that?" The memory of Suzanne in her child-disguise, pressing an identical stone into her hand, prickled unpleasantly at her brain.

"This is a Stone of Power. One of the three most powerful demonic artifacts ever created. The European royals gave one to the old queen—I won it from her when I defeated her. According to my mate's father, the lords Kesh was fighting in Maine had another, but the goddess who visited you yesterday stole it.

"Kirigan is right, of course. The gods are devious, and whatever plans they have are rarely for the benefit of humans, and definitely not those of us mated to their arch enemies. But... I do find it curious that the thief of this second stone sought you out and attempted to force a mating between you and a member of the family that currently holds another such artifact." There was no accusation in the queen's eyes, just calm reassurance. She knew.

"She gave it to me in Maine, when she was pretending to be a child," Georgia whispered, the implications still too enormous to process. "I thought... I thought it was just a pretty stone. But I... I don't have it anymore. It was in my pocket when Kesh... He ripped my clothes. It's probably still somewhere in the rubble of the penthouse if you want it."

Selma's gaze sharpened. "If I want it? Do you not

understand—this stone is *power*. And it was given to you. Over the centuries, demons have fought and died for these things, but you would just... offer it to me?"

A flush rose to Georgia's cheeks. Unbidden, Kesh's derogatory words about her inability to take what she wanted resonated in her mind. But that was ridiculous. She didn't *want* some demonic artifact weapon—all she wanted was peace. A quiet life with someone who didn't hurt her.

"What would I use it for? I'm not at war—you are. Better you take it than me. I wouldn't even know how it works." Turning back around to the magnificent red gown laid out for her courting ceremony, she ran her fingers over the fabric once more, trying to find some softness in it. "As I understand it, all I can do is marry one of your allies to ensure your support doesn't crumble and you lose this war. Love was never in the cards for me, but if I can help in some small way to keep yours intact... that's a nice bonus."

"Georgia—"

"I don't want it. All I wanted at the start of this was for my brother to live. He did. Kesh cured him. I don't want any part in demonic relics, or war, or... or *Fate*. Or whatever that goddess thought was going to happen when she gave me that stone. Please, just... just let me try to find whatever peace I can."

Selma was quiet for a long time. Finally, her voice softer than before, she said, "The main thing I've wanted for our kind was agency over our own lives. If this is your choice, I will support it. But please know that you aren't alone, even when it may feel like it. If you ever need me in your new life, reach out. I will come."

————

THE RED GOWN WAS AS UNCOMFORTABLE AS IT WAS beautiful.

Georgia stared silently at her own reflection, trying to reconcile the perfectly decorated doll she saw in the mirror with the empty sense of despair gnawing at her insides.

She'd never given much thought to who she'd marry. *If* she'd marry. Sure, when she was young and had felt alone and overwhelmed with the responsibilities her mother had foisted on her, she'd harbored dreams of some modern-day prince sweeping in and taking her away from all the difficulties. But as she grew older, it just hadn't felt realistic. To fall in love? To find someone who understood her, cherished her? No, that had never been in the cards. Not for her.

A firm knock on the door pulled her thoughts to the present. She drew in a deep breath, steeling herself, and turned away from the mirror just as the door swung open.

Kesh stood in the opening, dressed in his leather armor and with an iron crown decorating his brow. In his human disguise, he looked like a beautiful warrior prince straight out of a fairytale, and the sight of him made everything numb tense up inside her.

For a long breath, they stared silently at each other. Georgia's pulse thudded in her temples, down her body and deep into her core where she still felt the sweet ache of their illicit union. A cruel reminder of those haunting moments where she'd thought...

She forced a breath through her nose and deep into her lungs, raising her chin in defiance. There was no point in poking that wound anymore, and certainly no reason to let him see how much it still hurt.

"Are my suitors here, then? Take me to them. I wish to meet my future husband."

40
GEORGIA

Kesh's only response was to hold out his arm in silent invitation to join him.

It felt like a mockery of chivalry, the way his posture remained arrow straight and his face a blank slate as he waited to lead her to her Courting. Like he'd never touched her, never been inside of her. Never called her *love*.

The skirt of her dress swished as she crossed the room and, hesitating for only a moment, placed her hand on his offered arm.

For a long breath, he remained still, frozen with her hand resting against his leather arm guards. She dared a glance up and met his eyes. And for a *moment*... for a single split second, she could have sworn she saw... *something* in those black pools.

It was gone before she could decipher what it was. If it was even more than a figment of her imagination.

Without a word, Kesh began walking, leaving her to keep up with his long strides.

He led her down long corridors with worn, red carpet still present from the days when the casino's upper floors functioned as a hotel. Apart from taking out the slot machines on the lower floor, installing his imposing throne, and boarding up the windows, the prince really hadn't done much to change its 90s-style *free lobster buffet* aesthetics.

As he pushed open the double doors leading to the stairs, a low murmur of voices drifted up from the throne room.

Her waiting suitors, no doubt.

"How many are there?" she asked, hesitating at the top of the stairs as she realized she'd never asked. Her previous courting had been just a handful of males. This... this sounded like a lot more.

"Just under fifty. Thirteen of whom were on the fence about whether to support us or the Europeans, until the chance at winning your favor arose." He began descending the stairs, expecting her to follow.

She did, despite the knot of anxiety in her tensing with each step.

"Oh. Well... That's good. Your brother must be pleased."

"Yes. He must."

He was such a fucking dick. Her cheeks pulled up in a mirthless smile. What the hell was she doing, aching at every clipped word he offered? He'd told her to grow a spine multiple times. It was time to do just that, because this? Fretting and worrying about a man who was happy to hand her off like a maiden of old in exchange for military support? This was beyond ridiculous.

"Right. Well, I guess we shouldn't keep them waiting any longer." She snatched her hand off his arm and brushed past him down the stairs, hiking up her skirts to allow for a fast descent.

Kesh made a displeased noise from behind her. She ignored him and continued to the bottom of the stairs and straight ahead, toward the double doors leading into the throne room.

"Georgia!"

Without looking back, she let her skirts drop and pushed both doors open with more force than needed.

They swung open with dramatic gusto.

There may have been just fewer than fifty demon lords present, but there were far more males in the large throne room. Servants, bodyguards... fucking goblet holders, for all she knew. Maybe three hundred, at her startled estimate.

Every single one of them turned to look at her, the murmur of voices dying to complete silence at her appearance.

There was a clench of terror at being their sole focus, a primal human need for self-preservation stirring somewhere deep down. The need of prey to flee and hide. She pushed it away with a force of will.

Women with spine didn't cower.

"Hello, boys." Georgia raised her chin and stepped forward, into the throng of demons.

They parted for her like the Red Sea, creating a clear path all the way to Kesh's throne elevated on the dais straight ahead.

Well, why the hell not?

She sailed forward, chin up, spine straight, regal as fuck. The only sounds that followed her were the swish of her dress and the clicking of her heels. When she reached the dais, she hiked her skirts to ankle height and took the two low steps up, then turned around and sat down on Kesh's throne like she belonged there.

From her new perch, she had a clear line of vision to the open double doors she'd just marched through. Kesh now stood in them, taking up the entirety of the frame. His face looked like a thundercloud.

Sick satisfaction thrilled up her spine. With just the tiniest hint of a smirk, she leaned back on his throne and cocked one ankle on her knee in imitation of how he'd sat when she was first brought to him, broken and terrified. Spineless, as he'd called her.

Asshole.

Kesh's nostrils pulled up at the unspoken provocation. Black eyes locked in hers, displeasure rolling off his wide frame in waves. Without a word, he stalked down the cleared path toward her with long, sure strides. Like a warship on smooth water.

He didn't stop until he was right in front of her.

Georgia tipped her head back to look up at him, but made no attempt to move out of his seat.

The silence in the throne room was deafening.

His eyes narrowed in warning.

She narrowed hers in response.

His lip curled up, bearing the faintest hint of what now looked like a blunt human fang at her, but before she could mimic the gesture, he grabbed her by the upper arms and hoisted her off the throne.

Georgia gave an indignant squeak, then a huff when he took his seat and placed her on his lap.

"I was sitting there."

"You were. And now, I am." His strong hand curled around her hip, holding her in place, before he directed his attention to the gathered demons.

"Forty-nine lords have been invited to court the most recent Pure Breeder to surface. Yet my throne room is packed with six times that number of males. If you are merely here to gawk at the girl, this is not the time nor the place. We're at war. My lords, please dismiss your entourages to the perimeter of the building. If you wish to court the Breeder, you will do so alone."

Mutterings rose from the crowd, then a stream of demons began filing out through the double doors. When movement finally stilled again, she could see guards stationed around the entire perimeter of the large hall. Fifty men remained in front of the throne. Like Kesh, all had that same air of barely concealed power thrumming under their skin. Bar none, each of them had his gaze fixed on her.

Georgia lifted her chin higher. They may look like barely leashed predators in human disguise, but she wasn't prey. They were here to win her favor, not tear her apart. Unlike the male whose lap she was perched on.

"Your Highness... The invitation stated there would not be an auction, but a courting of this lovely girl. Perhaps it would be prudent to explain what this will entail?" The one male in the center of the room whose eyes weren't glued to her bowed his head respectfully at Kesh.

The prince exhaled an annoyed sigh. "What does it entail, Governor Maell? Do our most powerful, most clever lords really need instructions on how to win a woman's favor? It's a courting. Present your case to her. Tell her why she would be happy at your side, in whatever manner you see fit. In the end, she will choose the man who most appeals to her. The only rule is that *you will not lie to her*. Whatever life you offer, you will be bound to provide. Should you be proven to have lied in order to gain her favor, you will lose your right to her. Claiming mark or no."

A murmur rose up among the gathered males. The shock was palpable in the room.

Something tried to soften behind Georgia's ribs. Something ridiculous that she wanted no more part of. But still. This stipulation...

Even if he didn't care about her in the way she'd been stupid enough to think for a few, precious moments, he did care enough to ensure she wouldn't be tricked into a life she didn't sign up for.

Yes, what a fucking hero he is.

The wave of irritation at her heart's attempt to soften for the brute who'd broken it only a day before made her able to push down the small spike of gratitude.

"*She* will choose?" a large, red-haired male asked from the crowd. His handsome but brutal face was drawn in outrage. Georgia made a mental note to stay far away from him.

"You would *break* an established mating claim!?" another gasped.

"Yes, the Breeder will choose her mate from among you herself." From behind the throne, Kesh's father stepped forward to stand by their side.

Without conscious thought, Georgia shrank back against Kesh, her newfound *no-more-fucks-to-give* attitude not quite matching up to the eerie aura this particular demon gave off.

Kesh tightened his grip on her hip, a soft rumble escaping his throat. It cut off abruptly, and she got the distinct feeling the soothing sound in response to her unease had been as involuntary as her instinctive urge to seek his protection. He did, however, keep his tight grip on her hip.

If Kirigan noticed the effect he had on her, he didn't

pay it any mind. "And yes. Your words to her today are a binding contract. You know the queen's wishes—this is the compromise that was reached with her. No one will break your sacred bond to your new mate if you ensure she is *happy*. Which was already the sworn duty of any male who claims one of our desperately rare Breeders.

"We have lost too many mates to careless treatment over the years. Yes, a broken mate bond is a fate that often leads to death. But at least it will only be *your* death. You will not end the life of a precious Breeder under your responsibility. She would instead be allowed a new Courting, and hopefully given to a more worthy male, capable of keeping his vow to his mate's happiness. I would think none here would have any qualms about this stipulation? After all—the mothers of our species *must* be protected above all else."

The man who had spoken first—Governor Maell—bowed his head. "Wise words. And wise of our queen to recognize the disconnect between our old customs and our Breeders' needs.

"My mating took place centuries ago, when times were... *different*. But I can admit in hindsight, things would have been... smoother over the years, had my mate chosen me willingly. Considering the blessing our king and queen's union has brought both them and us, it would be foolish to disregard the value of changing our practices, however challenging it may seem to realign our very nature, no?"

There was another murmur of discontent among the gathered lords.

"That's all well and good, but it doesn't change the fact that she has spent days alone with the prince," a man with long, black hair and a scar down his lip bit out, keen eyes remaining fixed on her, despite addressing Kirigan. "Days where he will have influenced her, given her pleasure... He branded her, did he not? How is this... *courting*... anything but a pretense to sanction another Pure Breeder falling into your family's hands?"

This time, the murmurs rose to angry shouts of agreement.

"It's unmatched corruption!"

"*This* is how you reward us for supporting your family's claim to the Americas?"

"*Silence!*" Kesh's voice boomed through the room, making Georgia jump. The gathered lords quieted, but the tension in the room was nearly physical. Lips pulled back in silent snarls, fists clenched. A sharp, pungent stench touched her nostrils, like a watered-down version of the smell that had encapsulated the sleepy fishing village in Maine during the battle there. The acrid spell of violent, dark magic, this time, waiting to be released.

"You abandoned the old king for his family's treachery in attempting to steal an illegitimate mate to their bloodline. If you are so easily convinced I would do the same, you have chosen your allegiances poorly."

Every word out of Kesh's mouth was tense, clipped. "I will not court this Breeder. She will choose her mate without a bid from me."

Icy talons pierced her gut as the hall erupted in calmer, though clearly surprised, murmurs. She straightened her spine until it hurt, letting anger wash away the throb of pain at his words.

"And what motivation does she have to choose *anyone?*" the redhead from before asked. "If the choice is purely the Breeder's, what's to stop her from simply staying here, unmated?"

Enough. Full stop. Enough.

"First of all, 'the Breeder' has a name. It's Georgia. Hi. That's me." She leveled the redhead with a stare. "As for what guarantees you have that I won't simply opt out of your little arranged wedding scenario—you're looking at him. Staying *here* would mean staying with this asshole. So don't you worry your pretty little head about it, 'kay? I'd quite literally rather poke out my own eyes than spend any longer than I have to with your so-called prince. I'm sure *one* of you can manage to scrape together some semblance of a decent personality and a non-rapey marriage prospect."

A low, dark rumble vibrated from Kesh's chest into her—nearly imperceptible to her human hearing, but she felt it everywhere her body touched his. Every hair on her body stood on end in response to the primal threat of that sound, but it was a sick thrill, not fear, that shot up her spine.

His thick fingers dug into her hip, hard, and for a short second, she thought he'd yank her back against his chest. Punish her.

A long, tense moment passed as the gathered lords stared from her to Kesh in utter shock at her open disrespect of their volatile prince. Awaiting his reaction.

Slowly, finger by finger, he relaxed his grip on her hip, then leaned back against his throne in utter dismissal, allowing her to get up.

Good riddance.

Georgia got to her feet, lifted her chin, and surveyed the forty-nine men there to court her.

Even blind to their true nature as she was with the mark Kesh had given her, it was impossible to pretend they weren't something *other*. The low hum of power in the room itched against her skin, and the way they watched her with singular, unified focus was as preternatural as it was unsettling.

But they were also her future.

Her choice.

"Well? Are you going to court me, or what?"

41
GEORGIA

Another moment's complete silence. Then, the black-haired lord with the scar rumbled a low laugh. "You're a spicy little thing, aren't you? Very well. Let's get you courted, Breeder." He stepped forward and bowed elegantly before the dais. "Please allow me the honor of a dance."

"There's no music."

His lips curved up in a wry smile. Music taken straight out of a Regency movie began playing in the hall, summoned from thin air. He held out a hand toward her, palm up.

"Well, that's certainly a more pleasant use for your magic than what I've seen so far." Georgia took the first step down the dais, studying his features. He was handsome in his human disguise, and the way he looked at her as if she were a surprising puzzle wasn't entirely unpleasant. If he *had* been human, no doubt he'd be several miles out of her league.

And yet, a knot of reluctance tightened her stomach at his outstretched hand.

Without meaning to, she glanced over her shoulder at Kesh.

He didn't even look at her. He was staring straight ahead at the gathered lords, chin propped up on one hand, looking regal and bored.

Georgia drew in a deep breath and turned her focus back to the waiting lord. Carefully, she placed her palm in his.

He closed his warm fingers around her wrist, carefully, and gently drew her down the final step and closer to his body. "Do you know the steps? Modern women dance to different music, I know."

She shook her head, and he smiled indulgently. "Don't worry, little Breeder. I'll show you."

"My name is Georgia." The tartness of her voice made him shoot her a chastised grin.

"My apologies, Georgia. Breeder is a title of honor, but I will use your lovely name if you prefer. Is it a shortening of Georgina?"

"Yeah. My mom was reading a book with a main character called Georgina at the time she found out she was pregnant with me." There was an odd twinge in her chest at the thought of her mother being pregnant with her. She remembered her excitement when she was carrying Larry, but somehow the idea that she might have felt similar joy with Georgia was... alien.

She pushed it down, with the rest of the tense emotions she didn't have the capacity to deal with. "And what can I call you?"

"I am called Arduk." He slipped his hand to her waist and pulled her in close. A snarl rose up from several of the other lords. One of them took a step toward them, his nostrils hiking up in a silent snarl that made Georgia's heart give an involuntary spasm of fear.

Arduk looked up over her head to the prince. "Your Highness—if we are to court lovely Georgina without... incident, may I request your tempering rule to avoid any interferences? I would so hate to rip the horns off Lord Haru and traumatize the sweet girl in my arms, but if he takes another step in my direction, I'm afraid blood will be shed in your hall."

"You are monopolizing the girl!" the male who'd stepped toward them—presumably Lord Haru—snarled. Growls of agreement from the others rumbled through the throne room.

"You are the most powerful beings on this continent. You are what stands between us and destruction at the hands of our enemies, demons and gods alike. Yet *this* is how you behave? One whiff of a Breeder, and you need to be reminded what I will be duty bound to do to you if you put the girl in any whisper of danger? Form a fucking queue! You get five minutes each. I am *not* losing some of our most valuable allies over a cunt."

Kesh's voice cracked like a whip, boredom giving way to irritation. Though his words weren't aimed at her, they still cut to the bone.

She sucked in a slow, deep breath and, projecting her voice with her whole chest, snapped, "And just so we're clear, anyone who would ever so much as consider referring to me as a 'cunt' doesn't need to bother with their five minutes. I will not be considering your courting."

"Noted," Arduk said, a playful smirk pulling at the corner of his lips as he led her a few steps away from the dais. "You wish to be treated with respect. It's a fair request."

"It's not a *request*," she growled as he began leading her in a few simple steps to follow the old-fashioned music. "It's a bare minimum."

"Hmm, a bare minimum? I'm intrigued. What else do you require from a suitor, sweet Georgina?" He moved her easily around the floor, making the others step out of their way. She *felt* their fury, though it was squarely aimed at Arduk, not her.

She arched an eyebrow at him. He was looking at her with equal measures of interest and amusement. She was beginning to get the uncomfortable impression he saw her as something akin to an exotic pet throwing a hissy fit in captivity. "Oh, you think I'm going to do the work for you? You're a demon lord. I'd think you'd be able to do better than your average human man putting in bare minimum first date effort."

This time, the rumble of his laugh was accompanied by a gleam of challenge in his dark eyes. "Oh, I most certainly am able to. Now, let me see... If you pick me, pretty Georgina, I will shower you with adoration. Not a day will pass without my expressing my gratitude that you are mine. I will kiss every one of your fingers, your toes. And I will kiss you between the legs before every mounting."

Heat flamed her cheeks as discomfort crawled up her spine. "Really? *That's* your idea of courting?"

His smile heated. "Naturally. You'll be spending a lot of time underneath me. I want you to know that I will ensure that time is... pleasurable to you."

Why was it always about sex with demons.

"That's great. And how about if I tell you 'no'? Will you respect that?"

Arduk's gaze remained fixed on hers. "Sometimes."

"*Sometimes?*" She narrowed her eyes at him.

"You have a lot of fire, my lovely. It's... *refreshing.* I suspect you would grow quite bored with a mate who caved to your every command, not to mention... it's an unnatural state for a female to dictate the terms of mating. So yes, Georgina. *Sometimes* I will respect your no. And sometimes, you will learn to enjoy the female pleasure of complete submission."

Considering her experience of Hell, it shouldn't feel like a punch to the gut to be told he would *sometimes* rape her. But it did.

She'd been a victim then—small and helpless and

tricked into signing a contract out of desperation. Here she was, in the prince's hall, in her beautiful dress, spine straight, head held high, and powerful suitors vying for their five minutes of her time... and this demon lord still felt completely comfortable telling her to her face that he planned on ignoring her 'no' when it suited him.

He had to know it would do nothing to endear him to her, but he still smiled down at her, confident that this would not make her reject him.

Before she could make her mouth produce anything more than a wheezing sound, another lord stepped in between them, closing a firm hand around Arduk's biceps. "Your time is up. Step aside."

The black-haired demon's lip curled up in a silent snarl at the other's touch. The music stopped abruptly. "Get your hand off me, or lose it. Your choice."

"Arduk. Play nice. You've had your allotted time. It's Iye's turn to court the Breeder." The deceptively gentle chastising didn't come from Kesh, but from Governor Maell.

Arduk's nostrils flared wider, but after a tense moment, he released his grip on her waist and stepped back, allowing the other demon to take his place.

"My beautiful lady, I am Iye." The demon took her hand in his, bowed deep, and placed a light kiss on her fingers. "Lord of the territory you know as Washington State. It's an honor to meet you."

"Um... hi." She tried to bring her focus from the

unsettling moments with Arduk to her present suitor. "Nice to meet you, too."

"Would you care to continue dancing?"

At least he was polite.

"Sure, why not."

He placed a hand on her hip and took her other in his, pulling her in closer—still keeping just enough of a respectful distance between them. New music flowed through the hall, a low drumbeat unlike any she'd heard before.

"Arduk gave you a taste of the music from his youth —this is from mine," Iye said, his dark eyes on hers, drinking in her every expression.

"Oh. It's... beautiful, but very different from anything I've experienced." She frowned slightly, trying to decipher the rhythm. It went up her spine, almost primal in its nature.

"It would be. I was born more than two thousand years before you graced this Earth, my lady."

"Wait—two *thousand* years ago?!" Georgia gaped up at the deceptively youthful-looking being. "That's... wait, is that... normal?" It struck her that she hadn't asked Kesh his age. She'd assumed he was around her age, but in hindsight... Perhaps that was why he found it so easy to detach from what they'd shared. If he were anywhere close to this lord's age, perhaps their time together barely registered as more than a blip in his conscience.

Without thought, she glanced up at the throne. He

wasn't even looking in her direction. His focus was on his father, who stood in front of the prince, bent to whisper something into his son's ear.

"Normal? Perhaps not quite. It is not common to reach my age. The older we get, the stronger our inherent power grows. There is... let's call it *incentive* to keep your rivals from growing too aged." Iye's smile held little warmth. "Unfortunately for my enemies, I didn't prove exactly easy to kill. And now I am among the eldest demons on this continent."

"That's, uh, quite an age gap." Georgia glanced at him before looking back up toward the prince and his father. Kesh's nails were dug into the armrests of the throne, drawing deep grooves into the wood. Whatever he was being told, it clearly wasn't sitting well. Probably something about their stupid war. "I'm not really sure what we would talk about. I must seem like a toddler to you."

His warm fingers moved from her hip to her cheek, turning her attention away from the dais and back to him. "I assure you, you do not. Do not concern yourself that I might be unable to sate your hunger for conversation, my beautiful. All my age will mean for our mating is that I am strong enough to keep you and our offspring safe. Age does not work on our minds nor bodies like it does on human men. You will be well tended under my care."

Perhaps this wasn't the worst offer she could get. He was polite, he was promising actual conversation, and considering how they were at war, someone strong enough to keep any children she might have with him alive seemed like a solid proposition, considering the circumstances. So long as...

"And if I say 'no' to certain parts of this... tending? What will you do?"

His lips curled in a small smile. With a gentle caress to her cheek, he moved his hand back to grip hers so he could swing her around, returning them to the rhythm of the ancient drums. "My beautiful, I know you will ask this of all of us, but courtesy of the courting rules the prince has implemented, we cannot lie to you. I will not mistreat you. I will not savage you. And yet, 'no' is not an option for a demon's mate. In time, you will learn to appreciate this."

"*Appreciate* it? Are you nuts?" Georgia dug her heels in, pulling her hand out of his light grasp in the process. "What I *appreciate* is having a choice! What I *appreciate* is not having my free will ignored!"

Iye bowed his head lightly, entirely unfazed by her anger. "I understand. A Breeder's lot is burdensome; but it is necessary for the mating bond that you learn to enjoy the power that lies in submission. If you become mine, I promise that any resistance will be met with gentle insistence, not brutality. You should ask your coming suitors if they can swear to the same."

Georgia gaped up at him, not managing to make her mouth form any sort of response before he stepped away. He was immediately replaced by another demon

—the redhead who'd been so outspoken about her right to choose her own mate.

"Pretty Breeder… aren't you lovely?" He gave her a slow look from head to toe that immediately made her skin crawl.

"No. I'm *not* picking you." She made to turn away from him—toward literally any other male—but his strong hand closed around her biceps, forcing her back around to face him.

"Do *not* turn your ba—"

He didn't manage to get another word out. One second his hand was around her arm; the next it was gone. Fine, wet mist covered her face as she stared at the bloodied stump of his arm.

The redhead let out a pained gasp, but it was drowned out by the *rumble* echoing through the throne room.

"You dare lay a hand on her? *Under my roof?*" The prince's rough voice was barely recognizable, the thunder of it vibrating off the walls. "You paw at a woman *under my protection?*"

Still in shock, Georgia turned toward the dais—as did the rest of the lords

Kesh was no longer lounging on the throne. No longer looking bored.

He stood at the top of the dais, both hands clenched into fists, and something bordering on insanity flaming in his black eyes. Dark shadows oozed from his hulking form and crept along the floor, slowly filling the hall.

"Lord Ithikan offers his deepest apologies. *Does he not?*" Kirigan stepped forward from his place next to the throne, placing himself between his son and the rest of the room. His eyes speared into the redheaded lord, who was clutching at his stump to stem the bleeding.

"Yes. My sincere apologies, Your Highness. I meant no disrespect," he managed to grit out.

Kesh's nostrils flared in response, but this time Lord Maell stepped in. "Your apologies are noted. Please allow the prince's men to escort you off the premises. Your presence is no longer required at this courting."

Ithikan's face twisted in anger, but another look at Kesh's darkly shadowed figure, and he bowed his head an inch. "Certainly."

A soft murmur spread among the other lords as four of the guards stationed along the walls approached the maimed lord to escort him out of the room.

"Please, my lords—don't let this little, ah, *incident* ruin the sanctity of such a joyous event. Who is next to court the lovely Georgina?" Governor Maell smiled widely at the room, ignoring the still-simmering prince behind him.

After only a brief hesitation, another male stepped up to Georgia, blocking her view of the dais, though being careful not to touch her.

"My lady. You are even more exquisite covered in blood."

He made it sound like a compliment, but it wasn't

until then that Georgia realized what the wet mist covering her face was: liquified demon hand.

"Oh, *ew!* Ew, ew, *ew!*" She wiped desperately at her face with an arm—it came back smeared in red.

"Servants! Bring the lady a bowl of water and a soft cloth!" her newest suitor demanded at no one in particular, swiftly clocking on that 'blood' wasn't her accessory of choice.

A bowl of warm water and a cloth made from silk arrived in seconds. She grabbed it without fanfare, dunked it, and for a good five minutes, her whole focus was on scrubbing demon off her face and arm. Once she was finally satisfied she wouldn't accidentally swallow a few drops of Ithikan, she handed the bowl back with a shudder and glared up at the dais, toward the instigator of her impromptu blood shower.

Only he was gone.

As was his father.

Lord Maell remained at the foot of the dais, hands clasped behind his back—clearly left in charge of the rest of her courting.

With a deep breath, she turned back to the demon who thought she looked lovely in blood. "And who might you be, then?"

———

After eight lords, it was becoming clear that Lord Iye was accurate in his prediction. So far she'd asked them all, point blank, what would happen if she turned down their advances once mated, and thanks to the rules of the courting ceremony, they answered her honestly.

Every single one confirmed that a 'no' from her when it came to sex would be ignored. They wrapped it in pretty words and promised she'd *enjoy it,* but at the core of each answer lay the same, inescapable truth: she would be raped. Repeatedly.

For the rest of her life.

The fire that had brought her into the room, head held high and determined to choose her own fate to the extent she could, faded a little more after each dance.

What choice was there to be had if the outcome would always be the same?

The queen may have done her best to lessen the trauma that came with being a demon's Breeder, but even she was not powerful enough to change their very nature. Whichever male she chose, he would never view her as a person. Just a Breeder.

She looked up at the many faces eagerly vying for her attention and desperately tried to cling to the strength that had allowed her to face them before. It crumbled the harder she grasped for it. The faces began to blur—turning into one looming mass of black eyes and smiling mouths concealing sharp teeth behind pretty promises of devotion.

This was her life. There was no way out.

"Georgia?"

She jolted when someone gently wrapped a hand

around her wrist. When she looked up, a familiar face frowned down at her.

Mallorn—Kesh's Second.

"Kesh needs to see you. *Now.*" The last word was growled at the nearby lord, who'd been about to step in for his turn to court her. "She'll be back shortly."

"What's the meaning of this? We're in the middle of the ceremony! This is preposterous!" her would-be suitor snarled.

"You should bring that up with the prince, then. But I'd suggest you don't—unless you also want to lose a limb. He's in a foul mood today, which should be pretty fucking obvious. Or you can wait for twenty minutes, then get your chance to court the lady with your eyeballs still intact. Your call. Georgia, *let's go.*"

Relief flooded her body. A small respite from the mass of males. As little as she wanted to see the prince right now, whatever Kesh wanted, it was serious enough to send the warrior he'd seemed like he wanted to murder only yesterday. And she was grateful for the intermission.

"Alright. Take me to him, then."

His grip on her wrist tightened. Without another word, he led her out of the hall and away from the lords.

42

GEORGIA

Mallorn's grip on her wrist remained gentle as he led her through the double doors and down a wide corridor. They passed several guards, each of them frowning at the demon by her side, but before any of them could open their mouths to ask, Mallorn growled, "Kesh wants to see her. Immediately."

No one interjected as he guided her around the corner and into a room that looked like it had once been an office. A few dusty filing cabinets still sat abandoned in one corner, but outside of that, the room was empty.

Georgia frowned and turned back to Mallorn as he closed the door behind them. "Where's Kesh?"

"He's gone." The demon finally released her wrist and went over to rummage through one of the filing cabinets.

Her heart did something strange in her chest. Lifted and dropped. "Gone?"

"He left. Alone. No guards. No backup." His voice was tight but controlled. "He asked me to bring you to him. Quietly."

Georgia stared at his back. This made no sense. The way he'd treated her, the way he'd given her up like she meant nothing to protect his family... "He... he asked you to, what? Smuggle me out?"

Mallorn paused in his rummaging. His shoulders tensed for a moment, then relaxed again. "Yes. Now, before it's too late. He couldn't do it alone—he'd never make it past the other lords with you. But I can. He asked for my help in getting you to him."

"But... why?" The words were out of her mouth before she could stop them.

He scoffed softly. "You know why. He was *inside* you, Georgia. For a lord—especially someone like Kesh—there's no coming back from that. It'd be easier for him to live without his lungs than to let you go."

The words hit her like a physical blow. Something behind her ribs cracked open—painful hope, too sharp and too sudden. Her breath caught, and she pressed a hand to her chest, as if she could hold the broken pieces of herself together long enough to almost believe him. "He... couldn't let me go? But... everything he said... about his family being his priority? He invited all these lords here to court me."

"He had to pretend to comply—his father wouldn't

stand for anyone or anything getting in the way of protecting Kain and his family. Not even Kesh. So this is the way it's going to have to be. He will take you somewhere safe and hide you until the war is settled and no one can force you apart." Mallorn turned back around toward her, now with a silky bundle of fabric in his hands retrieved from the old filing cabinet. He shook it out, revealing a gorgeous, smoky-silvered cape that looked like it'd been plucked straight out of a fairytale. "Here, put this on. It's laced with invisibility runes, but it will only last a few hours. We need to be far away once the magic wears off. Come, Breeder. Let's not dawdle."

Kesh had planned this. He... he had chosen her over his family, after all. Her broken heart ached as something deep behind her ribs began to mend.

But as she stepped forward to reach for the cape, a whisper of guilt made her pull her hands back. "If he leaves and takes me with him... what will happen to them? The king and the queen? Will the other lords abandon them? And if Kesh isn't here to help—?"

"You really are a soft soul," he cut her off, but his voice was quiet, almost gentle. He held the cape out toward her. "They won't know he took you. Once you are safe, he will return. And he will blame me, in league with the Europeans, for your disappearance. The other lords won't know of his betrayal, and another instance of European treachery will only serve to strengthen American alliances. Once the war is won and the threat to the king has been eliminated, he will pretend to find and 'rescue' you, claiming to have needed to mate you to save your life. No one will suspect the truth."

Her knees felt weak. This... this was real. Despite his pretenses not to, Kesh had felt it, too. The powerful pull between them. He'd broken her heart, but only to save them both, and his family, too. Breathing shakily, she let Mallorn put the cape around her shoulders and pulled the hood over her head. His finger brushed against her cheek, unnaturally warm despite his human disguise.

"And you... you are okay with taking the blame? What will happen to you?"

Mallorn exhaled, a joyless smile pulling on his lip. "My first loyalty, my first responsibility, is to my prince. The... *dust-up* we had yesterday may have looked serious, but it was only a moment of my instincts getting the better of me. Kesh knows that, and this is what he needs from me, and so this is what will be done. Don't worry for me, Georgia. I will be fine. Now, come. Let's get you out of here. I have a car waiting. Follow me and be as quiet as you can. If anyone sees me trying to steal you away, I will be executed on the spot, and you—you will be given to someone other than Kesh."

———

THEY PASSED SEVERAL GUARDS ON THEIR WAY THROUGH THE corridors toward the back exit. Georgia clung to the inside of the cape, her heart beating so hard against her ribs she feared one of the demons might hear, but while they acknowledged Mallorn, no one even glanced in her direction.

They made it unaccosted to the back exit tucked behind a loading bay area. Mallorn nodded at the two guards stationed there, but when he reached for the door, one of the guards stepped forward and placed a hand on his shoulder. "Halt. You know we are in lockdown until the Courting is over. Kesh's orders."

Mallorn paused. One eyebrow crept up as he slowly looked down on the guard's hand on him, then back up to his face. "Bold of you to presume you get to command me, Girak. Do not get in my way. You won't like the consequences."

Girak lowered his hand from Mallorn's shoulder, but he didn't step out of the way. "The prince was clear. *No one* leaves without his explicit directive to us. If he confirms, of course we will let you be on your way, Mallorn. But until then, it's our hides if we let anyone pass. Even you. And you know he's fucking literal about it. He's been a complete ball ache since the Breeder arrived."

Mallorn narrowed his eyes slightly. "My orders are urgent—and from Kirigan, not Kesh. So either you move, *now,* or I will *make* you step aside. Once I return, I will tell Kirigan that his pressing and time-critical business was delayed because of *you.* And trust me—once I do, you will long for the time before he learned your name."

There was a moment's tense silence. Then, without another word, Girak moved back to the side of the door with a short nod.

"Wise choice." Mallorn pushed open the door and stepped through. He held it open just long enough that Georgia managed to dart through behind him.

She followed him around the corner at the back of the old casino and into an alley, where a sleek, black car with tinted windows was parked.

"The backseat doors are open. Keep the cape on and the hood up until I tell you otherwise," Mallorn said softly.

She did as she was told, sliding into the leather seat and tugging the cloak tighter around her body, hood shadowing her face.

Once the door closed behind her, Mallorn slipped into the driver's side and switched the engine on. "Make sure you stay down until we're there. The runes won't last much longer, and I can't risk anyone catching a glimpse of you."

"Okay." Georgia slid down on her side, curling up against the backrest. Her heart still thumped unevenly in her chest, but when he pulled out of the alley and out onto the busy street, the first threads of relief started threading through her nervous system. They were going to make it. He was taking her to Kesh—Kesh, who had chosen that unnamed, unrelenting pull between them over honor, over duty. Over everything.

However confusing and horrible the past twenty-four hours had been, regardless of the hurt and betrayal she'd felt in his hands, it was worth it. *Would* be worth it. Because the one thing that had been brutally clear as she allowed the forty-nine lords to court her, the one inescapable fact she had refused to acknowledge, was that he was her only shot at happiness. Of a genuine connection—frail and fraught, but real.

Her one chance at true love.

———

Neither she nor Mallorn spoke for the next twenty minutes as he drove them through the city's streets. She couldn't see much from her low perch on the backseat, only the sides of indistinguishable buildings and occasional flashes of the sky, darkened by the window tint.

When the car finally slowed, then stopped, he pulled the handbrake and looked over his shoulder in her general direction. "You can remove the cloak now, Georgia."

Finally.

She pushed off the seat to sit upright so she could undo the cape and pull it off her body. "Are we there?"

"Yes." Mallorn plucked the silky fabric from her hand, folding it away in the glove compartment.

The car was parked in what looked like some sort of

industrial car park, but from the backseat she couldn't see much apart from a tall chain link fence and broken concrete.

Mallorn opened the driver's side door and slipped out of the car, then came around to the back and opened her door. It was only then she realized he'd had the child locks on.

"Come. He is waiting."

She got out and frowned as she looked around. This place... why did it seem... familiar?

The demon by her side grabbed her by the elbow, his fingers still gentle, but the tug he gave her was firm.

Automatically, she followed him as he led her around the car—and she finally realized why this place seemed so familiar.

Ahead of them was a grim-looking warehouse, its roof covered in rusting corrugated steel. Atop the singular door, the word *Hell* flickered in red neon.

He'd brought her back to the brothel.

"Wait..." Confusion and a gut-level hit of dread made her feet falter. "Kesh said to meet him *here?* That... that can't be right. Why would he—?"

His hand around her elbow remained firm, the gentleness of his grip waning when his steps didn't slow with hers and she was pulled along beside him. He didn't look at her. Didn't answer.

"Mallorn? Why are we meeting him here?" Her voice pitched higher, the dread solidifying. She dug in her heels. He grabbed her by the arms and slung her over his shoulder.

Too late, realization set in.

Kesh wasn't waiting inside.

"No! No, what are you doing? No! You can't do this, please, no!"

She screamed and kicked and fought to get off his shoulder. It was no use. He held her in place with no visible effort and carried her over the threshold, back into the nightmare she'd only narrowly escaped.

It was dark inside, the air frigid against her skin. No one sat at the reception desk this time, and as Mallorn's long strides carried her down the long corridor with the makeshift chambers of horror lining each side. But though the smell of sex lingered, no one occupied the fluid-stained beds inside. The brothel was empty.

"Why is she *screaming?*" There was a voice up ahead —unfamiliar, but authoritarian. Disapproving. "Tell me you haven't hurt the girl."

"Of course I haven't," Mallorn growled. He carried her the last few paces, then put her down on her feet in a horribly familiar room: Jimmy the Pimp's office. "She's just familiar with this place. No woman willingly steps foot in a brothel twice."

Georgia immediately tried to dart back out of the room, but Mallorn easily kept a hold of both her arms, rooting her in place.

"Let go of me!" She kicked at his shins, and connected, but he didn't so much as flinch. He did, however, give her arms a small squeeze, as if to settle her. It didn't have the desired effect, but the gentle contrast to the kidnapping he'd just performed startled her enough to cast a look around the room.

There were two men in there with them. One was heavy-set, wearing a pinstripe suit she recognized as easily as she did the calculating look in his eyes: Jimmy, in his human disguise. The other was a stranger—one with an intimidatingly tall and broad frame that somehow seemed to contain more mass than it could believably hold. A lord.

"She's *'been here before?'*" There was dark ice in the stranger's voice. Slowly, he turned his dark eyes toward Jimmy. "You *whored* a Pure Breeder?"

Jimmy swallowed and took a half-step backward. "N-no, of course not, Your Highness! I would never— There was a *misunderstanding,* you see. She was brought to me as payment for a debt. Once I realized what she was, *of course* I *immediately* changed any plans to work her. She's untouched. I swear it."

"Well. Not entirely untouched," Mallorn grumbled.

The stranger shifted his focus to him, his black eyes narrowing slightly. "Not *entirely...?*"

"Prince Kesh had her. Released inside her. He would have claimed her, had I not interrupted."

"The usurper's brother is no more a prince than his brother is king. If you wish to live under my family's benevolent protection, you will do well to remember this." The lord held Mallorn's gaze for a moment longer, then he turned his attention to her.

Instinctive fear ran up her spine the second his eyes connected with hers. They were cold, ruthless, despite the smile he offered her.

"Ah. Well. Mishaps happen, don't they, little Breeder? We'll have you tested for pregnancy, and should the mongrel's seed have taken root... Well, there are remedies for that." He inhaled softly, his smile tightening at the corners. "You reek of fear, sweet one. Please try not to. I don't much enjoy the urges it brings up in me."

Georgia stared up at him, the horror of his words filtering through her panic. *Remedies.* He was talking about... She hadn't even considered the possible consequences of her wild, heat-fueled time with Kesh. Hadn't had the presence of mind, with all that came after. But this stranger was right—she *could* be pregnant.

Her knees turned soft with fear, one hand finding its way to her abdomen on instinct alone.

The lord flattened his lips in an expression of overbearing annoyance. "Ah yes, my apologies. That was... indelicate of me. You are hard-wired to feel protective of any offspring, even if sired by a cretin. But worry not —if we *do* have to take unfortunate measures, you should be gestating again within your next cycle. Now, really. Do try to control your emotions. You're making my skin... itch."

"I... I don't understand. Who are you? If you wanted

to court me, why am I here? You could have come to the ceremony—?"

The stranger let out a short, sharp laugh. "Oh, my dearest girl. A *courting* ceremony? Precious. No. I am Prince Aragalan, first in line to the throne of the *rightful* King of Demons. And I will not be courting you. I will be bidding on you at your auction in Rome tomorrow evening. And I intend to win.

"But *my* family upholds traditions, and we will allow the lords who support us to partake in the bidding for the right to your womb. They may not stand a chance against me, but it's important they think they do to secure their continued loyalty. Keeping the lords loyal proved... *difficult,* once word got out that the American imposters had acquired a Pure Breeder they allowed to be courted by *their* supporters. But now, thanks to our friends here," he nodded toward Jimmy, "you belong to us. And our supporters will fall nicely back in line. Within a year, I will have a son to establish my lineage, just in time to take back the Americas from the scum who thought they could splinter *our* rule."

The rightful King of Demons.

Ice-cold dread slowed her racing heart as the full realization of Mallorn's betrayal set in. She turned to look at him. "You're *selling* me to the Europeans? Scheming with someone like *him?*" She indicated Jimmy with a weak hand gesture. "Why? You're his Second. I don't understand why you would do this."

A flicker of pain crossed Mallorn's features, quickly smothered with anger. "You are still blind to his true nature. Your heart makes you dumb. Loyalty did the same to me. I thought him my friend. He never was. He knew my deepest yearning—knew all I wanted was a mate, a child.

"And the second he got the chance, he used that knowledge. He dangled you in front of me, in front of all his men, to tighten our loyalty when all along... you were Pure. You could never have been ours. And he used you too, too.

"He made you believe he would protect you, didn't he? Did he perhaps even let you believe he loved you? The second I told you he was waiting for you, that he chose you over his family, over power, you came with me. But the truth is, Georgia, he will never choose you. You were never anything more than a pawn in his quest to maintain power for his family. *That* is where his loyalty lies, and where it will remain. So I did what I had to do to protect *my* future. *My* family."

"It is a shame the American usurpers don't understand the value of rewarding loyalty. But, I suppose, their mistake is our gain. You will both be richly rewarded for your efforts in bringing my family a Pure Breeder. A mate for you, young warrior. And safe haven as well as my family's royal stamp of approval to run your business out of Rome for you." Aragalan gave Jimmy a smile devoid of warmth before he turned back to Mallorn. "Now, come along. I want the Breeder aboard my jet within the hour. We have a long flight back to Europe."

43
KESH

"You need to get yourself under control. Now."

Kesh paused his pacing in the anterior room Kirigan had dragged him to after *the incident* with Lord Ithikan's hand and bared his teeth at his father's infuriatingly expressionless face. "You think I'm not? You think this... this *farce* would continue for so much as another second if I wasn't?"

Kirigan's expression stayed blank, but the weight in his gaze remained suffocating. "You look at her like she is your undoing. You show your vulnerability with every breath, every movement. You revolve around her, and it is obvious to any man not too bespelled by the promise of her to look. We cannot afford this *infatuation*, Kesh. Forget what would happen if our supporters realized you've had her—that the only reason you didn't claim her yourself was your Second's interruption. We're at war, and if your focus doesn't return to that singular fact soon, we're going to lose. You're distracted by this girl, by the promise of her pheromones, believing it's *love.* It's not, I promise you."

"And what would you know about love?" The words were out of his mouth before he could stop them. They hung in the air between them, thick and acrid; an old wound rotting at the center.

"What would I know about love?" Kirigan's voice was deceptively soft, but though his expression remained blank, something sick and unsteady flickered in the depths of his black eyes. "You ask me that, after what happened with your mother?"

"My mother? *Love* has nothing to do with what happened to her." The wound ripped open. Three decades worth of pus spilled out. "*You* happened. You *broke* her, just like I would break everything pure and light in Georgia if I let myself do what every instinct in me screams for. You think *I* think this is *love?* I know it isn't! I am not fucking capable of loving someone as good, as gentle, as her. Just like *you* were never capable of loving my mother.

"Because that's what we do, isn't it? We eradicate anything that feels good, anything that means something, until it's as empty and dark and disgusting as the act that made us. You raped my mother to create me, just like your father raped whatever hapless female birthed *you.* That's all we are. Generations upon generations of violations made flesh.

"I thought it was just *you.* Kain—Kain loves Selma.

He was willing to let her go, to let her be free. But it's not just you. It's in me, too, this... fucking sickness!"

Snarling with the tension coiling in his chest, he punched a fist into the nearest wall, desperate for any sort of relief. None came, even as the plaster cracked and crumbled around his knuckles.

"I could have killed her! When I smelled her, I didn't know—what if she hadn't been Pure? I would have killed her with my need. So no, Dad. This isn't *love* any more than you raping Mom until she took her life to escape you was love. It is nothing but a monster aching to ruin the only good thing it's ever encountered!"

For a long time, Kirigan said nothing. Only Kesh's ragged breathing filled the room. He knew he'd pushed too far, said things that should never have been voiced.

He didn't care.

He *couldn't* care about anything but the unbearable ache behind his ribs that had settled in ever since he realized what he'd done. How close he'd come to ending the creature of light who'd held him while he cried for his mother's death. A death he'd nearly replicated with her.

"When your mother died, she took a part of me with her," Kirigan said, the quietness in his voice anything but gentle. "Not because I loved her. I did not. What your brother found with his mate is not possible. *Love* for us is not possible, because it requires us to deny the very thing we are.

"No. The day I claimed her, she carved a slice of my

innermost being and replaced it with her soul. My penance for taking her freedom. The price we *all* pay when we claim a mate. When she died, she left a hollow in me that will never be filled.

"I can't stop Kain from giving a piece of himself away—it's too late. The damage is done. He's forever tied to this... fiery soul. And in her, he's found the one thing that was never supposed to be possible for our kind. *Love.*" His face twisted with the word. "He thinks it a blessing, but the truth is that it doesn't matter what he feels for his Breeder. She will always be a liability to him, a weakness he can do nothing to shed. Which means I have to do anything and everything to ensure she doesn't die. Because if she does... I will lose him.

"But as much as I can't let you throw away our alliances for this Georgia and risk his Selma's life in the fallout, I also can't risk *yours*.

"*If* you give this Breeder a piece of yourself, as I gave mine to your mother, then you risk losing it when she decides she would rather end her life than live it with you. And trust me—nothing is worth that. *Nothing.* There is a reason most demons who lose their mates don't survive it, Kesh. You've seen what I've become. I will not allow the same fate to befall you. Nor Kain. So yes, my son. You *will* get ahold of yourself. You will let one of our allied lords mate her. And if the need persists, then I will find you a female demon to slake your desires in. I will handle this, Kesh. All you have to do is let go of a future that could never have been anything but misery."

This was the closest his father had ever come to verbalizing that Kesh's survival mattered to him. That he cared.

It was possibly as near to love as he could ever come.

And it tasted like ash.

"I don't know how to let her go when the fate I'm surrendering her to is no better than what she would face with me."

And there it was. The shameful truth he couldn't suppress, no matter how hard he tried, admitted on a whisper so raw there was no place to hide.

Whoever mated his gentle little human would force her submission.

He was a monster; he would ruin her. His hands or those of some other monster, her fate was the same.

Yet his instincts screamed *no*.

His instincts promised him he would never hurt her.

But his instincts lied. He'd already hurt her.

"Kesh..." For a moment, there was a flicker of something almost like regret in his father's eyes, so brief he might have imagined it, before the usual dark nothingness slid back in place. "She can't be—"

A knock on the door interrupted whatever he was about to say.

"Come in," Kesh snapped, not wanting to hear his father's denial of what his entire being screamed for.

Sefron opened the door. "Your Highness, Governor Maell wishes to know if you will keep the Pure Breeder long? The lords are eager to continue the courting ceremony." He grimaced. "And by 'eager', I mean they're about five minutes from ripping the horns off each other with impatience."

Kesh frowned, his attention snapping fully to the guard. "What do you mean, *will I keep her long*? She's not with m—" Ice-cold dread crashed through his nervous system as realization hit his body before his brain. He was moving before the full weight of terror hit. "Who took her? When did they take her?"

Sefron blinked, shock filtering over his features. "Your Highness, no one *took* her. Mallorn came to bring her to you about half an hour ago. He said you needed to see her."

Mallorn.

The name rang through him like a hollow strike.

His Second. His most trusted friend, up until yesterday.

The man who'd accused him of using Georgia to manipulate him. Who'd seen him take the woman his friend had wanted for himself.

He'd felt fear before, especially since the gentle little Breeder came into his life, but nothing... nothing like this.

"Sound the alarm. Lock down my territory. No one gets in, no one gets out."

"Your Highness, surely Mallorn wouldn't—?!"

"Do it!" Kesh spun back around to his father. "Call Kain. Tell him she's gone. Tell him whatever the fuck he needs to know to deal with the fallout."

"She's disappeared under your care, Kesh. It's prudent for you to stay and—"

"I don't give a shit what's prudent! He *took* her. I'm getting her back. And so help me—if you try to stop me, you'll be the first thing I burn.

Only silence followed him as he strode out of the room to find the woman he could no longer pretend he was capable of letting go.

44
KESH

The doors barely survived when Kesh shoved them open. The corridor around him was empty save for the pounding echo of his footsteps. His magic clawed under his skin, demanding release, demanding blood—but he kept it leashed. Had to.

Until she was safe. Until she was back.

The two guards in the surveillance room jolted upright when he slammed inside, all *heat* and barely controlled rage.

"Footage. Storage corridor. Mallorn. Now."

"*Mallorn?* Why—?"

Kesh's snarl cut off the demon unwise enough to question his instructions.

Fingers fumbled at keyboards. A monitor flickered. After a moment... *there.*

Mallorn, with her.

Something ached below his ribs, like a wound. He leaned forward on both hands and stared at the feed until they disappeared into an old office—one of the few rooms in the building with no camera.

On-screen, Mallorn stepped out again a few seconds later, alone. His face was blank. But not empty.

"Slow it down. Half-speed."

The demon at the console slowed the feed. Kesh leaned closer. Mallorn's mouth was flat, but there—left eye twitch. Eye ridge movement. Again.

Three glances.

To the side. As if checking something. Or someone.

And then—

A brief moment with the guards at the exit. Mallorn approached without urgency. Said something too low for the cameras to catch. Tapped the clipboard Yerren held. Waited for a nod. Walked out.

He didn't hurry.

Didn't fidget.

Didn't look back.

Kesh moved.

The hallway blurred past in peripheral streaks. The door to the old office cracked when he shoved it open.

Silence.

He stood on the threshold, breathing shallowly.

His power stirred, reaching without his command.

There was... *something* just beyond sensation. Like the edge of a dream. Like reaching in the dark for someone who had just left the bed.

Not scent. Not magic. Not memory.

Presence.

It wrapped around his ribs like the ghost of her body in his arms. She had been here.

He growled low, chest tight, then stormed out.

———

OUTSIDE, YERREN AND THE OTHER GUARD JUMPED WHEN KESH approached.

"You let Mallorn pass. Despite my orders to let *no one* out," Kesh barked. "Tell me why. *Now.*"

Both guards flinched at the barely controlled smolder of their prince's volatile temper.

Yerren swallowed. "He claimed he had urgent business for Lord Kirigan. He said it had been cleared. W-was that not—?"

Kesh didn't let him finish. "Where did he go?"

"He walked straight out to the alley," the second guard said quickly. "Got into his car. Headed east, toward the ninth turnoff."

Kesh didn't wait for further directions.

He reached the alley within seven seconds.

The air was thick with motor oil and old brick dust, but beneath it, beneath everything, was her. Twisted and fading, but *real.*

And Mallorn's car had gone east.

Kesh's breath stalled in his throat.

That route.

The route to *Hell*.

He took her back to the brothel.

Back to Jimmy.

Back to *enslavement*.

His Second. His most trusted.

The betrayal struck like a blade to the spine. Not just a theft. Not just treason.

He had *delivered* Georgia.

To that place.

To that fate.

The air around him crackled with his darkness.

Minutes that seemed like hours passed in blur that felt like drowning, then the doors to *Hell* were giving way beneath his hands, slamming open with a groan that echoed through the dark.

Kesh stepped into stillness.

No lights. No movement. No scent of blood or sex in the air. Just cold, abandoned silence.

But she had been here.

That tether deep inside him pulled taut. Not her scent. Not her magic. Something else. Like the memory of her fear stamped into the walls.

He forced down the rage clawing at his throat. If he let go now, if he gave in before he had her—

She would be gone.

He moved deeper into the brothel, past empty booths and overturned beds. No bodies. No women. No demons.

Each step made it harder to breathe.

Then—

A sound.

Small. Muffled. From the back of the building. Jimmy's office.

Kesh stilled.

Heat bloomed under his skin, quiet and lethal.

He turned toward the door. And walked in.

THE OFFICE DOOR, UNLOCKED AND UNDEFENDED, CREAKED open under Kesh's hand. Inside, Jimmy stood with his back turned, crouched over his desk. A large suitcase lay open on the floor, glittering with jewels, and gold, and something small and wrapped in velvet that glinted in his hand—an artifact, maybe. Irrelevant.

The demon froze when he heard the door. Turned.

"Your Highness," Jimmy said, too quickly. "I didn't expect—"

Kesh's hand closed around his throat before the last syllable hit the air.

The room lit up with magic, raw and scorching. Power curled through his fingers like black fire given shape.

"You get one chance," Kesh said, voice low and lethal. "Where. Is. She?"

Jimmy's eyes bulged as he clawed at Kesh's wrist. "Wait—wait, please—just listen—" The velvet-wrapped artifact clattered to the floor as he thrashed. "I didn't hurt her! I didn't touch her—I swear on my blood—"

Kesh said nothing. Just watched. His grip didn't tighten, but the magic did. It seeped through Jimmy's skin like acid, slow and deliberate. The pimp gasped as steam curled off his neck. The skin around Kesh's hand began to blister, then split. Muscle smoked.

The stench of charred flesh filled the room.

Jimmy screamed.

"I'll talk—I'll talk, please—"

Kesh tilted his head, his fury held perfectly still in the iron grip of his hand around the slithery demon's oozing neck.

"She's gone," Jimmy sobbed. "Europe. Prince Aragalan. He's taken her back to put her up for auction for the lords who support the old royal bloodline—"

More skin peeled away beneath Kesh's palm. Jimmy shrieked.

"Please! It wasn't my plan! It was Mallorn—Mallorn brought her to me. Said you were going to kill me for whoring her, kill him for challenging you. That this was our only way out—"

Kesh's magic surged, and Jimmy choked on his own scream.

"*Where?*"

"Rome! To the palace! She'll be mated before nightfall tomorrow. Please, just—just let me—"

The words dissolved into howling when the magic dug into his flesh, flared like a pulse.

Kesh's breath stuttered in his throat.

Rome.

The palace.

Not just enemy territory. The poisoned, beating heart of the enemy that wanted him, his family destroyed.

Auctioned.

They wouldn't delay; they would want her secured to one of their supporters as swiftly as possible. No time for strategy. No window for siege.

And if the auction began—

He knew what they were like. The Europeans followed the old ways. A woman subjected to that would not come out the other side with the light in her eyes still intact.

Something *broke* inside him; dark and violent and *powerful.*

The ground shuddered beneath his feet, the floorboards splitting with a thunder crack. Jimmy's scream cut off mid-breath as he disintegrated, body turned to dust in a flare of heat and raw energy.

Then the room exploded.

Not outward. Not upward.

Every atom of the building detonated in every direction at once.

The blast hit every surface; stone liquefied. Metal screamed. Fire rose in a column a quarter mile high.

Hell was gone.

All of it. Reduced to a crater still glowing at the

edges, ash spiraling into the air like smoke off a funeral pyre.

At the center, Kesh stood alone.

Breathing.

Barely.

Eyes burning amber with only one thought left in his mind.

Save her.

45
GEORGIA

The royal palace was quiet.

Not the kind of quiet that comforted. The kind that made it hard to breathe. The velvet runner underfoot swallowing the sound of their steps, as though sound wasn't allowed in this place.

Georgia walked between her kidnappers. Aragalan on her right. Mallorn on her left.

She kept her eyes on the floor. The hallway stretched ahead, a gallows walk, an endless runway of opulence and excess. The contrast to Kesh's casino was stark enough to register through her numb horror as she was marched through the palace.

Somewhere over the Atlantic, once the realization finally set in that there was no way out, her mind had slipped from raw terror into the kind of cold, creeping dread that settled in bone. No more bargains to be made, and no rescues to be had. Kesh wasn't coming to get her.

Her heart gave a dull throb deep behind her ribs. How she was still capable of feeling something as ridiculous as *heartbreak* amid the despair, she didn't know. Mallorn had fooled her so easily, because he'd known exactly where to twist the knife: he'd fed her stupid heart hope, and she'd leaped at the chance to believe that Kesh loved her after all, despite all the proof to the contrary.

But now?

Even if he did care, he wasn't going to save her. Not this time. She was deep in enemy territory, and the cost of retrieving her was not justifiable to a prince with subjects and territory to protect.

She wasn't worth the price.

"I can still smell it," Aragalan's voice was almost soft; a velvet caress laced with poison. He didn't look at her, but his hand constricted slightly around her upper arm. "The sadness. The fear. I believe I have made myself clear that I do not tolerate pheromone manipulation, Breeder."

"I can't control my smell." In the past, she would have apologized, cowered. That girl would have done everything in her power to diffuse his anger, to make herself as small a target as she could.

That girl, who still thought there might be way to lessen the horrors that lay ahead, was dead.

"In that case, I'll make sure you stop stinking of fear

myself. There are ways, even if I can't yet twist that pretty little ring Jimmy said you've been fitted with," the prince said, almost lightly. "We'll make sure you enter your auction with the sweet smell of submission staining your skin instead."

Georgia didn't respond, couldn't. What was there to say? No pleas would spare her, so she said nothing.

They stopped in front of a set of towering double doors, carved from some ancient black wood and inlaid with a sigil she didn't recognize. Two guards stood on either side, unmoving, weapons held at rest.

Aragalan let go of her arm and turned slightly toward Mallorn. "You'll be introduced," he said to Mallorn, still without looking at Georgia. "Father will recognize your part in securing a Pure. That kind of loyalty does not go unrewarded."

Mallorn gave a short nod, nothing more.

Aragalan didn't wait for a response. "Stand aside," he said to the guards.

They obeyed immediately, stepping back in perfect sync.

The doors opened without a sound.

The room inside was vast, but not grand. Dim, quiet. No court. No ceremony. The king was seated behind a desk of black stone, but Georgia barely registered him. Her gaze was drawn to the woman on his lap.

She was naked. Still. Her body draped across his thighs with practiced ease, as if she'd spent centuries being positioned exactly like this. His hand moved gently between her legs, toying with the gleaming band of metal encircling a swollen red clit, elongated from years of misuse, but the woman's face didn't so much as twitch. Her eyes were open, but vacant—so utterly hollow it made Georgia's stomach turn.

There was no rage in her expression. No resistance. No shame.

Just the kind of silence that came after a mind broke and never came back.

Georgia froze, breath locked behind her ribs.

"Father. Mother. I bring good tidings from the Americas." Aragalan's voice was smooth. "The Pure Breeder was successfully secured."

Mother.

This... this was the King's mate.

A Breeder. Like her.

Georgia's stomach twisted. Her lungs felt too tight to draw breath. Her legs wanted to move—forward, backward, anything to get away—but she stayed rooted. There was nowhere to go, and nothing to do but stay and look upon the future that awaited her.

Kesh's anguished voice, as he told the story of his mother taking her own life, echoed back to her with blinding clarity. This was why, she realized as she looked at the King's mate's vacant eyes. To escape, because death was the kinder choice than what it truly meant to be mated to a creature of pure darkness.

The King didn't look up. He continued working his

fingers between his mate's legs, idle and absent, as if she were no more than a fidget toy. She didn't move. "How was the crossing?"

"Uneventful," Aragalan replied, his posture loose, casual. "Our new allies ensured a smooth transfer."

"Excellent." The King finally lifted his gaze to Mallorn. "And this is the one responsible for extracting our golden goose?"

"Yes," Aragalan said. "He served as Second to the imposter prince, but found his allegiance... *shifted*, once he realized the true deceit his former master is capable of, even toward a loyal servant."

"Ah. Yes. Their entire bloodline is incapable of loyalty. You will find I have no such confusion. You have brought us a Pure, and your reward will be as promised: the next non-Pure Breeder we source will be gifted to you. As a thank you for your invaluable assistance." The King's smile didn't reach his eyes. "Assuming, of course, you remain loyal."

Mallorn gave another nod. "Of course, Your Majesty."

The King leaned back slightly, fingers retreating from his mate's clit at last, resting instead on her thigh. "And the other one?" he asked, eyes flicking back to Aragalan. "The one who's already shipped his whores to Monti and given the palace guards a free night as a welcome bonus... *Jimmy*, was it? Where is he?"

Aragalan's jaw twitched with faint distaste. "He made his own travel arrangements. There were some last-minute financial arrangements he wanted to square off with the father before taking his exit, but I suspect he won't want to linger longer than necessary. According to Mallorn here, Kesh was...*attached* to the Breeder. No doubt he'll be looking for her with some intent. Which reminds me—we need to do a pregnancy test on her before the auction. I'm not interested in raising a spawn from the traitors' bloodline."

The King waved a hand dismissively. "There's no way of knowing if she's carrying until the fetus disables her blinding mark, and the auction is tonight. When you win her, if she sees through the disguise within 2 weeks, we'll test for paternity, once she's given birth. If it's not yours, kill it and breed her again."

Bright fear struck through her numb horror at the casual cruelty. No. No, that was too much. Even for these creatures. Surely no, they couldn't, they wouldn't—

Her eyes fell on the King's mate, still draped over his lap. Her body and blank face had the same ageless appearance as her captor, but the signs of wear were unmistakable: stretch marks from births—multiple, from the looks of it—bruises on her hips blooming in shades of fresh purple to faded yellow, and puffy nipples from too much attention. Mercifully, her sex was currently shielded from view by her thighs, but it was more than obvious that here she would be a vessel only. And they would treat any baby she may have conceived with Kesh with even less regard than they would her. Of course a child produced from her womb, not of their lineage, would be considered nothing but a faulty product.

"Mallorn, please." Her voice came out as a strained whisper, fear for a child she that may not even exist overriding her numb acceptance that there was no way out.

He ignored her. They all did.

Georgia choked back the sob threatening to spill out and pressed her hands to her lower abdomen, not to shield a fetus that might not even be there, but to hold in the gut-splitting terror. "Mallorn... you can't let them do this. Please. *Please.*"

No one so much as looked in her direction.

"We have much to prepare for tonight," the King continued, as if she hadn't even spoken. "Show our new friend to his suite, then prepare the Breeder for her auction. We can't have her reeking of fear when our allies come to make their bids—we need them in a good mood to ensure they take the other news... with the correct understanding. If their attention is on the possibility of a submissive little mate, the peace treaty I've brokered with Kirigan should sound... more like victory than compromise."

Kirigan?

No. That couldn't be right.

She must have misheard. Misunderstood. The name echoed again—clear, deliberate—and the cold started at her fingertips this time, creeping up her arms like frostbite.

Not Mallorn.

Not Jimmy.

Kesh's father.

"I still don't understand why he would offer this deal," Aragalan said, gaze sliding to Mallorn. "Offering the Breeder, agreeing to limit Kain's territory to North America. They have one of our Stones of Power, the other is gone... We've lost two lords in direct combat to the younger son. Without this auction, if we didn't secure a victory within the year, our support might have begun to slowly dwindle. So what incentive did he have to suggest giving us not only a ceasefire, but a Pure Breeder as well?"

"He offered for the same reasons I accepted. Kirigan is only a few centuries younger than I," the King said, turning his black eyes to the broken woman on his lap. "I fought him at your mother's auction, and even then, no lack of cunning, merely his youth that ensured my victory. Had he been older at the time, stronger... he might have taken her. He is... clever. The costs on both sides are already racking up, and no matter who wins in the end, this conflict depletes our numbers.

"The gods are watching us. Waiting. The second they see their chance, they will strike. Whoever is left standing will be wiped out. So, in the end, this is better for us all. Especially for you. Now go—take your mate-to-be to recover from the journey. She will need all her strength for tonight. Her submission underneath you after you win will be a beautiful seal to our new peace treaty.

Georgia barely registered the large hand curling around her arm and pulling her out the door. Acid shock churned through her system as the full scale reality of what he was saying sank in.

Kirigan hadn't brokered peace with diplomacy.

He'd traded her for it.

46
KIRIGAN

Kirigan had liked the city, once upon a time. The noise and human decay had proven decadent hunting grounds and, as all demons, he'd been happy to indulge.

Nowadays, it was all static. Relentless impressions against his fraying mind.

He didn't sit as he stared out the window at the bustling life outside, at the humans going about their lives. He hadn't sat for hours. Not because he was tense. He didn't *feel* tension. He simply didn't trust what might surface if he allowed his body to relax. Right now, there was no room for the madness. No room to lose his grip on the carefully laid dominoes, lest one fall over too soon and spoil the picture.

Governor Maell entered behind him. No fanfare. They hadn't bothered with that in centuries.

Kirigan didn't look over. "I've heard what I needed to."

Maell stepped further into the room. "They're unified. Lords who haven't been able to share a battlefield now trade intelligence. Half the court is tapping surveillance webs that haven't been touched in years. Even the Lord of Nevada is in."

Kirigan's jaw flexed once. His gaze tracked a mother pushing a stroller on the pavement below, unaware she was passing so close to a demonic court.

Maell poured a drink from the dusty cart by the wall. "The Breeder was a catalyst. They'll follow Kain blindly now. Whoever took her did more for your son's consolidation of power than a decade of rule."

Kirigan kept still. The darkness tightened around his spine. "Convenient."

Maell watched him over the rim of the glass. "Yes. Almost suspiciously so."

The mother disappeared around a corner. Kirigan finally turned around to look at the governor. Flat. Unblinking.

Maell didn't press it, only leaned back against the edge of the bar cart. "I suppose, even if she *were* to turn up somewhere... unfortunate, say, mated to one of our enemies... she would be out of reach for good. This would likely keep them united under Kain's rule. He *did* offer her to them, after all. If someone managed to sneak her out under their collective noses, Kesh can't very well be blamed for losing her."

Kirigan didn't respond. The silence sank between them. Then his phone buzzed. The screen lit up.

Kain.

He extended a hand. "Leave me."

Maell didn't argue. He studied him for half a second too long, then slipped from the room.

Kirigan answered, pressing the phone to his ear. "Kain. You have heard—the Pure Breeder has been—"

"Kesh is gone."

Kirigan's breath stilled.

Kain's voice was taut, clipped. "He's already in the air. Headed for Rome. He took a jet, shot me a text from over the Atlantic. The Europeans have her. They're gonna auction her tonight. I called, told him to wait, to let us plan... He said 'no', then hung up. Hasn't picked up since."

A silence settled. The kind that didn't hum, didn't echo—just expanded.

Something unfamiliar tightened in Kirigan's chest.

He hadn't planned for this.

He'd expected Kesh to be furious, for his instincts to send him into a frenzy. But once the trail turned cold and his hormones had burned out, he would return to his duties.

The carefully aligned dominoes hadn't been laid out with this outcome as a possibility. For his son to act as if the Breeder was...

No. It couldn't be love. That would make the risk

incalculable. That would mean... he'd gambled his youngest son's life in exchange for his eldest's.

"He's going to get himself killed," Kain continued, voice rougher now. "I'm going to get him, before it's too late. I need you to take over all official duties until I'm back. Tomren will help with all administrative tasks. I've already briefed him—"

"*No.*" His voice cut through with enough snap to make Kain stop talking. No. No, no, *no.* The tightness in his chest clenched at his lungs, and something cold crept up from his tailbone. Not one son's life gambled. *Both.* "You can't—"

"I'm coming with you." It was Selma's voice now, coming from close to Kain. "If you go alone, you'll die, too, and I'm not about to let that happen. Besides, I owe Kesh for helping me save you last year. So yes, I'm going. You need me, you need my magic, and you need my Stone of Power." Her voice was bright and razor-sharp, and had a tone of ruthless commitment Kirigan had heard before.

"*Selma*—" Kain began.

"*Enough.*" Kirigan barked. "You will *both* stay where you are. I will retrieve Kesh. Alive. You have my word. Do not follow. Do not abandon your responsibilities here—or your *child.* I will fix this."

"Kiri—"

He hung up before Selma could finish her protest.

He would. Fix it. The mistake of not accounting for

the true strength of Kesh's attachment to the Breeder was his.

The dominoes were already falling. But he'd lay down another path—bend the line back, if he had to. He wasn't about to let either of his sons die for his miscalculation.

47
GEORGIA

The door shut behind the prince with a soft click. He'd brought her to an opulent suite, with gold and marble on every surface, and a view of the ancient city through the large windows that would have stolen her breath during any other circumstance.

"Come, Breeder. Eat. You will need your strength tonight." The demon led her by his grip on her arm to an overstuffed sofa, where a platter of food was laid out on the glass-and-marble coffee table in front of it. Piles of sliced meat, bowls of olives, loaves of honey-smeared bread. None of it did anything but turn her stomach.

"I'm not hungry."

"Unfortunate that you will still need to eat," he said, with no inflection of regret. "Sit."

She considered refusing. Her eyes slid from the

platter of food to the prince, who was simply watching her—waiting for the rebellion.

Georgia sat. There was no point in fighting, not about this. Possibly not about anything at all anymore.

She didn't eat. Not until the prince sat down next to her, picked up a piece of bread between two fingers, and pushed it to her lips. "Open."

She hesitated for a second, then obeyed. The food tasted like ash, and Aragalan's satisfied expression, when his fingers brushed her lips and she began mechanically chewing, raised goosebumps of revulsion along her skin. And still, she ate.

Memories of the first time Kesh fed her tried to surface. She didn't let them.

Mouthful after mouthful slid down her throat, tasteless and invasive.

"You're beautiful like this," Aragalan purred, his black eyes turning hooded as they greedily swept over her face and lingered on her mouth. He forced a green olive between her lips and rumbled something akin to a purr when she accepted it. "Submissive. My father tells me my mother took a few weeks before she surrendered fully, but that won't be a problem with you, will it? Your weakness seems fused into your blood from birth, hmm?"

Georgia glared at him as he pressed another olive—black this time—to her mouth, but there was little fire left in her gaze. "That's truly what you desire? A hollow shell by your side? Your mother *birthed* you, and yet you are content to see her like she's nothing more than a meat puppet for your father to use? That's all you want out of your wife? A mindless husk?"

"Wife." The word came out on a mocking rumble. Aragalan swiped his thumb over her lips, then dropped his hand to her thigh, squeezing high. "A truly *human* concept. You will be my *mate,* little Breeder. Your sole purpose will be to spread your legs, to receive me, and to birth my heirs."

He stroked his hand all the way down her leg, then back up under her skirt. His skin was scalding against hers, revulsion crawling up her thigh as he reached her panties and stroked his fingertips against the fabric. "Did you know getting fucked by a demon lord will kill a woman unless she's a Pure Breeder? Or a demoness, of course. But they're... not nearly as soft and pliant as human pussy."

"I'd heard." She managed to keep her voice steady and her gaze straight ahead, even as his fingers slipped underneath her panties and stroked through her cleft. Only when he found her clit and pressed in did he manage to wrest a shudder from her body.

She clenched her jaw when he began toying with the metal-encircled organ and tried to will her mind away from the screaming of unwilling nerves. Begging now, crying now, would only make it easier for him to snuff her spirit when the true horrors began.

"You will be happy to know, it doesn't mean I'm inexperienced. My mother has trained me well. I won't even need to activate your ring." He plucked at the metal circle, making it scrape cruelly against her clit. "Not after the claiming ceremony. You will be fully conscious as I wring orgasm after orgasm from your quivering flesh until that soft little mind of yours simply... gives. Within a week, you'll be on my lap, open and receptive to my every demand. Mine, and mine alone."

Aragalan gave a soft chuckle before pressing his thumb firmly to the tip of her clit, ignoring her involuntary jump. "Well... until our sons are old enough to need training, of course. Then you will service them, too, until they win their own mates, like my mother did for me and my brothers. Isn't that a beautiful thought, hmm? The circle of life and servitude you Breeders were born for, fulfilled to its fullest potential. Now, why don't you close your eyes and relax, my pretty? Let's get you nice and warm for your auction. The more times you come now, the less it'll hurt when I claim you at your auction tonight.

———

The door clicked shut behind him, the sound far too soft for the violence it left behind. Georgia stayed where she was, sprawled across the couch like a discarded doll, breath shallow, muscles trembling from exhaustion and shame. Her skin was slick with sweat, the ghost of his hands still burning on her thighs, her throat, the curves of her breasts. The aching nub of her trapped clit. She couldn't stop shaking. Couldn't stop remembering.

The room was silent now. Rich with gold leaf and velvet and polished stone, as if opulence could disguise what it was: a cage.

She dragged in a breath that tasted of salt and fear. The prince's parting words echoed—"you'll be fetched soon"—and she hated how her heart stuttered at the sound of imagined footsteps. Next came the auction. And then...

Georgia closed her eyes against the truth, but it didn't stop the knowledge of what came *after* the auction.

A shimmer broke the stillness—soft at first, like heat haze rising from scorched earth. Georgia froze, breath caught in her throat, muscles seized in terror. *The servants.* She wasn't ready. She'd never be ready.

But it wasn't the prince's servants come to fetch her for auction.

The glow sharpened, gold bleeding into every shadow, until the room seemed to hum with it. And then—Georgia's heart stuttered, confusion overtaking fear—Suzanne stood before her.

For a moment, Georgia could only stare. The goddess looked exactly as she had in Maine: barefoot, slight, an innocent child in face and stature.

The goddess smiled faintly, as if they were old friends sharing some harmless secret.

"Suzanne." The name rasped out of her worn throat.

"Well," the goddess said lightly, head tilting, "this is disappointing."

Georgia forced herself upright, every muscle screaming in protest. She clutched the edge of the couch, naked, trembling, glare sharp beneath the weight of everything that had been done to her. "Disappointing?" she rasped. "Do you know what they'll do to me? What they're planning? Please, just help me get out."

Suzanne regarded her like one might a smudged painting—once promising, now ruined. "I thought you'd help me," she said, almost gently. "I thought you'd be like Selma. Powerful. Capable of bending demonic darkness toward the light. But Kesh didn't claim you, so... I guess I was wrong. I'm afraid you're of no use to my plans. Rescuing you now would just draw too much attention to what I'm doing. The demons can't know, not until I'm ready. I'm sure you understand."

Georgia's breath shuddered. "Please. Please don't let them do this to me. You're a goddess. You could—"

"I *could*," Suzanne agreed, voice light as air. "But why would I? Saving you risks everything I've built. And you've already failed me." She tilted her head, as if remembering something important. "The Stone of Power I gave you. I need it back, so I can give it to my next hopeful."

"I—I don't have it." The words tumbled out of her mouth, stilted and frail as the callousness of the divine being in front of her sank deep. "I didn't—it's back in America."

Suzanne rolled her eyes. "You don't have it? You were gifted one of the most powerful artifacts on Earth, and you simply... didn't think to hold on to it? Right. I guess the pieces of my mistake are certainly forming a picture, aren't they? Well. I'd best be off. Stones to recover, evil power structures to destabilize. Good luck at your auction, Georgia."

The soft light folded in on itself and she was gone.

Georgia was alone.

A tremor worked its way up her spine as she stared at the place the goddess had stood.

When the door to the opulent suite opened some ten minutes later, and the servants arrived to lead her to her auction, she followed them without a word.

48
GEORGIA

When the King arrived in front of the large, opulent doors shielding the auction hall from view, the servants had already attached a gold chain to lead her by.

Gold encircled her wrists in ornate shackles and her neck in a collar inlaid with shimmering rubies, but the leash was attached where they expected her true submission.

"You look like a picture-perfect mate already. My son is a lucky man." The King let his gaze sweep over her, lingering on her bare breasts and sex before he plucked the chain from his servant and gave it a light tug. The motion traveled through the leash to the ring fixed between her legs, pulling her clit taut. Sharp, deep sensation seared through her pelvis, low and brutal. Georgia swallowed a hiss, refusing to give him the satisfaction.

"Come along then, Breeder." The doors ahead of them began to open. The hall beyond was bright with firelight, a circular room with an arena in the center and seats rising around its perimeter, like an amphitheater of old. The King tugged on her leash again, harder this time.

Georgia didn't manage to stem a small cry this time. She stumbled after him, powerless against the pull of the ring. As she would be for the rest of her life.

The chain pulled again. Georgia winced and followed, bare feet skimming polished stone, the clink of her shackles swallowed by the rising sound ahead.

When they crossed the threshold, the noise hit her like heat.

A roar.

Dozens of demon lords filled the coliseum stands, their voices thick with hunger and triumph. Not reverence. Conquest.

The King raised the chain slightly as he guided her forward, making sure she stayed a step behind him like a prized beast on display. Every movement of the leash sang along the nerve in her clit, sending sharp reminders of where she was, *what* she was.

They crossed the center of the arena floor. The lords above leaned forward in their seats, hungry-eyed, leering.

She didn't meet any of their gazes. Her chin stayed up, but her insides curled tight.

On the far side, steps of white marble curved

upward. The King took them without pause, tugging her behind, until they reached a raised platform with gilded railings and a single, low pedestal.

He tugged on the chain, guiding her up on the pedestal with the deep, sharp humiliation of the ring forcing her to flinch and adjust until she stood like he wanted her—arms behind her back, chest thrust forward, legs apart. Naked and visible to every eye in the coliseum.

The King waited for silence to fall over the gathered demons, as every eye fell on her body, displayed like meat on the platform. Then he stepped forward, his voice carried, rich and clear and perfectly amplified without need of a microphone.

"Brethren. Loyal subjects. Warriors of our future." He paused, letting the crowd's energy still before continuing. "Today, we mark a turning point. The Americans—our wayward kin, drunk on chaos and weakness—believed they could keep the rarest prize our kind knows to themselves."

A soft hum rolled through the room. Georgia kept her gaze fixed on the far wall.

"They thought her their salvation. Their rebellion's seed—a vessel to sire a new generation of traitors. But in the end..." He reached behind him and gave the chain a casual tug, making Georgia raise up on her toes with a whimper. The crowd laughed. "In the end, they saw reason. They understood they could not stand against us. That to do so, would be to perish."

He let the leash fall slack again.

"This Breeder is a symbol of their weakness. Their defeat. With the surrender of a Pure mate, I announce the end of the war with our traitorous cousins in the West. There is once again only one true court, and I will remember each of you here today. You who remained steadfast. You who did not waver."

He turned slightly, gesturing toward Georgia with an open palm. "And now, as promised—your reward.

"You all know the rules," the King said, letting his gaze sweep the crowd. "We begin with a display of wealth. A show of what each of you believes she's worth to your bloodline—what monetary value you place on the fruit of her womb."

A ripple of sound—low, eager—passed through the arena.

"Once the first bid has been placed, it may be challenged, either by currency or by a show of strength." He turned then, pausing to let his gaze wander up Georgia's trembling form. "A challenger may choose to fight the current bid holder instead of increasing the monetary value. Blood, spilled for the right to breed her. A worthy cost."

Georgia's stomach twisted. The weight of the gathered demons' attention pressed down on her like a second collar.

"Once a victor is named, his reward must be claimed before us all. Twist her ring to claim her cunt, seed her womb in the arena to cement your victory, and none shall be able to challenge your right as her mate for the rest of eternity."

A tremble worked its way through Georgia's body. Her throat felt too tight to swallow. Her first rape would take place in front of all of them. The subsequent ones would last for the rest of her existence.

The King raised his arm. "Begin!"

A voice rang out from the stands. "One million euros."

Another answered, fast and sharp. "One-point-two."

The crowd stirred, hungry for the game. The King said nothing, only stood beside her like a curator beside his prize.

Georgia didn't move. Couldn't. Her clit still ached between her legs from the last tug, nerves tight and raw. She swallowed the lump in her throat, the ruby-encrusted collar around her neck constricting the movement. Her wrists throbbed in their gold shackles. She kept her gaze on the floor ahead, on a crack in the marble no one else would notice.

"Three-point-four," someone called, raising another rumble amongst the lords.

Then a third voice—smooth, certain—cut through them. "I challenge."

Silence fell.

From the front row, Prince Aragalan rose. He adjusted his leather bracers and stepped down toward the arena floor, his eyes never leaving Georgia.

He smirked at her as he passed her platform. No leering. No filth. Just confidence. Like he already knew what her body would feel like submitting under his.

The lump in Georgia's throat became too big to swallow past the collar. Tears stung her eyes, and she blinked rapidly, willing them away. It didn't help.

The other demon lord—the one who'd bid three-point-four million for her—stepped into the arena after the Prince.

The two faced each other, nodded once, then looked to the King, waiting for the signal.

The King raised his hand, then dropped it sharply.

The arena erupted.

The two demons surged toward each other, bare fists crackling with shadow. Magic spilled from their skin like smoke—black and thick, twisting around their limbs as they collided. The sound of flesh meeting flesh echoed off the marble walls. Georgia flinched.

A fist connected with Aragalan's side, sending him skidding across the blood-slick floor. He snarled, rising to his feet, mouth already smeared with red. The magic around him coiled tighter, denser now, wrapping him like a second skin.

The other demon advanced, but too slow. Aragalan moved like a blade. He ducked the next blow, caught the other's arm, and drove his elbow up into the joint with a sickening crack. The man screamed. Then, Aragalan shoved him back with a blast of shadow, slamming him into the ground so hard the stone beneath cracked.

The crowd cheered.

Blood streaked the arena floor now. The other demon lay groaning, one arm bent wrong, blood leaking from his mouth.

Aragalan turned toward the stands, chest heaving, hands still dripping.

"Challenge me," he said, voice low and thick with triumph. "And I will use your blood to lubricate my cock when I claim the Breeder as mine. There is no besting me. There is no outbidding me. There is only defeat."

Silence stretched, heavy and taut. No one moved.

Then—"Four million," someone called from the upper tier.

The crowd stirred again. All eyes turned to Aragalan.

His lip curled. "Then come and take your chance," he snarled, already pacing toward the center, blood still slick on his hands.

The challenger rose, stepping down the marble stairs with deliberate calm. His gaze locked with Aragalan's, power rising in dark tendrils from his skin.

But he never reached the arena floor.

With a sound like the sky tearing open, the ceiling above them *shattered*. Stone and dust exploded inward, the air ripped apart by a force too sudden to prepare for. A heavy *thunk* followed, and a crack split stone floor, racing from the center of the arena in two directions, setting the pedestal wobbling.

Georgia cried out, stumbling to keep her balance. The King's hold on her chain yanked her back with a brutal tug as he raised a wall of dark magic around the platform, shielding them from the rain of debris.

Choking on an agonized sob, she squinted through the smoke and dust to the arena below.

Something moved in the haze—something black and burning and terrible, and...

No. No, it couldn't possibly be—

Fear gave way to mind-numbing shock as the smoke cleared and the large outline of a man turned crisp and clear and undeniable.

Kesh.

He crouched amid the rubble where he'd dropped through the ceiling, his body sheathed in pulsing shadow, power seething off him in waves. Eyes burning with a fury too vast for words.

Every demon in the room went still, but he paid them no mind.

Straightening slowly, his gaze found Georgia's. His lip curled in a snarl at the sight of her shackles. The humiliating chain. The deep sound rumbled through the broken coliseum, rich and deep and preternatural.

"You have one second to release what's mine, King of Nothing. *One.* Before I pull this palace down on your skull and erase your city from existence."

49
KESH

The European king didn't flinch.

He stood tall on the marble platform, one hand still loosely gripping the gold chain dangling from between Georgia's legs. Kesh didn't let his eyes follow to where it was tethered. Rage pounded in his temples and pressed at his skin, his bones, his *teeth* at the sight of her naked and trembling.

"What a dramatic entrance," the King said, voice smooth as glass. His eyes gleamed with nothing but dark amusement as he took in Kesh's dust-covered figure, standing amidst pieces of the broken ceiling. "But alas, need I remind you, you stand before me defeated, youngling? As you well know, the Breeder was surrendered in exchange for my mercy. Don't come here now, cloaked in borrowed fury, and pretend that wasn't the deal you struck."

Kesh narrowed his eyes at the lying king, so

haughty on his platform, clearly entirely confident in his belief that Kesh posed no threat. That he didn't possess the strength to take back what had been stolen. His guards and the lords in the room shifted, restless with the intrusion, but none of them moved. None of them interrupted. They thought the king's lack of concern signaled they were safe.

They were mistaken.

Kesh didn't look at the king. He looked past him to the tiers of stone seating above. The demon lords who now sat silent, watching. Waiting. Weighing power.

His voice, when it came, was low. Steady. Sharp enough to cut flesh.

"He's lying."

A murmur rippled through the chamber.

"Those of you who've met us on the battlefield—those of you who've bled beneath our blades—you know the truth. We are not losing." His gaze swept the crowd. "We are winning."

He took a step forward, smoke curling off his shoulders. "I would never surrender my female. This Breeder is mine. Aragalan stole her from my court, just as his brother tried to steal the last Pure. This—" He motioned toward the platform, toward the chain, the shackles, Georgia's trembling frame. "This is not a show of strength. It's a farce."

Silence.

"You think he intended to let any of you win her? That this auction is anything beyond theater?" He scanned the rows of watching lords. "Stay out of my way, and you will keep your territory. Your title. Your bloodline."

His magic pulsed, slow and dark.

"Stand against me—and you'll die with the false king and his spawn."

Kesh turned back to the platform, his eyes flicking to Georgia before he could stop himself.

Naked. Shackled. Collar gleaming at her throat. Ankles spread just so. And between her legs, the gold chain—still held in the King's lazy grip—running taut to the ring that encircled her clit.

Everything inside him locked. Every instinct, every tether, every inch of restraint.

Her eyes found his. Blue, wide, wet with tears she hadn't let fall.

Her lips moved, and though no sound passed them, her words still reached him.

You came.

The disbelief in her wet eyes sank deeper than his own fury. The fragile hope. The grief. She didn't think he could win. Not against all of them.

She didn't believe he would survive this. That he could save her.

His gaze shifted—to the male still holding her leash.

The king looked smug, prepared to speak again, to gloat again.

Kesh didn't let him.

"You're out of time."

The magic erupted from him like a detonation—black and vicious and absolute—with no warning and no chance for the King to react.

One moment the ancient ruler stood haughty and sovereign, hand still wrapped around Georgia's leash. And the next—

A blast of shadow slammed into him, ripping through flesh, through bone, through centuries of entitlement and rot.

Blood and ash sprayed the platform, coating Georgia's bare skin, her shackles, the marble beneath her feet. A hunk of something—part of a rib, maybe—hit the golden railing and skidded away.

There was a sound, wet and final.

The king was gone.

The leash clattered to the ground, chain swinging limp, one of the king's fingers still attached by scorched flesh welded to the metal.

For one breathless second, there was only silence—the kind that follows a cataclysm. Thick. Stunned. Disbelieving.

Then chaos cracked the stillness open.

A roar split the air, and Prince Aragalan launched from the stands with a burst of power, his black magic already coiling in thick, oily ropes around his arms.

He struck hard and fast, driven by fury and panic, the certainty of bloodline collapse driving him forward.

Kesh met him head-on.

A second impact lit the arena, shadow clashing against shadow, sparks and smoke and the stink of raw magic flooding the space.

Guards surged from the outer ring, blades drawn. Some of the gathered lords rose too—most to fight, some to flee—but not all chose sides. Not yet.

Those who did hurled themselves from the stands like animals.

The arena descended into slaughter.

Kesh moved like fury made flesh, power pouring from him in waves that cracked marble and split stone. Every blow he landed left ruin behind—demons thrown, guards crushed, the scent of seared flesh thick in the air.

He tore through them.

Aragalan came at him again and again, relentless, and Kesh met him each time with the deep-seated knowledge that if he lost, Georgia would face eternity as this monster's breeding slave. He could not fail her.

Not again.

He propelled his body forward and finally managed to catch Aragalan by the throat. Before the European prince could get free, Kesh slammed him into the ground hard enough to crater the arena floor. Blood trailed from his temple.

But there were too many.

Before Kesh could finish the job, magic exploded against his side. A sword found his ribs. Another slammed into his back. He staggered but didn't fall.

Until he did.

A blast hit him square in the chest, ripping through shadow and armor and skin. He crumpled to one knee, blood slicking the ground beneath him.

Another strike. Then another.

The last burst of magic threw him backward, slamming his body into the shattered remains of the central platform. Columns collapsed. The ceiling cracked.

Stone rained from above as the palace began to break apart.

Dust settled around him. The stone beneath his back burned hot with dark magic, and his every breath was a blade in his chest.

Kesh pushed up on shaking arms. He had to move. Had to stand. He couldn't fail her, he couldn't—

Before he could lift more than his shoulders, a black whip of magic slammed into his spine, forcing him flat. He snarled and tried again, but another lash struck, then another. Power lashed from every direction, from the surviving lords who'd chosen the Europeans' side.

Aragalan limped into view, blood streaking his face, one arm held stiff, but his eyes burned with fury. Behind him, two more lords, hands raised, magic coiled and ready, closed in. Together, they bound Kesh down. Power wrapped around his limbs, his chest, pressing harder the more he fought it.

He snarled and strained against it until his muscles screamed and his veins burned. The marble cracked beneath his body with the rumble of his magic, fighting to break free, but the binds held. There were too many.

He'd lost.

Through the haze of blood and dust, his gaze found Georgia again. His heart ached more than his body ever could at her wide, sorrowful eyes, fixed on his. She hadn't looked away during the entirety of the battle. Nor his defeat.

In her blue gaze, he saw everything he'd lost when he let fear and weakness reject the woman who'd shown him what it was to know love. If he'd claimed her, like every instinct in him had screamed to do, like even she'd known he was *meant* to do, none of this would have happened.

Instead, he would now die with the knowledge that his failure to protect the one who should have been his mate meant an eternity of debasement for her.

The magic pinning him tightened. A crack in his ribcage sent blinding pain through his bones, but it was nothing—*nothing*—in comparison to the rending of his heart as the final vestiges of strength bled from his broken body.

In the end, he didn't get to tell her how bitterly he regretted his cowardice.

His vision blurred, and as she faded into the darkness, all he managed was to mouth the last, inadequate words that mattered.

I'm sorry.

The magic constricted. Kesh's spine arched with the

force of it, nerves blazing in white-hot agony. He heard Aragalan's snarl—something guttural and victorious—and then the pressure grew sharp, focused. The unmistakable crack of vertebrae beginning to split.

This was it.

His body failed, muscles twitching against the stone, breath a thin whistle in his throat.

Somewhere beyond the noise in his skull, he heard it. *Her* voice. Desperate. Shattered.

"*No!*"

And then came the light.

Blinding, pure. It exploded through the darkness behind his lids like a sun bursting open, searing into what little consciousness he had left.

And then...

Nothing.

50
GEORGIA

Georgia came to on her knees.

The air was hot. The ground beneath her was hotter; fractured marble that steamed where it still held the imprint of her body. Her legs shook. Her hands trembled. One of them was closed in a fist without her remembering how, the smooth curve of the stone Suzanne had given her back in Maine pressed tight to her palm, still pulsing like a second heart.

She couldn't hear anything, and her vision blurred at the edges with the bright light thrumming all around her. Her skin screamed in places—her neck, her wrists. Her thigh. She looked down.

The shackles were gone. Melted. Only the burns remained—rings of scorched flesh where gold had seared against her skin. Her wrists were red and blistered. A raw mark ringed her throat like a brand. And across the tender skin of her inner thigh, a single raised line burned furious and sharp, where the leash had swung and branded her.

There was... a *power* pulsing through her body. Bright and dull, like pressing on a bruise that ran the length of her veins. Woven through every cell of her body.

The stone in her palm thrummed in time with it, as if synced in perfect, volatile harmony. She blinked down at it, mind still slow. Where had it come from? Last she saw it had been... Kesh's penthouse. Before...

Images flooded her: the heat, the agony, the need. Kesh, as wild as she. On top of her. *Inside* of her. The broken hollow in her chest at his rejection. The courting ceremony, Mallorn, Europe. Despair.

The leash. The fight. *Kesh.*

Terror lanced through her. Her head snapped up, eyes desperately scanning...

And there he lay.

In the center of the ruined arena, among rubble and dust and smoke.

His body. Half-buried in broken marble and streaked in soot and the charred remains of the demons who had taken him down, blood drying in the cracks of his armor, skin death-pale beneath the grime. His chest didn't move. His eyes didn't open.

The world dropped out from under her.

"Kesh." Her voice broke in her throat. *"Kesh!"*

Her legs moved before her mind could catch up. The

stone clutched in her hand burned hot, pulsing harder now. Light broke from her skin, shooting down her arms and legs as she stumbled toward him across the debris. The air around her thickened, power bleeding off her body in radiant waves. She fell to her knees beside him with a sob, light pooling from her chest, her hands, forming a shimmering cocoon around them both.

A shield. A ward. A desperate prayer. The magic bled from her veins, pulled from nothing but raw instinct to keep his broken body safe.

Her prince didn't move. His mouth was parted, his body slack. There was so much blood...

"No," she whispered, and the bubble tightened, sealing them inside. "No, no, no— Please. Don't leave me. Please, please..."

She reached for him, tears already spilling down her cheeks. He couldn't be gone; he couldn't.

Please, please no.

Georgia gripped his face with shaking hands. One palm cradled his bloodied cheek, the other pressed hard over the wound at his side where the armor had split. Light, from the deepest parts of her she hadn't even known existed before he stood in that arena, before he came to lay down his life for hers, curled between her fingers. It was *right there.* She felt it—the thrum of power far beyond her mortal comprehension, but she didn't know how to use it.

"Please." Her voice cracked apart. "Please don't

leave me. Not again, not like this. I can't—" Her mouth trembled. "You don't get to do this! You're mine, you bastard—*mine!*"

The tears came harder. Her forehead dropped to his, lips brushing the bridge of his nose. His skin was cooler than it had ever been before, the fire in him nearly gone.

Her power didn't build. It broke. Crushed open under the weight of her grief and poured into him without direction or shape.

Not a spell. Not skill. Need. Her love. Her terror. Her hope, ragged and bleeding and still somehow *alive.* It poured from her chest and her hands and her tears, spilling into his wounds like molten light, threading through torn muscle and shattered bone.

Something inside her cracked wide open. Not breaking—connecting. To him.

A tether pulled tight between them, so sudden and fierce it stole her breath. A current of knowing that split through the fog of panic. Like lightning. Like it had always been there. Dormant. Waiting.

Now, it surged.

Magic rose around them in a spiral of light. His body jerked, and she *felt* him in that primordial current flooding every part of her being.

He was still with her.

The bond pulsed once. Then again. And she clung to it, to him, with everything she had left.

"Come back to me. Come back," she whispered, forehead pressed to his as her trembling hands smoothed over his body and arms, again and again, the light in her filling him until he radiated with it.

Slowly, his skin warmed. Then his breath hitched beneath her hands. A pull of heat beneath her palms, subtle but sure. She choked on a sob and gripped him tighter.

Then his eyes cracked open, just enough for her magic flooding him to shine through his black eyes, turning them molten charcoal.

"Stop," he rasped, voice torn and ragged but *his*. "Georgia, stop. I'm here. Don't... don't give me any more. You're pulling... from your life force." His fingers, weak but steady, lifted to cup her cheek. "I'm here."

She let out a broken, gasping sound, half-sob, half-laugh, and leaned into the warmth of his touch. Her whole body shook. Her light flickered wildly around them, dimming and surging without rhythm now, the bond still pulsing between them like a third heart. He was *here.*

"I thought I lost you," she whispered.

"You brought me back," he rasped. His thumb brushed her cheek, reverent. "My beautiful, strong female. I always knew... from the first time I saw you, I knew..."

His other hand reached up slowly, gingerly, pulling her down. Their lips met, the kiss a tremor, not passion. Fragile and slow and sacred.

Kesh pulled back, eyes clouded with regret as he searched hers. "Georgia, I—"

"Kesh!" The voice cracked across the crumbled arena like lightning. Georgia whipped around just in time to see a swirl of smoke and shadow stop, materializing into a figure.

Kirigan stood where the auction platform had once been, eyes wide and face drawn. His mad gaze swept over both of them, hands trembling before he clenched them into fists. His face turned ashen as his eyes lingered on Kesh.

Behind him, Kain and Selma followed, she glowing with the same golden light still flickering around Georgia, he with the full power of his demonic force billowing like a cape around them both.

Selma moved first. No hesitation, no fear. She stepped into the center and took up a stance in front of Georgia and Kesh, the Stone of Power raised in one steady hand. Light flared from it, golden and sure, echoing the pulse of light from Georgia's stone. Kain followed her, one large hand on the small of her back as they stared down the few remaining European lords. A united shield.

"The old royals are dead. Your king is ash. The last of their princes is gone." Kain's voice boomed through the wreckage, his power swirling dark and solid around him. "We control two of the Stones of Power. If you bend the knee now, you'll retain your territories. If you resist..." He let the sentence hang, sharp and terrible. "You'll join your false king in death."

A long moment of tense silence followed as the

lords looked from the powerful demon and his magic-glowing mate to the half-vaporized, half-gutted remains of the lords killed by either Kesh or Georgia before the American King and Queen even arrived.

One by one, they dropped to their knees.

Kain began issuing orders. Georgia didn't pay attention to what he said. Letting the knowledge that they were safe, that there were finally no more battles left to fight, settle in, she turned her full focus back to Kesh. His eyes hadn't left her face since he first opened them. He drank her in as desperately as a thirsting man who has finally knelt by a fresh stream.

"The power of you..." he murmured, voice hoarse. "I have never seen anything so beautiful."

She smiled softly at the reverence in his tone, her thumb brushing instinctively across his cheekbone. "You always did say you wanted me to grow a spine. I think this might count."

His eyes darkened, this time with guilt. "I'm... so sorry. For everything. For how I treated you, for... for letting you go. I thought I was saving you. I thought... anything would be better than eternity bound to me, to my darkness. But the truth is... I was such a coward, I nearly—" His breath hitched with pain. "Because of me, you were hurt." His hand reached toward her neck, slow and shaking, and hovered just beside the burn there. Not touching, just near. "You were always meant to be mine, and I *knew*. In the most foundational parts of me, I've known since the first moment I saw you, and

I let my cowardice hurt you. I will spend the rest of eternity on my knees for you. I will never stop begging for your forgiveness. Even though I know I don't deserve it. I know I can't ever undo—"

She kissed him before he could finish. A press of lips, light as breath, trembling as she cupped his face. "You came for me," she whispered against his mouth. "You gave up everything to try to save me, and in doing that... You unlocked the strength in me that everyone else has always tried to stamp out. Including me." She pulled back enough to look him in the eye. "Your love unlocked this power. Your love saved me." She touched her forehead to his. "I choose you, too, Kesh. Still."

He let out a breath that shook through his whole body, eyes closing as his hand closed tighter around the back of her neck, as if every instinct in him wanted her as close as she could physically get. "I love you."

"I love you, too," she whispered, lips brushing over his once more.

For a long, blissful moment, nothing existed but the taste of Kesh's mouth and the warmth of his touch. Finally, *finally,* for the first time in her life, there was calm, the background sensation of uncertainty and fear faded, replaced with a warmth that took her several heartbeats to put a name to.

Belonging.

She belonged here, to him, *with* him. In his world, by his side, soul bound to his. The magic his love had awakened in her flared, as if in agreement.

"What *is* this?" Kirigan's voice, low and cracked, broke through the bubble of peace.

Georgia turned to see Kirigan make his way toward them, eyes fixed on her with an unsettling intensity. Disbelief mixed with something dark and unsteady. Kesh's grip on her tightened, and a low, involuntary growl of warning left his throat.

The mad demon paused at his son's warning, hand half outstretched toward her. "You don't understand, Kesh. Fate has marked our bloodline. That goddess knew—I need to learn how she knew before we did. *How* she knew. What is it about this girl that made you offer your life? The answer is inside her. It *has* to be."

He took another step forward, as if proximity might help him understand what had taken root inside her. What had fused her to his son.

Kesh's lip curled back, but it was Georgia's magic that stopped him in his tracks. It flared up around her, gold turning white at the edges, and Kirigan froze mid-step.

"Don't even *think* about touching me," she hissed, anger curling in her gut as she glared up at him.

Kirigan's hand lowered, just barely. His eyes flicked from her face to Kesh, then back again.

"I know what you did," she continued. "You *sold* me to them! They told me. Mallorn was just the courier. *You* were behind it all. You traded me, like I'm just... a piece of meat? Like my life doesn't matter, so long as, what? The people *you* love are safe?"

There was a moment of complete stillness.

Kain, who'd been busy with the other lords, turned slowly back around to stare at his father. Selma's lips parted. Kesh...

Kesh went still as stone beside her. "You did *what?*" he whispered, breath like icy steel. His fingers tightened at her waist, barely restrained.

"It was... a mistake," Kirigan said. His voice was soft, devoid of emotion, even if his disturbing gaze still held some unnamable darkness. "If I had realized what you were to him, I would have found another way, but I didn't... You are Fate-sworn to my son, little Breeder, just like his brother's mate was to him. Two in one family? It is... preposterous. An impossibility.

"You were supposed to be nothing more than instincts. And infatuation that threatened my family's safety. I saw my youngest lost to desire, at the brink of shattering our support, had he acted on it and claimed you for himself. The gods are stirring, plotting... We wouldn't survive a war on two fronts, so I did what I thought I had to, to secure peace with the Europeans."

Kesh's expression didn't shift. He didn't snarl, didn't growl. He simply looked at his father like something inside him had gone cold and permanent. "You chose eternal rape and enslavement for the woman I love?" His voice was low. Quiet. Deadly. "You thought you knew best? You thought getting rid of her would... what? Make me a useful tool again?"

His nostrils flared with a deep, deliberate inhale, his

grip tightening around Georgia's waist as if she was the only thing keeping him from ripping out Kirigan's throat. "You are dead to me," he said flatly. "If you ever come near her again, I swear—"

Kirigan cut him off. "This isn't over. You have no idea what's coming. The gods don't care for love, or mates, or kingdoms. Whatever they have planned, whatever interest they have in our family, it will only have increased tenfold now that another Pure Breeder's powers have been awakened by our bloodline. I acted only in the interest of survival—yours, and your brother's."

"You nearly cost my brother his soul," Kain said. His voice rang out clear, sharp. He stepped fully into the ruined arena, eyes narrowed to slits. "You nearly cost my kingdom its strongest warrior. You nearly cost me *my brother*. That is not survival. That is *cowardice*. And in your hubris, in your arrogance, you miscalculated. You could have cost us *everything*, Father."

"You sacrificed a Seer," Selma seethed by his side. "You sacrificed one of *my* subjects, my sisters, to a fate so brutal, women have taken their own lives just to escape it."

Kain took one slow step forward, shadows curling at his feet, voice like thunder striking ice. "You betrayed us. All of us. You are my sire, and that is the only reason you are still breathing. Leave—now. You are banished from my kingdom. Do not return."

The silence that followed rang louder than any explosion.

Kirigan stood there for a moment, perfectly still. Then he bowed his head. Not in shame. Not in remorse. Just... acknowledgment. A nod to consequences. His gaze swept over them—his two sons, and the human women Fate had chosen for them. There was no apology in his eyes.

Then he turned, stepped into shadow, and was gone.

The four of them stood in the cratered silence he left behind, the remains of the decimated royal palace smoldering around them.

Above them, the sky still shimmered with the echo of what had been unleashed. Ash spiraled through the air like snow. The wind carried the scent of smoke, blood, and magic.

In every direction, there was nothing but rubble.

The city of Rome was gone.

In the distance, sirens blared.

"Well," Selma said, hands on hips as she took in the devastation. "I don't think we're going to explain this one with a gas leak."

51
KESH

The still-smoking seven hills that had once held one of the cradles of human civilization slowly disappeared from view as Kain's jet put distance between them and what would undoubtedly prove to be the biggest disaster in demon history. Not that Kesh had it in him to care about the fallout. Not now. Not yet.

"Okay, all done." The golden glow around Selma's hands faded as she pulled back from Georgia's wrists, gentleness in her eyes as she looked her over.

"Thank you. The pain is gone. This... magic we have, how does it work? How do you control it like this?" Georgia asked, her focus more on the other woman than her freshly healed skin.

"The scars? Will they linger?" Kesh cut in, pulling her onto his lap now that he could do so without causing her more pain. His thumb grazed the pink line around her throat. A fresh wave of self-loathing and shame washed through him. *His fault.* Her skin was marred because of his failings.

"I don't know. I'm not a doctor, Kesh," Selma said, her voice laced with overbearing patience. "This is what my magic could manage. Anything more than this might need divine magic. Or, hell, plastic surgery might do the trick."

The thought of some arrogant human taking a scalpel to wrists and neck, let alone a god putting hands on her, made an involuntary snarl rip from his throat and his muscles constrict tighter around her body as instincts to protect her with his own flesh kicked into highest gear.

"Ugh, Kesh!" Georgia's protest came as a muffled whine against his chest; slender hands pushed at his biceps in protest. He didn't ease his grip—couldn't. Not while shame and regret and fury pounded in his temples and poisoned his veins.

"Kesh. She needs to *breathe.*" Selma's sardonic tone belied any seriousness to her words, but they speared through him with urgency, nonetheless. He loosened his arms just enough that Georgia managed to pop her head up, hair mushed from his embrace.

"Kesh. I'm *fine,*" she said, blue eyes capturing his. They were patient and tender and, in their depths, understanding. She knew the shame he felt, under-stood it because she was burdened with empathy so deep she was incapable of withholding forgiveness for his cowardice.

"My heart," he whispered, face twisting with pain as he pressed his forehead to hers, desperate for the connection she should deny him, but never would. His fingers trembled against her throat, brushing the scar again.

"Shh." She raised her hand to cup his cheek, soft and tender still. So at odds with the raw power she'd unleashed to save him. "These scars aren't a memory of enslavement—they're a reminder of breaking free. That I'm not helpless. Because of you."

"I should never have doubted your strength," he murmured, lips finding her cheek, her jaw. "From the moment I saw you, you've commanded every part of me. Your ability to care for everyone, even the demon who had to lie to himself to pretend he still had any say over his own heart... It was never a weakness. I will never let anyone tell you otherwise again." Nor would anyone take advantage of her kind heart again. A hot spike of vengefulness rushed through his chest at the thought of the person responsible for his female's cowed demeanor. *Her wretched mother.*

Once he'd found Mallorn and made him pay for his betrayal, he'd relish turning his attention to the woman who'd broken down her own daughter's sense of self so she could be a better servant.

His body hardened at the thought of peeling the cunt's skin off in slow, even strips. Georgia inhaled sharply in response to his erection rising beneath her and pulled her head back to glare at him, cheeks flushed a pretty pink. "Whatever you're thinking about right now—stop it."

He would never tell her, of course. She was too gentle, too prone to giving second- and third- and one-hundredth chances. The vengeance he'd extract on her behalf would only horrify her, make her plead for mercy for someone who, by all the stars in the sky, did not deserve another drop of her empathy.

"I'm simply thinking about how well I'm going to take care of you. *All* of you," he murmured, nudging at her jaw with his nose to coax her into baring the sensitive spot at the side of her neck.

"You almost *died* less than two hours ago!" she growled, shoving at his chest with absolutely no result.

"I'm fine. But if you insist on coddling me, you could always let me feed on your energy, hmm?"

"For fuck's sake." Georgia planted both palms on Kesh's face and pushed again. This time, he let her put a few inches of distance between them, if only to better enjoy the deepening pink in her cheeks. "We're in a confined space *with your brother and sister-in-law*, the *whole* of Rome got turned to ash from your fight with the European royals, and *I* turn out to have magical powers *and* somehow summoned a powerful stone that has everyone fidgeting. I think we have more important things to focus on right now!"

Kesh's expression sobered as he took in her irate

expression. She didn't know. She thought the ancient city had been blown off the map by his battle with the lords. She didn't realize...

Gently, he closed both hands over hers and guided them to his cheeks. Her glare softened, her thumbs rubbing lightly over his cheekbones, as if the light he brought out of her couldn't be contained by a scowl for more than a few seconds. The same light that, in her desperation to save him, had summoned the Stone of Power imprinted to her, and turned an entire city to dust.

Silently, as she looked up at him with a tenderness he still struggled to comprehend, he swore to himself that she would never learn the truth. The cost to her soft, human heart would be too much for her to bear. Because, while she could forgive *him,* he knew her conscience would never let her absolve herself. Initial reports from Kain's men suggested a large proportion of the human population had survived the blast, even as their homes had not, but there were still casualties. *Many* casualties.

No. He would carry that burden for her.

"Speaking of the events in Rome," Kain broke in. When Kesh glanced at him, he'd pulled Selma into his lap, his hand resting on her hip to anchor her to his body, but his eyes were on Kesh. "There are many urgent matters for us to discuss. First and foremost how we navigate the containment with the humans. The local lords are working several angles to control the narrative, but we have to acknowledge the very real risk that we won't be able to hide our existence after today.

"Add to that the precarious political position we find ourselves in, the urgent need to unite the kingdom across the Atlantic, the unknown factor of the gods' plans, our father's betrayal... and the yet un-claimed Pure Breeder our lords had hoped to court..."

White-seething fury slammed shut over Kesh's mind. His arms clenched Georgia tight to his body without conscious thought—but the rage-fueled snarl that ripped from his throat was entirely deliberate. "If you think I'm going to let *anyone* court my female—"

Kain raised a hand, interrupting him. "Of course not. I am neither blind, nor an idiot. But if we want to avoid further complications or challenges to your right to her, I will suggest that we take care of the... formalities... before we land."

"Formalities?" Georgia's voice was once again muffled by his chest.

"Kesh. Oxygen," Selma admonished.

Kesh gave her a half-hearted glare before he eased his grip on Georgia's body. Her head popped back up again.

"What sort of formalities? *I* get to choose. You're the good guys—and frankly, even if you weren't, I am one thousand percent done being a political pawn. I'm not marrying anyone but Kesh. I've made my choice."

Soft heat flooded through his chest, easing some of the rage. He looked down at the woman in his arms, lids half-lowering with affection. Even if she still hadn't quite understood that demonic mating was something far deeper, far more lasting than the human concept of marriage, the steely determination in her voice that she belonged to *him* was unquestionable. "I like you like this. Demanding," he murmured, nuzzling at her ear with his nose. "You're even more lovely with that titanium spine fully polished. I'll make sure it never dulls again, I promise you that."

"Ugh, Kesh, knock it off. Now is not the time!" She squirmed against his affections, blush returning—undoubtedly at the knowledge that Kain and Selma were still present.

"Actually, little Breeder... I'm afraid now *is* the time," Kain said, his voice deliberately gentle. "Once you're claimed, in the eyes of our most sacred laws, no one can intervene. But if we land back in America and you are not, not even I will be able to stop challenges to your right to choose your own mate. It was difficult enough to get the lords to accept the original courting ceremony. After your kidnapping and the chaos in Rome, it will be impossible to control the situation. Kesh will be challenged, repeatedly. Violently. Immediately. And with no chance to fully recover his strength.

"Which is why it will be safer for you, for him, and for our rule, that he claims you now. Once you carry his mark, there will still be disgruntled males. Perhaps even some factions that oppose us on this basis, but nothing and no one will be able to pull you apart. So if you are certain my brother is your choice, Georgia, we will perform the claiming ceremony now."

"Oh... I... Well, yes. Of course I'm certain." She looked from Kain back up at Kesh, a shy smile on her lush lips. "A wedding in the sky, huh? That's... sort of romantic."

Selma let out a loud snort. "Oh, sweet summer child..." she pushed off Kain's lap, slapping at his hand when he was too slow to release his grip on her. "You hold on to that thought of *romance* for as long as you can. I'm gonna go tag in the co-pilot, so someone not in the family can bear witness. And I can... not."

Georgia looked after her as she headed for the door to the cockpit, a small, confused frown marring her brow. Kesh pulled her attention back to himself with a finger under her chin. His entire body thrummed with anticipation. This... this was what his entire life had been leading to. This moment. This woman. "I will make sure you spend the rest of your life never regretting your choice," he rasped, gently brushing a lock of her hair behind her ear.

The frown smoothed from her brow, and her eyes crinkled at the corners with her responding smile. "I'll hold you to that."

"Good." Unable to wait any longer, he tangled a hand at the back of her hair and drew her in for a deep kiss. Her breath hitched sweetly as their lips bruised together, then mingled with his when he flicked his tongue between hers to tease her open.

"Stars, even these lips taste like life," he groaned into her mouth.

She slapped his chest in admonishment and tried to pull back. He didn't let her. Rising to his feet, he hiked her up and made her spread her thighs for his hips before he put her down on her back on the carpeted airplane floor.

"M-pph!" Georgia protested, body going rigid under his.

"Shh, my love." He pulled back, pulse hard in his throat at the sight of her kiss-swollen lips and wide eyes. "Let me worship you like you were meant to be worshipped."

"Not *now*, you absolute savage! There are people here, and we're supposed to be getting marri... *oh*. Oh, no. Oh, you can't be serious!" He saw the moment the truth finally hit her, and her dreams of at least a semi-human ceremony aboard his brother's jet turned to vapor.

The startled, outraged look crossing her pretty features made him chuckle and press another kiss to her lips. "You're so fucking adorable. Don't worry, my heart. Once we have completed the ceremony, there will be no doubt in your mind that we are bound in soul and flesh for the rest of eternity. You may call me your husband once it's done, if you so prefer, but what we will be to each other is far more than a marriage could hope to encapsulate."

"Why is it always about sex with you demons—*ah!*"

Her growl broke on a soft gasp when his hand slid up underneath her shirt, her breath shuddering when he closed his fingers around her breast. She shoved at his shoulders and peeked over his back at Kain and the co-pilot, who'd taken Selma's spot by the king's side. "Seriously, can we at least not do this in front of your brother and whoever this guy is?"

"You are a Pure Breeder, Georgia. Witness must be borne," Kain rumbled, his voice soft and respectful. It still made Kesh snarl and jerk his head to the side, the sound of another male addressing his female making primitive instincts flare. "Do not speak to her!"

Kain raised both hands in surrender and bowed his head before leaning back in his seat. His brother was more than familiar with possessive mating urges.

Mollified that there would be no further attempts to distract her, Kesh returned his full attention to Georgia, gaze molten. "Normally, I would claim you in front of the rivals I defeated for the right to you. They would have to watch and bear witness as I took what they coveted. But nothing with you is ever simple, is it?" He flicked a thumb over her nipple and smirked when her front teeth dug into her lower lip in response. "So I will claim you here, now, with the king and Greg as our witnesses. And once I'm done, you will be mine in every way."

"*Greg?* Really? *Oh!*" Her protest died on a gasp when he pushed her shirt up over her head and clean off her body, baring her.

She instinctively clasped her hands to cover herself —one between her legs, the other across her breasts— her startled eyes darting back to Kain and the pilot, cheeks pink with embarrassment.

Kesh knelt back up, letting his eyes roam over her curves. The pink scars from the places her shackles had burned her glowed against her pale skin, fresh reminders of the abuse she'd endured at the hands of the Europeans. Her strength, too, yes—but he would never forget the sight of her on that platform, naked and scared and on display for the monsters planning to break her.

"I will never hurt you. I will never humiliate you. Everything we do together—even this—I swear on everything in this world and beyond, I will make sure you want it. All of it." His voice came out in a rasp, his throat tightening with the weight of responsibility. This woman, this gentle creature who'd trusted when she had little reason to, had offered him kindness when he'd deserved nothing but hatred... she was his to protect, body and soul. He'd die a thousand times over before he'd do anything that might turn her into a hollow shell, like so many women before her. Like his mother.

Georgia's eyes flicked back to his at the sound of his plea. The tension in them softened at the raw promise in his.

"I love you," she whispered, and it wasn't just the words themselves that struck through him like lightning—it was everything they represented: forgiveness, hope, trust. Kesh groaned like a wounded beast and flung himself down on top of her again, mouth seeking hers with a desperation he could do nothing to rein in. Hard, desperate kisses fell on her lips, her chin, her cheeks, her eyelids, then lips again. His tongue flicked against the seam, begging for entrance. He groaned again, deep and needy, and when it was granted and wet, soft heat enveloped him.

She mewled underneath him, sweet, feminine surrender, and clung to his shoulders, all thoughts of hiding her naked body from the onlookers forgotten as she embraced the firestorm of his love. She would never have to shield herself again. He would always be there to protect her. Always.

"I will burn the world for you," he rasped, fist tightening in her hair. A tug and she bared her throat for his mouth with a soft whine. "And I will build it back up again, so you are surrounded by nothing but beauty and adoration. *Mine*. Always mine." His rumbling devotions came between heated kisses to her jaw, her throat, her collarbone, his brain fogging over with every brush of her skin against his lips. *"Georgia."*

She was his apocalypse. His everything.

Slim fingers tugged at his hair. He pulled his mouth from her collarbone with effort and groaned softly at the heat in her gaze as it met his.

"You're mine, too," she whispered. "Always."

His breath left him in an explosion. "I can't wait. My

heart, I need you—I need to have you, claim you. Tell me you want it, tell me you want me—"

Her hands slid to his face, framing his jaw. "Yes."

His last vestige of control broke.

His hand found the softness between her thighs as he descended on her breasts, mouth hungry and fingers shaking with need to feel her—

"Fuck!" He snarled the word into her flesh as his fingers slid through her cleft and found her already soaked and swollen open for him. Darkness descended from all sides, narrowing his focus to the hot little cunt pulsing under his digits. Everything male and monstrous in him roared up from within, obliterating anything but the need to *claim.*

Her sheath clung to the two fingers he pushed up inside, and he groaned with her as her hips bucked to accept the intrusion.

"Kesh—!" His name broke on a moan that went straight to his groin, her fingernails digging into the plush carpet. "Ah, *deeper—!*"

He obeyed on fevered instinct alone, curving for her G-spot with frantic reverence. The fleshy spot pulsed under his touch, warm slickness coating his fingers every time he dug into the cushioned bundle of nerves.

"S-*hit!* Don't stop, don't stop!" Her syrupy mewls rang in his ears as he kissed his way down her stomach, desperate to taste her need. Her clit lay swollen between her splayed labia, pressing against the ring confining it, begging for him.

"Nothing and no one's gonna make me stop," he growled, the gravel in his voice making it sound like a threat. It wasn't.

The second his tongue flicked over the bared tip of her clit, her entire body arched up and her hands released the carpet to wind into his hair instead.

"Fuck yes! Kesh, yes! Kesh, Kesh, Kesh!" She sang his name like a filthy prayer, yanking on his hair to force him harder into her pussy. Her legs wound around his ribs, holding him to her as she rocked up against him in rhythm with his fingers and tongue, riding his face like the shameless slut she'd always bloomed into underneath him. If he hadn't known she was meant to be his since the moment he first laid eyes on her, he'd have known it now, with her pussy pressed to his face and her limbs clutched to him like he was the center of her whole world. Like she lived for the pleasure only he could give.

His lips closed around her clit. On the first suck, her fingernails bit into his scalp.

Fuck, she smelled like life. Tasted like Fate. Felt like redemption.

He forced a third finger up inside her fluttering cunt and was rewarded with a hard gasp and a buck up against his mouth for *"more!"* The word rang through the cabin, pleading when he sucked her clit hard, demanding when he teased with long licks. When a fourth digit speared into her, her sweet voice took on a hoarse note, the demands finally turning soft and submissive.

"*Shit,* that's—oh, Kesh, please, *please...!*"

Every instinct in his body understood what she needed. Snarling, he pulled her clit into his mouth, let the metal of her ring catch on his teeth to trap the base—and then sucked her so hard and fast, the tip of her small nub of nerves pulled long and taut within the hot cavern of his mouth.

She *shrieked* and arched off the floor, knees slamming closed on his ears, and hands shoving at his head instead of pulling in. He didn't let her dislodge him, didn't falter for a single second, because he was hard-wired for her, *made* for her, and nothing and no one would stop him from bringing her to completion—not even her.

It took seconds.

One moment she was frantically writhing to escape, the next, her pelvis bucked hard three times in a row, her back arched—

The second her pussy pulsed on his hand, he curled his fingers in against his palm and pushed deep, forcing his knuckles through her spasming opening until his thumb caught on her flesh.

"Ah-*ow!* F-*ah!* Kesh, n-*naah!*" She shrieked, clinging to his hair, and finally, mercifully, *came.*

His name thundered in his ears as he fucked her on his hand, instincts ensuring he opened her pelvis for every thrust, even as his full focus remained on the tortured clit between his lips, the apex of her pleasure.

The smell of her release, rich and deep and *Georgia*, flooded his nostrils and lit up every cell in his body until there was nothing left of him but pulsing, aching *need*.

His female went boneless beneath him, thighs splaying wide and arms flopping down next to her body. Even her pussy eased its bone-breaking grip on his hand, the soft wetness of her turning pliant and submissive once more.

Releasing her clit from the vacuum of his mouth, Kesh pulled back up to his knees and stared down at her.

She was flushed and spent, mouth pulled up in a lopsided smile. Eyes dazed and full of worship. For him.

There was nothing he could do to hold back any longer.

Georgia let out a gasp of surprise when he grabbed her by the hips and flipped her onto her stomach, and a mewl of protest when he yanked her to her knees, ass toward him.

"Wait, Kesh—"

Her cunt was swollen bright pink between her thighs, still soaking from her orgasm. Her entrance flushed open in anticipation.

"*No.*"

His voice was not his own. His body was not his own.

Kesh kept her anchored with a hand curled around her hip. He ripped his leathers open with the other, ruining them in the process. His cock sprang free, and the relief of it made a hoarse moan tear from his throat. It throbbed with his pounding heartbeat, the pronounced ridges nearly purple with the need to claim what was his.

He didn't have a single drop of patience left to spare. Growling, he palmed her pussy, forced her thighs wider apart until her cunt gaped like a little mouth for him, pressed his knees between hers to keep her spread, and sank his cock into her without a moment's hesitation.

"Ah! Sh-*it! Fuck!*"

He pushed the cartilage ridges on his crown through her opening in one, smooth push of his hips, and she screamed and cursed and smacked the floor with one hand.

He didn't stop—couldn't. He pushed deeper, forcing her pelvic bone to give way with the brutal shape of his cock. Everything was sharp, deep bliss, so powerful he could barely contain it.

He reached the narrowest part of her pelvis, and her hips jerked forward, instincts to escape briefly over-riding trust. He caught her around the waist, fingers gripping tight, and held her steady as he slowly pushed through her final resistance.

She cried out again, but this time, the pain was

laced with pleasure-laced submission as the tip of his cock finally kissed her cervix. "Kesh...!"

He fell on top of her, one arm trembling around her middle, the other barely holding his weight. Every inch of his cock screamed with sensation, the wet, tight heat of her more than he could take, yet nothing—*nothing*—would ever make him separate from her again. This was redemption. This was home.

"I love you so much I can barely breathe, Georgia. You are my everything, my reason, my soul." The words spilled from his lips, raw and unfiltered, pulled from the bliss of their connection.

"As you are mine," she whispered, one hand briefly lifting to skim his arm in a caress before she planted it on the plush carpet again. Bracing for what her body knew came next.

His first thrust was slow, reverent. It didn't last.

White-hot pleasure raked through his blood as her pussy grasped at his cock and squeezed his ridges. There was nothing left of his control. Nothing left in the world but burning, all-consuming *need*.

She screamed as he fucked her, bucked and writhed and clawed at the floor, first to get away, then in an orgasm that had her cunt fluttering and squeezing on his thrusting cock in maddening spasms.

It didn't so much as slow him.

His hips slapped a hard, brutal rhythm against her ass, every hard-wired instinct in his body determined to wring the strength from her trembling form, until the power in her blood could no longer hope to resist his claim.

"Mine!"

"Mine!"

"Mine!"

She came again, and this time, when her pussy seized on his girth, he surrendered.

"Fuck! Fuck, Georgia—!" His magic came in a torrent, the darkness sweeping through his blood as his balls drew up tight. And released.

He cried out, blind with ecstasy, gone on the bliss of orgasm and instinct. Everything was heat and relief and tight, maddening perfection. He pounded her pussy through their shared orgasm, snarling with the maddening sensation until, finally, she collapsed underneath him, wrung of the last ounce of her strength.

Then, he struck.

His teeth clamped shut around the back of her neck as the most primordial part of his power flooded from him and deep into her, searing her skin and marking her blood.

Only some long minutes later, when his magic finally ebbed and his cock had no more semen left to give her cervix, did he relax his jaws and gently lower them both to the floor, bodies still locked together.

Georgia panted softly underneath him, eyes rolled back, barely conscious. But when he kissed her nape and curled his body on top of hers with the instinctive need to protect her while she recovered, she let out a soft laugh.

"That... *hnngh...* wow."

"Agreed," he murmured softly, as lightness slowly swept through his body, replacing the wave of dark madness of the mating high.

This... this was what it felt like to claim his mate?

'Wow' was as good a word as any, because none would ever come close to describing the molecular remaking of everything he'd ever been, and everything he'd ever thought he'd wanted. Now, there was only her.

The woman who, in defiance of his very nature, he loved with his entire being.

The woman who, in defiance of reason itself, loved him in return.

And finally, finally... she was *his*.

EPILOGUE
GEORGIA: TEN DAYS LATER

"This is a terrible idea."

"So you've said. Repeatedly." She reached over to pat her mate's arm, half to soothe him, half to aggravate him with her sweetly patronizing tone.

Kesh clenched his hands around the steering wheel and gave her a glare out the corner of his eye. "Perhaps, then, you should consider *listening.*"

"Nah."

"Fuck's sake, Georgia—!" Kesh's growl died at the involuntary grin spread across her lips at his predictable response. Softness edged into his expression despite the annoyed sigh. "You enjoy playing with fire a little too much, mate."

Warmth fluttered in her chest at his use of the word 'mate'. It had been less than two weeks since he claimed her, and it had taken her less than a day to realize how inadequate 'wife' sounded in comparison. Being his mate was something far more foundational, far more eternal. She leaned over to kiss his arm. "It's not my fault you're adorable when you get cranky. Nor that it's extremely easy to light this particular fire."

A flash of darkness passed through his eyes before he returned his full focus to the road. "Careful now. There are *other* fires you tend to stoke with your sass, and I am more than happy to arrive at your family's home with you wearing my semen around your pretty neck, little one. Are you?"

"You're such a brute." She huffed with faux annoyance. But despite the clench of well-used muscles down below, she pulled back to the safety of the passenger seat. Seeing Larry again was going to be emotional enough without first getting pelvicly, emotionally, and spiritually wrecked by a roadside sexathon with her enthusiastic mate.

"Hmm," he agreed, without so much as the good grace to sound remotely ashamed of this fact.

TWENTY MINUTES LATER, KESH PULLED THE CAR TO A STOP IN front of her mother's house. What had been her home, too, up until very recently. Funny, in a way. As she peered up the path to the front door from the passenger side window, the thought that she'd never really felt like it was *hers* in any meaningful way struck. She just hadn't realized until the day she'd carved herself a space to call her own among demons and darkness.

In this house, she'd always been a supporting role.

Kesh's large, warm hand cupped her cheek and gently guided her face back to meet his gaze. His beautiful, human features were pulled into a soft frown. "Your scent tells me you are worried. I won't let anyone hurt you, ever again, Georgia. Not demons, and certainly not these people."

The distaste in his voice as he spat out the word 'people' made an involuntary smile ghost across her lips. "My family isn't about to attempt to sell me off in exchange for world peace or anything. We're good."

His eyes narrowed. It was only slightly, but it was enough for her to see the anger buried deep in his black gaze. "You were harmed before you ever came to me. The people responsible live behind this door. And I need you to know, mate, that you will be safe in there. In every way."

She hadn't been aware of the tightness in her stomach until it eased under Kesh's protective declaration.

"I love you," she murmured, leaning forward to rest her forehead against his.

His free hand slid to the back of her neck, pulling her in closer. "It still takes my breath away. I don't think I'll ever stop marveling at hearing those words from your lips." He bent lower, mouth seeking hers with the desperation usually following confirmation that she truly did love him.

Georgia gasped softly against his lips, the heat of him overwhelming as always, but when he flicked his tongue for entrance, she combed her fingers through his hair and pulled back. "Okay. We both know how this tends to end, and I'm *not* fucking you parked outside my mom's house. Come on. Let's go in."

Kesh arched an eyebrow, clearly not convinced about the need to not fuck her in the car, but when she reached for the handle to get out, he relented. He was around the car and taking her hand before she'd fully managed to climb out of the passenger side.

Together, they walked up the path to the small house.

The door opened before she could knock. Larry rushed out and, ignoring Kesh's instinctive growl of warning—ignoring Kesh entirely—wrapped both arms around her and hugged her so tight, her feet came off the floor.

"Georgie," he whispered into her hair, voice hoarse and deep. "Oh my God, I thought... I thought I'd never see you again."

"I know. But I'm here now." The past several weeks might have put her upbringing into sobering perspective, and she'd finally come to accept that how she'd been made to care for her younger brother as his second mother hadn't been fair to her. It didn't change how every part of her lit up and softened at the same time as she wrapped her arms around the back of his neck and clung on.

"I missed you, Baby," she cooed, in a tone so soft Larry let out a raspy laugh and pulled back enough to look at her with sparkling eyes, the same shade of blue as her own.

"You know I've been half a head taller than you for like... Three years, right? *Baby* is a bit ridiculous, sis." His smile softened, the corners of his lips trembling before he finally looked up at Kesh. "You've brought her back. That means she's free?"

Kesh's eyes narrowed to slits, but Georgia quickly intervened before he could say something that would undoubtedly ruin the mood. "I'm free. As for being back... perhaps we better talk inside?"

"Yes. Of course. Sorry." Larry finally released her, but reached for her hand as he stepped back to lead them into the house. Kesh let out another disapproving rumble and claimed the other, shutting the door behind them as they entered. The house suddenly seemed even smaller than she remembered it, with his huge frame taking up most of the hallway.

Georgia looked into the living room. Everything was as it had been before she left. The pictures on the walls—mostly of Larry, many with her by his side. More without. Her mother, when she was younger, in pretty makeup and posing for the camera. Mike was an avid amateur photographer, and ever after the pictures of him had been taken down, the ones he'd shot of her through the lens of an enchanted man remained.

"I'll... make some coffee." Larry turned to Kesh, hesitance painted across every feature, but politeness won out. "Do you take milk or sugar...?"

Kesh just stared at him.

Georgia gave her mate a minor glare out the corner of her eye, but she supposed she should be grateful he wasn't currently growling like some sort of overgrown terrier. "Kesh doesn't drink coffee. But I'll have a mug, thank you Larry."

"Oh. Okay. Um... tea?"

"No." Kesh more or less grunted his response but at least it was a word.

"Right. Well, we're fresh out of blood of virgins, so..."

Kesh rumbled a laugh—a surprise to him as much as it was to Larry, judging by his raised eyebrows. "I ate before we got here. No virgins needed."

Larry paled, no doubt imagining every gory way a creature like the big male by her side might eat. Georgia, who knew exactly how he'd fed and how there'd definitely been no virgins involved, smacked his arm. "We'll wait in the living room."

Her brother disappeared into the kitchen, and Georgia steered Kesh into the living room.

He took in the small room with a blank expression. "Quaint."

"Not really. Most people don't grow up in a palace.

This is normal." She gently nudged him toward the couch. He obediently sat down, immediately making the old piece of furniture look doll-sized and ridiculous.

Then she spotted the throw blanket on the armrest. New.

"I didn't grow up in a *palace.* My dad had an estate in Idaho." His eyes landed on her face, then followed her gaze to the throw blanket.

"It's new," she said softly. Then, because putting words to the hollow feeling blooming low in her gut was easier when he was near, she sat down on the sofa by his side and ran a hand over the soft blanket. "My mom was talking about how it would spruce up the room to get a cashmere throw blanket, back before Larry got sick. I guess she celebrated his recovery by finally treating herself to one. I just... I guess a part of me expected everything to stay the same. That she'd be too distraught with my disappearance like she was with Larry's illness to consider home decor. Which is petty and selfish, of course. I'm glad she's been able to find little joys."

"No, you're not." Kesh cupped her cheek and turned her face to his. His eyes were calm and gentle. "And that's okay. You're allowed to be hurt, Georgia. You're allowed to expect a mourning period. You've not been gone that long. But you know what she is. You've known for a long time. You're simply still getting used to acknowledging it out loud to yourself, and so it still hurts.

"But you're not replaceable, Georgia. You never were. Ache for the mother you so richly deserved to have—pity her if you must. Once we leave here today, you'll never feel second best ever again. I promise."

Wordlessly, she pressed her head into his shoulder and let his warmth wash away the ache of what never was.

Larry found them still tightly embraced when he returned from the kitchen with two mugs of coffee. He hesitated on the doorstep, eyes flicking between them. The question mark painted across his face was nearly audible.

Georgia gave him a small smile and pulled back far enough from Kesh's shoulder to hold a hand out for her coffee mug. "You can ask."

Hesitantly, Larry crossed the floor and held out her mug for her to grab. His attention remained mostly on Kesh. "I thought... you made a bargain. Like Rumpelstiltskin."

"Rum...what?"

"Rumpelstiltskin. Since you... left. I've been researching, about demons." Larry's lips pinched as he took a cautious seat on the edge of the armchair facing them. "That's what you are, isn't it? A demon? That's what she's been seeing all these years? She made a bargain with you in exchange for healing me."

Kesh nodded once in confirmation.

Larry looked back to Georgia, his eyes searching hers. "You don't seem... in distress, like you did at the hospital. Have you been... magicked? Mind controlled?"

Georgia gave him a soft smile. He was brave, her baby brother, to ask in front of the male who'd just confirmed his demonic nature. And concerned enough about her safety to risk his own. "No. I haven't." She shot Kesh a fond look. "He can't—even if he wanted to. I'm immune, as it turns out. And also... we're married."

"Married?" Larry placed his mug on the coffee table with a clonk, eyes wide in alarm. "You *married* one of them? That was the bargain? Oh, Georgie, no—"

She held up a hand before he managed to say something that might offend her mate. "No, no. Nothing like that. I married Kesh because I love him. It's been... a bit of a whirlwind. A lot has happened since I've been gone, but... it's been good. *This* is good." Then, because there was still a distinct look of alarm on her brother's face, she added, "I'm happy, Lar. Really, truly, happy. You don't have to worry about me anymore. I promise."

"You always said that." His voice was soft. "That I shouldn't worry about you. You know I always will, right? You're my sister."

"Your *big* sister. It's my job to worry about you, not the other way around."

"No. It isn't. It wasn't." He frowned and looked down at the mug in his hands for a moment. When he raised his eyes to hers again, for the first time, she saw the young man he'd become, rather than the child she'd raised. "What happened when we were kids wasn't okay, Georgia. You deserved so much better. Even if I'll forever be grateful for everything you sacrificed for me."

"I know." Her voice was quiet, choked by the unexpected lump in her throat.

The silence stretched across the living room.

Finally, Larry looked at Kesh. "If you ever hurt her, I will find a way to kill you."

"Larry!"

"If I ever hurt her, I'll let you." Kesh ghosted his hand down her thigh and closed his fingers gently around her knee. "My kind doesn't find love easily. Be assured that I will protect her against anything and everything—in your world, and mine."

Larry nodded once, clearly understanding the demon's words as the solemn promise they were. "Good. I will hold you to that."

"Well, this sure is a nice family visit. Anything *else* you'd like to threaten my new husband with, or...?"

"Considering you brought back a *demon,* I think it's going pretty well," Larry shot back. He took a sip of his coffee and shook his head.

She chuckled, the unexpected levity nestling in like a warm blanket. This moment? This was more than she'd ever thought she'd get.

"So... are you still in town? Can we... hang out more often?"

She grimaced and shook her head. "Not for a while. We're moving to Europe. I don't know how long for, but at least a few years. But... we can email? Maybe video call, if you'd like?"

"Yeah. I'd like that." Larry smiled at her. "I could even try to save up and come visit over the summer?"

Kesh squeezed her knee in warning. She ignored him.

"You're always welcome wherever I am."

By her side, her mate swallowed an annoyed sigh.

Larry, however, lit up. "I can't wait. Do you know where you're going yet? Please say Paris."

"Milan."

"Oh." He bit his lip, his easy smile fading. "Is it... related to the... Rome-thing?"

The Rome-thing. The human world was still beside itself from the disaster. Understandably. There were not logical answers to be found, no explanation for what had happened, and while governments were still searching through every possible explanation involving terrorism or freak accidents, the internet was split down the middle on an alien super weapon, and magic. No matter the combined efforts of the demon lords around the globe, there was no stopping this. It was only a matter of time before the truth came out and Breeders were no longer the only ones who knew about the demons who lived among humanity.

Until then, however...

"It's not... *not* about that."

"Ah." The frown was back on her brother's face. "But... you'll be safe?"

"She'll be safe," Kesh rumbled. He exhaled and nudged gently at her shoulder. "It's time for us to leave, little one. We have a long drive home."

Home. He meant the casino where they temporarily had their base while he and his brother prepared for their trip to Milan where they were to take point on the clusterfuck that was 'the Rome situation.' It didn't matter, though, that they didn't have a comfortable house or a place that was truly theirs yet. Her home was with him. Always would be.

"Alright." She placed her coffee mug on the table and got to her feet. "It was good to see you, Larry."

"You don't want to stay a little longer? Mom should be back from work in half an hour or so." He stood, too, and followed them to the hallway, clearly reluctant to say goodbye.

"No, that's alright. But you give her my best." There was an ache in her chest again, but softer this time. Lighter.

"I will." He pulled her into a hug again, tight and long enough for Kesh to start making impatient noises. When he finally released her, she took his face between her palms and gave him a reassuring smile. "We'll email. And video chat. And you'll come to Milan this summer, and fall in love with a pretty Italian girl."

Larry let out a chuckle and lifted his hands to cup hers where they bracketed his face. "I love you, Georgia."

She brushed her thumbs over his cheeks and finally

took a reluctant step back, releasing him. "I love you more."

***

"For a human, he's not... the worst."

"You just liked that he threatened you. You big weirdo." Georgia leant her head against the car window as the city lights passed them by. Exhaustion that had little to do with anything physical flirted at the edges.

A large hand found her thigh, anchoring her. "I like that he's protective of you. Even if you *are* stronger than most other beings on this plane of existence."

An involuntary smile quirked her lips. "Thank you. For taking me to see him. It meant... a lot."

"If it makes you happy, it's my job to make it happen, little one."

"*Well.* I hope you don't expect me not to take advantage of that for the rest of our lives." She turned her head from the window to give him a tired grin. "Which reminds me... I seem to remember something about a pumpkin pie situation you were trying to resolve. Ya know, before you blew up your penthouse, and—I assume—the million squashes along with it."

"Hmm. You remember correctly. I suppose I will have to rectify that—in between political and global chaos." He gave her thigh a squeeze.

"Yup. Gotta learn to bake. It's in the mate handbook. I'm certain your brother bakes for Selma, too."

"I have absolute faith you're correct about that," he

mumbled, just the slightest sardonic note sneaking into his deep voice.

She paused as something struck her. "Speaking of Selma... Why did it never occur to you that *I* might have been Pure, too? From day one, you were all 'you are not for me, Breeder. Only the purest of Breeders can withstand the might of my dick.' Yet apparently your dad knew the moment I shook off his restraints, back when I, ah... tried to climb him like a tree. Due to evil ring manipulation, I will hasten to add. Wouldn't it have been prudent to, I don't know... tickle me with magic or something, just to make *sure?*"

To her amusement, a flush of pink colored his cheeks. "Yes. In hindsight. Obviously, that would have been helpful. But Pure Breeders..." He glanced at her out the corner of his eye. "You are *rare*, Georgia."

"Yes, *I know.*"

"I don't think you do. With you, there have been three within this past century, globally. That's unheard of. Before that, it was perhaps one per century. You being Pure... it was impossible. And testing you..." His expression turned agonized, and his fingers tightened around her thigh, as if afraid she'd vanish if he didn't cling on. "It would have required me to entertain the possibility that you... that you *could* have been mine, only to then face the very real possibility—the almost guarantee that you wouldn't be compatible. I couldn't face that. So no. I didn't test you."

Her heart did something stupid and mushy in her

chest. Gently, she placed her hand on top of his, warm into the marrow of her bones. "Well. I guess you'll just have to make it up with monthly—no, *weekly*—pumpkin pie baking."

Kesh rumbled a soft laugh. "I guess so."

"Maybe you don't buy a whole field of dick-shaped gourds every time. Your feeder kink is a little out of control," she teased, the lightness in his voice nestling in deep behind her ribs.

"Is that a *complaint* in how I care for you, mate?" His tone turned to a playful rumble. "You know what else those *dick-shaped* gourds can be used for, if you have objections to eating them, hmm?"

A scandalized gasp escaped her throat when the implication—and the exact, huge shape of his last pumpkin-heist hit her. She turned fully to face him, mouth agape. "You wouldn't!"

"I'm afraid you're wrong on this one, my love. I absolutely will."

KIRIGAN
FOUR DAYS LATER

"...destruction of Rome. Two weeks on, officials still have no explanation for the event, though pressure is mounting across intelligence and scientific communities. The UN's special subcommittee on anomalous threats continues closed-door sessions in Geneva, while Italy's own inquiry—led jointly by military and forensic analysts—has yet to release findings from the blast zone. Surveillance data from multiple agencies remains classified, though sources confirm coordination between ESA, NASA, and private satellite firms is ongoing.

The working term remains 'non-nuclear mass energy event' but behind the scenes, language is shifting. Quiet references to 'targeted survival patterns' have surfaced in internal NATO cables, though no official body has acknowledged the growing suspicion that the effect was selective.

In the absence of answers, theories continue to spread. Government messaging emphasizes calm and scientific integrity, but civil unrest in several countries suggests public confidence is eroding. Italy has extended its state of emergency. The Vatican enclave in Bonn has yet to appoint a new interim pontiff."

Kirigan sipped his glass of whiskey, his eyes remaining on the screen as the news anchor cut to an interview with one of the survivors. A young man with wide, trauma-deepened eyes telling a story the world had heard a thousand times since the calamity in Rome, and would a thousand more times while the humans tried to make sense of what had happened that day.

The persistent, creeping sensation at the back of his neck finally made him sigh softly and turn off the TV. Silence settled in the apartment, heavy and still.

"If you're here to kill me, you really should get on with it." He took another sip of whiskey, eyes remaining on the now black screen. "I am in no mood to stop you. I can't guarantee that will remain the case."

A light, twinkling laughter brushed against his nape. Primordial instincts raised the hairs on the back of his neck, shoulders twitching as his muscles instinctively tensed up in expectation of an attack. It never came.

"What a melodramatic boy you are." The voice was light and sweet and childlike, mocking in its innocence.

It grated against his spine like claws. "Alas, I have to disappoint you. I'm not here for a bit of light murder, however tempting. I'm here to talk about your two daughters-in-law."

Numb darkness flirted with the edges of his vision. He pushed the madness down, carefully placed his whiskey glass on the side table, and finally turned around.

The goddess stood at the other end of the room, with the sofa between them. She was in a child's form, with bare feet and a white, flowing dress, the innocent roundness of her face contrasting the sharp wariness in her eyes.

"Hmm. I take it you are the divine creature who stole the Stone of Power from the battlefield in Maine?" His eyes swept over her lithe form. Beneath the numbness, instincts twisted and snarled to snap her neck.

She gave him a thin smile. "*Stole* is such a nasty word. I prefer *liberated*. And, may I add, selflessly gave it to the young woman under your son's care."

"*Selflessly,*" he echoed softly. "Interesting choice of words. Did you plan for her to destroy Rome? Was that always the intent? Expose us to the humans? It's a matter of weeks before they'll know the truth of us now. And of you. There's no hiding our existence, our influence over them, not after a calamity of that magnitude."

The goddess grimaced. "Not... exactly. Mind, you can't deny, her innate magic over that cursed stone is fascinating. By all accounts, a demonic artifact unleashed to that extent should have eradicated all life, but it didn't. It only culled the wicked. Such power is... quite something."

"You knew that already. Since Selma. That's why you targeted the girl in the first place. You wanted to unleash that power in her, too. How you think that would benefit *you* in any way, I am... curious about. Both Breeders are fiercely loyal to my sons. Any power they gain will not be used for your schemes, so it begs the question...why are you so interested in my bloodline?" He narrowed his eyes slightly, taking in the goddess's every micro expression. She was old. Far older than he. Deceptively powerful. This was the second time she'd snuck past his defenses—not an easy feat for most divines.

"Ah, yes. Your bloodline." She picked at her dress, voice light. "Things seem to be going well for your spawn. I hear even the objections the other lords had about another Pure Breeder being swept off her feet by one more of your sons faded quickly enough, when they realized what kind of power that union brought their side. Keen to kiss the ring, turns out. And, certainly, the sudden opening of territories in Europe after the sudden, ah, death toll, among the old royals' supporters seems to have helped as well. Supposedly Kesh and Georgia are headed to Germany any day now, to govern the continent through the power shift. Tell me... will there be a going away party? Are you buying a nice set of luggage for the newly-mated?"

Kirigan narrowed his eyes. The venom behind her barbed question didn't penetrate. There was nothing left for the poison to anchor into behind his ribs. Only darkness. "I grow tired of your games. If you had a point to make by coming here, make it."

The goddess snapped her fingers. "Ah, yes. That's right. You had a little falling out with both your sons, didn't you? Tsk tsk. Such a shame."

He took a single step forward. A silent warning. Despite the smile on the goddess's youthful face, he caught the slight tension in her body at the movement.

"Now, now. There's no need to get unpleasant. I'm simply here to sate my curiosity. You see, your sons have caused ever so much chatter amongst us gods. First a young, unknown lordling *falls in love* so profoundly, he awakens a power thought lost in the female of his affections. He loves her so much, he's willing to sacrifice his own wants, his needs, for her. Not exactly usual demon behavior, I'm sure you agree.

"And then, what do you know, despite all odds... his baby brother goes and does the same. Only this time, it's not just *your* power structure that's been shattered in the process—it's the entire magical world that's been cracked open. But not... all the way. Not *quite*. A few of the sigils are still holding, if only barely."

Kirigan narrowed his eyes. *There.* Finally. The reason

beneath this treacherous creature's incomprehensible actions. "You wish to break the ancient wards? That's why you stole the Stone of Power and gave it to Georgia? In the hopes of awakening enough power to destabilize magic itself? Why? Your kind were the ones to seal the other realms off in the first place. Demons were the only magical beings you couldn't displace from this plane. Reopening the portals will only further undermine your power."

The goddess gave him a small smile. It held no warmth. "Don't you worry your pretty little head with the *whys*, demon. That's far above your pay grade. No, your role in this is far more... shall we say grunt-level—"

"You truly think I will be a pawn in your schemes?" he interrupted, voice flat. "That Fate's touch on my bloodline means I will help you break the last sigils? Tell me then—what do you think will happen? *Love?*"

The goddess let out a tinkling laugh. "Oh, no. You misunderstand. I'm well aware of the blackness in your heart, Lord Kirigan. Remind me what happened to the last woman to suffer your affections... suicide just to escape, wasn't it?"

Tight, clawed darkness climbed up his spine. Not pain—he wasn't capable. Just emptiness.

Kirigan exhaled softly. "Is that your plan, then? Convince me to break another Breeder so her sons will know pain so early that they might crack open just enough to be capable of love through sacrifice?"

The goddess's eyes sparkled with something akin to mischief. Or perhaps malice.

"Something like that, yes."

"And you plan to convince me to play along... how?" He tilted his head, detached curiosity at the creature's brazen confidence just barely breaking through the hollow. "There is nothing I desire. No bargain you could tempt me with. No threat to leverage, not if my sons are so powerful, their unions with their mates have cracked the sigils holding back the fabric of reality itself. Surely, you don't need Fate's touch to break a woman bound to a demon lord."

"Ah, but that's the thing. I don't believe Fate has touched *your* bloodline, demon. You didn't claim the girl after I activated her ring, despite how her scent must have hit every dark, primal part of your base brain. No, you were capable of scheming and calculating how to best strengthen King Kain's hold on the throne, even as the little thing was begging for your dick." The goddess picked at a perfect fingernail before she looked up at him through her lashes, that infuriating smirk still in place. "No, I believe Fate has touched your late mate's bloodline. Your sons are Fate-bound, but you... well, *you* are more circumstantial. A catalyst, if you will."

He stared blankly at her. Uninterested in taking the bait.

She placed her hands on her hips, impatience

crossing her childish features. "Your sons are not the only ones whose mother you killed."

"I have killed countless mothers. What is your point?"

The goddess tilted her head, the smirk returning. "You'll see. Mercy has a way of coming back to haunt us. Ah, but I'd best be going. Fate seems to need just a *teensy* extra nudge to get things rolling—and I have a bit of a deadline to meet. See you soon, lord Kirigan."

A soft twinkle of light and she was gone.

Kirigan stood still in the darkness, letting the prickles of irritation along his skin from the divine presence fade.

Mercy? He had never shown anyone mercy, not before his mate's death, and certainly not after. Whatever the goddess's plans, she had revealed very little. Not that he would expect anything more from such a treacherous being.

What had she hoped to gain by coming here? She'd pried no secrets from him, and whatever her reasons to crack the wards that kept the magical worlds separated—

A hot, sharp flash of pain along his veins interrupted his thoughts. He stared down at his forearms, but nothing broke the skin.

What the—?

Searing agony split behind his ribs, like the organs behind them ripped open. Kirigan let out a gasp and sank to one knee, one arm clutched across his ribs. It was then, as he knelt on the floor of the dark apartment, the goddess's words finally pieced together.

His sons were not the only children he'd left motherless.

Fate hadn't touched his bloodline, but his late mate's.

Another gasp tore through his throat, hoarse with pain, as something old and filthy clawed its way up through the madness.

A memory swallowed up by the void in his mind. A little girl, curled up on the floor at his feet. Body wrecked, eyes glassy.

His mate's first daughter, orphaned twice over by the same monster.

And the magic he'd buried in her bones that day, formed in the blood of her freshly killed father.

ALSO BY NORA ASH

DEMON'S MARK

Branded

Demon's Mark

Prince of Demons

The Mad Demon*

ALPHA TIES

Alpha

Feral

Protector

(Holiday) Intrusion

THE OMEGA PROPHECY

Ragnarök Rising

Weaving Fate

Betraying Destiny

ANCIENT BLOOD

Origin

Wicked Soul

Debt of Bones*

DARKNESS

Into the Darkness

Hidden in Darkness

Shades of Darkness

Fires in the Darkness

MADE & BROKEN

Dangerous

Monster

Trouble

www.ingramcontent.com/pod-product-compliance
Lightning Source LLC
Chambersburg PA
CBHW031729180726
48283CB00005B/1430